D0194924

THE NATANZ
DIRECTIVE

Also by Mark Graham

The Harbinger

The Missing Sixth

The Fire Theft

Nonfiction

Parents Are Diamonds—Children Are Pearls

THE NATANZ DIRECTIVE

A JAKE CONLAN THRILLER

Wayne Simmons

and

Mark Graham

THOMAS DUNNE BOOKS

ST. MARTIN'S PRESS

NEW YORK

This is a work of fiction. All of the characters, organizations, and events portrayed in this novel are either products of the author's imagination or are used fictitiously.

THOMAS DUNNE BOOKS.
An imprint of St. Martin's Press.

THE NATANZ DIRECTIVE. Copyright © 2012 by Wayne Simmons and Mark Graham. All rights reserved. Printed in the United States of America. For information, address St. Martin's Press, 175 Fifth Avenue, New York, N.Y. 10010.

www.thomasdunnebooks.com

www.stmartins.com

Design by Omar Chapa

ISBN 978-0-312-60932-0 (hardcover)
ISBN 978-1-250-01347-7 (e-book)

First Edition: September 2012

10 9 8 7 6 5 4 3 2 1

To the Superpatriots in my life: my wife of thirty-five years,
Corinne, whose love for me and our family is and always has been
unwavering; to my daughter, Alison, and son, Wayne, who will
always be my greatest source of intense pride; and to my mom,
Dean, whose love and drive instilled in me at a very early age,
"I can do it," and my father, Wayne, whose courage, strength,
and conviction I continue to draw upon today.
—WS

To Nobuko, Erin, Colin, and Chuck
—MG

ACKNOWLEDGMENTS

We would like to thank the following people for their enthusiastic support, superior talents, and unbridled energy: Brendan Deneen; Peter Rubie; Lt. Gen. Tom McInerney; Lt. Col. William V. (Bill) Cowan; Mario Acevedo; Mark Stevens; Kerry Patton; Keith Urbahn; Jed Babbin; Carrie Nyman; Dave Payne; Gerald R. Molen; Clare Lopez; Judge Andrew Napolitano; and all of Wayne's buddies of the U.S. Air Force Special Tactics Squadrons, the 1st SFOD-D, and the CIA. This book would not have been possible without every single one of you.

AUTHORS' NOTE

With regards to certain CIA designations, we chose to use "Directorate of Operations," "Deputy Director of Operations," and the acronyms "DO" and "DDO" instead of the current "National Clandestine Service" and "Deputy Director of NCS" to create continuity for the reader and an ease of understanding of the CIA hierarchy during the years Mr. Simmons was active in the Agency.

THE NATANZ DIRECTIVE

CHAPTER 1

WASHINGTON—DAY ONE

I pulled into the parking lot of the Georgetown dock and saw a double-decker river taxi overflowing with people getting ready to leave. I peeked at my watch. Two minutes. I found a short-term parking space, threw on the parking brake, and jogged to the ticket counter looking the part of a businessman on the verge of missing an afternoon meeting.

The guy at the ticket counter had seen plenty of guys like me, so he had my ticket ready and was holding up ten fingers. I handed him a ten, nodded my thanks, and headed down the ramp. The gate was already closed, but the attendant saw me coming.

"Just in time." He put a crack in the gate, and I slid through.

"Thanks for waiting," I said, even though I knew he hadn't.

The *Cherry Blossom* looked like an old-time riverboat scudding down the Mississippi, the paddle wheel churning off the stern, spray gently showering the deck. I walked through the lower deck as the boat headed downriver. An eclectic gaggle of tourists crowded along the filigree railing as their guide's voice rang out over the loudspeaker.

I looked for disinterested parties. I looked for a sidelong glance. I looked for a man dressed like a librarian or an accountant. I climbed the stairs to the second deck. The view improved, and I ignored it completely. A man in a tweed coat

1

with a neck scarf tucked under his chin stood alone off the stern end, watching the paddle wheel turn. It was probably by chance that he was stationed next to the American flag dancing in the breeze, but I kind of doubted it.

"You look cold," I said, standing next to him.

"When you're seventy-six you'll be cold pretty much every minute of every day, too," Mr. Elliot said. I'd always called him Mr. Elliot. I always would.

"Then why the hell did you pick a water taxi in the middle of the Potomac for a get-together? I kind of miss our room in the Holiday Inn."

He stared at me with blue eyes as challenging and icy as they'd been during our first meeting nearly thirty-five years earlier. His grin had taken on an ironic twist over the years, and I suppose that was inevitable given the business we were in. "A room at the Holiday Inn costs money. A senior's pass gets me a view of the river for five bucks."

"I paid ten," I said.

"Your time will come, kid."

He'd aged, to be sure, but the fire was still there. How many people could you say you trusted with your life? Well, with Dad dead and gone I was down to one. And here he stood. I could only hope that he felt the same.

"So. The White House chief of staff and a three-star in the same room," he said with a chuckle. "Bet that lunch was a barrel of laughs."

He was talking about an impromptu and rather extraordinary get-together at the Old Ebbitt Grill with my longtime friend Lieutenant General Thomas Rutledge and a political animal named Landon Fry, only the most powerful man in the country save the president himself. I didn't like politicians. Fry was no exception. "I had the Monte Carlo, the general had a Cobb salad. Fry probably munched on the silverware."

Mr. Elliot chuckled again. "You always have the Monte Carlo." He drew his coat tightly around him and stared at the water churning below us. "They didn't give you the details, of course."

"They used *The Twelver* in the same sentence with *critical mass* and *catastrophe,* so I assume I'm going in headfirst," I replied.

The Twelver. That's all the general had needed to say. "The Twelver" was a two-word reference to Mahmoud Ahmadinejad, Iran's president and the Agency's least-favorite person. The Twelvers were the largest Shiite Muslim group in Iran. They believed the Twelve Imams to be the spiritual and political successors to Muhammad. It was an extraordinarily powerful position, because the Prophet's successor was thought to be infallible. It was no secret that Ahmadinejad fancied himself the Twelfth Imam, even if few others did.

"You'll go in headfirst *and* without a net," Mr. Elliott corrected.

"So what's new?"

Mr. Elliot turned and faced me, gimlet eyes burning, dead serious. I'd seen that look a hundred times before, and it always meant the same thing: showtime.

My longtime case officer said, "You're back on the clock. Headed for the badlands. Boots on the ground."

"I wouldn't have it any other way."

"You know we don't call a guy out of retirement unless no one else can do the job, Jake," Mr. Elliot said plainly. Then he got down to business. "Your mission is to develop indisputable intel proving that Iran has nukes and the launch capabilities to use them. We also want you to provide coordinates to support military strikes and covert assassinations inside that country. And you have two weeks max to do it."

I wanted to say, *Oh, is that all? No sweat.* But I didn't, of course. Mr. Elliot did not appreciate sarcasm. I started doing the math: two days to prep, eight days on the ground, and four days for the inevitable complications.

No sweat.

Mr. Elliot fished a pack of Chesterfields from his coat pocket, shook a cigarette out despite a NO SMOKING sign not twenty feet away, and used an old Zippo to light it. He smoked, and I watched the water. A gentle wake crested behind the boat, but I could just barely hear it over the riverboat's engine. I heard voices, laughter, and footsteps as excited tourists moved to the starboard side of the boat. I followed their movement. The George Washington Monument pierced the air like a giant spike. The dome of the Thomas Jefferson Memorial seemed to hover like a flying saucer above columns of snow-white marble.

That's how people reacted when they came to D.C. They saw the White

House and the Library of Congress. They stared into Lincoln's eyes and marveled at the names on the Vietnam Memorial. They gazed into the Reflecting Pool and tipped their heads to the sea of white at Arlington Cemetery. And they felt something. These were the symbols of their country, and they felt something. Pride, freedom, security. Who knew? But it was my job to protect that something. And if it meant a black op in the heart of most dangerous country on earth, well, so be it.

"I'll need the MEK," I said. The Mujahedin-e Khalq was Iran's most powerful antigovernment group. They would do anything to topple the current regime. I knew their leadership as well as anyone in the Agency. I didn't trust them any more than they trusted me. If I could aid in their movement, they would allow themselves to be used. "Which means starting in Paris."

"Good. Because we have a little problem in Paris that needs taking care of."

I didn't like the sound of this, not with a two-week-timetable already staring me in the face. "So? Lay it on me."

"There's a leak." His voice was a half-octave lower than it had been three seconds ago. "It begins with a member of the Senate Select Committee on Intelligence and ends with a French drug dealer who's decided to try his hand at extortion. And so far he's been damn successful. The leak needs to disappear, Jake. Your mission depends on it."

He turned and looked across the water. I stared at the side of his face and said, "Details?"

"You'll have them before you leave." Mr. Elliot used a polished leather shoe to put out his cigarette. Now he vouchsafed me a look that was just this side of sympathy. "I know what you're thinking. What about the senator? A rat sitting on one of the most powerful committees in the government. Who silences him?"

"And?"

"I'll take care of it. You put your guy in Paris out of business, and I'll put mine out here." He fished out another smoke.

"Thought you were quitting," I said.

"That was before they dragged my favorite operative out of his rocking chair, and I had to take up my babysitting duties again." He grinned. The grin turned into a snakebitten chuckle. I may have been fifty-six, but I still looked forty-five—that being my own humble opinion, of course. Well, maybe if the lighting was just right. I could still dead lift five hundred pounds and run a marathon in five hours. What was all this about a rocking chair? "Okay, granted, you still look like you've got a couple of miles left in the tank."

"Helluva compliment. Thanks a bunch." I gripped the railing as the river-boat inched toward the dock at Alexandria. "Any more surprises?"

"The DDO will be sitting in on your meeting tomorrow at the Pentagon. Be nice. You're going to need him," Mr. Elliot advised.

The Agency's deputy director of operations was a politician through and through, but nothing went down without his approval. I would need him: Mr. Elliot was right about that. But he was just part of the op. I would run him just like I did every other asset, as if he were a blink of an eye away from slitting my throat. I said, "How much will he know?"

"He'll know the op, but he won't like it." Mr. Elliot slipped a hand into his coat pocket and came away with a disposable phone in his palm. When the riverboat lurched to a halt, he grabbed my arm for balance, and the phone slid into my hand. The exchange was so quick and seamless that it reminded me of the old days. "It's good for three calls."

I looked into his eyes. He had something else to tell me, and it wasn't going to be pretty. I made it easy for him. "And . . . ?"

"That obvious, huh?"

"We've known each other a long time."

"I've made contact with the Russians in Saint Petersburg," he said.

The Russians in Saint Petersburg. That could mean only one thing: the Russian mafia. I was right. Not pretty at all. In fact, downright ugly.

I turned to go. "This your stop?"

"Nah. I bought a round trip."

"A round trip for five bucks!" I caught his eye one last time. "I gotta give the AARP credit."

Last I saw him, he was lighting another cigarette with his Zippo, and it did my heart good to know that he had my back again.

I went in search of a taxi. Everything from this moment on was a full-blown black op.

CHAPTER 2

The deputy director of operations of the CIA was three or four years Mr. Elliot's junior but looked at least ten years younger. His name was Otto Wiseman. He and Mr. Elliot were contemporaries, straight out of the Helms era, when nothing in our business mattered more than HUMINT, a less-than-inspiring moniker for the most important tool a man in my position would ever use: human intelligence.

It's pretty straightforward: HUMINT is the kind of intel that's collected by human sources—guys like me—and provided by other human sources.

During my years in the Agency, that source of intel could have been anyone, from an arms dealer in Honduras to a drug runner in Key West, a broken-down call girl in Washington, D.C., to a money-laundering financier in New York. It didn't matter where the intel came from. It mattered only if Mr. Elliot and his team could use it to put down a drug ring in Florida or take out a black marketer in Jersey; target a terrorist cell in Alexandria or a meth lab in Alabama. We'd done it all during my rather auspicious tenure as an outside paramilitary operative.

Officially, HUMINT was a product of conversations or interrogations with persons of interest. Very civilized. Yeah, right. Unofficially, it was most often a product of deceit, cunning, or treachery. How else were you going to get what you needed from a narco-terrorist with the endearing habit of slicing up his own people with a butcher knife, just to make a point? Walk up and ask him whether he was in possession of two tons of marijuana or a hundred pounds of uncut heroin and would he mind giving up the location? Better to convince him that his drugs didn't compare to your drugs and set him up for a raid by a bunch of DEA guys with MAC-11s and body armor. I never knew how my intel was used. I only knew when the dirt balls I'd been setting up weren't there anymore.

HUMINT requires boots on the ground. There is nothing more effective in gathering relevant and pertinent intel. Too bad fashion got in the way back in the early 1980s, when satellites became all the rage and people actually started to believe that you could spot a bad guy from 150 miles in the air. No more Cold War, no more need for HUMINT. At least that's what the politicians thought. Too bad the end of the Cold War hadn't signaled an end to people who wanted to destroy America.

Come 9/11 and the reality of satellite intelligence gathering hit us square in the face. Without the HUMINT to back up our love of technology, we weren't going to win any kind of war, much less a war on terrorism.

Being contemporaries didn't make Mr. Elliot and DDO Wiseman two peas in a pod. Wiseman was a politician. He had an agenda, and it wasn't always in line with that of the guys in the field. As a matter of fact, he'd have let me burn in a second if it had served his precious agenda.

The DDO reminded me of my eighth-grade math teacher, Mr. Boggs. They were both short, wiry men with skin pulled so tight over their cheeks that I swear you could see the bone punching through. Unlike Mr. Boggs, DDO Wiseman sported a military buzz haircut and a suit tailored in Hong Kong.

"I'm being straight. I don't like the op," he said to me. He paced. General Tom Rutledge and I sat. There was an oval table between us, good for a dozen or more people and typical of Pentagon furnishings. It was just the three of us and a pot of coffee. A leather briefcase contained my travel papers, three completely untraceable passports—those were the DDO's words—and money.

The travel papers I needed. You didn't hitch a ride with an air force jet without papers. The "completely untraceable passports" would go into the trash the minute I reached Paris. When DDO Wiseman said "completely untraceable," he meant by everyone except him and his band of European field operatives. No, thank you. I'd already placed a call to a Parisian associate from days gone by, and the passports he'd promised me would truly be untraceable. Sorry, Mr. Wiseman, but you're not the one guy in the room that I trust.

"What's to like," I said to him. "It's essentially a suicide mission."

"Exactly. So maybe what I mean is I don't like the odds of the op. That sound more realistic?" He looked from me to the general. Tom was like a stone-cold statue: he could have had pigeons perched on his shoulders and never moved a muscle. The DDO could rant and rave all he wanted; the mission was a lock. The sooner the meeting was over, the better. "I want every detail of your plan, Conlan. I can't protect you and I can't help you if you're not straight with me."

"Yes, sir," I said. The DDO probably didn't hate my guts, but he hated not knowing who I really was or what I had really done for the Agency for twenty-seven years. And what he probably hated even more was the certainty that I had run the kind of black ops that he had only dreamed of running, even while he turned his nose up at outside undercover guys like me. That's what you did when you spent your career shining a seat with your ass: you talked down to the guys in the trenches.

Not me. I had total respect for the deputy director of operations of the CIA. I had total respect for how a guy in his position could torch a mission— even one as vital as this one—just to show how much power he wielded.

"You communicate straight through my office. You got it?" he said, leaning against the table. "I'll decide what the general and his team need to know. We clear on this, Mr. Conlan?"

Oh, so now it was Mr. Conlan. How very interesting. No problem. I had anticipated this request, and I wanted to demonstrate my sincerity. I reached into my pocket and palmed a fifteen-dollar dual-band Hop 1800 GSM disposable phone. I slid it across the table and into Wiseman's bony hand. He held it up as if I'd offered him a peanut butter sandwich when he was expecting caviar.

"What's this? A joke?"

"I want to be able to get you on a secure line at a moment's notice," I said. "I know you're used to people going through channels, which I'm happy to do, but our timetable might make that difficult."

I nodded in the direction of the phone. "Do you mind? It means keeping it with you at all times." I didn't say, *Take it or leave it,* even though it may have entered my mind to do so.

"I want to hear from you every day, Jake," he said. Now I was Jake. Pretty soon we'd be sending the general out of the room. "Do we have a deal?"

"Count on it," I said. I pushed back my chair and came to my feet. Tom did the same. "Now I've got a plane to catch. Thank you, gentlemen."

The deputy director of operations shook hands with Tom and placed a hand on my shoulder as we exited the room. "Show the bastard," he said. I assumed he meant The Twelver, but maybe I had missed something along the way.

"Keep that phone close," I said as he shuttled down the hall with two waiting aides.

Tom and I went in the other direction. I heard him chuckle. "Say, you wouldn't have one of those really cool disposables for me, would you?"

"And waste another fifteen bucks? Forget it."

We were outside and a long way from the building before he said, "You'll have a phone waiting for you when you land. It's got everything on it that you asked for. And some things you didn't." He looked at me. "You didn't say anything about a weapon."

"Already done," I replied.

"Send me a postcard." Translated: you know where to send intel.

"We'll do lunch in a couple of weeks," I said and headed for my car. I turned over the engine and put some music on: The Who's "Goin' Mobile."

CHAPTER 3

CHARLES DE GAULLE AIRPORT, FRANCE

It was five thirty in the morning. A sliver of gray light bleached the horizon. Perfect timing. You don't bring a plane like the Blackbird SR-71 into one of the busiest airports in the world during the middle of the day if your goal is anonymity.

The plane taxied onto the brightly lit parking tarmac and halted.

We had crossed the Atlantic at Mach 3, with my six-foot, 185-pound frame crammed into the copilot's chair in the cockpit of a plane I would have sworn had been put into mothballs years ago. No pretzels, no hot coffee, no bantering with flight attendants of the opposite sex. But the average commercial flight to Paris from D.C. takes a good eight hours, and we did it in close to three and a half, so I wasn't complaining. After all, how many people can say they've experienced Mach 3 speeds with one of the best pilots on the planet at the controls. And most important of all, the nuclear clock was ticking, and we had to shave every second possible.

My canopy popped open. A couple of U.S. Air Force techs pushed a gantry up against the sleek, viperlike fuselage. One reached into the cockpit and helped me undo my seat harness and uncouple the oxygen fittings from my helmet and bulky pressure suit.

"Good trip, sir?" she said, easing me out of my seat.

"'Surreal' doesn't really describe it," I quipped. I clambered out of the cockpit and onto the gantry. I descended the metal steps with the visor of my mirrored helmet cracked just enough for me to get some fresh air. This way, I was just another flyboy back on earth; no use drawing attention to myself.

Two guys in flight suits escorted me from the gantry into the back of a nondescript cargo van. They weren't wearing name tags. The techs hadn't been, either. No surprise. We might as well have landed in Area 51, because you don't exist on a mission like this.

A guy with sergeant stripes helped me out of my helmet and pressure suit. He said, "Welcome to France, sir," and slid a plain black carry-on out from under a bench.

"Good to be here. Thanks for the ride." The van was already in motion. I opened the carry-on and unpacked a dress shirt, business suit, and black wing-tips. An American businessman on the streets of Paris might not be as common as an American tourist, but no one gave a second glance to a guy with a brief-case in his hand.

I fished my NSA-modified iPhone from the carry-on, did a quick function check to make sure the apps I'd requested were there, and dropped it into my pocket. I tucked an envelope stuffed with euros and dollars into the interior pocket of my suit jacket. I examined two passports with two well-vetted IDs and found a pocket for them as well.

"Hungry?" the sergeant asked.

"Starving." My last meal had been six hours earlier, at Langley, and not much of one at that.

"Thought so." He handed me a sandwich. "Chicken salad. Best I could do."

"You're a godsend." I unwrapped the sandwich and devoured it. He poured coffee from a thermos and passed me the cup. "You're fast becoming my favorite person," I told him.

"Enjoy it. ETA ten minutes," he said.

I counted the minutes off in my head—an old habit—and hit it right on the number. As the van came to a halt, I checked my tie and ran my fingers through my hair. The sergeant gave me a thumbs-up and threw open the van's rear doors. They opened onto a service door at Terminal 1. A maintenance tech—by the looks of him, an agent from the Direction Générale de la Sécurité Extérieure, the French equivalent of the CIA—held the door open and acted as if I were invisible.

I towed the carry-on along a narrow corridor and exited through a plain door into the terminal lobby. I'd been dropped on the other side of customs, free and clear. I was leaving the womb of safety and emerging into the cold world of peril. It was game on, and I could hear music inside my head: Lynyrd Skynyrd's "Free Bird." Showtime.

I melded into the crowd and walked toward the passenger-pickup zone. For the casual observer, I projected the nonchalant air of an American businessman back in France, yet every fiber of my being was on high alert and would be for, well, as long as it took.

I stopped for coffee and a newspaper at a small kiosk, paid in euros, and carried my cup to a deserted seating area with a view of the sun breaking above the horizon. I had ten minutes to kill. I opened the paper, but only for show. I hit the Eavesdropping app on my iPhone, clicked the browser, and checked e-mail. There was only one, and only one word at that: *pristine*. Excellent. My backup was in place.

I opened a secure line on the phone. I sent a text to a longtime contact in Amsterdam named Roger Anderson. There wasn't a piece of equipment in the world that Roger couldn't get his hand on, and I would need his procurement skills in the next forty-eight hours. The text was three short words: *Halo. Two days*.

I finished my coffee and headed for the exit. I stepped outside. The air was cool and moist; it was going to be a typical spring day in Paris. I discerned a pattern among the people streaming in and out of the airport: hurried and self-absorbed; typical airport behavior. I was on the hunt for that one anomaly. That one person whose glance lingered a blink too long, that one airport employee who seemed a step out of place, that one face with a sheen of anxiety.

I stopped and observed the line of taxis waiting for fares. Most of the drivers looked Arab. I spotted a tall, light-skinned man with exceptionally pronounced cheekbones—he looked Ethiopian or Somali, but I knew different—standing against a less-than-pristine sedan third in the queue. He watched the swarm of arriving passengers with the laconic eyes of a veteran while I watched him. He was a veteran all right, but not of the taxi-driving kind.

When I was sure I was the only person taking an interest in him, I dragged my carry-on his way. This didn't make me particularly popular with the cabbies at the head of the line, but that was not my problem.

He turned my way. He smiled and his eyes flicked in recognition. I studied them, plumbing them in an instant for any sign of trouble. His name was Hammid Zoghby; he was an Algerian operative and an old friend. But in the shadowy world of black ops, alliances can turn in a moment, and old didn't necessarily mean trusted.

He stuck out a large paw. "Monsieur Green! *Bienvenue à Paris,*" he said.

Charles Green was one of three aliases I had invented for this mission. As far as the world knew, a guy named Jake Conlan was having dinner in his Annapolis home and sipping a nice chardonnay.

Zoghby threw my carry-on into the trunk and offered me the rear seat of the taxi. There was a blue gym bag with an Adidas logo on the floor, just as I had instructed.

He pulled away from the curb and traded some choice Arabic with the cabbies at the head of the line. Then he laughed, as if screwing a couple of Iraqis was about as much fun as an African could have. He glanced at me in the rearview mirror and in English said, "Where to?"

All Zoghby knew was that he was to pick me up at the airport with a blue gym bag in tow. "Head for the city and take your time." At this time in the morning, we would have the road more or less to ourselves, and I was in no hurry. My rendezvous wasn't until midmorning.

"You got it, boss." Zoghby kept a close eye on his rearview mirror as we made our way out of the airport and gave me a quick nod as we merged onto the highway. "Looking good," he said. He sat back and turned on the radio.

I set the gym bag next to me and zipped it open. Hidden underneath a layer of folded towels was a Mauser 7.65 mm pistol—not my gun of choice, but acceptable for the work I had to do here in Paris—and an aluminum tube: a silencer. I checked the magazine. Another two magazines were tucked inside a black nylon pouch. I slid the pistol inside my waistband and the spare magazines and silencer into the pockets of my suit coat.

There were also two Cartier jewelry boxes inside the gym bag, and I set them on the seat next to me. I discarded the lids, pushed aside the interior cotton, and removed two stainless steel memorial bracelets with the names of two former comrades laser-cut into the bands. Paul Redder and Clayton Spriggs were operatives killed in Afghanistan four years ago. Good friends. Superpatriots. And, yes, the bracelets memorialized their sacrifices, but they weren't the work of Cartier or any other jeweler. They were hand-tooled by an explosives expert in Marseilles named Fabian Tomas. I'd known Tomas for twenty-three years, and there wasn't anything he couldn't turn into a weapon.

These particular bracelets were coated with a minute amount of Semtex, a relatively stable explosive until it came in contract with a spark detonator. In other words, I wouldn't want to rub the two bracelets together unless the situation absolutely called for it. Perfect for locks. Perfect for diversions. Perfect for close contact. I'd never gone into an op without them. I wasn't about to start now.

I fitted Paul's bracelet around my left wrist and Clayton's around my right. Hopefully, I wouldn't need to use them.

Stopping The Twelver meant I'd have to work with Iranians, people I preferred to keep at a distance, preferably in the crosshairs of a .300 Winchester Magnum sniper rifle. To get inside Iran and to gather the kind of intel I needed, I had to enlist the one group that wanted Mahmoud Ahmadinejad and the mullahs who had his back to fail as much as we Americans did. That group was the Mujahedin-e Khalq. The MEK was the most powerful Iranian resistance organization in the world. The irony of the situation was that they were still tagged as a terrorist organization by my own government. Go figure.

Sure, there was a fair share of upstanding patriots in the MEK membership, though most operated in the foggy middle ground between insurgency and organized crime. They bankrolled their operations by dealing on the black market, which meant that their activities also attracted some serious scoundrels. I didn't mind your average scoundrel. I just wasn't particularly fond of the kind who looked at patriotism as a marketable commodity.

A Renault coupe slid up next to the cab on our left, close enough for me to recognize the guy riding shotgun. His name was Davy Johansen. Davy was a former SEAL Team Six operator and freelance counterintel specialist, another buddy from the old days. I didn't recognize the driver, but if he was sitting an arm's length from a man as cautious as Davy, then he'd been properly vetted. These two were charged with watching my back. Zoghby didn't know they were there; he wasn't supposed to know.

As the Renault dropped back a couple of car lengths, the taxi approached the Boulevard Périphérique, the main artery encircling Paris proper.

Zoghby shot me a look in the rearview mirror. I gave him an address in the Tenth Arrondissement. His eyes crinkled. Exactly the reaction I'd expected. We were a stone's throw from the center of Paris, yet parts of the Tenth Arrondissement made for the roughest neighborhoods in Europe.

"Sounds like fun," he said.

"A barrel of laughs." I checked my watch. A quarter to eight.

A block from my destination, we crossed a broad, shimmering canal, and I told Zoghby to take a right turn onto a narrow street crowded with cars and delivery trucks and working folk. It was the kind of place where people scratched out a living and seemed to be enjoying their plight. I could hear radios blasting, people laughing, and the occasional horn sounding. A taxi on these streets hardly warranted a curious glance, but that's exactly what I was looking for: a curious glance, a face in a window, an idle worker. So far, so good.

"Right there," I said. I leaned forward and pointed to a dingy apartment building at the end of the block. "Make a left and pull up at the entrance."

Zoghby did as he was told, though I could see by the look on his face that he was trying to make sense of it. I handed him an envelope with five thousand euros in it, payment for the pistol and the ride and his silence. I left my carry-on in the taxi; it had only been for show as I passed through the airport. If I needed anything, I'd buy it.

"Be well," Zoghby said with a distracted wave. "You know where to find me if you need me."

I waited until the taxi was out of sight before setting out. The café I was looking for was a block and a half to the west. I headed that way.

My meeting with the MEK was at ten. My contact was one Sami Karimi. The DDO had supplied me with some background, and Davy had done some digging on his own. I had to go through Sami to get to the right people in Amsterdam. I didn't like it, but my choices were limited. The MEK had their rules, but their rules didn't mean a thing if they didn't conform to mine. The solution was easy. I may have needed them but I had to convince them they needed me more.

The truth was, I needed Sami for more than just his Amsterdam contacts. I needed him to point me in the direction of the drug dealer Mr. Elliot had mentioned—the one who had overplayed his hand by extorting money and information from a member of the U.S. Senate Select Committee on Intelligence; the one who was screwing with my mission.

Inside the café, I ordered a cup of coffee and a croissant and took a seat by the front window, where I could observe the rather dingy storefront across the street. The windows of the storefront were streaked and plastered with ragged posters. Graffiti covered the metal entrance door. The MEK loved these kinds of dumps for their covert meetings, so I wasn't surprised when Karimi suggested it.

I fished out my iPhone and scrolled through Karimi's dossier. I stared at his face.

His head was heart-shaped, with a pronounced forehead and a receding hairline brushed into short curly locks looping behind small ears. He had a typical Middle Eastern nose: long, sharp, and thin. His chin was surprisingly weak, which didn't help with the bucktoothed look. Not a handsome guy.

The dossier told me that Karimi was a "fund-raiser." He earned his keep in the MEK by smuggling contraband such as beluga caviar, Chinese cigarettes, computer chips, and stolen car parts. Odds were he had a network populated with some very nasty characters, and if he showed up with fewer than two of them in tow, I'd have been shocked. "Come alone" didn't mean a thing to a guy like Karimi.

At 9:47, Davy Johansen's Renault rolled past. Ten seconds later, my phone signaled an incoming text. It was from Davy. It read: *He's got company. Front and back, 100 meters.*

I grinned. *So much for orders,* I thought. I finished my coffee and had just enough time for a refill. I held the empty cup up to my waiter.

At 9:52, I got a second text from Davy: *In position.* He had a clear view of the street and a ten-second dash to the storefront. His driver was holding down the alley out back.

At 9:56, a last text read: *One in, one out. Watch yourself.* In other words, one of Karimi's men had taken up a position inside the building and one was stationed in the alley out back.

Karimi appeared ninety seconds later, ambling down the sidewalk with his hands in the pockets of a dark windbreaker and a cigarette dangling from his lips. He wore jeans and looked fitter than I had expected.

When he reached the storefront door, Karimi pulled keys from his pocket, unlocked the three dead bolts, and opened the door with a kick to the bottom. He didn't go in. He turned and waited, just another merchant getting a late start on the day.

At 9:58, I left the café, crossed the street, and masked my approach in the bustle of pedestrian and vehicle traffic. My pistol pressed against my hip with reassuring heft.

Our eyes met. *"Bonjour, monsieur,"* I said. "Cigarette?"

"You dress like a bookkeeper," he said in English.

"And you dress like a pimp."

Satisfied, he breathed a sigh of relief. I didn't. I said, "Let's go inside, Mr. Karimi."

Karimi tossed his Gauloises into the street gutter. He opened his palm toward the door. "Be my guest."

"Thanks." I even smiled. But Karimi had no sooner crossed the threshold and closed the door than three things happened in as many seconds. First, I horse-collared him with one arm. Second, I pressed the barrel of my Mauser against his temple. And third, I said in the calmest voice he had ever heard, "Didn't you get the message, Mr. Karimi? We were to meet alone. Not with a couple of your buddies hanging around."

"And so we are." Karimi gagged on the words. "We are meeting, and I am alone. Just as you requested."

I had to give it to these Middle Eastern types: they really knew how to split hairs. "Have your friend come out, Mr. Karimi. Now."

The office was crammed with cheap desks covered by a jumble of desk lamps and open cardboard boxes. Computers ten years past their prime were tied together by extension cords and cables that snaked across the room in search of a functioning electrical outlet. Overhead, a row of fluorescent lamps buzzed and flickered and painted everything with an anemic, greenish cast.

I pushed him through a doorway into an open bay. Car tires and cardboard boxes in various sizes were stacked on sagging plywood shelves. The place smelled of grease and grime like a neglected auto garage. I said: "We're wasting time, Mr. Karimi."

I increased the pressure on his esophagus, and a single word squeezed from his vocal cords: "Aziz."

I didn't suffer fools well. Never had. But in a voice as calm as a placid lake I said, "Your friend outside has been waylaid by my friends outside, so let's quit playing games."

The man named Aziz stepped out from the shadow, his right hand holding a pistol at the ready. A Walther .380. Good gun. Enough to blast a hole through his partner, but probably not through me. Not that I would have bet my house on it.

"Tell him," I said to Karimi.

"Put the gun down, Aziz. Let's talk."

Aziz was a lanky, hard-looking man, maybe thirty or thirty-five if you gave him the benefit of the doubt. The gun dropped to his side. "On the counter," I said, easing my gun away from the side of Karimi's head.

Aziz laid the Walther on the counter next to a toolbox. I loosened my grip on Karimi's throat. "Hell of a way to get an operation started," I said in English.

"We needed to make sure that we could trust you," Karimi answered.

Smart thinking, weak execution.

I pocketed the Mauser and picked up the Walther. I released the magazine and let it clatter to the floor. Racking the slide, I emptied the chamber. I tossed the pistol to the floor. "Okay, now you can trust me."

I pointed to a card table and four folding chairs. "Sit. Now that we're acquainted, let's get to business." I took the chair with my back to the wall. Karimi and Aziz sat opposite me. Stacks of paper littered the table. I saw bills of lading, customs documents, and shipping manifests, all counterfeit of course. I got out my iPhone and shot Davy Johansen a coded text: *Shipshape*.

Next, I dipped my hand into an interior coat pocket, withdrew an envelope containing fifty thousand euros, and tossed it in Karimi's direction. "For your time."

He opened the flap and thumbed the bills in the envelope. He glanced at Aziz. Then he pushed the envelope inside his windbreaker. "That's a lot of money. What does it buy?"

"I have to get into Iran. I have to do it quickly, and I have to do it with absolutely secrecy. Who better than the MEK. We've worked together before. We've both benefited. Same deal."

His brow wrinkled. "When? Why?"

"When is my business. Why is obvious. Regime change," I said. Those were the magic words with the MEK. They harbored no shortage of hatred when it came to Mahmoud Ahmadinejad and the mullahs on the Supreme Counsel. If the words *mortal enemies* ever applied, this was a perfect example.

Karimi's stare deepened. His face bunched into a tight knot. "Regime change. And you can make that happen?"

"Hah!" His friend Aziz was disgusted. He jumped to his feet and threw his arms in the air.

"Have your friend sit down." I didn't say this to Aziz. It was an ultimatum that I expected Karimi to use to reestablish his footing in the meeting.

He said, "I wouldn't presume to tell my friend how to express his indignation."

"Then tell Mr. Aziz he has two choices. He can sit, or I can help him sit. Please tell him that my definition of *help* and his definition may not be the same."

Karimi twisted his head in Aziz's direction. He gave a classic Gallic shrug and opened his palms to his friend as if to say, *You decide.*

Aziz stood his ground for three face-saving seconds, then trudged back to his chair and sat.

"Thank you." I was still looking at Karimi. "I need contacts. I need cover. I need transportation."

"Why come to me? If my sources are correct about you, you're a phone call away from our leadership. Why come to me?" he asked again.

"Because I respect the chain of command," I said. I was lying, of course. I couldn't have cared less about the MEK's chain of command. What I respected was the fact that the guys on the ground—guys like these two sewer rats— were the ones in the know about every other sewer rat in Paris, and that's what I needed.

"Listen, Karimi, you want your country back, then we can't play games. You have to trust me, and I have to trust you." Total bullshit. I trusted this guy about as far as I could throw him. "Make a call to Amsterdam. Set up a meeting for me tomorrow. Noon. Tell them Mr. Green respects the MEK hierarchy." I was making myself ill. "Tell them these are the most important times in the MEK's history."

I paused and let the words linger. Karimi wasn't stupid. He negotiated for a living, and he knew the negotiations weren't complete. "And?" he said.

"And I need the immediate whereabouts of one of your esteemed colleagues, Mr. Karimi. A complete and total waste of humanity named Reza Mahvi."

"Reza." He couldn't hold my eye. His gaze shifted to Aziz, who used the moment to inch to the very edge of his seat. Karimi drew a noisy breath, glanced back, and said, "Why?"

"Because he's peeing in my government's cornflakes, that's why," I said. "And because he's selling the information to your sworn enemy. Any other questions?"

CHAPTER 4

It was a black night. Moonless. Ideal.

Not that I had planned it that way.

I'd been given the word. Mr. Elliot said the Iranian had to disappear. My mission depended on it. He didn't say to wait for the perfect night.

Disappear was one of the many euphemisms guys like Mr. Elliot used. You know, one of those words that's maybe just a little less offensive or distasteful than coming right out and saying, *Kill the bastard.*

Politicians love euphemisms. I guess we like them all right in our business, too. We used the term *special ops* when what we were really talking about was burning down unsavory governments, sabotaging narco-terrorist operations, torturing people who may or may not know things we needed to know, assassinating the rottenest apples in the barrel. Controlling a little war in Africa or a well-meaning skirmish in the Middle East. You get the picture.

But this kind of thing was done neither haphazardly nor irreverently. Every operation, every assignment, every action was plotted with purpose and clarity. Some people might look upon sabotage or assassination or insurrection as indefensible, but nothing could be further from the truth. They were acts with a singular purpose, acts bent on defending the American way of life.

I had no problem putting a gun in the face of a drug dealer suspected of

23

blackmailing a member of the Senate Select Committee on Intelligence, and I had no problem pulling the trigger. You play with fire you pay the price. But I did have a problem with a U.S. senator who lacked the pluck and the self-control to keep his cocaine problem behind closed doors. Now he was jeopardizing my mission, and now I was being asked to clean up his mess.

The drug dealer's name was Reza Mahvi. I'd known him back when he worked as a captain in a swank restaurant on New York's Upper East Side and owned a little piece of a crowded honky-tonk bar in the Village. Reza knew half the politicians in D.C. back then, and the senator from Massachusetts was just one of them. Reza had fixed up dozens of congressmen with expensive women and nearly as many with enough pot and blow to keep them high twenty-four hours a day.

The last time I'd seen the Iranian, I was undercover in New York, and he was bragging about the women he dated as if half of them were movie stars and the other half were United Nations staffers instead of call girls and political wannabes. I remember his making a federal case about the orange Corvette he drove back then, as if he'd plunked down forty grand in cash for the thing instead of digging himself further and further into debt the way all his Iranian buddies did.

Yeah, I'd known Reza Mahvi well enough. Did I like him? The truth was, liking him or disliking him wasn't part of the job back then, even though I'd acted like he was my best buddy every time I went into the club. Reza wasn't a big enough fish or a ballsy enough player to trade heavy in the hard stuff, but he knew the guys who did. Part of my job for the twenty-seven years I'd spent running black ops was to find them.

Apparently, somewhere along the line, Reza had relocated to Paris and graduated from drugs and women to extortion and blackmail. The senator from Massachusetts had become one of his favorite targets. But now Reza wanted more than the senator's money: he wanted the kind of information that only the Senate Select Committee on Intelligence was privy to. I didn't know which of them was more stupid or more careless, the guy doing the blackmailing or the guy with the target on his forehead. I had my opinion, but it didn't mean much under the circumstances.

When Mr. Elliot said that Reza Mahvi had to disappear, I knew immediately that the order had come from the highest level. No one had to say another word. I understood completely. Reza and his once benign dog-and-pony show had stepped over the line, and the most important mission of my career was in jeopardy. Wasn't going to happen.

I didn't like carrying a gun in a foreign city, especially with a fake passport in my pocket. I didn't like using MEK sewer rats for my source information. It also wouldn't have been my first choice to make the hit on a street as busy as the Rue de Pantin, but I didn't have the luxury of waiting for Reza to take a midnight stroll in the Luxembourg Gardens.

The Iranian had taken up residence in a seventeenth-century apartment house within spitting distance of the Seine, but just far enough away to keep the rents reasonable. He was on a month-to-month lease. It was 11:30 P.M. when I cruised down the street the first time. I was driving a beat-up Renault that Davy Johansen assured me could not be traced. It was Thursday night, and I had the windows down. The fragrance off the Seine hinted of an early autumn, my favorite time of year in Paris. Too bad I wouldn't be around long to enjoy it.

Lights blazed from a dozen or more windows across the face of the complex. I heard music drifting down from a third-floor balcony, and I saw a half-dozen people with wineglasses in their hands. I made two more passes. Then I toured the parking lot out back and found the space reserved for unit 19, Reza Mahvi's place. Cars filled half the other spaces, and most were newer models owned by twenty- and thirty-year-olds who probably saw themselves as "upwardly mobile." Too bad Reza had given up his orange Corvette: it would have stood out like a sore thumb and told all his neighbors that an Iranian pimp lived in unit 19. These days he drove a white 1984 Mercedes convertible, as if that were less conspicuous.

I got on the radio. Davy Johansen and his partner had taken up positions on either end of the block and were there mostly to see to it that Reza didn't bolt. He wasn't going to bolt.

"Status," I said. "Alpha?"

"At the table," Davy said. He was positioned east of the complex on Rue de Pantin, with eyes on every piece of transportation moving in my direction. "At the table" was typical tradecraft. We always spoke as if the target had a scanner with the capability of monitoring our conversation, no matter how long the odds were.

"Bravo?"

"Table clear," the one posted at the intersection west of Reza's place said. I didn't know him. I didn't want to know him. Just do the job and say good night.

"Roger that," I said.

I didn't want the Iranian using the visitors' parking spaces out in front of the apartment house, and a dirtball like Reza wouldn't think twice about doing that if he thought it would save him a dozen steps to his front door. Visibility out on the street was way too risky, especially with people hanging out on their balconies, so we'd filled the empty spaces with rental cars. Just in case.

"Sit tight," I said in a voice so calm you would have thought we were delivering a pizza. "Not a chance in the world this guy'll miss dinner. Momma's cooking up a classic. He'll be here." All this really meant was that I knew how Reza operated. I knew he was a creature of habit. And I knew he'd make an appearance eventually.

There was something else I remembered about Reza Mahvi. He was nothing if not a big talker. He couldn't wait to regale you with his puny exploits. If there was a name to drop, he dropped it—anything to put a fresh coat of paint on the image of a second-rate street hustler. Clearly, he'd taken a step up in the world. From hustling drugs and women for U.S. congressmen on the prowl to putting the squeeze on the very guys he used to pimp for. Give the guy credit.

"Action!" Bravo called, his voice as cool as a mountain stream. He had Reza in his sights. "ETA thirty seconds. I'm putting a lid on it on this end."

"Likewise on my end," Davy said.

"Ten seconds to the table. Fifteen to the chair. Good luck," Bravo said.

"Roger that," I said. And those were the last words we would ever say to each other.

I saw the headlights before I saw the Mercedes. I was parked in the space reserved for unit 16, two cars away from Reza's space. Naturally, Reza spun his wheels navigating the parking lot; he may have climbed the criminal ladder a rung or two, but he still conducted himself like a second-rate drug dealer.

The Mauser 7.65 mm rested on my lap, and I gripped it loosely with a gloved hand. It was fitted out with an aluminum silencer and was untraceable.

Mob-style. That's how Mr. Elliot wanted it done. A clear message needed to be delivered to anyone else thinking about blackmailing an American official, and the 7.65 caliber, the silencer, and the parking lot—everything was designed to make it look like that.

I opened my door, slipped the Mauser into the pocket of my jacket, and climbed silently out. I walked along the back of the cars to Reza's Mercedes. The music inside the car was still blaring, and Reza was drumming the steering wheel, waiting for the song to end. I kept my back to the apartment house even though all the balconies faced the Seine. I walked without a sound between the Mercedes and a gray Citroën. I stopped next to the driver's-side door and wrapped on the window with my left hand. Reza sat bolt upright at the sound, like a man fending off a blow. Then he saw my face, and the slow dawn of recognition caused his brow to furrow. I smiled, but the furrows only curled into lines of dark suspicion. I beat on the window again. He finally rolled it down, shaking his head and trying to look pissed off.

"What the fuck? That you, Jake? What the hell you doing in Paris, man? You scared the shit out of me," he said, sneering.

"Yeah, sorry about that," I said, easing the Mauser from my jacket pocket. "But we need to talk."

Reza shook his head; he was clearly partied out. "I got no blow on me, man. Nada. And besides, I've been out of that business for years."

"Do an old friend a favor and turn down the music, Reza," I said calmly.

Perturbed, Reza reached for the knob on the radio. I raised the Mauser. The end of the silencer came up next to his head, and I pulled the trigger. Two times in less than a second. The Iranian slumped sideways. I didn't wait to see if he was dead. He was.

I launched the Mauser toward an overgrown hedgerow, turned, and walked with unhurried steps back to the Renault. I was opening the door on the driver's side when two women came out the back door of the apartment house and started across the lot. I didn't glance back and didn't hurry. I slid behind the wheel but didn't close the door until I saw the women duck inside a red Fiat parked a dozen spaces away. When I heard their doors slam, I closed mine. I waited until the Fiat was out of sight before turning over the engine.

I wasn't concerned. I'd be on a plane for Amsterdam in an hour. And by the time the French police identified the Iranian, I'd be headed for the most danger-ous place on earth and Reza Mahvi would be the very least of my worries.

CHAPTER 5

AMSTERDAM—DAY FOUR

I never forgot a name and never jettisoned a possible connection, including Arman DiCiccio.

I entered the Merry Times café, a serious dump on a side street just off Warmoesstraat Boulevard. Pungent smoke clouded the air. A bunch of college-age kids crowded the closest table and shared hits on a bong. Most of the other tables were occupied by couples nursing lattes and puffing on joints. Glass cabinets sat atop the wooden counter along the back of the café. A chalkboard above the counter advertised prices for the café's daily specials: Silver Haze, seven euros; Thai stick, six euros; Isolator hashish, eight euros. Ah, Amsterdam! No place on earth quite like it.

I wore a tie-dyed hoodie with a tattered denim Jerry Garcia cap and mirrored sunglasses. I looked like an over-the-hill Dead Head and fit right in.

I was here for a reason, and it had nothing to do with getting high. There was a link that everyone digging into Iran's nuclear capabilities failed to make, and that was the funding that supported both their worldwide terrorist movement and their weapons research. A serious part of that funding came from their monopoly on opium production, and their influence stretched from Afghanistan and Turkey to Burma and Cambodia. It meant billions of dollars, and you can get a lot done with billions of dollars.

29

The Merry Times was the domicile of one Arman DiCiccio, a man I had befriended during my first op, over three decades ago. Arman had gotten wounded in a crossfire outside a Newark nightclub, shot in the thigh and stomach by his own people. His subsequent convalescence hadn't worked out so well. He'd gotten himself addicted to morphine, and that had drawn him here to Amsterdam, the junkie capital of Europe. Since then, Arman had kicked the habit, or so I'd been told. That was the good news. The even better news, for my purposes, was that he had plied his many and varied contacts in the drug business to open up this coffee shop and smoke hole.

I took a seat near the counter and ordered an espresso from a rail-thin waitress with bronze-and-gold hair. I had a new weapon under my hoodie; Davy Johansen had arranged a pickup the minute I landed in Amsterdam, and his choice of the Walther PPK/S had put a grin on my face. The Walther .380 was my favorite pistol. Davy knew that. What he didn't know was that he'd earned himself a bottle of fifteen-year-old Dalmore for his efforts.

Five minutes passed before a curtain of plastic beads guarding the doorway behind the counter parted. A very large, very pudgy man with acres of tattoos limped into the room with a cardboard box in his hands. I studied him with a crooked grin on my face. His thinning, wiry locks were gathered into a ponytail, which only served to emphasize a receding hairline. His forehead was a knob of smooth flesh creased by shallow pink wrinkles. Bushy eyebrows hooded dark, deeply set eyes. It had been years since I'd seen that face and the years had taken a toll, but it definitely belonged to Arman DiCiccio.

Arman's arms had once been thick with hard muscle, but these days they were fleshy and slack. He rested the box on the counter and sorted through buttons of hashish in plastic wrappers. I came to my feet and stepped up to the counter. I set a small backpack on the counter and pretended to be interested in the contents of the glass jars in one of the cabinets.

"Alles wat ik u kunnen helpen met?" he said in Dutch.

My Dutch being pretty nonexistent these days, I tried a grunt and a short shrug.

This was a gesture he had apparently witnessed before, because he switched to English and tried again: "Interested in our specials?"

I removed my sunglasses, kept my voice low as I said, "Got any Specter Six?"

Arman went statue-still, like his bones had turned to ice, and his face knotted into a ball of hard concentration. Specter Six had been the code name for one of the many counternarcotics teams that I ran back in the day, and Arman DiCiccio had been one of my assets.

"Damn!" It was a sneer. Then he rose to his full height and spread his shoulders, as if the memories of his past service invigorated him. Well, maybe "service" was overstating it.

I extended my hand before he could get out another word. "Charlie Green." Two words and he knew I was undercover, as if my ridiculous outfit weren't hint enough.

We shook. I read his grip, looking for signs of anxiety. "How have you been, Arman?"

His hand was warm and loose, but not without some of its former strength. A good sign. I let it go.

He smiled and slapped that proud gut of his. "Too good. Way too good," he said. "Man, it's been . . . hell, it's been a bunch of years."

With his gaze fully on me, I studied his eyes: steady and clear. I measured the timbre of his words and found nothing but warmth and camaraderie.

His gaze flickered to my cap, and the old habits of our clandestine operations came back. He would no sooner give away my identity than he would betray his mother. I had once broken the neck of a Colombian drug dealer who had the muzzle of his Glock .380 screwed to DiCiccio's temple, and he owed me. At least, that's what he thought. Who was I to argue?

He said, "Here on business, Mr. Green?"

"Always."

"I have some kick-ass Purple Skunk in the back. Let's have a taste." Arman waved in the direction of my waitress. "Maaje. Mind the store, will you?"

31

My old comrade shoved the hashish buttons under the counter and limped through the beaded curtain. I stepped around the counter and followed him into a stockroom thick with the smells of coffee, teas, and hashish.

Arman continued through another door into a small office. An open laptop sat on a desk between neat stacks of papers and magazines. Muted cheers from a soccer game murmured from a flat-screen TV on the wall. A wipe board on the adjacent wall was covered with columns and numbers listing the shop's eclectic inventory.

He stood to one side and ushered me in with a flick of his fingers. He closed the door behind me. I took the pulse of the room; it was three seconds before I judged it clean.

"Sit, my friend," he said. I chose a green leather chair with a view of the door. I placed my backpack on the floor. DiCiccio took his place in an Aeron executive chair behind the desk. He propped his right foot on a wooden crate and massaged the bullet wound on his thigh, the product of our last job together.

"What gives? Mr. Green?" He cocked an eyebrow. I knew he wanted to say "Jake" but stayed with my nom de guerre.

I inched my chair closer to the desk and winged a thumb in the direction of the TV. "Turn that up a bit, will you?"

Arman aimed the remote at the flat screen and pumped up the volume. I had no reason to believe that anyone would be eavesdropping on us, but there was no such thing as being too careful.

He laid the remote back on the desk and knitted his fingers. Then he leaned forward. His voice dropped an octave. "I figured you'd be retired. Not too many guys like you beat the odds."

"I was retired. I opted back in."

That piqued his curiosity, and he raised his eyebrows, anticipating, I imagined, some type of enticing explanation.

I dodged his unspoken question and got straight to the point: "I need your help, Arman."

He gestured with open hands. "Whatever you need, Mr. Green."

"The Iranian opium connection," I said simply.

Arman DiCiccio, a veteran of way too many close calls, puffed his cheeks and leaned back into his chair. He exaggerated a long sigh and rubbed his face. Then he leaned forward and anchored his elbows on the desk. "You're deep in it, aren't you, Mr. Green?"

I didn't answer right away. Finally, I said, "Deeper than you think."

Arman DiCiccio's eyes narrowed, and he hunched over his desk. I sensed a strain of concern. He was putting two and two together. He knew I hadn't come here to talk about the opium trade. I wouldn't have come out of retirement for that. He probably also figured that whatever I was up to was bigger than one guy trying to connect the dots between Iran's stronghold on the opium market and their blatant funding of terrorist groups from Japan to Algeria. That left only one thing: weapons development. When I saw him shake his thick head and massage his ruddy face with two hands, I knew he'd made the connection. "Okay. So, I'll ask you again. What do you need?"

"One plus one. A name here in Amsterdam and a name in Tehran. An open door to the money pipeline. Something I can track," I said. "And I don't have time to work my way up from the bottom, Arman. Top dogs only."

With immense sarcasm, he said, "Damn. Is that all? Hell, why didn't you say so."

I waited. He had every right to be pissed. Here he was, running his little hole-in-the-wall enterprise, just making enough to stay comfortable, and some guy from a past he'd do anything to forget shows up and asks him to ID someone who could put him out of business with a single phone call.

"This make us even," he said. "Right?"

"You've never owed me a thing, my friend."

DiCiccio smirked. Whispered, "Same old Jake."

He clicked the keys on his laptop and turned it around for me to see. The monitor displayed a local newspaper, *Schuttevaer*. Centered on a page of the business section was a photo of a round-bellied man with a trim beard, and dressed in a dark suit. He stood grinning on a balcony overlooking the city. The caption identified him as Atash Morshed, and the adjoining article described the extraordinary success of his online banking business, investment firm, and brokerage house. Well, I had to give Mr. Morshed credit. What better cover for hiding and diverting money.

I said, "A well-respected investment banker. Makes sense. Do me a favor. Cut and paste this link into an e-mail message." I gave him the address of an anonymous Yahoo account.

He turned the laptop back around and clicked a series of keys. "Done," he said, then sat back with his hands folded over his belly. "You won't get close to the guy, you know. Especially now. One of his buddies—a real model citizen by the name of Reza Mahvi—got whacked yesterday in Paris, so his crew has tightened ranks, from what I've heard."

News travels fast, I thought. But that was no reason to let Arman know that Reza's death was old news to me. I said, "Thanks for the heads-up. Now who's the guy pulling Morshed's leash in Tehran? That's who I'm really after."

"Out of my league." DiCiccio shook his head. He chewed on his lower lip. He was done talking, I could see that. He said, "If I knew that, I wouldn't be running a coffee shop on Bloom Straat, would I?"

Actually, I believed him. And even if I hadn't, a knock on the office door saved him from explaining himself any further. A crack opened in the door, and I heard my waitress say, "Arman, I've got an order here for three ounces of Moonshine Dominator. I can't find it on the shelves."

"Hold on," DiCiccio called to the door. Then he looked me up and down. "Well, business calls, Mr. Green."

"You've been a big help," I said quietly.

DiCiccio nodded. He reached for the remote and lowered the volume on the soccer game. He rose to his feet and extended his hand. "It's been a pleasure. Don't leave town until we've had dinner."

"I'll try," I said, taking his hand. I pumped it once. I was a nice invitation, but we both knew I was the last person on earth Arman DiCiccio wanted to have dinner with just now. "Keep your head down."

"You, too. Good luck, Mr. Green." He pointed to the back door. I scooped up my backpack and let myself out. A cobbled alley led me back to Warmoesstraat Boulevard and tourists trying to look discreet as they prowled among Amsterdam's many temptations.

I turned south and settled my pack on my shoulder. Now I had to throw Atash Morshed's name into the National Security Agency's hopper and hope that their computers could find a link with that one special name in Tehran; they'd know by the amount of money that was being funneled through this special person's account. The rest was up to me.

The safe house the MEK had procured for me was on Bergstraat, but I never intended to use it. Instead, I'd paid cash for an upper-floor room in the Golden Dutch Hotel on Singel. It was a twenty-minute walk from Arman DiCiccio's café, and I spent most of that time checking my tail. There were bicycles by the hundreds on the street, and this added to my dilemma.

It's hard not to love Amsterdam. They say it began as a medieval fishing village. Thankfully, the canals are still there to remind you, and the extraordinary quality of a floating city prevails. These days it still holds on to a good amount of the seventeenth-century magic of its heyday, and the buildings that crowd the canals look as ancient and proud as the stone they were built from.

The Golden Dutch Hotel was one of these buildings, though half of its patrons were full-time residents. I used the back stairs instead of the lift and climbed to the fifth floor. A musty scent followed me to room 523, and I used my key to let myself in. I went straight to the window. I studied the street, then the Singel canal. The banks were cluttered with colorful houseboats, and a floating market was bursting with the colors of what looked like a million flowers.

I sat on the bed and used the iPhone to activate the secure linkup to route my call through the CIA's encrypted connection. I sent a conference request to General Tom Rutledge. The text reply came back immediately: *confirmed*. *Good*, I thought. He was making the mission his top priority, and I guess that only made sense.

The conference-call program gave a beep prompt, and I oriented the iPhone toward me. Rutledge's face appeared on the screen. A sheen of sweat glistened on his forehead and a white towel was draped over his shoulders. The collar of his gray U.S. Army T-shirt was ringed with perspiration. It was 1416 hours here in Amsterdam. With the six-hour time difference, I must have caught him in the middle of his morning racquetball game.

He looked at me and said, "Things are well?" He would never use my name, and I would never use his. No matter how secure the line was supposed to be, you didn't use names.

"Smooth as silk."

Tom nodded. This was his way of acknowledging the hit against Reza Mahvi. Even though the video of our call was highly encrypted, a man in Tom's position couldn't afford to implicate himself on a sanctioned assassination. I waited. He wiped his face with a corner of the towel. "Lay it on me."

"I've got a lead here in Amsterdam. Look for the info in five. I need our friends at Fort Meade"—in other words, the NSA—"to give it an Alpha Sigma Nova priority. My instructions will be in the e-mail."

"Done," he answered. "What's the terrain like?" By this he meant the danger level.

"Pretty flat right now. But I'm on for tea in the afternoon." This confirmed my meeting with the MEK's leadership in two hours. "I'm going on a walkabout after this call."

"Good. Keep me posted. Anything else?"

"Not at the moment."

"Then I'm out." The call disconnected and the screen went blank.

I composed the e-mail and forwarded the information on Atash Morshed. The NSA had decades of practice tunneling into banking operations, but even their supercomputers would take time. I'd check on their progress later.

I didn't want to talk to Deputy Director of Operations Otto Wiseman, so I sent him a voice text. Three words: *See Tom Run.* In other words, "Talk to General Tom Rutledge. He'll give you an update."

Last but not least, I sent a text to Roger Anderson, my longtime contact here in Holland. It read: *On track. Drinks at ten.* This confirmed our rendezvous at a dive bar we both knew called Tracks at 1800, two hours earlier than my message suggested. His reply was instantaneous: *With bells on.*

After closing the communication links and the associated apps, I put my Jerry Garcia cap back on, hitched my pack over my shoulder, and went outside for a recon of the area. I strolled in what seemed an aimless pattern along the canals and made my way toward the center of Amsterdam. I did a couple of tourist things. I bought coffee from one street vendor and a braut from another. But it was all for show. I was on the prowl, vigilant, wary, suspicious of even the most ordinary of details. So I spotted the two guys following me fairly quickly.

They were good. Not great, but good. Did that make them MEK or DDO or someone else? I couldn't tell.

I ducked into a pub and headed to the men's room with my backpack. I swapped my hoodie for a blue golf jacket, my denim cap for a khaki hat with a floppy brim, and the mirrored sunglasses for tortoise-shell wraparounds. I stared at myself in the mirror. It was a simple but effective change, from stoner to tourist.

I used the back door and walked halfway down the alley. I entered a second pub via the kitchen, gave a nod to a startled chef, and ordered a glass of Rauchbier from the bar. I carried it out to an empty table on the outdoor patio and slouched in a chair. I sipped the beer, toyed with my iPhone, and watched the people coming my way.

The two men strolled on the adjacent sidewalk. They had glossy black hair, swarthy complexions, and trim beards; definitely Middle Eastern, but Amsterdam was replete with them. Their gazes swept the patio and passed over me. One of them was talking on a cell phone as they passed by.

He was speaking Persian. Mine was still a little rusty, but I understood him when he said, "We've lost him. . . ."

CHAPTER 6

AMSTERDAM—DAY FOUR

I watched the two men halt at the entrance to the pub's patio.

The one with the cell phone was doing more listening than talking now, which meant that someone was not real happy. The questions I was asking myself were pretty straightforward. Who did these guys work for? And who was giving them hell right now on the other end of the phone?

I'd been tag-teaming with a couple of Wiseman's Amsterdam agents since I'd arrived, and they were waiting for my call in the lobby of the Amsterdam Hilton. So I felt relatively confident in assuming that these two were not more of Wiseman's men; and that if they were, then the deputy director of operations was not playing it straight with me.

I had to assume they were MEK. If so, I had a problem. My meeting with the MEK leadership wasn't for another hour and twenty minutes, and the location hadn't even been confirmed yet.

The two men passed through the patio and entered the pub. I put my glass of beer on the patio table and left. I crossed the street and watched the pub from inside a souvenir shop. I scanned both sides of the avenue, checking for signs of a second team: a shadow checking to see if the first team was being shadowed, so to speak. This was typical overkill in the cloak-and-dagger business; if you didn't know if you were being tailed, then you shouldn't be in the business. Fortunately, these two were alone.

They reappeared outside the pub less than a minute later, looking confused and pissed. The taller of the pair made another call on his cell phone. I took three pictures of the pair with my iPhone for later reference and waited.

It was a short call and very one-sided. The two hurried away from the pub and headed north. I stepped out of the souvenir shop. When they were halfway down the block and had put a good number of pedestrians between us, I started after them. They were still on the hunt, heads swiveling, peering into every storefront, stopping at every intersection and gazing down every alley.

I stayed with them, a half block behind, wary of the possibility that they could be leading me into a trap. At Bloedstraat, they turned left. Here the street narrowed through a residential neighborhood restricted to foot traffic and bicycles, and there were plenty of both. The tightly packed apartment buildings made this place way too convenient for an ambush. I watched their progress from the end of the street. I had no intention of venturing forward until I was dead certain of what they were doing.

Ten seconds later, they turned left at the cross street and disappeared around the corner. I plunged down the avenue. This was the kind of street the tourists never saw, which meant they never really saw the heart and soul of the city. The scent of baking bread filled my nostrils. A neon sign flashed over the door to an apothecary. I heard laughter.

I was a dozen paces from the cross street when an older-model Volvo sedan sputtered into view. I could see the shorter of the pair at the wheel. His taller partner rode shotgun.

I got to the cross street just as the car sped up. I had just enough time to memorize the license tag and take a second photo with my phone before the car was gone, lost in the chaos of traffic. Not that either the photo or the license-plate number would be of any value.

An hour earlier, I had been certain that I had arrived in Amsterdam unnoticed. Now I was high-profile on someone's radar. I wasn't particularly eager to return to my hotel room, but leaving my backpack was not an option. Bad move leaving it there in the first place, and now I had to risk going back. I made a call to the front desk and asked for the head bellhop. In my experience, there was very little a bellhop wouldn't do for twenty American dollars, and this one delivered my backpack and duffel bag to the loading dock out back of the hotel for exactly that price.

I kept a list of additional safe houses in my iPhone. My backup was a tiny apartment in Hartenstraat. The landlord knew me only as an American businessman who insisted on privacy during his sporadic visits to the city. I sent a text asking if my room was available. Moments later, he answered that it was. Good. Maybe things were looking up.

I walked the several blocks to Hartenstraat and scoped the neighborhood, a strip of shops and apartments crowded together on opposite sides of the street. All clear.

The front door to the safe house was tucked between a women's clothing boutique and a bakery. I tapped the entry code into an electronic lock beside the entrance, let myself into the tiny foyer, and shut the door behind me. I paused at the bottom of the stairs. I listened to every sound. There was only the chatter of people passing by on the walk outside, the ring of a bicycle bell, and the echo of a television on the first floor. Nothing else.

A row of mailboxes hung from the foyer wall. I turned the tumbler lock on the mailbox assigned to my apartment, opened it, and removed the room key stored inside.

My room was second to the left on the landing. Standing to one side of the door, I slipped the key into the dead bolt and turned the key until the lock snapped open. I listened for the rustle of clothing, the shifting of feet. Nothing.

I swung the door open and peeked inside. Again, nothing. I locked the door and activated the iPhone app that searched for surveillance bugs. Nada. I checked the rest of the apartment, the closet, under the bed, the shower stall. The upside was that the bathroom was stocked with toiletries; the downside was that I wouldn't be here long enough to use them.

I threw a couple of pillows against the headboard of the bed, got as comfortable as I intended to get, and scrolled through my incoming messages. General Tom Rutledge wanted a videoconference ASAP. Had to be about the online banker Atash Morshed and his Iranian connections. I sent my reply: *Ready now.*

I stared at the phone for nearly a minute before the conference-call app beeped. I held the iPhone up to my face. Tom's visage appeared. He was in full dress uniform, and I wondered why. A fruit salad of ribbons decorated his left breast pocket, and three silver stars glittered on each of his shoulders.

He said, "Sit rep?" Rushed. Even a little harried. Interesting.

"My situation is this. I was shadowed earlier today by two Middle Eastern types. I'm sending you their photo right now." I transmitted the image and waited.

"Got it. Hold on. I'm doing an NSA cross-check," Tom said. I waited again, counting the seconds off and betting I wouldn't get to thirty. I didn't.

"The picture's coming through," Tom said, twenty-six seconds later. His brow wrinkled as he examined the photo. "The tall guy is Kia Akbari. An MEK operative."

"If he knew I was in Amsterdam, that means our security has a big hole." I felt the sting of anger because someone had been careless, or worse, traitorous.

"His boss is Kouros Moradi."

"The guy who runs the MEK cell here. The guy I'm supposed to be meeting within two hours. Not good," I said, even though I could read Tom's expression.

Not good, but also curious. I'd dealt with Kouros Moradi a dozen times back in the old days. He was smart and crafty. Smart and crafty enough to use any opportunity to put a chink in the armor of the current Iranian regime, and he was also resourceful enough to help. That's why I was starting with him here in Amsterdam. All well and good, but it didn't change the fact that two of his guys had been following me unannounced and uninvited.

I didn't like this. A key to my survival was knowing more about the other players than they knew about me. Back in the day, this would have been enough for an agent in my position to cut bait and call the entire operation off. Retrench and regroup. But I didn't have that luxury. The clock was ticking.

"Okay. My problem. I'll take care of it. Any word on our online banker and his contacts?" I said. I was talking about Atash Morshed, the moneyman for the Iranian drug industry, and I'd assumed that's why Tom had called.

"Plenty. Didn't take much for the NSA to plow through his records. The guy's up to his gonads in drug money, and a significant part of the cash Morshed is laundering makes a beeline right into the hands of some character named Sepehr Tale."

"Don't know him?" I said, shaking my head from side to side.

"Iran's undersecretary for economic development."

"Economic development, my ass," I said. The only economic development that the mullahs and The Twelver were interested in was military development, and that meant we'd scored a hit on the guy in charge of channeling drug money into the government's nuclear weapons program. "We're onto something. Good work."

"It's a crack in the door, but it's only as good as you can make it," he said. He was right. An official like Sepehr Tale could not be bribed or reasoned with. He was a tool of the regime. He might have believed wholeheartedly in what the mullahs were selling, but probably not. And it didn't matter. He was controlled by a single element: fear. Who knew how many men and women he had seen hung up by their necks at the end of a derrick crane. Who knew how many people he had seen die in Evin Prison. Sepehr Tale was a means to an end. A tool to be used and discarded. I looked forward to doing both. "Listen, report back after your meeting with Moradi, right?"

I said, "Right," but by now I was working every angle, including the possibility of a loose cannon in the Pentagon, General Tom Rutledge's own backyard. I was watching his face. His gaze tightened, and his presence was so electric that it was like he had teleported into the room beside me. I almost smiled. Instead, I said, "Lay it on me."

"This probably goes without saying, but I'll say it anyway: everyone seems pretty darn convinced that the Iranian government and the MEK are like oil and water. Serious foes, blood enemies. All that crap. But you and I know there's a lot of overlap when it comes to agendas and loyalties. Watch yourself, okay?"

The general had it dead on. It didn't matter what side of the fence they were on—progovernment or antigovernment—they were all more or less criminals, no better really than the narco-terrorists I'd hunted for two-plus decades. I looked at the three-star general on the other end of the phone and grinned. "Keep those chest medals polished, my friend."

"Will do." Tom signed off.

His e-mail had come through and provided a local telephone number and a couple of recent head shots of Kouros Moradi, the MEK kingpin. He'd changed since I'd last seen him. In the first photo—probably a passport shot—he was facing the camera in a stiff pose. A deep crease down his forehead bisected unkempt eyebrows that almost touched. His wavy black hair was smoothed back and needed combing. Wide jowls met with a thick neck. A dense mustache hung beneath a proud nose. In the other photo he was looking past the camera and seemed to be walking in a hurry. It was a candid shot, grainy, as if taken from a security video. Appearances aside, I knew better than to underestimate a guy with as much influence as Moradi had in this town.

I sent him a text confirming our meeting, and we finally settled on a warehouse in the Haarlemmerbuurt district. I wanted to arrive at least an hour early, so I took a quick shower, dressed, and went downstairs and grabbed a taxi.

It was a fifteen-minute drive, and I used the time to send a brief e-mail to Mr. Elliot. I didn't use the iPhone. I used a disposable I'd bought at the airport. *May need backup. Current cast dirty.*

His e-mail reply was almost instantaneous: *So what's new!* And then: *Look for the color blue.*

I broke the phone apart and tossed it piece by piece out the window. I saw the taxi driver watching me in his rearview mirror. I said, "Bad connection."

We drove west from Central Station and turned west into the Haarlemmerbuurt. The district was old even by Amsterdam standards and was now a place where shops and cafés and restaurants had turned quaint into fashionable.

Where else could you find a candy store, a vintage shop, a nightclub, and an abandoned warehouse on the same block, all illuminated by streetlamps and gaily decorated storefronts?

I paid off the cabbie and scouted Haarlemmerstraat for ten minutes, just another tourist enjoying a "not to be missed" section of the old city. I crossed the street to a bistro with "Glazen Huiz" written above the entrance. I followed two couples inside.

About twenty customers occupied the bistro, all pleasantly oblivious to the high-stakes game in play. I allowed an extremely attractive maître d' to lead me to a table near the back. I had a dozen other diners between myself and a window and a clear view of the warehouse entrance.

It was six thirty. Time for another text. This time I invited Moradi to bring along Kia Akbari, the man who had been following me earlier. It was a not-so-subtle message that I knew I'd been tailed and had given his bloodhound the slip. Moradi replied to this with a not-so-subtle question mark. A question mark and nothing else. Interesting.

While I waited, I ate a light dinner and drank coffee. Right on time, a Volvo—identical to the sedan I'd seen earlier—halted along the curb before the warehouse. The tall, lanky Akbari exited the front passenger's-side door. He adjusted the hem of his jacket, a telltale sign of the gun he was trying to conceal, and scanned the street.

A man emerged from the backseat of the car. He was powerfully built, with a thicker chest and a big, lumpy face. *Kouros Moradi.* Older, but no less menacing. He wore a black woolen coat and a cloth hat. Older, but still a fashion disaster. He held a cell phone in his hand. I imagined he always had a cell phone in his hand.

Just then, a second car pulled up, the door to the backseat flew open, and a third man jumped out. This one was almost as tall as Akbari. Sunken eyes and wildly dramatic eyebrows dominated his slender face. I recognized him at once. The MEK's second-in-command in Amsterdam, Ora Drago. Drago hadn't been so well placed when last we'd met, but even back then I'd made him for an up-and-comer.

The cars moved away and disappeared down the block. Moradi and his team turned toward the warehouse entrance, but I put a halt to their progress with another text: *Tell Akbari to stay where he is. You and Drago go to the middle of the street.*

Moradi read the screen, then lifted his gaze to sweep the area. He said something to Akbari. Then he and Drago walked into the street again and stopped. Moradi opened his palms as if to say, *Happy?*

I sent another text: *The bistro. Come inside.*

Moradi read the text. He looked into the Glazen Huiz's windows and searched for me among the patrons. He tucked the phone into his pocket. He and his second-in-command advanced into the bistro, arms hanging by their sides, hands loose, faces calm. Old hat, these kinds of clandestine meetings.

The maître d' approached them, but the two acted as if she didn't exist. Ignore a woman who looked like her? Crazy. Well, to each his own.

Moradi unbuttoned his coat and looked across the restaurant. We locked eyes. His jaw tensed, and his eyes slitted with unabashed mistrust. I used one hand to motion him and Drago to the empty chairs at my table and kept my other on the table. I was armed. I didn't intend to hide the fact, but it wasn't necessary to make two guys who lived just this side of paranoid any more paranoid than necessary.

Moradi placed his large, hairy mitts on the table. The gold band of an expensive watch clasped his wrist. I wondered how much of the MEK's budget was diverted to personal expenses. His eyes crinkled in amusement, like we were playing five-card draw and he was holding all the cards. He said, "Mr. Green," with just a hint of sarcasm. "So that's the name you're going by these days."

"It's been a long time, gentlemen," I said, looking from Moradi to Drago and grinning crookedly. "You've taken a couple of steps up the ladder, Drago. I'm impressed."

"Last we heard, you were dead or put out to pasture," he replied coldly.

"Negative on both counts," I said. "Glad to see that we're playing on the same side of the ball again." I saw the blank look on Moradi's face. "It's a football expression."

"I hate American football," he said. "Are you armed?"

"Damn right. When things get twitchy, I find a Walther PPK/S makes me feel just a little more secure. And things have apparently gotten a little twitchy."

"I assume you're referring to Kia. Let's begin there." He arched his thumb in the direction of Kia Akbari, who hadn't moved a muscle since his bosses moved inside. "He was following you, you say. Are you certain?"

I opened my iPhone to the picture I had taken of Akbari and his driver. I held it out for the man across from me to see. "Look familiar?"

"This is troublesome," he said, glancing at Drago.

Drago shook his head as if "troublesome" didn't describe it. He looked at me. "I put Kia on the tail. No offense, but you were coming into our house, and I wanted to make sure a meeting like this wasn't compromised."

"And you did so without my consent," Moradi said flatly.

Drago looked at Moradi, opened his palms. "I thought you had enough to worry about, *moaellem*."

Moaellum? Teacher? Master? I wasn't sure, but it seemed to be a statement of respect, and Moradi seemed satisfied, as if his second-in-command had taken initiative. He turned his gaze back to me and shrugged. "Okay?"

I didn't reply. What was I going to say? *You're both liars. That's what you do. Lie.* Instead, I said, "Let's discuss why we're here."

Moradi chuckled sardonically and answered in Farsi. "You're going to enter our country. You need help. And once you're in, you'll need more help."

I also switched to Farsi, clumsy as it was. "Good guess."

"There are only two reasons why a man like you would want to get into Iran." Moradi placed his weight on his elbows and crowded the space between us. "One would be to assassinate Mahmoud Ahmadinejad. How grand would that be! The other would be to stop his nuclear weapons program. Not an easy thing to do."

"Let me get into the country first, then we can get into the details of why," I said evenly.

Moradi laughed, showing big teeth, as shiny and white as the dinner plates. "Fair enough." His cheeriness vanished. "Mr. Green, let's you and me come to an understanding. I want Mahmoud Ahmadinejad gone. I want the mullahs who keep him in power gone. I want my country back."

"On that, you and I agree." Did I really think the MEK would be any better? I wasn't so sure.

"If you're going to ground in my country, you'll need contacts. I can provide those for you. If you need a way in, well, we have the people for that, too."

"Good. I knew I could count on you. How soon?"

He shrugged. "Tomorrow. Maybe the next."

"Tonight, Moradi. I need the contact info tonight. I don't plan on being here tomorrow."

Moradi's eyebrows arched above his thick, fleshy face. "Fine. Tonight. But not here. Not in public. We'll use one of our places." He started to reach for his cell phone. "I'll get my driver."

"No. We'll do the caravan thing. You, Akbari, and me in a cab. Drago in his car. Your driver in his," I said. "Give me the address. I'll make a call."

Moradi shrugged; caution was not something he disapproved of. He wrote the address on a napkin, showed it to me, and then crumpled the napkin in his fist. It disappeared into his coat pocket. I checked the address with my iPhone. The location was in the Dapperbuurt district, a neighborhood of apartments and small businesses just east of here.

I called a taxi, stood, and motioned to the door. Moradi and Drago started out, and I kept two arm's lengths behind them.

When we emerged from the restaurant, Akbari straightened. His hand moved exactly four inches closer to his jacket, and therefore four inches closer to his weapon. It wasn't those four inches that worried me.

"Kouros?" he called. "Everything okay, boss?"

"Your boss and I are getting along fine," I answered. "But even so, keep your hands where I can see them, if you don't mind."

"Do it," Moradi ordered. "This is a friendly party."

He glanced at Drago. "Stay close, but not too close."

"Got it. Both cars are on the way," Drago replied.

Our taxi arrived thirty seconds before the MEK cars. Moradi and I climbed into the back. I took the seat behind the driver. Akbari sat up front, on the other side of the partition. Nothing like a little bulletproof glass between you and the man you least trust, especially one with a gun in his coat.

The cab made two quick turns and pushed through a yellow light onto Prins Hendrikkade. I looked back. Drago's driver got caught at the red, and I didn't know whether this was good news or bad. To our left, a sprinkling of green, red, and white lights blinked off the surface of the canal, and music spilled out from a houseboat overflowing with college-age kids. To our right, multistoried buildings built of stone the color of dull bronze rose like a gauntlet next to the street. Double-decker buses, bicycles, and bright lights made the city sparkle like a theme park.

I kept mindful not only of what was ahead of us but behind as well. I could see a set of headlights drifting from lane to lane, and it didn't take more than a quick moment to recognize who and what they belonged to. I was expecting Drago's Saab, but it wasn't. It was a Volvo sedan Moradi had arrived in.

"Why is your guy driving like a maniac?"

Moradi turned his head toward the rear window. "What do you mean?"

"Your driver."

Moradi's eyes and eyebrows bunched together in a tight knot, and his slack mouth curled into a scowl. Something was wrong. We hadn't gone another block when the Volvo began flashing its headlights. Something was definitely wrong, and then Kia Akbari was shouting from the front seat.

"Watch out!" He was pointing at the oncoming traffic.

I saw it then. A delivery truck was rumbling over the center median and careening toward us. My first thought was to bail, but we were traveling too fast. My second was to grab Moradi and jam him against the back of the front seat.

The taxi's brakes screeched, and the horn blared.

It was too late.

CHAPTER 7

PRINS HENDRIKKADE, AMSTERDAM

The delivery truck careened over the median and plowed headlong into us. I had three thoughts that more or less raced through my head at the same time. One, this wasn't a drunk driver or an overzealous commuter; the driver of the delivery truck hadn't touched his brakes or made the slightest attempt to swerve. Two, Kouros Moradi's driver knew something bad was afoot, because he'd been trying to run us down for nearly a block; but if he knew something, why not use his cell phone to warn us? And three, I could have been at a barbecue in my own backyard instead of playing bumper cars with a three-ton delivery truck.

Our taxi was slammed backward, metal crunching, glass shattering. The crash rattled pretty much every bone in my body. The instant everything stopped, I bolted upright from behind the front seat and took stock of the situation. Up front, Kia Akbari and the taxi driver blinked in dazed shock, their faces chopped up by the rain of sharp glass fragments from the shattered windshield. At least they were alive.

Around us, cars were screeching to a halt. I heard shouts and screams echoing from the sidewalks.

The delivery truck sat before us, the front bumper and grille smashed in and a fountain of radiator fluid spewing into the air. Light from the streetlamps tricked across the strewn wreckage, and shards of glass glimmered like uncut jewels. Kouros Moradi uncurled himself from the floor, his face contorted and pale.

"You okay?" I didn't need the head of the MEK in Amsterdam dying just then. I still needed him.

"Okay. I think," he said.

A man clambered out the passenger's side of the truck cab, pistol in hand, and shouted in Farsi, "Find the American."

I'm not normally a betting man, but I was willing to lay odds just then that he was talking about me.

"We gotta move," I shouted at Moradi.

I jerked open the door and grabbed him by the collar. We spilled out of the car and he landed on all fours on the asphalt. I fell in next to him.

"Go! They want me, not you. Go," I shouted, pushing the huge Iranian toward the curb. He shambled into a crowd of astonished pedestrians who, not five seconds earlier, had been out for an evening stroll and were now witnesses to some very serious mayhem. If it were me, I'd be diving into a doorway for cover right about now.

I drew the Walther from inside my jacket and popped the safety. At the same moment, I heard the taxi's front door swing open and caught a glimpse of Kia Akbari darting around the back of the taxi, gun drawn.

He looked straight at me. At this range, I was a sitting duck, and all I could do was berate myself for a lack of good judgment. *Well done, Jake.* But of course the Iranian was a sitting duck, too. But rather than empty a full magazine into my torso, Akbari flattened himself against the trunk of the car, held his pistol in a two-handed grip, and aimed at the truck.

"Go. Go," he yelled at me. "I'll cover you."

The driver of the runaway delivery truck jumped out and drew a Glock; I imagined it was a Glock by the burnish of the metal, but it could have been any 9 mm. He and his partner used the truck's doors for cover and opened fire. Relatively professional, but sloppy. People screamed and dived for cover. About time. I heard music blaring in my head, Lynyrd Skynyrd's "Call Me the Breeze." *Time to play, Jake.*

Bullets ricocheted from the pavement close to my feet. I fired two shots, taking out the window glass of the truck and sending the two gunmen ducking for cover.

Akbari scooted along the back of the taxi and put himself in the line of fire. He yelled over his shoulder, "Get the hell going!"

Akbari fired out his magazine, riddling the truck and keeping the two men at bay. He crouched behind the taxi and groped in his jacket for a fresh magazine.

I hated these kinds of decisions. Run in favor of the mission and leave a soldier with zero chance of survival, or risk the mission and take a stand by his side. I heard sirens. "Move," Akbari screamed. So I did, and hated myself for it.

I sprang to my feet and ran. The sidewalks were filled with fleeing people, and I pushed a woman and her child into a nearby stairwell. I glanced back. There was a motorcycle darting down the thoroughfare, and it wasn't the cops. I saw bullets splash around Akbari's feet. One hit his ankle, and he crumpled to the pavement. I was raising my gun when the next bullet tore into Akbari's leg and another ripped into his belly. His head lolled back, and the pistol spun from his hand to clatter on the asphalt. Goddammit. The man had sacrificed himself for me.

A flood of police cars raced onto Prins Hendrikkade. The two gunmen charged around the taxi, guns raised, and paid no heed whatsoever to the police. They raced into the crowd with one aim, and that was to find and kill me. That wasn't going to happen today. I painted a picture of both of them in my head even as I ran. The passenger: a burly Persian with a bald head and a thick nose, snorting like a bull in heat. The driver: a skinny, dark guy with spiked hair and a Hulk Hogan mustache. I wouldn't forget them.

I had a fifty-yard head start and dashed left into a side street, dodging pedestrians and hurdling a baby stroller. I could outrun the shooters or taken them down in a firefight, but my bigger problem was the motorcycle.

I looked over my shoulder. On second glance, it looked more like a dirt bike as it zigzagged through the street. The rider wore a black-and-red helmet. He locked in on me. He had a very nasty-looking machine pistol dangling in front of him—probably a MAC-11 purchased from an American arms dealer—and I saw him gripping it with his right hand. All hell was about to break loose, and I had to end it fast.

When I reached the cross street, I tucked myself around the corner of a four-story stone apartment house. I gripped the Walther with two hands, stepped around the building, and triggered three shots in less than a second, all low and aimed at that midlevel point where the biker's knees and the bike's gas tank came together. I didn't wait to see the results. I dipped back behind the building and listened as the bike skidded across the pavement.

Now I looked. The motorcycle had tumbled onto its left side, pinning the rider's leg beneath it. He lay dead still, arms spread apart. I dashed out into the street and straight for the motorcycle. I hadn't ridden a bike in years, but I figured it would come back to me.

It wasn't to be. The next wave arrived, heralded by a chorus of blaring car horns and a beat-up Renault screeching to a halt on the cross street. The right-side doors opened and the two shooters bounded out. A second motorcycle circled them. The rider goosed the throttle and pointed the wheel directly at me. I was in serious trouble.

My one chance was straight ahead, across the street, to the canal. I had maybe three seconds. I dodged a Mercedes coupe as it swerved in front of me and braked to a halt. The driver stared moon-faced at me, fear and surprise bleaching him of color. I bounded over the hood and onto the sidewalk. I saw a houseboat cruising the canal, left to right. I was probably too old to attempt what I was about to attempt, but I didn't stop to think about it. I grasped the steel railing that bordered the canal and launched myself toward the boat. I hit the canvas canopy dead center. The canvas ripped apart under my weight, and I fell on my ass on the deck. A dozen partygoers stared, their faces blanched with astonishment. Who could blame them. A man dropped his glass of wine. A woman screamed. Dinner plates went flying.

I levered myself upright and shouted in my very rusty Dutch, "Get down on the deck. Down on the deck. Now!" I pulled an older couple to the deck and several others followed.

An instant later, gunshots popped above us. Bullets punched through the canvas and raked the boat's beautiful wooden hull. Anyone who hadn't dropped to the deck did so now, all except a woman in a cocktail dress with a wine goblet stuck to her fingers. She was paralyzed with fear, and I couldn't blame her. I dragged her to the deck, looked her straight in the eye, and said, "Don't move."

Another salvo of bullets clawed through the port-side windows, shattering wine bottles and turning dishes into shards of porcelain. Wine and food splattered the deck.

A speedboat skimmed toward us from the right, bounding over inky water dappled with the yellow reflections of streetlamps. I saw a man take up a position on the bow. I saw him raise what looked like an AK-47 to his shoulder. The muzzle let loose a ball of fire, and bullets sprayed the houseboat.

At the front of the galley, a flight of stairs rose to the bridge. Someone begged for help over a radio. I sprang up the steps. Two crewmen wore blue jackets, khaki pants, and matching baseball caps. One looked completely panicked at the helm; the other was gripping a radio handset and screaming into the mike. Their faces beamed in shock when they saw me climb onto the bridge.

"Down, down, down," I shouted, physically throwing the radioman to the floor of the bridge deck and pushing the helmsman aside. I grabbed the wheel. I shoved the throttle to its front stop, and the houseboat surged forward.

Our sudden wake rocked the speedboat, knocking the shooter off-balance and into the canal. Now it was two against one. Better odds. Not great.

The pilot of the speedboat gave his motor a squirt of gas and turned the boat toward us. Another man crawled from the cockpit, a fresh AK-47 at the ready.

The houseboat lumbered forward; no way could we outrun them. Our advantage, if you could call it that, was size and heft.

I turned the helm to the left and motored into the middle of the canal. The speedboat pilot was so fixed on getting into a good firing position that he didn't notice that I was nosing him toward the canal's opposite wall.

The shooter raised his gun, but I drove him off the hull with three quick shots from my Walther. I had seven bullets left and a fresh magazine in my coat pocket. I fired two more in the direction of the speedboat's pilot. He eased off the throttle long enough for me to nudge him closer to the canal wall. We were now thirty feet away and closing.

The speedboat pilot finally realized the danger and hollered in panic. He jerked the throttle and tried to reverse his engine. The boat didn't respond.

I spun the helm to the left. Now there was nothing to cushion the blow with the canal wall except the speedboat trapped between us. That was the plan.

A surge of water lifted the speedboat, and the houseboat slammed the tiny hull against the concrete. The speedboat splintered, taking both pilot and gunman down with it.

I didn't look back. I eased the throttle back on the houseboat and guided it into the middle of the channel, toward a second canal on the left and a stone bridge. I heard sirens. I saw patrol cars with blue lights flashing on their roofs. One parked close to the railing on the opposite side, and a searchlight lanced across our flotilla of gondolas.

From what I could see, there was no sign of the gunmen on the thoroughfare by this time. I filled my lungs and took note of my heart rate: sixty-six. A little high, but not bad given the excitement.

I urged the houseboat's two crewmen to their feet. "Take the wheel," I said to the helmsman. I pointed to a wooden pier jutting out into the water a hundred yards ahead. "That's my stop. Get me close."

Then I caught the radioman's eye. "Alert the channel police. And get an ambulance over here. Then get downstairs and check on your passengers. If you've got a first aid kit, I'd bring it along." He just stared at me. I snapped, "Now, sailor!"

He jumped to it, powering up his radio and tapping an area-wide emergency number. We were closing in on the pier. I gestured at the helmsman's jacket and hat. "Mind if I borrow those?"

"What?"

My Dutch sucked. I switched to English. "Your hat and jacket."

I realized the Walther was still dangling from my hand, and I stuffed it into my shoulder holster. I fished a roll of euros from my pocket and gave him half. I stripped off my coat. He did the same. It was a poor disguise even with his baseball cap, but the police would be looking for brown suede, not sailor blue, so it was better than nothing.

The helmsman cut the power and turned the nose toward the pier. "Ten seconds," he said.

"Sorry about your boat," I said. What else could I say? I half expected him to say, *Screw you,* but he didn't. In fact, as I was jumping from the bridge to the main deck, he said, "Good luck."

He swung the stern within two feet of the pier. I jumped. I looked back long enough to raise a hand, but by then he was busying steering his shattered boat back into the middle of the canal, his world changed forever.

In the distance, I saw the spires of an ancient church illuminated by a gibbous moon. *When in need of a hiding place, look for a house of worship.* Mr. Elliot must have said that to me a dozen times, but I'd always thought he was kidding. Maybe not.

I walked. Running might have felt like the right thing to do, but running had one very negative side effect: people took notice. I also thought people might take notice of the helmsman's jacket—not exactly my style—so I shed it as I walked along a cobbled walk lined with gift shops and street-side cafés. I saw an empty table on the patio of a coffee shop and took a seat facing the walk. I hung the jacket on the back of the chair. I powered up my iPhone. I entered Roger Anderson's phone number and typed a short text: *Trouble. Change of plans. Nieuwe Kerk. One hour?*

I waited, allowing my eyes to drift from one end of the block to the other. By now the police would have my description. By now the guys in the delivery truck would have called in reinforcements. But they'd had their opportunity and blown it. You only get so many chances at the perfect ambush. They'd played it poorly. Too much drama. I'd learned one thing a long time ago: guys with guns love making a big show of things, but the best kills were the ones no one sees coming.

My phone vibrated. Two words: *Roger that.*

I got up, left the coat, and tugged at the brim of my newly acquired hat.

The Nieuwe Kerk was only a thousand yards or so from where I was standing as the crow flies, but I took the back streets. I hadn't spent much time in Amsterdam, and when I had, it had always been work related. I never really had the chance to appreciate the ancient melding of wood, brick, and stone that carried from building to building or the houses fronting the maze of tree-lined canals. I could see the romance that drew couples here. Oh, yeah. And of course, everyone knew that Amsterdam's red-light district had few rivals, and their lax drug laws were the stuff of legend, so maybe there was an appeal to the college kid on holiday or someone looking for an uninhibited place to drown his sorrows. Me, I'd take a quiet stroll on a New Jersey beach any day.

I crossed under the viaduct and into a residential district populated with multistory apartment buildings with latticed windows and graceful gables. Here, the bottom floors were crowded with the offices of lawyers and dentists. A trio of muscle heads, vapor steaming from their thick necks and sweat-soaked jerseys, ambled out of a gym. To the north stood the Montelbaanstoren clock tower with its white-columned top and matching spire. Lumbering on my right was the itinerant water of the Oude Schans canal.

I stopped in the shadows of a magnificent elm and sent Moradi a text. He replied that he was okay and asked me where I was. I didn't reply right away. Moradi wasn't my problem, I was sure of that, but the problem was too close to him for me to work that side of the street again.

I would need the MEK again once I reached Tehran, but for now I needed some distance. But Moradi deserved at least one last communiqué. If Kia Akbari hadn't put himself in harm's way tonight, I might not have survived. His death was worth a couple of words, so I typed: *I'll make sure Akbari didn't die in vain.* Then I pressed the send button.

I was a block from the Nieuwe Kerk when my phone vibrated again. I stared at the screen. General Tom Rutledge. His message read: *The chief of staff needs a word. See the map.*

CHAPTER 8

NIEUWE KERK, AMSTERDAM

This wasn't a good idea.

I'd just seen a man killed. The mission was compromised by sources I hadn't yet determined, but I knew for sure I couldn't trust the DDO's men any more than I could the MEK's.

The answer was to play one against the other, but that kind of counterintelligence took time and resources. Right now, I just needed to get to Istanbul and make damn certain I covered my tracks into Iran. And here I was waiting for a phone call.

Politicians. They always needed to be front and center. And anyone who tried to tell you that the president's chief of staff wasn't a politician had been living under a rock for a very long time.

"The chief of staff needs a word," General Tom Rutledge had said exactly six minutes and twenty seconds earlier. I was sitting in the back pew of the Nieuwe Kerk, a Gothic masterpiece that history dated back to the fifteenth century and more or less made it hard to justify that Nieuwe Kerk translated literally into "New Church." Well, maybe not so new, but way back then it served as the replacement for a slightly smaller house of worship called Oude Kerk. You guessed it: "Old Church."

I loved architecture and could have gazed at the arched ceilings and the gaudy mosaic and stained-glass work for hours. Too bad I didn't have the hours to waste. In fact, I didn't have the six minutes and twenty seconds I had already wasted while a politician who needed a word got around to delivering it.

My phone vibrated. The church was a beehive of activity. Mostly tourists, and mostly tourists who weren't impressed with the need for silence. I was glad for their lack of decorum.

"Go," I said into the headset microphone. I powered up the real-time-map application on my iPhone. It allowed anyone with authorization to input data germane to my mission at anytime. I could see that General Tom Rutledge had done so ten minutes and fifteen seconds ago.

"Sorry if I kept you waiting," said a voice from Washington, D.C. I recognized Chief of Staff Landon Fry's voice from our previous meeting, and the voice-recognition app confirmed it.

"No sweat. You're a busy man," I said and managed to keep the sarcasm out of my voice. "Is your 'need for a word,' as our mutual friend put it, worth the wait?"

"I think it is. Our mutual friend agrees. He's here with me now."

I rolled my eyes. Two of the most powerful men in the world sitting side by side, playing messenger boy. What a waste! I imagined that Tom was rolling his eyes, too. At least I hoped so. I said, "So?"

"We've picked up some information. It's pressing. I wanted to deliver it myself," Fry replied. I heard two things. The information should already have been delivered, and it should have been delivered through the most expedient channels, that being the link the general and I had already established. Since it hadn't been, the chief of staff apparently didn't trust that Tom and I would see the information in the same light as he did. Okay, fair enough. Not particularly smart, but fair enough. "We've received satellite imagery suggesting some increased shipping activity at one-bravo-one on your map. Can you see it?"

I used the zoom to zero in on Iran, and one-bravo-one hit on the city of Qom, ninety miles southwest of Tehran. It was located on the Qom River and was as old as the hills, seven thousand years old if my math served me. Now the Shi'a considered it one of their many holy cities. Population a million. Give or take. I said, "A million people and one of your satellites picked up enough increased shipping activity to raise a red flag. Okay. Coordinates?"

"North of the city center. Coordinates embedded." I recognized Tom's voice. Calm, but laced with purpose. I coded in the embedded coordinates, and the map zoomed in on a series of unimpressive buildings across from a corridor of railroad tracks. "A new development. Residential, warehousing, commerce."

"Industrial?"

"No. At least none we could pick up." In other words, not on the surface.

"A new development, you said. How new?"

The general answered again. "Ten years by the look of the foliage."

"What does that tell you?" Fry asked. Maybe he felt a little left out.

"It tells us that anything that new might have a dual purpose. Like hiding an underground factory or a research site or a chemical plant." I heard a very satisfying round of silence. I hated to break it. "Or it could be nothing. In any case, I'll put it on my radar. If I hear anything on the ground, I'll plan a personal visit."

You didn't ignore this kind of information. I wouldn't, and neither would the general. So I had to ask the chief of staff, "You're not very trusting, are you? Did you think our mutual friend and I would laugh this off?"

Landon Fry cleared his throat. "I know you're not a huge fan of IMINT or MASINT."

I looked up at the magnificent altar at the head of the church's nave and made eye contact with Jesus Christ, ignominiously crucified by a bunch of frightened, overmatched Romans. I shook my head. I just loved politicians who threw out acronyms; as if that made them bona fide members of the fraternity. He could have just said, *I know you're not a huge fan of high-resolution photography, or signature intel, or any other bullshit coming from a flying trash can one hundred fifty miles out in space.*

"I'm not a big fan when that's all you've got," I said.

Fry answered quickly, "That's why we have you."

59

And I was just as quick to say, "Then I guess we'd better cut the chitchat short. Send over your pictures. I'll see if I can connect the dots."

I signed off. I glanced up at Jesus on his cross again. "Politicians," I whispered, and figured he knew exactly what I was talking about.

I stood up and walked toward the transept and one of the most extraordinary pipe organs ever built. I followed a man in a wheelchair up the aisle. The ambrosia that permeated every house of worship in the world filled my nose and made me think of Cathy. I wasn't sure why. She was a spiritual woman, but not necessarily a religious one despite her upbringing. Her family was Italian Catholic, and family was at the top of her list, no question. We'd spent half our marriage apart, and she'd had no idea what I was doing back then. None. I could have been living on another planet. I had been completely honest with her the day I proposed. "You can't know what I do." Period. No apology. No equivocation.

I'd leave without a word and be gone for six weeks at a time. I'd take on the persona of one of the most corrupt, vicious drug dealers in the hemisphere, digging in so deep and doing things in the name of my country that only a man with the keys to the kingdom could get away with: drugs, arms, women, violence, death. And always, always with one goal in mind: intel.

I'd show up six weeks later, kiss her on the cheek, and go coach my kid's soccer game. Play poker with the boys. Make love to my wife. Run my limo business. Wait for the next assignment.

She thought it was over when I hung up my spurs five years ago. I'd told her it was over. Apparently, I had lied. And lied again when I walked out the door five days ago. All I could say was, "I have to be gone for a while."

I could see the look on her face as clearly as if she were standing in front of me right now. The look didn't say, *How could you?* or, *You said you were through.* To my amazement—but you know, maybe not my surprise—the look said, *It's okay. I'm proud of you. Go. I'll be here when you get back.*

So maybe that's why the lingering ambrosia of the New Church brought her to mind. Maybe getting back meant more than it ever had.

A priest stepped out onto the altar. A hooded white robe made him look more like a monk. It was hard to see his black beard, but I knew it would be neatly trimmed. I knew that a stubble of salt-and-pepper hair would be closely cropped and that his scalp would be sunburned. I also knew that the beard did a poor job of covering up the scar along his right cheek. I knew because I was responsible for the scar.

Roger Anderson was a retired air force master sergeant. An absolute badass, and one of the best soldiers on the planet. He'd made a career out of keeping the Stingers sharp for the Twentieth Special Operations Squadron, aka the Green Hornets. If a mission went to shit and you needed out *now,* his boys had been the ones you called.

Like a lot of the military's old hands, guys who'd called it quits but were eager to keep their hand in the game, Anderson had set up camp in Amsterdam, the crossroads of international intrigue and the mother lode for black markets from Marseilles to Moscow. No one knew more about High Altitude, Low Opening parachuting than Roger Anderson did. No one. And no one knew better how to get the latest gear. If I was going to get into Iran undetected, nothing could beat a HALO insertion. If I was going to HALO, I wanted the best in the business making sure I didn't die in the process.

I knelt at the altar rail. He stepped in front of me and offered his blessing. "You always did trust the wrong people, my son," he said, crossing my forehead with his thumb.

"Don't I know it."

"Who's hunting you this time? The usual suspects?"

I shrugged. "I didn't stick around long enough to find out, but I've got a couple of ideas."

A guided tour moved down the aisle behind us, and a woman speaking German was spouting facts about the church's hand-carved choir screen. When they were out of earshot, I whispered, "You got my message. Thanks."

"You mean the one about being in deep shit or the one about making a purchase?" He chuckled. "A bit of both, I guess, huh?"

"We both know you wouldn't have it any other way, Rog."

"As long as the money's right." He blessed me again and started to turn away, saying, "Meet me in the sacristy."

He was still chuckling as he walked back across the altar and disappeared through a door carved of some exotic wood that reminded me of Brazilian cherry.

I made the sign of the cross, got up, and circled the altar to a side door that led me straight into the sacristy. Roger was throwing off his vestment. Underneath it he wore blue jeans and a plaid shirt. There was a bottle of altar wine standing alongside a set of glass cruets, and he took a long, satisfying swallow. He smacked his lips and set the bottle back down.

He must have seen the disgusted look on my face, because he said, "Being a man of the cloth is tough work. Hell, what do think this wine is for? Follow me."

We walked to the back of sacristy. A set of double doors opened into a closet filled with vestments: chasubles, cassocks, stoles. Roger pushed them aside, and not with a particularly delicate touch. Behind the vestments hung a burlap curtain. Behind the curtain was a slab of thick wood equipped with a handgrip: a door. What the hell was a door doing at the back of the vestment closet in the sacristy of a five-hundred-year-old church? I was about to find out.

Beyond the door lay a pitch-black tunnel, but there was a pair of gas lanterns, which Roger struck up with a Bic lighter.

"Hold these," he said, thrusting the lanterns into my hand. He turned back, rearranged the closet and curtain, and reset the door. He grabbed one of the lanterns and headed down a tunnel built from heavy timbers and blocks of stone. "Watch your step."

He meant that literally, because less than ten seconds later we were descending a staircase made from roughshod lumber that looked as old as the church.

"What is this place?"

Roger grunted. "This church has gone up in smoke more than a couple of times, and it hasn't always been an act of God or a forgotten holy candle that caused it. Amsterdam may seem like the picture of peace and neutrality, but if you think the Catholics haven't been prepared for the occasional hostilities over the centuries, think again."

"This leads back to the canals, doesn't it?" I said. My logic was astounding, and obviously Roger thought so as well, because he answered with another less-than-reverent grunt. "So how'd an American expatriate with a suspect history find out about this place, Rog?" It wasn't really important, but my curiosity was getting the better of me.

"Two years ago I was minding my own business at a tavern in the old city when a guy sat down on the bar stool next to me. We got to talking. He'd been the caretaker of the church grounds since he was sixteen. Six beers later and he was telling me all his dirty little secrets, including the one about the imfamous sacristy tunnel. I toured it a couple of days later. Never know when you'll need an exit strategy."

We stopped talking. The tunnel leveled out. It smelled of mold and condensation. The ceiling dripped. I counted 687 paces. The door at the base of the staircase was a sheet of steel and badly rusted.

Roger took a deep breath, cracked the door, and peered out. A shock of blue and perfectly placid water stretched out across Singelgracht, the innermost canal in Amsterdam's magical ring of canals. I stepped up next to him and looked out. A dagger of ivory moonlight speared the water, and a line of houseboats was moored along the banks. Far more inviting was the twenty-two-foot-long motorboat tied up to a concrete landing no bigger than my back porch back home.

"Our ride," Roger said. "Climb aboard."

Three steps took me from the tunnel to the landing and into the hull of the boat. The outboard, I noticed, was a meticulously clean and highly polished two-horsepower Tohatsu. Leave it to Roger. He never settled for anything but the best, even if the launch looked like it would capsize in a light summer breeze.

I took a seat in the stern. Roger pulled the tunnel door closed behind him. He climbed aboard, positioned himself next to the tiller, and kicked the engine to life. It purred like a kitten.

"It's a twenty-minute ride," he said. "Let's hope we don't have to outrun anyone."

CHAPTER 9

AMSTERDAM—DAY FIVE

Roger piloted the launch away from the church dock and into the murky waters of Singelgracht. Houseboats crowded the canal as they did all the waterways in Amsterdam. I was grateful for the company—you didn't launch an attack from a houseboat—but I surveyed every one of the boats as if the rule was just made to be broken.

We passed Durgerdam on the left. A lighthouse perched on a steel-girder lattice, a sentinel of days gone by and a monument to Holland's perpetual battle with the sea.

He steered the dinghy into IJmeer, a lake and bird sanctuary, and eased back on the throttle. A family of ducks gave us a wide birth. Geese squawked and scattered.

"I'll bet you're sorry right about now that you chose Amsterdam for your coming-out party, huh, Jake?" Roger chuckled softly.

"Hell, man, I've worked with the MEK a dozen times in the past. So have you," I answered. "And I'm going to need them once I get where I'm going."

"It's not the MEK, Jake. At least it's not Moradi. But he's getting old. Hard to know who to trust these days. Me, I couldn't care less about the politics."

"Good," I said.

I studied the lowland terrain that seemed to stretch far into the night, like a shadow at the edge of dawn. Egrets stalked along the shore. Cars and trucks scurried on the roads, busy as ants. Something in the op had already soured, and the danger reeked like a toxic odor. Roger had always been a man to think on the fly—hell, that's what had kept him alive during some of the most harrowing dogfights in air force history—so I appreciated his sense of style in slipping out of Amsterdam via the water.

"Politics or not, I know enough about your MO over the years, Jake. I don't give a damn what you're up to, you know that, but it doesn't take much to connect the dots, I guess you know that, too."

A pelican bobbed in the water right in front of us, a head-on collision in the making. At the last second, it burst into the air, a blur of white-and-brown feathers skimming skyward.

I reached inside my coat and withdrew an envelope. I tossed it in Roger's direction and said, "See what you can connect with this."

Roger let the tiller have its own way for a moment and used both hands to collect the envelope. He hefted it, giving the weight of it his professional appraisal, and eyed me slyly. He opened the flap and peeked inside. His posture stiffened just slightly, which was a good sign coming from a man who had seen as much as Roger had seen, and a soft whistle wafted across the water. He closed the envelope and took control of the tiller again.

"Let me guess. This brick of cash means you're looking for either a Mark Six or a Mark Seven."

"The Seven."

"You're going deep."

I didn't say anything, and Roger had the good sense not to ask what or where "going deep" meant. He knew, more or less, and knowing less was always better in his business.

Our launch chugged out of IJmeer and into Markermeer, a huge lake contained by the Houtribdijk dike, a massive wall of earth and stone spanning the middle of the horizon and threatening to block out the sky. With the egrets and the pelicans behind us, Roger advanced the throttle, and we picked up speed.

"The Seven is a rig for extreme altitude," he said, tucking the envelope inside his windbreaker. "Let's talk logistics."

My original plan had gone to hell. Roger seemed to be the only piece of the puzzle that was holding together, and I shouldn't have been surprised. It didn't matter now how things had gotten so mucked up; it didn't matter whether the DDO was compromised or whether the MEK had sprung a leak. All bets were off. If I was going in via HALO, I needed a staging area. I needed one or two good people who I could trust for at least twenty-four hours. And if not trust, then use up quick and dispose of quicker.

I could find both the staging area and the help in one place: Turkey.

"I need to get to Istanbul, Rog, and not by the usual methods," I said. "Any ideas?"

"Yeah," he said, nodding his head. "Istanbul works. Good choice. Maybe your only choice, now that I think about it. And, yeah, I can get you there. You got the dough, I can get you just about anywhere."

I winged a thumb in the direction of Amsterdam's fading city lights. "Off the grid." I meant no airports, no train stations, and no water taxis.

Roger looked at me as if the obvious was something he had no time for. He said, "Is there any other way?"

"What do have in mind?"

"Jake, you work your magic, and I'll work mine." He pulled a cell phone from his jacket and punched in a number.

"Think I'll make a call myself," I said to him. He gave me a nod.

I moved from the stern to the bow and planted myself against the railing. The closest boats, all pleasure craft, were a good hundred yards away and mere outlines in the deepening night.

First, I had to finalize my entry into Iran. I needed a location within reasonable driving distance to Tehran, but not so close that someone could spot my drop. I'd done a preliminary search back in D.C., but that had been with three or four people looking over my shoulder. I didn't need three or four people times three or four other people knowing anything about my entry. I pulled out my iPhone and activated my mapping app. I plotted three possibilities, all north of the city and all deep in the mountains. Google Earth allowed me to study the sites from above, and the hills outside the village of Fasham looked ideal.

I noted one landing point in a broad valley crossed with an unpaved road moving east to west and a two-lane piece of asphalt that traveled north and south. I marked the coordinates in the phone's memory. This would be my diversionary landing point. Then I zeroed in on a less-trafficked valley a kilometer to the northwest and hidden by a low-lying ridge. The high-desert terrain was passable, and it would need to be. I marked those coordinates as well.

Next, I opened the secure-communication app. While I waited for the protocols to signal the all clear, I glanced back at Roger. He was still busy chatting on his phone.

The first prompt from the app told me that General Rutledge was unavailable, so I activated a recording feature that would ensure he had a transcript of the call.

The second prompt patched me through to the phone I had given to the CIA's deputy director of operations, Otto Wiseman. It was the middle of the day in D.C.; he picked up after a single ring. "You're not much of a communicator, are you, soldier? What happened to our deal?"

"How's the saying go? Deals are like babies: easy to make, hard to deliver. Especially when the shit hits the fan the way it did in Amsterdam," I remarked.

"Yeah, I heard about your troubles," Wiseman said deliberately.

A shootout in downtown Amsterdam struck me as a bit more than "troubles," but maybe the DDO was used to a bit more action than I was.

The less Wiseman knew about my plan the better, but he was the only one with the assets I needed for the next stage, assets that neither Rutledge nor Mr. Elliot could provide.

No use beating around the bush. "I need a C-17. One of the high-altitude jobs."

The venerable C-17 had gone through any number of variations, but the Globemaster III was built for high-altitude clandestine missions of the max variety, and that's what I needed.

"When and where?" Wiseman said without missing a beat. No *Are you out of your mind?* or even a *What the hell for?* I had to give him credit.

This was a $250 million airplane I was requesting, crewed by highly trained and combat-seasoned aviators. Wiseman's casual tone made it sound like I was asking for a neighborhood delivery of groceries.

"Field Twenty-seven." That's all I needed to tell him. Field 27 was a remote airstrip in Turkey where, during the Cold War, the CIA used to launch U-2 spy planes for look-sees over the Soviet Union.

"You sure about that?" Wiseman asked. "Twenty-seven's not exactly in prime condition. In fact, it's desolate as hell."

Even better. "I'll be ready at 0100, local time. Day after tomorrow."

"You're not cutting yourself much slack."

"Can you have it there, yes or no?" In other words, don't waste my time with small talk.

"Consider it done. Day after tomorrow, 0100 local time."

"Good. And the less noise the better."

"I guess that goes without saying," the DDO said. In his eyes, maybe. Not in mine. "What's your ten-twenty? Amsterdam?"

Yeah, he was the deputy director of operations for the CIA, and one of the most powerful men in the world, but he really didn't need to know where I was at the moment. When I didn't answer, he threw out another question: "How will you get to Turkey?"

At the moment, I didn't know, so I said, "Director, just make sure the C-17 is ready, okay?"

"I think we've already covered that ground," he said. "What's your MO once you get in the country?" Inquisitive guy.

I had to know if there was a leak in his office, and the bait was entrance into the country. I said, "Have your people at this location at dawn. And tell them to keep their eyes open. Once I touch down, we'll want to move fast."

I transferred the coordinates of the first landing point, at the crossroads just outside Fasham. I waited. Heard computer keys clicking on his end.

"Fasham?"

"Yeah, basically the middle of nowhere."

"Where a shitload could go wrong. You know that, right?" Wiseman said.

"Yeah, well, plenty has already gone wrong." It was a lure. I wanted to see how he'd respond.

"There's still time to abort. We've got other options."

I wondered for a split second whether the DDO had ever heard the term *superpatriot*. Not likely. I said, "Actually, we don't. And I've got my orders. And it's only a round-trip ticket if I succeed."

Wiseman cleared his throat. He was basically a desk jockey. Desk jockeys didn't like being reminded that, for some of us in the national-security business, a mission screw-up had consequences a helluva lot more damaging than a black mark on an efficiency report.

"Anything else?" he asked.

I wanted to say, *You do your job and I'll do mine,* but I'd probably pushed the envelope far enough for one conversation. Instead, I said, "No, sir. Field Twenty-seven. Day after tomorrow. Thanks for your help. I appreciate it."

I terminated the call before he tried to fit one last word in, which I knew he sure as hell would. I quit the recording function, a fraction at ease knowing that Rutledge now had a copy of the conversation.

Next, I palmed the last of my disposable phones from my jacket and punched in Mr. Elliot's secure number. I expected him to let it go to voice mail, but he answered three rings in, saying, "Good to hear your voice, young man."

"Likewise," I replied. That was the sum total of our niceties. I gave him a quick summary of my plans going forward: requisitioning the HALO gear, transportation from Amsterdam into Istanbul care of Roger Anderson, and my arrangements with Wiseman for the C-17 drop into Iran, including the misdirection about my landing point.

"Straightforward. Direct," he allowed. "I approve. And the less you-know-who and his morons know, the better."

"So here's what I need," I said and sent him the coordinates of my second landing point.

We waited for the message to go through. Here I was communicating from the bow of a launch in the middle of one of Holland's biggest lakes and getting impatient because our communications were subjected to the laws of physics.

"Got it," Mr. Elliot said a split second later. "Looks good. Dawn, the day after tomorrow."

"Affirmative. And I'll need transportation."

"No shit. In the middle of goddamn nowhere. I would have never thought of that." He chuckled, and I let out a slow breath. "Look for a guy on a camel."

I grinned. "See what I had to put up with for thirty-odd years."

"And you loved every minute of it," he said, doing what a good case officer did to keep things on an even keel. Then he got back to business: the challenge code for my contact. "Ask him for Marlboros. He'll say he prefers Montecristo coronas."

"Got it."

"How's your finances?"

"I'm burning through money like a roadrunner on crack."

"I'll send a care package." He paused. When Mr. Elliot paused, you knew something important was coming. "Hey, listen. Watch your six. There are a lot of people who want to see you fail."

"I'll do my best to disappoint them."

"You do that. Take care."

His phone beeped, and the line went dead.

I turned off my phone. There was a sense of finality to the decisions we'd just agreed to. I could feel the heat on my face and liked it. I could hear a song lyric coalescing in the back of my mind: "You can't always get what you want, but if you try some time, you might find, you get what you need." Yeah, every once in a while the Stones came through. Nice job, Mick. Very appropriate. You go in, doesn't mean you come back.

I broke apart the disposable and dropped the parts into the lake. I stepped back to the stern. Roger had the tiller in his hand and a satisfied look on his face.

"So?" I said.

"Your ride is on the way. Amsterdam to Istanbul, direct," he said. "I wish

70

I could say I got you a real good deal, but I thought quality was a tad bit more important than bargain shopping."

"Someone you trust?"

He smiled, a perfect wave of irony filling out his face. "This guy has the same view of politics as I do. You pay, he performs."

"My kind of guy."

Roger veered from the middle of the lake toward the entrance near Stede Broec and the dike that signaled landfall northwest of the city.

We were one of three boats queued to cross through the dike. If anything bad was going to happen, this was the place. You couldn't find a more perfect spot for an ambush than the narrow concrete passage connecting Markermeer with Lake Ijsselmeer. And if Roger Anderson, an apolitical man of profit, decided to sell me out, no better opportunity would present itself. I tossed him a cautionary glance and made it look as if I were studying the dike.

My paranoia was unwarranted: all I saw was a man tending to the details of our crossing. We squeezed through the watercourse without so much as a short pause and continued across Ijsselmeer to the end of the peninsula and the commercial shipping district of Den Helder. Container ships as big as apartment buildings and frigates with rust from one end of their superstructures to the other were berthed here. Loading cranes towered over the ships, and night crews worked in the shadows of yellow spotlights.

Anderson pointed us to a pier south of the main port. There were two other boats moored here, both similar to ours in their insignificance. Our launch tapped against the dock, Anderson shut off the motor, and I helped a deckhand with our ropes.

Anderson clambered onto the dock beside me. He seemed in a hurry. He said, "This way," and moved down the pier.

Like all commercial harbors, the scale of the facilities and the vessels that used them dwarfed everyone and everything. Huge cranes serviced enormous ships. Stack after stack of pallets marked seemingly endless rows of giant warehouses. The immensity created an ambience that was at once eerie and humbling. We crossed over a set of railroad tracks, passed through a chain-link fence, and headed to a shabby, redbrick warehouse. There were two doors: a wide bay door flanked by a regular-size door made of steel. Anderson halted outside the steel door and punched a code into a cypher lock.

A lock buzzed. Anderson pushed open the door and I followed him in. He reached for a light switch, and the ceiling lamp directly above us illuminated the corridor. Metal bay doors on opposite sides receded into the gloom. A forklift sat idle, like a sleeping beast, the concrete floor around its tires marred by skid marks.

As we proceeded down the hall, the next set of overhead lights would blink on, and the ones behind us switch off. The effect was like walking in a tunnel collapsing to the beat of a metronome.

Roger halted at the fourth door and fished a set of keys from his pocket. He opened three stainless steel padlocks that secured both sides and the bottom. He grasped the bottom handle and gave the door a yank. It scrolled open with a tinny rattle. The familiar, musty odor of military equipment wafted out.

He reached to the left and flicked a switch. Overhead fluorescent lamps sputtered on. Shelves filled with boxes and crates and duffel bags in shades of military green lined a wall to the left. Roger knew exactly where he was going. He walked straight to a shelf in the middle of the wall, bent over, and dragged out a metal crate the size of a footlocker. The lid was stenciled USMC FORCE RECON, SPECIAL OPS TEAM TANGO.

"Here you go." He snapped open the latches and swung open the lid. "This shit is so new, the jarheads don't even know it's missing."

I crouched beside the crate and inspected the gear. A Mark Seven HALO rig. Harness. Instrument module fitted out with GPS, radio, altimeter, and clock. An MC-5 ram air parachute. Reserve chute. I was liking it already. Pressure suit with electrical heater. Gloves, also heated, and very cool the way they plugged into the suit. Helmet with oxygen mask and regulator, microphone, and ear speakers. Goggles with built-in display and a direct feed to the instrument module. Did I say cool?

Touching this equipment made my nerves tingle with anticipation. Yeah,

I admit it: carnivores like me were adrenaline junkies even at my age and completely unapologetic about the fact.

"Got everything but the oxygen," he added. "There will be a fresh tank when the time comes."

I arranged the equipment back in the crate. "Weight?"

"Come on, hotshot. Take a guess," he said.

I shrugged. "In pounds, a 102.5, give or take."

"More like 104. You're rusty."

"Rusty or not, I can't see myself dragging this gear from here to Istanbul. And a couple of miles down the road from there as well."

"You tell me where, and it'll be there."

"What's this? You taking a sudden interest in my mission?" I said.

"Let me guess." Anderson quirked an eyebrow. He tapped his windbreaker over the spot where he'd pocketed the envelope. "If I'm wrong, well, hell, you got a full refund coming."

"Yeah, right."

"A C-17 Globemaster. Am I right?"

"Time to go," I said, shaking my head.

"Not yet." Roger pulled back his sleeve and read his watch. "Not yet. First we eat."

"I'll eat when the mission's over."

Roger cracked up when he heard this. "Same old Jake."

"I keep hearing that. 'Same old Jake.' What is that? Like a compliment?"

"A compliment, my ass." Roger led me over to an improvised kitchenette, meaning a coffeepot, a cupboard filled with canned soup, and a microwave. The coffee was strong and the soup was hot. We ate it standing up. When he was done, Roger tossed his dish into a tub sink and looked at his watch again. "Now it's time to go. Finish your coffee. You got a plane to catch."

He locked up. We retraced our steps through the warehouse district and made our way back to the boat. Motoring past the Channel Islands and into the North Sea, Roger switched on the GPS mounted on his instrument console.

The readout counted down the distance to the location, which was apparently in the middle of nowhere.

One thousand meters. Five hundred. One hundred. Fifty.

Roger pulled back on the throttle, and we came to a slow stop amid gray and blue swells. Behind us, the Channel Islands were smudges in a sea of haze.

"Nice," I said, with an undisguised bite of sarcasm in my voice.

"Patience, my son."

I heard the drone of the airplane five seconds before I saw it. I craned my neck and studied its features as they came into view. Twin turboprops, a high-mounted wing, floats adjacent the engine nacelles, a V-shaped fuselage. Very impressive. The airplane circled once, displaying the lines of a Bombardier 415 amphibious flying boat, painted light gray with only black buzz numbers on its rudder fin. My ride to Istanbul. Excellent.

The flying boat descended, skimmed the water, then sliced across the surface with plumes of spray dancing in its wake. The Bombardier settled into the water and glided toward us, propellers slowing, engines whistling. A hatch opened in the fuselage behind the left wing. Roger advanced the boat's throttle and guided us to the airplane. A crewman in a white helmet, yellow life vest, and blue overalls waved from the hatch.

"Let's move," he shouted.

"Well done, Rog," I said.

"We aim to please. Now get your ass going," he replied.

"Thanks." I snapped off a salute, knowing it would piss him off, and it did.

"Don't salute me." He winced. "I was a sergeant, not some candy-ass officer."

Roger nudged the bow of the boat up against the open hatch of the plane, and I climbed aboard. I turned and gave Rog a thumbs-up. The crewman swung the hatch closed.

"I'm Lauflin," he said, his accent very German. He led me up a passageway to a cabin aft of the cockpit. He pointed to the man in the left-hand seat. "He's Darby. Best pilot I know without a license."

Darby glanced over his shoulder and gave me a nod. "You bring the money?" he shouted. I patted my pocket. "Let's see it," he called. "No offense."

I reached for my stash and peeled off twenty-five hundred dollars. I handed it to Lauflin, and he pointed to the four empty seats in the cabin. "We're in business. Have a seat."

He handed me a headset. "Get comfortable. It's seven hours to Istanbul. We've got sandwiches and coffee, and plenty of both. Let me know."

"Thanks. Think I'll catch up on some sleep first."

I took a seat on the far left next to a window. Lauflin strapped into the right-hand seat next to the pilot. The turboprops roared, and the airplane surged forward. I sank into the seat. The flying boat bounced across the water, accelerating until we broke free. The pilot put us in a gradual climb and we turned southwest and back over Amsterdam.

We leveled off. I closed my eyes. Sleep came so fast that I didn't even have time to dwell on how exhausted I was or how risky it was to go to sleep in the company of two guys I'd never met before and would never see again. Especially after the really great time I'd had dodging bullets in Amsterdam.

When I woke up, we were over water again. The Black Sea. It had to be. The sun was breaking over the horizon, a sliver of pale orange light. My headset had slipped down around my neck. I reset it. "Where are we?" I said.

Darby answered. "We're an hour out," was all he said.

"Any chance that coffee's still hot?"

"We just brewed a new pot."

I unbuckled. Stood up and stretched. Lauflin turned in his seat and held out a steel thermos. "Sandwich?"

"Thanks."

There was a cooler between their seats. Lauflin popped it open. The sandwiches were wrapped in tinfoil. He handed me two. "My sister made these. Can't say with what exactly. But I've had worse."

Some endorsement. I thanked him again and went back to my seat. I ate both sandwiches so fast that the taste eluded me. I sipped my coffee and watched the morning of my fifth day on the job open up below me. I saw fishing boats and a cruise liner.

Morning painted the water emerald green.

We were descending over the Sea of Marmara, south of Istanbul, on the flight path into Nuri Demirağ International Airport. Our flaps squealed. The landing gear whirred, and the wheels clunked into place. We passed over the beach, our shadow spilling across the Turkish coastline.

The pilot eased us onto a runway reserved for planes of lesser size and import than the steady flow of commercial flights coming from all corners of Europe and the Middle East. We landed with little more than a jostle and taxied toward the terminal.

"We'll get you as close as we can," Lauflin said, "But you'll still have a bit of a walk. The tower wasn't real thrilled with our flight plan."

"Imagine that," I said, as the plane came to a halt on the tarmac. I slipped my gun under the seat and stood up. I felt naked without the Walther, but only a fool would have tried to slip a gun past the very suspicious folks in Turkish customs. Besides, the streets of Istanbul were a virtual cesspool of illegal weapons, so arming myself again would be matter of a phone call or two.

Lauflin wasted no time cracking the hatch and dropping a foot ladder to the concrete. There was a maintenance tech and a service truck waiting for them. That struck me as unusual for a plane this size, but then everything was striking me as unusual at this stage of the game.

"Thanks for the lift." I handed my headset to Lauflin and gave Darby a brief nod.

"Have fun," he said.

Oh, yeah. A barrel of laughs. I climbed down. The hatch closed behind me.

I walk to the terminal without looking back and followed a group of businessmen inside. I passed through security and entered the line for customs, a bedraggled guy with no luggage. I showed a Canadian passport identifying me as Darrell Swan, a businessman from Toronto, got the usual please-give-me-a-reason-to-stop-you look from the customs agent, and merged with a dozen other travelers into the main terminal.

Things were going well. Or, given my rather cynical view of the world: too well. My internal alarm sounded. *Careful, Jake. Watch your six.*

And sure enough, there was good reason. I stepped outside. My plan was to hail a taxi, just another weary businessman eager to get to his hotel, but I didn't have time even to reconnoiter the cabstand.

A line of Turkish policemen had fanned out across the walkway, and they were systematically inspecting passports. Okay; but why weren't they stopping any women? And why did they seem to be targeting men who looked like they'd just dropped in from Europe or America? Couldn't have anything to do with my recent arrival, could it? Just a coincidence, right? Sure. Absolutely. If only I believed in coincidence.

I stopped and leaned into the shadows cast by a nearby pillar. It was a lousy hiding place. One of the policemen looked in my direction. He was a large man for a Turk, and his uniform didn't fit him worth a damn. But he had a strong voice, and all his colleagues heard him when he shouted, "There he is. Arrest him."

He was pointing at me.

CHAPTER 10

NURI DEMIRAĞ INTERNATIONAL,
ISTANBUL, TURKEY—DAY FIVE

Like a school of piranha, the Turkish airport police swarmed in my direction, oblivious now to the crowds exiting the terminal. They had their target. Ten of them in black uniforms with silver accents and black ball caps, POLIS embroidered across the front. Hands on their holstered pistols. Advancing. Clumsy, but calm. One spoke into a handheld radio, and his face was etched with urgency.

I glanced back into the terminal. The glass reflected four more cops jogging my way. Nix that option.

To my right, cars and buses zipped along the passenger-pickup lanes. A three-story wall topped with a glass walkway ran the length of the road on the opposite side. No place to run. It didn't look good. All I could think about was the mission.

My guts knotted in anger. The cops had had plenty of warning; hell, they'd probably received an engraved invitation from someone. Which meant one thing: my operation's security didn't have a hole, it had a goddamn chasm.

The question was, why the police? What had they been told about me to warrant such a display of authority?

I knew one thing. Istanbul was no place to be arrested. Even Mr. Elliot would be hard pressed to spring me from a Turkish prison. And for all I knew, the DDO wanted me arrested; what better way to put an end to my mission. Wiseman knew I was bound for Turkey. He might not have known when or where, but he wasn't stupid. And if he was working the other side of the fence, then my problems were bigger than a gaping hole in my security.

I'd spent less than a second mulling my predicament, and that was too much time to waste. My feet were taking me away from the converging police and into a new wave of travelers disgorging from the terminal. I saw a hotel van waiting for anyone registered at the Istanbul Regency; the driver was standing outside the van. The motor was running. Hijacking the van was a long shot, but I wasn't averse to a long shot.

I had made up my mind and was about to make a break for the bus when I heard a car horn blaring. I glanced over my shoulder. A black Mercedes sedan appeared from behind a line of buses, breaking every moving violation in the airport. It caromed over a speed bump and past the cabstand. I heard shouting and saw people scattering.

The car turned my way. The driver hit his horn again. Every muscle in my body tensed. I reached for my Walther, knowing full well I'd left it on the floatplane. I was calculating the distance between the hotel van and the Mercedes when I saw the diplomatic plates on the front bumper. American.

The Mercedes screeched against the curb. Dark-tinted windows masked the interior, but the front passenger door swung open even before the car came to a halt. A man shouted, "Conlan! Get your ass in here."

The well-coordinated police line disintegrated into a mob, running and yelling in a garble of Turkish and English. I heard the word *Halt!* and several others that didn't sound quite so polite.

So I had a choice between an American-embassy vehicle that had pretty much shown up out of nowhere and a dozen or so very unhappy Turkish police. Now that I thought about it, calling it a "choice" probably wasn't fair.

I sprang for the sedan and dived through the open door. I landed headfirst on leather as supple as newly crushed velvet. I was still scrambling for a hand-hold when the driver stomped on the accelerator and the Mercedes shot from the curb. Very fancy driving. I folded myself onto the seat and jerked the door closed.

I tossed a backward glance. The policemen had slowed to a jog, their expressions rippling with disgust. The Mercedes bore diplomatic plates; there was no point trying to stop us. I did a split-second inventory. This one had my heart racing, if you could call seventy-two beats a minute racing. My baseball cap was missing. That pissed me off.

I glanced across the seat.

The driver was in his late twenties. He had straight blond hair falling midway over his ears, a slender build, a pressed suit, and a perfectly knotted tie. He might have looked like a surfer, but he guided the Mercedes with the expert touch of a NASCAR racer.

Without taking his eyes off the road, he extended a hand. "Trevor McCormick. American embassy. Or maybe that was obvious."

I shook it. Dry. Firm. Cool. If this was the enemy, he was very good. If he wasn't, then I was in good hands. I was betting on the latter.

"That was quite a welcoming committee back there." McCormick checked his mirrors and switched lanes. We gained speed as we turned onto the overpass linking us with Ataturk Boulevard, heading north from the airport and into Istanbul. Thirty seconds.

"Who are you?"

"Just a guy doing his job," he answered.

"Just a guy doing his job. Is that a fact? A guy who shows up with his diplomatic plates and takes pity on a poor sucker tap-dancing with the Turkish police."

He rolled his eyes my way, said, "Consider this an unofficial favor from a friend back home."

I could have asked, *Who?* but that would have been a dumb question. The chances of his knowing "who" were exactly none. Plus, I already knew who. It wasn't General Rutledge; Tom didn't keep company with the State Department.

Mr. Elliot, on the other hand, kept company with anyone who mattered when it came to his guys. I said, "Never mind."

McCormick chuckled. "Somebody with some juice, that's for sure."

His nonchalance did little to put me at ease. First, a rat within the MEK had tried to grease me in Amsterdam. And now, the Turkish cops. Any other day of the week, they wouldn't give a rat's ass about a guy like me. Unless, that is, they were spoon-fed bad intel. Maybe I'd been pinned with an international warrant, or maybe someone was calling in a favor. A very big favor. And if that was true, it had to be someone very high up the food chain.

Could have been Wiseman. Or someone close to him. If so, he'd have to play his cards close to the vest and avoid any clumsy moves.

Could be Moradi. If so, he was playing both sides of the fence, and that didn't sound like Moradi.

"I'm reaching under my seat," McCormick said.

We locked eyes for three seconds. "Go ahead and reach," I said.

He did. No jerky movements, no change in facial expression, no blush or blanch. Eyes on the road. Easy in, easy out, and came away with a shoulder harness fitted with a 9 mm pistol. Another Walther PPK/S. How much better could it get! He handed it over. "A Walther guy, huh? I didn't know they still made those."

He grinned. I scowled. "Hey, don't get smart, kid. This is a man's gun."

He was still grinning, so I said, "Silencer?"

"They said you'd ask."

"Too predictable for my own good."

He reached down again and came away with a flat cardboard box the size of a safety deposit box. "Ammo, silencer, the works. Oh, yeah, and a back-up phone. Just a precaution. Take a look."

McCormick returned his full attention to the road and gave me a chance to examine my new toys without the commentary. I started with the iPhone. Did an app check. The five or six I needed and a shitload more I didn't. Excellent. The aluminum silencer fit the Walther like a sucker on a stick.

McCormick followed the wide boulevard through the western sprawl of the city. High-rises towered over low neighborhoods and city parks. Although Turkey was a proud Muslim country, its attitudes were decidedly relaxed, judging by the billboards showing women in bikinis. Not that I minded.

Out of habit, I glanced into the passenger-side mirror. A BMW motorcycle darted behind a cargo truck trailing us by four car lengths. The rider wore a black helmet with a tinted visor and black leathers. If the guy wasn't following us, he was following someone else. Or maybe he was just an asshole who thought the entire road was his playground, traffic be damned. I doubted it; not the way my luck had been running.

I knew one thing. Riding blind behind a truck was a dangerous thing for a guy on a motorcycle. Unless he was hiding.

"You see him?" I said to McCormick.

"The Beemer tucked in behind the truck like some kind of stunt rider?"

"That's the one." I was supposed to be deep cover and now it was like my itinerary had been broadcast on the evening news. "What was your plan?"

"The plan was a safe house." He shrugged. "Won't do much good with that guy on our tail, I don't suppose. Let's see what we can do about that."

McCormick engaged the cell phone attached to the center console and activated the voice control. He said, "Chelsea."

The phone replied, "Dialing Chelsea."

McCormick snatched the phone from the console and put it to his ear. "We're being followed. BMW motorcycle. Single rider." He listened for a moment, replied, "Okay," and dropped the phone back into the console. He glanced my way. "Got it covered."

He accelerated, switching into the fast lane and moving three cars ahead. Then he eased back into the traffic lane and took the O-3 interchange east. The motorcycle didn't miss a beat, staying three cars back and looking far too obvious.

A quarter of a mile ahead, a dump truck merged onto the interchange, and McCormick said, "That's our guy." Not five seconds later, a white van fell in behind us, and McCormick's cell phone rang. He punched the speakerphone and said, "That's us behind you. The Mercedes."

"What else would you be driving?" a voice from the dump truck quipped.

"Got the bike?"

"Yeah, I got him. A real yo-yo."

"Let's play."

McCormick kept the phone alive. He checked his mirrors. The BMW jumped one car; now he was two back, including the white van. When McCormick saw this, he pulled the Mercedes to the left, gained speed, and slipped in front of the dump truck. The guy on the Beemer responded, jumping the van and settling in behind the dump truck.

McCormick barked into the cell phone, "He's all yours."

Two things happened simultaneously. The white van slid into the fast lane and came up next to the motorcycle, boxing him in behind the dump truck. At the exact same moment, the bucket of the dump truck jerked upward, the rear gate opened, and a curtain of dirt sloughed off the back and onto the road.

The motorcyclist had nowhere to go. As the dirt rained down over him, he had no choice but to put the bike down. The bike tumbled through the wall of dust, smacked the pavement, and disintegrated. The rider slid across the concrete on his back and spun to a halt in the soft dirt.

I tipped my head back and laughed. "I love you guys," I said.

McCormick shrugged. "It's not usually this exciting."

I glanced out the back window again and saw the white van skidding to a stop. Two men in civilian clothes jumped out and jogged in the direction of the fallen biker.

"They're with us," McCormick said with a grin. "U.S. Marines and OJKB detailed to the embassy."

OJKB. Özel Jandarma Komando Bölüğü. Turkish Special Forces, and the very last people on earth you'd want interrogating you. "I have a feeling our friendly biker is going to wish he'd followed someone else," I said.

"I can pretty much guarantee it," McCormick said. He took the O-3 south into old Istanbul.

I was tempted to ask McCormick exactly who in the embassy he worked for, but I decided to respect his anonymity. All manner of people were assigned to the embassy besides the boot lickers from State. DIA. CIA. NSA. FBI. It was a cook's stew of more or less meaningless acronyms. It was no wonder nothing ever got done. But I had to give McCormick credit: he had acquitted himself well.

At the next intersection, he cornered onto a busy thoroughfare and a collection of mixed neighborhoods. An open market on one corner, a mosque on another, a meeting hall on yet another. I could see that we were headed for the tip of the peninsula.

McCormick made a right at Kennedy Street, a wide boulevard that paralleled the coast of the Sea of Marmara. The Mercedes slowed as we approached a three-story hotel at the end of the block. The building was a simple boxy structure slathered in white paint with pastel-blue trim. Plain and dowdy: perfect for a safe house. We parked outside the entrance. A sign read: HOTEL MARMARA.

"It's not five-star," McCormick said, "but it's got plenty of what you need most. Security." He handed me a business card. "Tell the front counter I sent you. They have your room ready."

"You coming in?" I asked. There were two points to this question. If he said yes, it told me the American embassy wanted me watched and more people knew about my arrival than was healthy; that was not Mr. Elliot's style. If he said no, then I could take a deep breath and maybe even enjoy a drink and a hot shower.

"Why? You need a chaperone?" He shook his head and his expression turned serious. "Duty calls. I want to see if our mysterious biker has a name."

"And maybe you could ask him real politely who his employer is," I said. McCormick grinned. "Thanks for the lift."

We shook hands, and I let myself out.

The Mercedes pulled away and disappeared around the corner.

I walked empty-handed into the hotel, realizing how good a change of clothes would feel right about now. The lobby was floored with terracotta pavers and wainscotted in pink tile. Palms and lush plants grew from planters fired a brilliant blue. Arcs of light painted the walls beneath amber sconces.

The tropical colors and garden fragrance gave the lobby a relaxed, festive ambience.

I told the front desk clerk that McCormick had sent me. He didn't ask for my name and didn't bother with ID. He just handed over a key card. "Room 203. Enjoy your stay," he said simply.

I decided on the drink before the shower, and said to the clerk, "There a place nearby where a man could get a drink?"

The concierge overheard my query and hurried over. "Yes, sir. A drink? Right this way." He pointed to an arched door that led to the hotel restaurant. "It's not fancy, but it is comfortable."

"That's all I ask." I followed the tile floor to an open staircase that rose to a mezzanine. I took a corner stool at the bar, close to a wall of beveled-glass windows that allowed a view of the greenway on the other side of Kennedy Street. The silvery waters of the Sea of Marmara trundled toward the horizon.

The bar looked like a cross between an Irish pub and an English public house, all dark woods and brass, beveled glass and Tiffany lamps. A huge mirror ran the length of the bar, and shelves of liquor bottles reflected in the glass. Wine goblets and cocktail glasses hung from overhead racks.

It wasn't crowded, but then it wasn't even lunchtime yet.

There were three men and a woman gathered around a tall, round table and perched on backless stools. They were speaking Italian, which wasn't a huge surprise. Istanbul had always attracted the Italian tourist, though these four didn't strike me as the tourist kind. The men were casually attired, but they looked more like locals. The woman wore a loose, blue dress cinched around her waist, and its plunging neckline immediately caught my attention. A pair of very nice legs caught my attention shortly thereafter.

There were three guys tending bar, and that seemed a bit excessive for this time of the morning, but maybe they were expecting a rush of unkempt Americans fresh off a car chase. The one intently polishing a glass was quintessentially Turkish: heavy mustache, meaty shoulders, thick neck, and looking semidapper in a red vest over a white shirt and black trousers.

His buddies were hunched behind the bar, one skinny and amped up, the other calm and build like a welterweight. Both fussing with glasses and liquor bottles, and looking preoccupied.

The barkeep put his glass and polishing cloth down and set his elbows on his side of the bar. "What'll you have?" he asked in English as guttural as the broken water pump in my dad's old Chevy.

"Whiskey sour. Maker's Mark." Eleven in the morning; what else?

The barkeep nodded and got to work.

Me? I got to work thinking about my next step. Sending a status report to Rutledge could wait. I had transportation to arrange out to Field 27, and the thought of renting a car was making more and more sense. "Trust no one" had taken on new meaning over the last twenty-four hours.

I felt confident that Wiseman would deliver the C-17. If he or someone in his office was intent on bringing me down, then I'd know the moment I landed in Iran. I half expected the landing coordinates I'd given DDO to be compromised; it was just a gut feeling. I hoped I was wrong.

My arrangement with Roger Anderson was another matter. Roger was not in the business of screwing people over. The HALO gear would be there when I arrived at Field 27. I could check that off my list.

On the other hand, I didn't know quite what to make of the MEK. Someone had ambushed a car carrying the head of their Amsterdam chapter, and Moradi could easily have been killed. Why would they do that? If it was a ruse, it was a damn risky one. If someone didn't care whether Moradi lived or died, then the MEK had real problems.

I took a deep breath. I heard the woman at the table next to me laughing, a deep, melodious laugh that reminded me of Cathy. The woman's very nice legs also reminded me of Cathy, and I let my imagination wander for a moment. I looked at my hands and imagined my scarred fingers slipping down Cathy's spine to the small of her back, then lower. I imagined her scent and her . . .

It was the skinny, nervous bartender who placed a napkin on the counter and set the whiskey sour in front of me. Wrong! Dead wrong. Three decades of training and black-ops insanity threw up about a dozen red flags. I reached out and grabbed him by the front of his shirt. I yanked him across the bar, hard.

"What the fuck!" he hissed.

The bar went silent. Everyone was looking—everyone except the barrel-chested Turkish barkeep who had originally taken my order. He was nowhere to be seen.

I stared into the skinny one's eyes. Twitchy. Very twitchy. He had the rank odor of nervous sweat about him. It wasn't hot in the bar. Not hot enough to sweat. The other one, the welterweight partner, made a quick move toward the end of the bar, and I shouted, "I'll break his neck."

He froze. My eyes flicked his way. "I'll break his neck. And then I'll find you and break yours. Please tempt me."

He didn't. Not an amateur. Not a seasoned pro, but worthy of my attention.

"What's going on?" one of the Italians at the table said.

"Shut up! And don't move," I snapped. I could do the thing with my voice that pretty much froze people in their tracks, and he did exactly as he'd been told.

With my free hand, I snared the cocktail glass. I held it up to my nose. There was nothing to smell, but I knew. I'd bet my next paycheck on it, if only I was on someone's payroll. I held the glass up to the skinny one's face and jammed it against his very prominent nose. "Drink it," I said. "Drink every drop."

He shook his head. Panic: I could see it sweeping over his ugly, olive-colored face. "No. Why?"

"Because I want to see how long you last. A minute. Five minutes. Maybe ten. Now drink it," I said in a low, dusty voice. He struggled, but he was no match for my strength, and certainly no match for my annoyance. I jammed the glass against his lips, sloshed the liquid into his mouth, and he immediately spit it back out. "What kind of poison?"

"Ricin. I'm sorry."

I let the drink tumble to the bar. The glass splintered. I dragged him onto the bar. I pulled out the Walther. The woman at the table gasped, but I didn't have the heart to tell her to shut up. The welterweight made a dash for the door. I wanted to shoot him in the back, but this was not the time or place for gunplay.

I put the barrel of the gun against the skinny one's temple. I knew I had less than ten seconds before all hell broke loose. "Who do you work for? Tell me!"

"I'm a believer," he said. "Kill me. I know my fate."

"I don't need to kill you. When your employer finds out how you botched this job, he'll use something a lot more painful that a bullet." I smashed his head into the bar top and stowed the gun in my jacket. I pushed away from the bar, took a last glance at the Italian woman's legs, and walked out. At least the morning wasn't a complete loss.

CHAPTER 11

ISTANBUL, TURKEY—DAY FIVE

So much for the Hotel Marmara. And so much for a stiff drink and a hot shower. I was probably better off without the drink, now that I thought about it, but the shower still sounded damn good.

I stepped from the bar into the lobby, walking as if I had all day. Of course, the welterweight had just sprinted out the door ahead of me, so it was hard to be completely nonchalant. The bellhop, the concierge, and the guy at the registration desk stared at me as I crossed the tile floor, my shoes as sound-less as my breathing. The elevator music playing in the background seemed louder. The song sounded vaguely familiar—like a Viennese waltz I might have heard on my honeymoon—but then that was the whole point.

"Sir?" The concierge hurried my way. I studied his face. The worry lines were genuine. So was the imploring tone of his voice. "Is everything all right?"

Maybe the look on my face wasn't as unreadable as it should have been. I'd been caught off guard. Not enough to cost me, but enough to remind me that I'd been out of the game for five years. *You're a step slower, Jake, and you might as well admit it.*

Admitting a shortcoming isn't a bad thing, Mr. Elliot used to say. We all have limits. Know what they are; know when they're about to kick your ass; know how to lessen the blow. It's the man who thinks he's infallible who ends up with the bullet in his head. Yeah, or a lethal dose of ricin in his Maker's Mark. Not a respectful way to treat a man's favorite whiskey.

"Lousy service," I said to the concierge. My mouth was dry. I tasted something metallic on my tongue. A headache squeezed the front of my skull. My guts felt like they'd been shredded. All good signs. All reminders that I had better right the ship and right it damn fast before my mission went any further south on me.

Back home, I was a regular at a gym frequented by government types, mostly agents from the various arms of Homeland Security. Free weights had always been my thing. Outside paramilitary work took a devastating toll on the mind and the body, and staying in shape wasn't just my rule; it was Mr. Elliot's rule. When the body goes, the mind and spirit aren't far behind. In my line of work, if the mind and the spirit falter, you're a dead man. I believed that back then, and retirement hadn't dulled the belief.

These days I liked testing myself against the young carnivores hanging around the place; it was a testosterone jungle, and I had to admit that I hadn't tired of the competition. Yeah, I could still do the weight, but not the reps. And these days, my routine took fifteen minutes longer than it had ten years earlier. The upside was that I knew more about the limitations that Mr. Elliot had talked about, and I also knew more about maximizing my strengths. I guess that's called experience.

"Is there anything I can do?" he said.

"You could hail a cab for me," I said.

"Right away." He hustled out ahead of me. I still had three pressing needs: nourishment, sleep, and a few minutes of privacy when no one in the world knew where I was. I was running on empty.

I stopped at the door and looked back at the guy at the registration desk. I said, "Turn back the sheets in my room for me, will you? I'll be back in a couple of hours."

Of course, I had no intention of returning, but I didn't want them alerting Trevor McCormick to my sudden departure. If I needed the help of someone from the American embassy again, it would be on my terms, not his. I honestly didn't believe that McCormick was a party to the Maker's Mark incident, but his hotel of choice clearly wasn't the safe house it was intended to be.

I went outside, stopped, and scanned for any sign of the welterweight. He didn't look smart enough to muster a counterattack after the fiasco at the bar, but failure motivates people in strange ways. Especially when the people holding you accountable have a low and often deadly tolerance for failure. The MEK definitely fit that description. And now I was wondering if the Revolutionary Guard or someone else inside Iran was onto me. If there was a traitor inside the MEK, it was very likely that he or she was betraying me to the Iranian government, and their influence had few boundaries.

I stepped past the entrance. There were three taxis in line along the carriage drive, a yellow one, a green one, and another yellow one. The concierge was at the head of the line, holding open the back door of the first yellow one. I walked over to the second cab instead, the green one.

"Green's always been my color," I said when I saw the confused look on the concierge's face. It was just a precaution, but I planned on taking every precaution going forward.

I ducked into the back. The cabbie glanced back at me, a thick, fleshy man with round glasses. His English had a second-grade quality to it, but my Turkish was preschool at best. He said, "Where to?" and it was all I could do to put the two words together.

"Old town. Hotel Sultanhan."

His expression in the rearview mirror said, *You're leaving one hotel for another. Who does that?* But he merely shrugged and said, "A fine choice, sir."

He put the cab in gear and drove. I had stayed at the Sultanhan two decades or so earlier, when I was negotiating an arms deal with a very nasty group of Syrians. Small and classically Turkish, it was a stone's throw from places like the Blue Mosque, Sofia, and Topkapi Palace, all the hot spots for American and European tourists. Very easy to blend in.

But it wasn't the Sultanhan that interested me; it was a tiny motel two blocks away, where I'd met the Syrians. Quiet, indiscreet, and completely off the grid. Exactly the kind of place I needed before my rendezvous at Field 27.

I closed my eyes for five seconds.

Inventory time. Pulse? Fifty-four. Acceptable. Breathing? Normal. Head? A little woozy, but clear. State of the mission? Despite everything, more or less on track. Allies? Two, rock solid. The rest, questionable at best.

I opened my eyes. The Istanbul skyline filled the cab's windshield. Where had all the skyscrapers come from? From a distance, modern Istanbul looked like Chicago or Seattle. Closer, a maze of red-tiled roofs, gold-domed mosques, and needle-shaped minarets signaled the Istanbul of old: "old" meaning ten thousand years in the making and still as vibrant and broken as it had been in the days before it was even called Istanbul.

The cab jogged along Peykhane Cad in a battleground of traffic. He cut off at Piyer Loti and snaked along behind a tourist bus until he came to Piere Loti Cad and a carriage drive in front of the hotel. I handed him an American twenty-dollar bill and climbed out.

I stared at the whitewashed facade, the arched windows, and the narrow balconies and remembered the company I had kept there for three nights. It seemed like another lifetime, and yet I could recall every detail. The Sultanhan was meant for romance and quiet dinners with just the right woman, not for international intrigue. But that was then.

I waited for the cab to disappear from sight, then crossed Piere Lot to Boyaci Ahmet and spotted the Column of Constantine. It wasn't much, but you couldn't take your eyes off it. It was a stone tower rising a good hundred feet into the air that you realized was constructed nearly two thousand years ago by a Roman emperor. It looked its age, but was even more impressive for it. A crowd of people and hundreds of pigeons clustered around it.

For me, it signaled a cobbled alleyway on the far side of the square that led to a two-story, shacklike building called the Burnt Column Inn. It sounded quaint, but it wasn't. I walked through a rickety screen door into a shoebox-size lobby where a woman in a head scarf was working an ancient-looking adding machine.

I should have been surprised at how good her English was until I calculated the number of Americans and Europeans she had to deal with every day. "Room?" she said.

I nodded. "With clean sheets."

She smiled at this. I didn't know if the smile meant, *Of course the sheets are clean,* or, *What the hell are clean sheets?* She said, "How many nights?"

I held up one finger. She smiled again and said, "Euros?"

"Dollars." She nodded. The price was eighteen dollars per night. I gave her twenty-five and said, "No calls, please."

The room key was actually a key attached to a plastic card that read "23." Room 23 was a flight of stairs up and down a narrow hall. I passed a community restroom and realized my shower wasn't going to be as private as I'd hoped. I plunged the key into a standard dead-bolt lock, pushed open a hollow-core door, and stepped into a room that smelled of lavender and curry, a very odd combination.

I didn't care. I walked straight to a four-poster bed, built high off the floor, and pulled back the covers. The sheets sparkled they were so white. Hallelujah. I took the Walther from the shoulder harness and laid it on the bed. I set the alarm on my iPhone for 1500 hours and set the alarm in my head for the same time. I plugged the phone into a wall socket, knowing that even with my Mophie it could be a long haul before I was able to charge it again.

I could hardly get my shoes off before I stretched out on the bed, fully clothed. I gripped the Walther in my right hand and closed my eyes. Sleep was instantaneous and dreamless. My internal alarm woke me up two minutes before the iPhone's alarm sounded. Two hours wasn't much, but I felt 100 percent better.

I retrieved my iPhone. It was 0800 in Washington, D.C.

I activated an app called the Listening Bug. It was a sweeper program. I wasn't expecting to find anything in a room in the Burnt Column Inn, but the way my luck had been going, I did a thorough scan anyway: bed, lamps, window frame, closet. All clear.

Mr. Elliot first. I punched in the new number he'd given me during our last session. It rang four times—twice longer than usual—which meant he was tracking the call via GPS. He answered, saying, "You're not at the Hotel Marmara. Trouble?"

"My middle name these days," I answered. I backtracked, starting with a quick account of the attempted poisoning. I rehashed the unexpected police reception at the airport and my introduction to Trevor McCormick, and ended with the motorcycle rider tracking us from the airport. "Your guy was Johnny-on-the-spot at the airport, and he handled the bad guy on the bike about as well as a man could. Maybe too good. You sure about him?"

"Shit, man, if you can't trust him," Mr. Elliot replied, "then we're fucked. I trust him like I trust you."

Good enough, then. I said, "Alright. Then I need him for the ride out tonight. Can you arrange that?"

"Already done," he said. Over the course of our thirty-plus years together as case officer and operative, I'd heard him say "already done" maybe a couple of hundred times. It didn't mean exactly that; it meant, *You can count on me. Don't give it a second thought*. And I learned never to give it a second thought, because he always came through. Always.

"Good." I filled my lungs. He waited. "I was a split second away from drinking that drink."

He read my mind. "Five years is a long layoff."

"No excuse."

"No excuse at all," he said matter-of-factly. "But it begs the question, do we move to another option?"

He didn't mention what that other option was, but I knew what he was getting at. That I pull up stakes and return home with my tail between my legs. Meaning, the HUMINT part of the op inside Iran failed. Because of me. Wasn't going to happen.

"I'm still in," I said calmly.

"You sure? There's no pressure from this end."

Total bullshit. I fold and I'd never be able to look Mr. Elliot in the eye again, not to mention my relationship with General Tom Rutledge. But pressure had nothing to do with it; neither did my self-esteem. I'd been charged with developing indisputable intel supporting military strikes and covert assassinations inside the most dangerous country on the planet. Imagine coming home and telling my kids I couldn't hack it. A superpatriot no more. No chance.

"It's a go," I said. "I'll wrestle a gorilla if I have to."

Mr. Elliot chuckled. "I'll put your driver on full alert. Give him thirty minutes' notice."

"Roger that." We hung up. I powered up the videoconference app and dialed General Rutledge's number. The call went through a series of clicks—security cues—and Tom answered. He was wearing a black warm-up jacket. "Caught me on the way to a tennis game," he confessed, as if me being here in full-op mode and him being in D.C. playing tennis just didn't feel right. "News?"

I didn't bother with a full report: too much melodrama. "I'm a day away," I said, knowing he would understand that I would have boots on the ground in the badlands tomorrow. "I need an ID infusion." Meaning new passports with completely revised travel packets. I wanted to go in without any of the baggage I'd accumulated in Amsterdam and Turkey. Tom didn't need an explanation.

"They'll be in your deployment kit."

"And my transportation?" Meaning the C-17 Globemaster III.

"Ready for a pickup, 0100 tomorrow morning, your time. Rendezvous point is seven hours away," he said, referring to Field 27. "You better hustle."

"And you'd better put in some time on that serve of yours. My daughter's got more juice on her serve than that weak-kneed thing you were sending over the net last time we faced off," I told him.

"Is this the same daughter who's been kicking your ass since she was fifteen?"

I grinned. "Touché, my friend. Touché."

Tom's grin didn't last. We were separated by thousands of miles and our images were nothing but tiny dots on an electronic screen, but I could still feel his concern.

"Godspeed, my friend."

Honestly, that was the problem with working hand-in-hand with a friend: the emotional baggage couldn't possibly do either of us any good. I said, "Thanks," and the screen went blank.

Time to go. I fished Trevor McCormick's card from my jacket and dialed his cell phone. It rang once. I could hear by the tone of his voice and a quick intake of breath that Mr. Elliot had put him on the alert. I asked how soon he could get to me. He said twenty-five minutes.

"Good. I'll be across the square from the Column of Constantine. In the gift shop."

"What? Why there? What's up?" he wanted to know. So, Mr. Elliot hadn't told him about the screwup at the Hotel Marmara.

"I'll explain when I see you," I said. "And if you can track down some coffee, I'd appreciate it."

I spent ten minutes washing up at a communal sink at the end of the hall. I'd used a lot worse. There was a bar of soap attached by a piece of rope to the faucet. The water was lukewarm and only slightly rusty. There was an empty paper-towel dispenser and a cloth towel that looked as if it had been used by a construction worker or a gardener. I walked with wet hands and face back to my room and used a corner of the bedsheet to dry off.

I spent the five minutes rechecking my Walther. I spent another minute composing a text to the DDO, asking him to set up a safe house in Tehran, as close to Jomhuri as possible. Jomhuri was located in the city center, and I only knew about it because that's where everyone went to buy their computers and cell phones, and the bazaar there was apparently overrun by the younger generation. The request would keep Wiseman busy, even though I had no intention of using one of the Agency's safe houses, except perhaps as a diversion.

I checked myself in the mirror hanging over the dresser. I needed a shave. But other than that, the news wasn't all bad. At least there were no dark circles looming under my eyes. I shared an ironic grin with my reflection and headed for the door.

The woman behind the reception desk was still working the keys of her adding machine; apparently running a motel the size of the Burnt Column was more complex than I'd imagined. She smiled at me and her round face came to life, eyes bright, as if running a motel the size of the Burnt Column was a blessing.

Her smile compelled me to say, "Thank you," but when I was outside the motel I still turned in the opposite direction, away from the square surrounding the Column of Constantine. I walked down the cobbled alley, turned left, and circled the block. I ducked into the gift shop I had mentioned to McCormick, thumbed through a local newspaper, and watched my tracks. I bought a copy of the English version of *HaberSkop*. I turned away from the counter, stopped to put the change back into my pocket, and saw two policemen patrolling the walk.

Ten-to-one they had nothing to do with me, but I got out my iPhone and called McCormick anyway. "Change in plans. Come down Isil Street. Slow down when you see the Yildiz Market. It'll be on your right. But don't stop."

"I'm sixty seconds away."

I stepped through the gift-shop door. I rolled the magazine in my palm and fell in behind an Asian couple with a map of the old town opened in front of them. The police were looking in the direction of the square and the ever-present crowd taking in the sights. I turned down Isil Street and heard a car rolling up beside me. I dropped the magazine into a curbside trash can. I walked into the street just as the Mercedes rolled past and slowed. I heard the door locks click. I jerked the door open and slipped into the front seat.

"Everything okay?" McCormick asked.

"Just a couple of cops in the square. Better part of valor, if you get my meaning."

"If you mean you're not overly enamored with the Turkish police, yeah, I get your meaning," he replied. He took the first turn away from the square. "So why the change in location? The Hotel Marmara not to your liking?"

I wasn't going to mention anything about the poisoning. The embassy would learn what had happened when I filed my after-action report. Although McCormick and I were on the same team and Mr. Elliot had vouched for him, he really didn't need to know anything extraneous to the task at hand.

"Nah," I said casually. "I was just in the mood for a little sightseeing."

McCormick stared across the front seat at me. I didn't move. Then he said, "Okay. Where to?"

"We might want to start with a full tank. We got a helluva drive ahead of us."

I flicked on the navigation app on my iPhone. Field 27 was due east, nearly 400 miles away. I plugged it into the GPS on the Mercedes dash. It popped up on the navigation screen. McCormick studied it. Shrugged. "Glad I brought coffee."

He reached into the backseat. The thermos was stainless steel and good for ten or twelve cups by the looks of it. The cups were paper. I poured. He drove.

We stopped for kebabs and manti at a food stand near Korfez. Typical Turkish fast food served with hot tea. I was famished, and even food on a stick tasted good. McCormick tried to make small talk, but I spent most of my time retraining my mind for a HALO jump from forty thousand feet in the air.

I offered to drive, but McCormick shook his head and smiled. "You're in good hands," he said. "If I were sitting in that seat and had my choice between the Turkish landscape and sleep, I'd already be sleeping."

"In good hands, huh? That's what a friend of mine said, too." I looked across the console for three seconds. Made a decision. I lowered the back of the seat and closed my eyes. "Wake me up when we get to Sorgun."

He did. I opened my eyes, repositioned my seat back, and stretched. My eyes went immediately to my watch. The time was 12:22 A.M. An hour and twenty minutes of solid sleep.

"Thanks. I needed that," I said, and he seemed to know what I meant. I gazed into the pitch black of a moonless night. Two minutes later, I pointed to an exit leading into the low hills off the E88 highway. "Left here."

The road angled north through plowed fields set against shallow clay hills. Lights from farmhouses shone within the draws surrounding us. Clusters of stars peeked through a ghostly layer of feathery clouds.

I followed our progress on the iPhone map, searching for the road to the airstrip. It had been years since I was last here. It was dark as the inside of a gun barrel, and the rugged terrain was not marked by a plethora of outstanding landmarks. At least not ones that I recognized.

Always have an escape route in mind in case of trouble—basic tradecraft—and McCormick and I were mindful of both the potential trouble and the potential exit strategy. He slowed to a crawl and shook his head at the same time. "We're shit out of luck if this goes south," he said, but his voice was calm when he said it.

We rounded the bend, and our headlights shone against the back of a pickup truck parked beside the road fifty meters ahead. Its lights were off, but the vapor wisping from its tailpipe told me the motor was idling.

I slipped my hand under my jacket and gripped my pistol.

McCormick eased off the gas. "We expecting company?"

The placard on the tailgate of the truck came into view. It read: MINISTRY OF THE INTERIOR.

"What the hell's a government truck doing out here?" he hissed. "Coincidence?"

"Like hell." My chest tightened.

A man in a dark uniform stepped into the road from the left side of the truck. Strips of reflective tape glowed on his jacket. He cradled an MP5 submachine gun and called us to a halt with a raised hand.

"He's got company," I said, seeing the silhouette of a second man in the truck. "Passenger side."

McCormick whispered, "Okay. Excellent. Now what?"

My mind flipped through a dozen possible action plans, none of which had a chance in hell of working. We could run the guy over and come back for his companion, but that made less sense than seeing what the hell he was doing out here, not a half mile from Field 27 and my transportation into Iran. In any case, it was a good bet the landing zone had been compromised and my mission was dead in its tracks anyway.

"Keep cool. Let's see what he wants."

The cop put up his hand, and McCormick eased to a stop.

The cop came around to my side of the Mercedes. I thought that was kind of odd, but maybe that was the way they did things in Turkey. He kept his head down and skirted the periphery of the light created by our headlights.

I wrapped my hand around the Walther's grip and kept it nestled along the door panel. Safety off. Finger on the trigger.

If there was something urgent or out of place happening here, the cop gave no indication. His step was even. His posture was relaxed. Of course, he had a machine gun capable of displacing twenty rounds in a split second, so maybe he had a right to be nonchalant. Then I got a glimpse of his face, and my memory traveled back in time nearly fifteen years.

He made a circle with his hand, telling me to roll my window down. I pressed the window control on the side of the door, and it opened. The cop leaned in. I recognized him.

"Atif! Jesus! What the hell?" I said. Atif Hakan. An operative from the Turkish State Security Bureau. He and I had worked together for nearly six months, busting narco rings and cracking heads from Izmir to Budapest. He was as ruthless as I was and just as dedicated. "You're still alive."

"You sound surprised." He extended a hand. "Jake Conlan. I shouldn't be surprised to find you in the middle of nowhere."

"What's an old fossil like you doing out here?" I replied. I was still gripping the Walther. This was weird. McCormick had used the word *coincidence*, but coincidence didn't explain this. "Who'd you piss off?"

"Duty calls. You know the drill." His grip was firm, pleasant. His tone easy and relaxed.

"The last time we met," I said, "you were wearing the uniform of an air force colonel. That's quite a fall to flatfoot cop."

Hakan laughed. "Well, with all the cutbacks, I'm lucky to have a job. This time it's something really important. Like making sure a certain airstrip is clear of stray goats."

"You're kidding?" I was genuinely surprised.

"Would I do that?" He straightened. "Follow me up the road."

Hakan climbed into the cab of the truck. Its headlights came to life. A spray of white illuminated the road, and the truck rumbled out ahead of us.

"Who is he?" Trevor McCormick wanted to know, and rightfully so.

"An old colleague."

"Is that why you were gripping your gun like a man holding on to his last dollar?" He glanced over at me.

"He's Turkish. Turks take it as an insult if you trust them," I said.

The American embassy attaché shook his head. "Our guy back in D.C. didn't tell me you were completely full of shit."

A half mile ahead, we turned off the road and followed a dirt path bordered by slender poplars, through newly turned fields, and up and over a rocky slope. The air outside was chilly and smelled of rain, but I kept the window down. The road dead-ended in a small wooded valley. The truck stopped and turned off its lights. Hakan got out. The airfield was just beyond the crest of the hill.

"Cut the lights and motor," I said to McCormick.

I combed the surroundings. The trees were a tangle of black against the purple of the night sky. The night had fallen under a spell of dead silence. All I heard were Hakan's footfalls approaching. He had left the MP5 in the truck and instead carried a radio.

He touched the side of his wristwatch. A dim yellow glow chiseled his features with soft light. "The bird is ten minutes out. Better get going."

I looked over at McCormick and shook his hand. "Thanks. I'll put in a good word for you when I get back home."

He grinned when he heard this. "I'd say, 'Stay out of trouble,' but I know that's not going to happen."

"Probably not." I climbed out and slid the Walther into my shoulder harness.

Hakan and I hiked up the draw to the top of the hill. In the darkness, I felt a rush of old memories storming back—distant missions and fallen comrades—and told myself this was no place for a walk down memory lane. Actually, if I never walked down memory lane again it would be too soon.

We crested the hill and found ourselves at the southern end of a long, wide strip of flat concrete, like a section of highway someone forgot to connect with the rest of the world.

Hakan adjusted the volume of his radio. The speaker crackled.

A groan echoed from the distance. To the west, a black form cut through the clouds. Cigar-shaped fuselage. Four turbo props. Long, narrow wings that raised the C-17's operational ceiling from thirty-three thousand feet to a height well over forty thousand. Fuel tanks hanging between the engines that allowed the plane to stay aloft pretty much all day.

Hakan raised the radio to his mouth. "Tango-tango-sierra-five. Have you in sight. Status. Victor."

A voice replied, "Roger."

In the early days, for a mission like this, we'd have to guide the airplane in with radar vectors and radio beacons and mark the landing strip with portable lights. Now, with GPS, the crew could plop the machine within one foot of any location, no sweat. Supersensitive radar allowed the pilot to thread a needle if that's what he had in mind. Night-vision systems gave the crew a clear-as-day view of the terrain. Electronic countermeasures made the airplane practically invisible to radar and infrared detectors. About the only thing the Globemaster couldn't do was clear the landing zone of stray farm animals.

The plane began a steady descent, wings level, landing gear extending. No navigation lights, no landing lights, just a black shape getting bigger and bigger. Very cool.

Seconds later, the C-17's huge tires touched the pavement, and puffs of smoke feathered skyward. There was some protesting from the engines and the brakes, but the pilot got the plane stopped, and did so with runway to spare.

The big airplane crawled toward us. The thunderous noise, the sense of urgency, and the sudden realization that I would be jumping out of the tail end of this behemoth made my blood pulse with anticipation.

The C-17 rolled to a stop. The ramp dropped to the ground.

Hakan slapped my back and shouted, "Good luck, Jake. Next time we meet, you better be retired and knee deep in grandkids."

"I'm working on it."

I ran toward the C-17 Globemaster.

Next stop. Iran.

CHAPTER 12

IRAN—DAY SIX

I stood at the rear of the C-17's cargo deck, feeling like a stuffed pig.

An air force staff sergeant named Dooley checked my HALO rig for the umpteenth time, and I had no intention of complaining. He fussed with the harness. He ran his hands over the main parachute and did the same with the reserve chute. He scanned the GPS monitor on my instrument console, the O_2 equipment on my right hip, and the jump bag banded around my waist. He checked the breathing regulator attached to my oxygen tank and the seals where my helmet, gloves, and boots fit into a pressure suit, a necessity at this altitude: forty-two thousand feet. One leak and my blood would literally boil. Dooley gave me a thumbs-up.

"You're a thing of beauty," he said. Normally, you have to write everything down on a dry eraser board or a pad in a situation like this, but we were on comms and using a bone mike.

"I owe you a beer," I said.

"Oh, hey. I nearly forgot." He reached into his back pocket and came away with a folded piece of paper that looked like it had been torn off yellow legal pad and not very gently. "This was tucked inside your suit when I unpacked it."

He handed it over. I opened it with gloved hands.

103

It was handwritten and clearly in haste. It read: *Enjoy the ride, old man. Try coming back in one piece. Roger.* I grinned out of the side of my mouth and offered Roger a mental thanks. Dooley took the note back and found a pocket for it.

"Let's check the numbers," he said, nodding toward my helmet and visor.

The digital readout from the instrument console hovered inside my visor: Pressure Altitude. Absolute Height Above Ground. GPS location. Distance and compass heading to the LZ (landing zone). Time Elapsed. Oxygen Count. Not a lot of light reading.

This time I gave Dooley a thumbs-up.

"Better you than me," he said. I felt like a man in a fishbowl, and the hollow sound of his voice didn't help.

Dooley wore a helmet and pressure suit similar to mine only with a monkey strap that secured his harness to the airplane. The fuselage interior lamps reflected across his visor. He squinted at his wristwatch.

"Showtime, Mr. Conlan. All set?" Now his voice was all business. So was his expression.

This was a critical step of the HALO protocol, switching from the airplane's oxygen system to my personal tank. For the last hour and a half, I'd been "prebreathing" to purge nitrogen from my bloodstream. Falling through the rarefied atmosphere could induce an embolism, though not as extreme as what could happen to a deep-sea diver. I wouldn't suffer the bends, but I could sure as hell get disoriented and lose track of what I was doing. Not a healthy mindset when you're dropping through the night sky at one hundred twenty miles per hour, counting every second, and maneuvering like a bird of prey in free fall.

If the oxygen switch wasn't done correctly, even one breath of regular air would be enough to contaminate my system, and I'd have to start all over. Trouble was, there would be no starting over. We didn't have the time. It was a one-shot deal.

The sergeant puffed oxygen from my tank to purge the regulator and made the switch. The readout on my visor blinked from Standby to 100%. All good. I had twenty minutes of oxygen, and the countdown had already started.

Even though I was being dropped from 42,000 feet Pressure Altitude, my LZ was 6,292 feet above sea level. That meant I would have to open my main chute at 8,792 feet Pressure Altitude, which was actually 2,500 feet Absolute Height Above Ground with an Elapsed Time after jumping of four minutes and fifty-six seconds. This was not a give-or-take situation. Give-or-take meant you were squashed against a mountaintop like a bug against a windshield. I wasn't afraid of dying, but that was no way to go.

"Okay, Mr. Conlan," Dooley said. "Six minutes, and we're going to open her up."

The sergeant gave me the once-over, and I gave him a thumbs-up. The jump light on the bulkhead panel glowed red.

Six minutes. My mind looped through the commands drilled into me by the Black Hats at jump school in Fort Benning. The one that stood out was: "Don't get all amped up. You're only going one hundred twenty miles per hour. A walk in the park." The Black Hats were renowned for their sarcasm.

Six minutes: get ready!

Six short minutes; 360 seconds that tightened my nerves like a ratchet. My mouth went dry, but my heart rate hadn't jumped two beats. Nice, easy breaths. Nothing too deep.

I did a slow, methodical equipment check. Not that I wasn't confident in Dooley's handiwork. But it was a good way to pass 360 seconds.

I stepped through my mission. The Iranians had made an art out of hiding the key components of their nuclear weapons program. You could apply only so much science to ferreting out hidden factories and industrial plants. The way to crash any well-orchestrated shell game was to dig under the shells. You did that with boots on the ground and people. The plan was to link up with the MEK inside Tehran, but the operation had been plagued with double crosses from the start. So I turned to a back-up plan, one that I would stitch together on the fly, using a guy whose life I'd once saved from an ambush perpetrated by one of the most ruthless drug dealers ever to invade American soil.

Charles Amadi. Nephew of Abbu Amadi, known publicly as the prime minister of the Republic of Iran; known privately as an ardent foe of President

Mahmoud Ahmadinejad. Charlie was just as ardent, and I planned to tap his zeal.

Charles hadn't followed his uncle's footsteps into politics. Charlie had spent a few years in America running errands for the Iranian drug cartel in the 1970s and had returned to his native land after the revolution, intent on maximizing the black market that was the inevitable result of a nation run by a tyrant. Over the years, he'd built an underground network that smuggled and sold everything from electronics and booze to hard cash and information. Charlie wasn't picky about what he sold as long as the bottom line was drenched in black.

He and I hadn't seen each other in years. No matter. He would listen to my pitch because that's how men of honor acted when it was time to repay a debt.

Dooley disconnected the umbilical cord that connected me to the airplane's electrical power. He switched off our handheld comms and relieved me of mine. Now the static inside my earpiece went silent and the drone of the C-17's turboprops replaced it. The console battery had thirty minutes' worth of juice to power my GPS system and to heat my suit and gloves.

A battery of servos groaned. The hull at the back of the fuselage cracked apart. A pair of thin, bright lines connected together by a quirk of physics appeared. The lines widened into a parallelogram framed by the aft cargo doors and ramp. The sky shone white and brilliant, like a glimpse into a different dimension.

I blinked and felt my adrenaline surging. The plan was to land in predawn darkness. This was more like the glare of an early-morning sunrise, the kind that made driving east a royal pain in the ass. The split second of alarm passed as quickly as it had come when logic set in, and I realized we were forty-two thousand feet above my landing sight. Up here, dawn was already a reality. By the time I'd enjoyed the ride of my life and deployed my parachute, I'd be nicely masked by twilight.

The ramp descended until it was level with the cargo floor. The sergeant held up an index and middle finger. *Two minutes.*

One hundred twenty seconds. Okay, I'd successfully navigated for four minutes and Mother Nature still hadn't called. I guess I was up the creek if she did. Dooley was still staring at me, waiting for some sign that I had gotten his message, so I gave him a brief nod.

He gestured toward the ramp ominously hinged to the cargo deck. The gesture meant: *Take your position.* Dooley stepped up to the door and stood beside me. He put one hand on my shoulder, and we both stared at the jump light.

My heart rate spiked—ninety-one beats per minute by my calculations—and I found myself breathing too deeply. *Settle down, Jake. You've done one hundred six jumps. What's one more?* Other than the absolute need for pressurized air, the subzero temperatures and the fall from eight miles above the earth into the lap of America's most vehement enemy, hell, this was a cakewalk.

Dooley gestured. *Thirty seconds!*

Adrenaline pumped into my muscles and made me hyperaware of the details around me. The rhythmic drone of the engines. The hum of the cargo deck. Lights blinking. The sweat glistening on the sergeant's face. The way his eyes were pinched in concentration. Oh, yeah, and the void of space staring back at me like a black hole.

I saw the jump light blink from red to green. Dooley slapped my arm and pointed out the aircraft. *Go!*

With so much gear, there was no graceful way to navigate to the edge of the ramp, so I resorted to an exaggerated waddle. I peered out at the glistening blue black of a new day. The earth below was a big gray ball.

I tapped the button on the instrument console to start the Elapsed Time stopwatch, then raised my arms and leaned forward. I tumbled out into space. I arched my back and stretched my arms and legs into a rigid cross position. There was a momentary whooshing sensation as I passed from the plane's sphere of influence; the calm that followed was total and complete.

I steadied myself in weightless free fall. I used my hands and feet to weathervane around and give the C-17 a farewell glance as it shrank farther and farther away. If I never saw another high-altitude plane again, it would be too soon.

I spun around until the visor readout put me on a straight shot to my destination. *Into the lion's den, Jake. Let's do this.*

I don't know where the music came from. But there it was, ZZ Top's "Sharp Dressed Man," pounding in my head. The music was usually a heat-of-battle thing. Then again, if this wasn't the heat-of-battle, then what the hell was?

Clouds blanketed the ground. No matter. I navigated using my GPS. I drew my arms into a V shape, steered with my feet, and maneuvered by twisting my body. I'd been dropped twenty miles north from my LZ, and the body position I'd assumed allowed me to track two miles more or less horizontally for every mile that I fell. The sensation was like an out-of-body experience, but I didn't have time to enjoy it. I'm not sure I wanted to. Just get on the ground and go to work.

Pressure Altitude: 38,924 feet and whistling through the air at two miles per minute. My heart raced in time to the numbers scrolling on the readout.

I tracked on course and plunged through the clouds. White vapor masked my visor. I felt the chill against my face. All I could see were the yellow digits of the instrument readout shining on the inside of the visor.

In what was essentially the blink of an eye, I had suddenly punched through the clouds and was streaking through a layer of air so clear and clean that I stopped breathing for a split second. It was like being reborn.

The sun rolled below the horizon and I was instantaneously shrouded by twilight; it was as if I had stepped into a time machine and been transported back in time. In a way, I guess I actually had been.

Pressure Altitude: 22,956 feet. Time Elapsed: one minute, thirty-nine seconds.

I followed the GPS reading as it counted down the Distance to LZ. 16.8 miles. I sliced through another bank of clouds.

Altitude: 17,217 feet. Absolute Height Above Ground: 10,925 feet. Time Elapsed: two minutes, fifty-four seconds. Distance to LZ: 8.3 miles.

I kept on track until my Distance to LZ read one mile. I checked the terrain against the geo maps I had memorized. My landing point was a shallow draw five hundred yards northwest of a hilltop that looked down on the fork in the Fasham–Tehran Road, a ribbon of asphalt that traversed the rugged Alborz Mountains. The tops of the hills were light gray and serrated—like broken teeth—and the valleys between them were black and forbidding with dense vegetation. Lights twinkled from the village of Fasham, just north of the fork. Smoke plumes vented upward, straight as the strokes of a crayon, meaning no wind.

Altitude: 7,571 feet. Time Elapsed: four minutes, forty-six seconds. Distance: zero. I was right over the LZ and resumed the cross position to stop my horizontal movement. What a way to travel!

I rotated slowly, reconnoitering the area and separating it into grids. Along the eastern horizon, a band of azure heralded the new sunrise. To the west and north, tiny lights peppered the gloomy mountains. Headlights trickled along the Fasham–Tehran Road to the spiderweb of highways north of Tehran. To the south, far in the distance, the illuminated sprawl of the city caused a shiver to sprint along my spine. Below, my landing point centered on a gash of tawny-colored ground flanked by shrubs and trees.

I grasped my rip cord and watched the Absolute Height Above Ground readout:

3,358 feet.

2,912 feet.

2,695 feet.

2,500 feet. I pulled my rip cord.

The main chute unfolded with a rustle of cloth. The chute billowed into a square, and the harness tightened around my torso and thighs to absorb the tug of the opening shock. Spot on. I gave Dooley a quick thanks and checked my rate of descent against the horizon. All good. Grasping the steering toggles on the front risers, I swung in a wide spiral to complete my ground reconnaissance.

Still no sign of life. The LZ looked clear of rocks and fallen timber. Thank God for satellite imagery.

I unclipped my jump bag and felt it jerk against the end of the tether hooked to my harness.

I took aim at the landing point. I held my legs out, knees bent, and hips loose. It's all about absorbing the impact, the Black Hats preached. You walk away with a broken leg, just hope the walk's not too long. The Black Hats were full of great advice.

At the last moment, I pulled both steering toggles to flare the parachute and touched down no harder than stepping off a porch. *Nicely done, Jake.* But this was no time to celebrate.

Landing was the time when I was most vulnerable. If the bad guys were onto me, I was dead. I scrambled to gather the parachute, unsnap the harness and instrument console, and step free. The readout in my visor blinked off. Releasing the latches of my helmet, I gave a twist and pulled it off. Cool, humid air rushed into my nostrils, and my lungs celebrated the rush of good, old-fashioned air.

I zipped open the jump bag and dumped out the backpack with my mission equipment and provisions. I bunched the parachute and harness into a tight knot and crammed it into the jump bag. I forced the helmet in and zipped it closed.

One more detail. I extended the self-destruct lever on the side of the instrument console. A pull on the lever sent a surge of electricity that fried the circuitry and erased the software. Not something the NSA wanted laying around.

Jump bag in one hand, backpack in the other, I hustled into the trees for cover, a voice in my head shouting, "Move your ass!"

I ducked into the darkest shadows and shrugged out of my pressure suit. I had civilian clothes underneath, jeans and a shirt. I carried the Walther and an extra magazine in a shoulder holster.

I plopped onto the ground and swapped my HALO boots for a pair of black cross-trainers from inside the backpack. I slipped into my jacket—new passports in one pocket, envelopes of money in another—and put a baseball cap on my head.

Finally, I dug the iPhone from my shirt pocket and turned it on. I activated the satellite-communications app and sent encrypted text messages to General Rutledge and Mr. Elliot: *Feet dry.*

I stuffed all the HALO equipment into the jump bag. I dragged the bag into a thicket of junipers and jammed it deep into the bramble. I camouflaged the spot with loose branches. This gear was easily worth a quarter of a million dollars. Well, no skin off my nose. If the government really wanted it back, they could send a battalion of marines in to get it.

I traversed the hill, staying in a low crouch, and inched my way to the crest. I dug into a hollow between two low-lying junipers. From there, I had an open view of the Fasham–Tehran Road and the fork that I had designated as my diversion LZ, the spot where I'd told Deputy Director of Operations Otto Wiseman I intended to land at daybreak. Thirty minutes from now.

My thirst caught up to me. I guzzled one of the water bottles from my backpack. Then I munched on an energy bar. I pulled a Zeiss digital telescope from the backpack and connected it to my iPhone to survey the area.

Exactly two minutes passed before I spotted a line of vehicles approaching from the south on the Fasham–Tehran Road. I spotted two small 4×4s with machine guns mounted on top, followed by two cargo trucks. They reached the fork in the road and fanned to the west about a hundred meters, a wake of fine dust marking their passage. The trucks halted. The back flaps of each were pushed aside and a squad of black-bearded Republican Guards jumped with easy steps and full combat gear to the ground. The cargo trucks retraced their tracks to the Fasham–Tehran Road and drove until they were out of sight. The soldiers melted into the surrounding brush. The 4×4s crawled beneath a canopy of trees that made them invisible from the air. They trained their machine guns on the fork in the road and waited.

I plugged a line jack into the side of my iPhone and fitted an earbud into my right ear. I tuned in to the radio-scan mode that the NSA techs had modified for the phone. The scan latched on to the strongest signal. The signal was close. Very close.

My Farsi was rusty. But I recognized it when I heard it, and I managed to interpret an irritated voice saying, "Okay, the sun's coming up. Where's the target? He should have landed by now."

I shook my head in disgust. I'd been right all along. Somebody close to the DDO had leaked my plans; or maybe the DDO had leaked them himself. *Who* didn't matter to me at that moment. I'd fended off the ultimate double cross. I was alive. The mission was still intact.

CHAPTER 13

IRAN—ALBORZ MOUNTAINS

I taped another thirty seconds of the growing frustration among the Republican Guard troops who were expecting Jake Conlan to parachute at any second into the crossfire of their machine guns. The tape would provide General Rutledge with sufficient evidence to institute an investigation into the security breach apparently infecting my operation. I would forward the audio link the first chance I had.

Either someone in the MEK had tipped off the Iranian government or someone in DDO Otto Wiseman's sphere of influence had leaked word of my HALO drop. I still hoped I was wrong about Wiseman. After all, he and I were supposed to be fighting the same fight, right? To keep the land of the red, white, and blue safe from scumbags just like the ones hiding in the bushes not a hundred yards from me.

Of course, I was also acting under the assumption that the leak wasn't coming from the office of my good friend General Tom Rutledge, something I could hardly bring myself to consider. But since I also knew that Mr. Elliot had no such prejudice, I would send him the same audio link. Mr. Elliot would leave not a single stone unturned, including the general's entire staff. I told myself it was a case of better safe than sorry and had nothing to do with my friendship with Tom.

I switched off the radio scan. I'd heard enough. I also had no idea whether or not the Republican Guard had the capability of scanning radio signals this far from Tehran, but I had no intention of giving them the chance.

I shifted positions, lying prone under the dense foliage of the junipers with only my left hand peeking out with the Zeiss digital telescope. I panned the entire area and followed the image through the iPhone. I hit the zoom function and zeroed in on the wooded area where some very serious soldiers were waiting. Bastards were in for a very long wait.

I switched modes on the Zeiss to the thermal viewer. I counted twenty red-and-orange images clumped inside the brush. As the minutes dragged on, the images became restless and shifted positions, clearly as undisciplined as they were impatient.

True, I may have escaped the Guards' less-than-professional trap on this inauspicious morning, but now I had to consider just how much they knew about my mission. If they had any idea I was headed for the suspected nuclear weapons facility in Qom—information Chief of Staff Landon Fry had shared with me—then their security there would be on high alert. If they knew I was onto the money-laundering pipeline that ran from an online banker in Amsterdam named Atash Morshed to Sepehr Tale, Iran's undersecretary for economic development, then they would be blanketing Tale with security. Contingencies. Always work the contingencies, Mr. Elliot preached. Make them work for you.

The sun crested the eastern hills, and an already bright sky became an incandescent blue. A helicopter thumped in the distance: a Huey with Iranian military markings. How ironic to see an American-made helicopter on the hunt for an American CIA operative. Well, hell, what would war be without the dispassionate contributions of arms dealers and defense contractors?

The copter made a pass up the valley, zooming to within five hundred meters of my position before circling back to orbit the diversion point. I flipped on the radio scan. There was a fresh volley of heated radio chatter, and I could tell that the ringmaster of this circus was definitely pissed off. Good. Glad I could accommodate.

114

The helicopter made another pass up the valley and raced south, back toward the city. New traffic barked over the radio, orders for the men to rally. *Sorry for the disappointment, chumps.*

The 4×4s with the machine guns emerged from the trees. The foot soldiers followed. The two troop trucks returned from wherever the hell they had gone. They gathered the troops, formed a column behind the 4×4s, and headed south along the Fasham–Tehran Road.

I kept still for another fifteen minutes. When I was sure the bad guys hadn't circled back, I opened a channel on my iPhone. I sent a new message to General Rutledge, which read: *Bear waiting. Went home hungry.* I attached the audio link from the Revolutionary Guards' radio transmissions.

I e-mailed a second message to Mr. Elliot. This one read: *Leak confirmed. Too many suspects to count.* I attached the audio link again and hit the Send button.

I was repacking my backpack when Mr. Elliot replied: *I'm on the hunt.* I was glad to hear that, of course, but there was almost no chance he would ferret out the leak in time to aid my mission. Then a second message appeared. It read: *Russian delivery in transit. Coordinates and codes to follow.* I stared at the words and shook my head. If it came to that, I was a dead man. But at least the mission wouldn't be a complete loss.

I shut down my phone. Now for my ride, whoever that was. I slithered out from under the juniper and hiked back to my original LZ, the rendezvous point for Mr. Elliot's contact. I tucked myself under the brush and waited.

At ten o'clock, a battered stake truck rumbled up the draw and came to a halt. A Chevy. A total waste of metal, if the exterior was any measure, but there was a healthy purr to the engine. The driver got out. He circled to the rear of the truck. He dropped the tailgate. A half-dozen goats hopped out and scampered into the grass. Very believable.

I watched for thirty seconds, waiting to see if the man had any company. He was alone. I resorted to the Zeiss telescope again and zoomed in on the man. He looked to be about six feet, tall for a Persian. He wore a rumpled khaki coat over cotton drawstring pants that might have been white in a past lifetime. He carried a wooden staff. Was that supposed to convince the world that he was a goatherder? Who knew?

I made him to be in his late thirties. He bore the leathery skin of a man who spent most of his time outside. He sported the scraggly, unkempt beard so common to Iranian men and wore a red-and-black kaffiyeh on his head.

I spent another thirty seconds scanning the area in case he had been followed. I switched to the thermal viewer to pierce the foliage. Nothing on both counts.

The man walked up the trail. He fished a small device from his coat pocket and I switched back to the Zeiss. I couldn't tell for sure, but it looked like a GPS. He walked to the exact center of my LZ and stopped. He pocketed the GPS and loitered there, stabbing the ground with the staff. He played the part well, giving all his attention to his goats, but his demeanor shouted: *I'm your guy. Do you want a ride to Tehran or not?*

I stored the iPhone and the Zeiss and slung the backpack over one shoulder. I palmed the Walther in my left hand. I pulled a pair of sunglasses from my jacket pocket, put them on, and emerged from the shadows of the junipers. I started down the slope.

The man must have caught the sound of my footsteps. He turned almost casually. It was clearly not a defensive move, not a surprised one. Good. He tipped his head in my direction as I marched toward him. He tried to act disinterested, but the charade wasn't necessary. Two guys meeting in the middle of basically nowhere? Oh, yeah. Happens every day.

I stopped ten feet away, asked, "Got any Marlboros?" My Farsi sucked.

"No, sorry." He shrugged. "All I have are Montecristo coronas."

Right response, right demeanor. All good. But if he thought I was going to drop my guard, he was sadly mistake. I did offer my hand, however. "Those will have to do." I gave him the name from my French passport: "Richard Moreau."

He shook my hand. His was as dry and cracked as an old tree trunk. "Amin Panahi." He smiled. Then he glanced skyward and quipped in English, "Nice of you to drop in. Looked like fun."

116

He'd obviously seen my parachute. "A barrel of laughs," I said with per-haps a touch too much sarcasm. I nodded in the direction of his truck. "Thanks for the lift. We'd better get going."

He whistled. The goats perked up their ears and trotted toward us. Panahi herded them with his staff in the direction of the truck; he'd clearly done this before. One by one, the goats leaped into the back, their pointed hooves drumming the cargo bed. He closed the gate and secured it with a bent coat hanger. The weathered and rusted Chevy looked older than me. A real high-class ride. I'd have to give my compliments to Mr. Elliot. The guy really knew how to treat his operatives.

We climbed into the cab. A small plastic bucket of sunflower seeds rested between us on the tattered bench seat. The engine started with a wheeze and a grumble, then purred like a kitten. We made an about-face and headed down the rocky draw. The dirt path bisected a pair of low-lying hills and fell in with the Fasham–Tehran Road. We headed south, mimicking the path traveled by the 4×4s and the troop trucks of Revolutionary Guards. The road paralleled a fast-moving stream. Sporadic traffic became a steady flow the farther south we drove. The skyline of metropolitan Tehran loomed on the horizon and grew in stature with each passing mile.

Panahi offered the sunflower seeds. I shook my head and hoped I wasn't insulting him. He shrugged, dipped a hand into the bucket, and tossed a hand-ful into his mouth.

"I will drop you near the grand bazaar," he said, grinding the seeds be-tween yellowed teeth. His hands gripped the wheel like a man wrestling an alligator. "The room you've been assigned is a three- or four-block walk. That's all I know. The exact address has been sent to you."

"Good. Thanks." I dug my iPhone from my pocket and powered it up. I opened my secured e-mail account, found messages from both Tom and Mr. Elliot, and started with the general's. *District 12, Harandi, 125, Tic-Tac-Toe.* District 12 was the municipal location of the Grand Bazaar. I remembered that. The address of the safe house was 521 Harandi. Tic-tac-toe meant my GPS would signal the right room when I arrived.

Mr. Elliot's e-mail was typically Mr. Elliot. One word: *improvise*. Oh, don't worry. I had every intention of improvising.

I closed down the phone. "We good?" Panahi asked.

"Good as gold," I said.

Panahi looked at me a bit strangely. He was probably dying for an interpretation of "Good as gold," but then the allure of gold was the same in pretty much any language. After about two seconds, I think he got it. He huffed what I took to be a less-than-enthusiastic endorsement of my affinity for clichés and gripped the wheel even tighter.

He stayed quiet. I wasn't interested in small talk either and did my part to reinforce this, staring at the grid of skyscrapers waltzing along the horizon.

Panahi busied himself with the task of keeping his rattletrap on the road while his gaze flitted nervously from mirror to mirror. We passed through the village of Roodak and three kilometers later merged with the main highway for Tehran. The more we drove, the more frequently Panahi dipped into the sunflower seeds.

Traffic backed up, and now I could see why. Orange cones funneled all southbound traffic into a single lane. Men in police uniforms with AK-47s checked each vehicle coming through.

I'd spent my career talking myself out of tight corners. As the moment of deception approached, I'd learned to cope by smothering any possible doubts or fears with self-confidence and faith. Meanwhile, Panahi munched nervously. Damn guy might as well have tattooed the word *suspicious* on his forehead.

"Relax, my friend," I said in a voice that was far more businesslike than it was friendly. "Take a deep breath and relax."

When it was our turn to advance to the checkpoint, he spit the wad of chewed husks out the window and let the truck roll forward. Two policemen. One stood out in front of the car with his hand resting lazily on the butt of a pistol riding high on his right hip. Panahi halted the Chevy next to the second policeman and rolled down his window. The cop leaned in. He was overweight and sloppy. He wore sunglasses and chewed on an unruly mustache. He wasn't nervous—I saw that—and he didn't carry himself like a man expecting trouble. All good.

I managed to catch snippets of his exchange with Panahi. I heard the words, but mostly I was studying his tone, his inflections, his tempo. Same conclusion.

"What is your business today?"

"What do you mean?" Panahi played it well. He cocked a thumb to the goats in the back. "You think I'm taking my flock out for a joyride?"

The policeman ignored the sarcasm and extended an open hand through the window. "Papers."

Panahi handed the cop his ID. He studied it. Flipped it over. Studied it some more. "What is your destination?"

"The Grand Bazaar."

The cop returned the ID and looked at me. "And you?"

"He's from the French Ministry of Agriculture," Panahi answered. "Here to study how we raise animals."

The policeman beckoned with his fingers. I gave him my passport.

He flipped through the passport and read my name. He pronounced it, "Ri-charde Mora?"

"Close enough," I replied in French.

The cop studied me, eyes narrowing as if deciding what to do next. I looked at him with eyes so calm and warm that he might as well have been my best friend. My message was simple: don't cause trouble. Which translated into: don't make me shoot you between the eyes. I had already triangulated my position between him and his partner. If I had to, I could drop them both in a single heartbeat. After that? I'd have to ditch Panahi and commandeer a car. Things would get hairy. Again.

The policeman returned my passport and then did a rapid-fire exchange with Panahi, talking too fast for me to catch any of it. The cop took a step back and waved us through. Panahi dug into his cup of sunflower seeds and shoved a fresh handful into his mouth.

I looked into our rearview mirror. The policeman stared at us. His partner joined him. They exchanged a dozen words, then his partner spoke into a hand-held radio.

A cataract of undeniable questions unraveled in my mind. Had Panahi given me away? Was the MEK—hell, or even the Iranian government—using him to shadow me? I didn't think so. He was Mr. Elliot's man. Mr. Elliot picked his people carefully. He trained them. He put them in the field only after they'd passed muster in situations a whole lot more dicey than a police roadblock.

"So?" I said.

"Tensions are high," he answered. He nodded toward the police. "These pricks have been warned to trust no one. A foreigner is a foreigner. Even when he's traveling with a local."

Great answer. Who could argue with that? He was right. Tensions were high in Tehran. They'd been high for thirty years, and the people had no one to blame but themselves.

We drove into Tehran, a city of fifteen million people with as much freedom as caged mice in a deceptively urban setting. Yeah, most of the world was quick to demonize Iran, but you couldn't tell it by the lush, well-manicured greenbelts lining the highway, and you couldn't tell it by the amenities and architecture as modern as Chicago's. You couldn't see the tension, not from the front seat of a pickup truck. But it didn't take much to imagine how much brighter this place would be without crazy zealots like Mahmoud Ahmadinejad and his gang of mullahs riding their people's back.

A cell phone chirped from Panahi's coat pocket. He answered it in Farsi. ". . . Just crossed the Hemmat Highway . . ." A sideways glance to me. "Safe and sound." He put the phone away and said in English, "All clear."

"Who were you talking to?" He could tell by the tone of my voice that full disclosure was his only option. "Who?"

When he glanced across the console this time, he looked me right in the eye. We held that pose for a good three seconds. Then he gave his attention back to the road. His voice was calm when he said, "Do you really think I'd drive straight into Tehran with someone as important as you in my care without eyes and ears on our drop zone, Mr. Moreau?"

Another good answer. "Not if you wanted to live very long."

"My life is not important. That we succeed is."

I wanted to say, *You're breaking my heart,* but I didn't.

Panahi turned from the highway onto Shariati Street. We rattled down the road and curled in the direction of the city's sprawling downtown. Like Istanbul and so many other cities in Mesopotamia, the old and the new could hardly be separated in Tehran. You had to remember that the area we were driving through had first been settled more than eight thousand years ago. That's a lot of years and a lot of time for humans to mess up whatever had been good about this ancient land in the first place. You could travel through Tehran and see a thousand-year-old mosque across the street from a twenty-year-old steel and glass high-rise, a piece of junk that wouldn't last another fifty. Guess which one got the nod in my book?

The streets were packed with cars and buses, taxis and minicabs, bicycles and motor bikes. And thousands of people. It was hot in the cab now that we were moving at a snail's pace, and I rolled down the window. A cacophony of motors and mechanization melded with the shuffle of footsteps and a wave of competing voices.

I saw soldiers. I saw police. I heard sirens.

Pedestrians darted between cars, and my insides squirmed. Someone could jog right up to us and put a bullet through my brain. Well, maybe that was a little melodramatic, but I reached inside my coat and grasped my pistol nonetheless. I clicked the safety off, index finger resting on the trigger. Panahi made a left onto a side street lined with boxy row houses.

The Grand Bazaar probably didn't have the benefit of road signs and billboards announcing its location back four hundred years ago, when the first merchant put up his tent, but now there was signage helping everyone from tourists to bankers to find it. Four hundred years ago, it was an outdoor market. Today it was housed in a remarkable domed affair with corridors meandering more than six miles and selling everything from copper and gold to cinnamon and coriander. You could borrow money in the bazaar or barter for cow's liver. You could buy a kite or a kitten. You could haggle over jewelry or hire a tailor. You could have your fortune read in one booth, drink coffee and munch homemade pastries in another, and negotiate a loan in another. You could see and do a lot of things in six miles' worth of booths and stalls. You could spend a week and not see everything.

I knew by Panahi's choice of side streets that he was headed for the north entrance to the bazaar. I said, "Circle around to the south entrance, will you?"

"Why?" he said. "We don't have any backup in place there?"

"I think I'll do some sightseeing," I replied. He knew what I meant. I didn't want his backup. He made a couple of turns, fought through trench-warfare-like traffic, and eased to the curb of an especially drab concrete building.

"This is as close as I can get." He nodded toward a wide arch that led into a maze of stone corridors. "Don't get lost."

"Take care of those goats," I said. I opened my coat and pulled out a stack of Iranian currency, rials worth about a hundred dollars. "Thanks. Keep the change."

Panahi must have seen enough American movies to get the joke. "Take care, Mr. Moreau."

I got out and stood on the sidewalk to watch Panahi and his truckload of goats drive away. I had no intention of entering the Grand Bazaar, though my stomach was growling from lack of food, and I would have paid good money for a bottle of water or a cold beer. Wasn't going to happen here.

Improvise, Mr. Elliot had advised. And that's what I was doing.

I started walking. I took the long way back to Shariati Street. In the shade of a café awning, I took out my iPhone. Flipping through my list of old contacts, I found the address of a woman who probably wasn't going to be thrilled to see me; it had been ten years, and we hadn't parted on the best of terms. She wanted me to stay. I had to go.

But if anyone could provide me with a safe haven, even for a day, it was her. And if anyone could point me in the direction of Charlie Amadi, it was also her.

I hailed a cab and recited a pair of cross streets close to the address. We drove west on Azadi Street and past the central metro station with its statue of a scowling bearded man on a plinth. That was something you couldn't help but notice about Tehran, and probably the entire country: it was full of homage paid to grumpy geezers who looked like they hadn't been laid in years. If they had wanted an objective opinion, I might have suggested lightening things up a bit and turning some of those billboards into twenty-foot-high advertisements featuring girls in bikinis, like the Turks did. Just a thought.

I glanced out the rear window a couple of times, saw a logjam of cars and mopeds two blocks long, but nothing struck me as suspicious. Eleven minutes into our journey, the cab took a left on Jalilabad and halted at the intersection I had requested. I paid the driver in euros and got out. A stream of exhaust followed him down the block, and I watched for fifteen seconds. The cab hit a green light at the next intersection, made a right turn, and disappeared.

I stepped into the doorway of a four-story apartment building and watched the traffic for nearly a minute. Then I started walking. Two blocks took me into a neighborhood dedicated to small shops and tenements. I stepped up to a street vendor, bought a bottle of water, and ducked into the shade of a cherry tree.

I spent a minute taking the pulse of the neighborhood. Much had changed since I'd last been here. And not for the best. If other parts of Tehran were showpieces of "progress," this area was a dead end of neglect.

The address I was looking for was a small market a half block farther on, located on the bottom floor of a forlorn two-story building. Long ago, that address had housed the Casbahye-Sorkh—the Red Casbah—one of the fanciest and hippest nightclubs this side of Bangkok. Now it was a freshly painted concrete shell with a colorful sign inviting locals to shop for the kind of things you might find in a 7-Eleven back home.

I looped my backpack over my left shoulder, keeping my right hand free, and crossed the street. A woman in a head scarf with grocery bags dangling from each hand hustled out the market's entrance, and I held the door open for her.

I crossed the threshold and halted. I peaked over the rims of my sunglasses and kept my face hooded by the bill of my baseball cap. Rows of canned goods and bags of rice crowded the shelves. A cooler filled out the far wall and glass doors opened onto milk cartons, water bottles, and soda. Fresh vegetables and fruit were arranged on a center island across from the counter.

A video camera faced the entrance and reminded me that there was always someone watching. It was virtually the same in every grocery store, train station, bank, coffee shop, and church in every major city in the world these days. All in the name of "national security," two words whose definition had been manipulated to fit the call of a thousand politicians. How often I cringed when I heard people say they'd be willing to give up a "couple of freedoms" to feel more secure. Stupid, fearful sons-a-bitches didn't realize that it was their freedoms that spelled out their security, not the other way around.

I stepped up to the cash register. A swarthy-faced man about my age gave me a nod. He had flecks of gray in his curly hair, a broad nose, and even broader shoulders. Twenty years ago, he'd probably been a bouncer or a jackhammer operator.

"May I help you?" He spoke Farsi, and I was only half sure I'd heard him correctly.

"Leila Petrosian?"

The man's eyes widened when he heard Leila's name, and he pinned me with the kind of glare that was one part suspicious and one part highly protective. "Who's asking?"

"A friend."

"A friend? I know all of Leila's friends. You aren't one of them." He reached for the telephone.

"I wouldn't do that," I warned in English.

"No? And why not?" the man answered in English.

"Because it would ruin his welcome," a woman's voice informed him. The owner of the voice stepped through a curtain that separated the front of the store from the back. As sleek as a dancer, as strong as an athlete. Blonde hair curled around brown eyes that stunned you with their radiance.

Leila Petrosian.

If anyone would know where Charlie Amadi was, it would be Leila.

CHAPTER 14

TEHRAN, IRAN—DAY SIX

Leila Petrosian's pillowy red lips curved into a where-have-you-been? smile. I took off my sunglasses, folded them into my shirt pocket, and tried my best to match her expression. It had been a long time. And our relationship was exactly the kind that made it as hard to be together as it was to be apart. I didn't know how else to describe it.

Life in Iran might not have been kind to Leila, but the years had. Her skin was as smooth and flawless as ever, and the voluptuous curves she had flaunted as a young cabaret dancer made a simple cotton dress look like a fashion statement in a magazine.

"You look . . ." I paused, sifting through any number of adjectives that seemed inadequate.

"Amazing?" She tried to help, and her smile told me she was teasing.

"I was thinking *sensational*, but *amazing* works, too," I said, smiling with genuine enthusiasm. This was the best I'd felt since leaving Washington, D.C.

I had met Leila three decades earlier, when she worked the floor show at a club called Sitta Al Sa'if. She was married. So was I. Back then, the nightclub scene in Tehran had made it a mecca of entertainment. Leila had proved as agile with money as she was in dance slippers, and by the time she was twenty-two she was part owner of the Red Casbah. But when the shah was chased out, the

125

mullahs took over and shuttered all the nightclubs for inciting immoral and dangerous behavior. Immoral? Yeah, well, that might depend on your perspective, I suppose. But dangerous? The most dangerous things to come out of a night at the Red Casbah were hangovers and regrets.

The religious police raided Leila's club—the pious hypocrites had been some of her best customers—and when the raids couldn't shut her down, the government stepped in. They confiscated her bank accounts. They dumped her liquor stock down the sewer. They issued a warrant for her arrest. What kept Leila out of prison were her connections to the Armenian community. We tried staying in touch. I couldn't get in back in those days, and she refused to leave. She once told me, "If I give up on my country, I give up on myself. The same way you feel about America."

After that, we met maybe a dozen times or so over the years. By then, she was a divorced woman. She wanted more from our relationship, but it wasn't possible. We didn't talk much about life under the heel of the Islamic regime, but every once in a while she'd tell me things. About the oppression. About the mood of the people. About the dwindling opportunities. It wasn't pretty. A land of progress and prospects had spiraled into a land of tyranny and stagnation.

I knew how risky it was meeting her like that. Risky for me, even more risky for her. But it was hard to resist. Here was a woman who made every day seem like a brush with spring. I hadn't seen Leila for ten years, not since surviving an assassination attempt in Kazakhstan. After that, I was called home permanently. I sent letters for a year, but she never returned them. I didn't hold it against her. There was no future. There never had been.

And now she was three feet away, and all I could do was stare.

The sparkle in Leila's eyes burned as mischievously as ever. The dress she wore hardly accommodated the Islamic dress code—Leila had no patience for the sad attempt of men to hold women to some standard they would never tolerate for themselves—and the way the fabric clung to her was a three-alarm fire waiting to happen.

"Rahim," she said to the muscle-head attending the cash register. "If anyone comes looking for me, tell them I'm out running errands."

Rahim shot me a jealous glare. I didn't need another enemy, so I said to him, "Relax. I'm just a guy visiting an old friend."

Leila held the curtain open and beckoned me through. I followed her down the hall, trying my best not to get distracted by the obvious distractions of her exceptional legs and firm, round bottom. The hall doglegged around the corner, and she glanced back at me, her grin just a bit mocking. "Just an old friend, huh?"

"He didn't look like the kind of guy you'd want to piss off," I replied.

"Rahim is very protective, that's all."

We approached a shelf stocked with bags of rice and cans of mango juice. Leila grasped a bracket on the shelf and pulled. The bracket clicked and the rack of shelves swiveled, revealing a secret door. She passed through, and I followed.

We entered a room furnished like a miniature Fifth Avenue lounge. A narrow wooden bar, polished within an inch of its life, ran across the far wall. It was backed by a beveled mirror, and bottles of top-shelf liquor were arranged in front of the mirror. A velvet love seat and leather chairs were positioned over a Persian carpet. Soft light spilled from wall sconces made of smoked glass. Leila swiveled the secret door closed again and turned a dead bolt.

I took in the room and tried to make sense of it. "Side business?"

"I supply beverages of the alcoholic kind for private entertaining," she told me. "You don't think running that little store pays the bills, I hope?"

I dropped my backpack onto a chair. Leila glanced at it but knew me well enough not to ask. Instead, she stepped close and clasped my hands. Her eyes smoldered with a look that brought back memories of long, sleepless nights and sweaty bedsheets.

"Jake, I missed you."

It would have been so easy, and so wrong. I had Cathy, kids, and a life that had taken me far from the world I had known for all those years. Still, I told Leila what she wanted to hear, and maybe what a part of me still felt. "I missed you, too."

She squeezed my hands and gave me a perceptive grin. "Thanks for saying that."

Then she let go and leaned against the bar. She studied me now with the eyes of a long-time survivor of turmoil and uncertainty. "Okay, now that we've got that out of the way, tell me what brings you to Tehran? Business?"

"Business," I said, gazing at the bar and the bottles. Liquor was contraband—strange for a city that had once been the cosmopolitan rage of the Middle East—so it was a safe bet that she was buying wholesale from someone with his hands deep in the smuggling business. And no one had his hands deeper in the rackets than Charlie. "I'm looking for Charlie Amadi, Leila."

"Charlie!" Leila chuckled. Then the chuckled faded, and her eyes flashed with an odd and enticing mix of concern and interest. "Why in the world would you have business with a man like Charlie Amadi?"

"I need his help. It's important."

"Important how?"

"I'm back on the job." She at least deserved a certain amount of honesty. "Where can I find him?"

"You can't. He finds you."

"I don't have that kind of time. Make it easy on me and tell me where he is."

"Charlie doesn't like surprises, Jake."

"He'll make an exception for me. We go back a long time."

Curiosity and surprise fanned out around Leila's eyes. "I didn't know that."

"Back when we were both young and stupid."

Leila turned and stared at her reflection in the mirror. It was like she was trying to put together the pieces of a puzzle I had just scattered across her already difficult life. After a long moment, her gaze slid to mine, and I could see she'd made a decision.

"He lives just east of Azad University on Malek. Very private. Very tight security," she said. Then she raised her shoulders in a reluctant shrug. "But this time of day you might just find him at the Park of the Reluctant Martyrs."

"Why there?"

She grinned. "There's a playground there. And swing sets."

"Charlie has grandkids!" Now I was grinning.

"I can drive you."

This brought me back to reality in no uncertain terms. "No," I said firmly.

She smiled at me, her head just slightly tilted to one side, like a statue filled with inspiration and sympathy. "I always liked your business, Jake. It was a business with a purpose. And I always liked the fact that you'd do whatever it took."

"Leila . . ."

"I know why you're here."

"No, you don't." I didn't want her to know why I was here. I didn't want her to know that my mission was to secure evidence worthy of an attack on her country. But then maybe it wasn't her country anymore, not really, not the one she grew up loving.

She touched my cheek. "I'll get my wrap."

It wasn't a wrap that she reached for but an abaya hanging behind the bar. It was black and gray and hung to the floor like a cloak. She made it look almost fashionable. It wouldn't stop people from seeing her with a man who had been banned from Iran many years ago, however.

"I have a car out back. It's not much, but it'll get us where we're going." She pointed to a door set against the opposite wall. "This way."

I picked up my backpack. The door led to a dimly lit hall that exited into a narrow alley. A gray Toyota Camry was crunched against the wall, leaving just enough room for another vehicle to slide by. There were five or six other cars parked exactly the same way up and down the alley. It was already hot and the air smelled of curry. I covered my head with my baseball cap and put on my sunglasses.

"I'll pull out," she said, sliding into the driver's seat. I watched her move with a light step and purpose. Then I searched the alley as far as my eyes would take me. I didn't want this woman's life in my hands. I didn't want her anywhere near my business. I wanted her safe and sound in her run-down store with Rahim watching over her. But I also saw that there was no way to say no to her.

She inched to the center of the alley. I opened the door and settled onto the passenger seat, the backpack on the floor between my cross-trainers.

As we eased down the alley, I flashed back momentarily to the bar and the wall full of liquor that Leila called her primary source of income. Liquor was banned under Islamic law, which made it a profitable commodity. It was a numbers game. A good $750 million worth of booze was smuggled into the country every year, but the government managed to track down only a fraction of that. I had to wonder if an operation as open as Leila's seemed to be benefiting from some type of protection. And if so, who was she beholden to?

Leila glanced over at me. She shook her head, as if she knew what I was thinking. "You're wondering about my place, aren't you? I'm small potatoes, Jake. Just a lady trying to stay above water. Half of my clients work for the government, so I guess they could shut me down in a heartbeat."

"But why would they?" I said.

"They've got a lot bigger problems than a renegade dancehall girl with a couple of bottles of whiskey behind the bar." She steered the car out into a steady flow of traffic. "You trust me, don't you, Jake?"

"I don't trust my own shadow, Leila," I replied. "But you I trust."

She smiled, but it was a sad smile. "Buckle your seat belt," she said.

"Yes, ma'am."

I pulled out my iPhone and sent General Rutledge a quick text. *Still alive and kicking.* I sent the same message to DDO Wiseman. I wasn't giving anything away. He would assume I was in Tehran, but Tehran was a very big city. I had no intention of mentioning Charlie Amadi to anyone, not even to Mr. Elliot. But then, Mr. Elliot would expect no less. "Need to know" was not just a cliché made famous by B-movies; it was a hard-and-fast rule in the world of black ops. Location was always a "need to know," because the fewer people who knew your location, the less chance you had of getting dead.

I changed apps. I used an NSA satellite app called Eyes to zero in on the Park of the Reluctant Martyrs. I didn't get the name. Wouldn't all martyrs be reluctant? Well, maybe not in a land of suicide bombers.

Eyes gave me a bird's-eye view of the park; it was real-time information, and the oblong terrain was filled with people. Too many. I don't know what I was hoping for. Maybe Charlie and a couple of grandkids doing their thing on the swings, all alone and waiting with bated breath for Jake Conlan to make a much-anticipated appearance. It looked like Grand Central Station. How many of them were Charlie's muscle only time would tell.

"Busy place," I said. "Don't people have anything better to do on a Wednesday afternoon?"

I zoomed in. Eyes allowed me to troll the park by using a series of walking paths to block out a manageable grid. It was obvious. Six guys standing like statues around the perimeter of a grassy knoll along the park's west side, with a sizable lake protecting the knoll to the east. They were either bodyguards or trolls. I was betting on the former.

Charlie hadn't stayed long in the United States after I'd saved his life nearly thirty years earlier. But he'd stayed long enough for the two of us to forge a working relationship. I never intended to use Charlie for anything more challenging than being the occasional bagman. Not because he wasn't capable. He was more than capable. The bag work was more or less my way of sending up a test balloon. I'd always wondered how light the satchels of cash would be after they passed through his hands. Every shipment came out to the dollar. He'd smuggled kilos of cocaine and heroin. Each and every time, every gram was accounted for at its destination. What I wanted from Charlie was intel. You get intel in small amounts just by being in the right place at the right time, but you can pile up the intel by the bushel if you get the right people to trust you.

Charlie began to trust me. I was a good teacher. What I taught most effectively was the art of survival. He learned it quickly. He became an expert in how to watch his back and cover his tracks. For his part, Charlie was an accepted cog in the Iranian drug cartel. He knew people. He was the son of the Iranian prime minister, himself a rogue of some note, and so he'd landed in the States knowing people. No one questioned his loyalty because of his pedigree.

After two years of milking Charlie of as much intel as possible, I suggested he return home. The operation targeting his people was coming to a head. When the shit hit the fan, he didn't want to be anywhere near New York or D.C. or any other place on the East Coast.

So he left with his very pretty wife and two beautiful kids and a serious knowledge of the streets. He used it to build a fortune in Iran. Drugs, alcohol, and arms. The big three. Then he diversified, smuggling in everything from electronics to foodstuffs. Then he learned to convert his profits into property on three continents.

Now he had grandkids and spent his afternoons in the park. Fair enough. I figured he owed me for his good life, and now it was time to cash in.

"How well do you know this Park of the Reluctant Martyrs?" I asked Leila as she steered the car into a commercial neighborhood crowded with shops, cafés, and streams of pedestrians.

"Well enough," she said. She glanced down at my iPhone. "Have you found him?"

"West side. Near the lake."

"Then the west side near the lake it is," she said.

We rolled to a stop at a red light. Downtown Tehran could have been a major downtown in any metropolitan city except for the number of police. And you might have been able to overlook that had it not been for the soldiers. And if you were really willing to turn a blind eye, maybe you could even ignore the fifteen- and sixteen-year-old kids armed with batons and clubs and strutting through the streets with orders to attack anyone who looked even remotely like a demonstrator.

"What the hell," I said as a group of four of them stopped in the middle of the crosswalk and sneered at the traffic.

"Oh, yes, Ahmadinejad's child army," Leila replied. I had never heard her sound so dispirited. "The Guards recruit them from the countryside because they know the regular police won't attack the demonstrators; after all, most of them have family walking side by side with neighbors. Not these boys. They're starving when they come here, and they're thugs when they leave. The Guards sees to that. The more brutal, the better. It's terrible, Jake. Just terrible."

The light changed. The traffic inched forward. But the tension over this city in chains could be felt even without the windows rolled down.

"Three blocks," she said, nodding toward a fork in the road and a forest of trees rising before us. "The entrance to the park is straight ahead. No cars allowed."

"I'll walk from here, Leila. You've done enough," I said. "More than enough."

She pulled to the curb and brought the Toyota to a halt. She reached over and grabbed my wrist. "Take off your sunglasses. Please," she asked in a low and husky voice. I did so, and she held me with her dark eyes, as calm and cool as a winter's eve. "I haven't done enough, Jake. That's the whole point. Not near enough. I've been a part of the problem, not a part of the solution."

"Leila, listen . . ."

"No, it's true. If I can help, let me. I know you'd do anything to protect me. I know that. But I have to stop being afraid. And maybe you can help me by letting me help you." Her fingers were pressing into my wrist, and she wasn't even aware of it. "Please."

I nodded. "Okay." How could I hear those words and say anything else? I hoped it didn't come down to needing her help, but I didn't say that, either.

She opened my fingers and pressed a key into my hand. "If you run out of places to hide or just need a cold beer and someone to confide in, this opens the back door to my place. I want to do this."

I leaned over and kissed her cheek. I grabbed my pack, opened the door, and climbed out.

I waited until she was safely away and then lost myself in the crowd. I saw a T-shirt shop with baseball caps in the window and ducked inside. I bought a gray one with a blue Nike swoosh on the crown and tossed the old one into the trash. I stepped back outside and into the shadows of the shop's awning. I surveyed the street. I was out of place, but at least the beard I had started back in the States was coming in.

The strip of commerce gave way to an upscale neighborhood, and a block farther on the entrance to the Park of the Reluctant Martyrs came into view.

I stopped under a shaggy, plain tree. The park was not as big as I had expected, given the satellite view from the Eyes app, but it was the size of three or four football fields, anyway.

Past the entrance, a concrete sidewalk ran along the perimeter of the park's west side. There was also a walkway that bisected the park from east to west. Knots of men looked to be loitering on all four street corners, but you could see the tension in their movements. Others paced along the sidewalk under the outstretched branches of elms and maples, and still others patrolled farther into the park. A pair of black Mercedes sedans were parked along the curb, and the men standing next to them didn't look like they'd come to the park for a game of boccie. They were Charlie's men. All twenty-one of them, by my count. That was a lot of sentries. Which meant that Charlie had extremely deep pockets and a reason to be paranoid.

Scattered trees provided shade over the grassy lawn. The lake formed a natural barrier to the south and east. To the north, low hedges and gardens spilling over with perennials, surrounded by a decorative fountain. Sunlight refracted through the water in a spray of rainbow colors. There was a play-ground and common area across from the fountain. There were three picnic tables, and I could almost hear the laughter coming from the family gathering there. I was most interested in the man sitting with his back to one of the tables, watching a half-dozen young children scurry through the playground.

I slid my backpack off my shoulder. I opened it and fished out the Zeiss digital telescope. I connected it to the iPhone and scanned the park in high magnification.

I studied Charlie's bodyguards. They all appeared to be cut from the same rough cloth. A couple wore thigh-length coats, unusual for such a warm day, a telltale sign that they packed Uzis, AK-47s, or M4 carbines. Heavy artillery for the man they protected.

I panned to the man on the bench. There he was. Charlie Amadi. He wore a sweater and khaki pants. The years had added a few pounds to his frame and rounded out his face, but he looked healthy and energetic. He was fully en-grossed in the activity on the playground, the kids darting from the slides and the swings to the carousel and a sandbox. Two more bodyguards: probably Charlie's lieutenants.

Time for our reunion.

I put the Zeiss away and sent Rutledge and Mr. Elliot the same update: *About to meet the hometown boy.*

I could feel the Walther in the harness beneath my jacket. I had no intention of hiding the fact that I was armed from Charlie's army. Pure stupid. I crossed the street and walked straight for the entrance, which was really nothing more than two stone pillars capped with statuesque eagles. I didn't see the significance.

I walked with an easy step. My arms hung loosely at my side. I was ten steps from the entrance when four of Charlie's men blocked my way.

"Sorry, private party," one of them said in Farsi. He was the tallest of the group and built like a linebacker. When I didn't respond, he was smart enough to switch to English. "Private party."

I stopped. I held my hands out in front of me. "No problem. I'm here to see Charlie. Charlie Amadi."

"Mr. Amadi's not here."

I looked at him like I'd seen smarter lab rats. "Oh, I see. That must be his twin brother sitting over there by the playground. How stupid do I look?"

I started forward again. They closed ranks. One of them put a hand on my shoulder. Bad move. I grabbed the hand, took it off my shoulder, and squeezed. Before any of his buddies could react, I looked at the linebacker and said, "Charlie and I are old friends."

I let go of the hand. Now I was attracting a crowd. I held my hands up again. "Under my right arm," I said. "A Walther. The safety's on."

Now they got rough. Two of them grabbing my shoulders, the linebacker doing a hard and very effective frisk. I let him. He came away with the Walther in his hand. I looked past my reception committee and saw Charlie's two lieutenants looking our way. Even from here I could see their lips curl in warning scowls. Charlie must have felt the tension, because he came to his feet, turned, and stared. I saw him issuing instructions.

I raised my arms high in the air. I wanted him to see that I was alone and pretty much helpless. "Go tell him," I said to the linebacker. "Tell him it's Jake."

The linebacker stared at me for five long seconds. Then he spit an order to one of his team, a short guy with a gaunt face and a blue-black mustache. He turned and hustled over to Charlie's lieutenants. Said something I couldn't hear. But whatever it was, it got Charlie moving, not fast, but steadily. His lieutenants were caught off guard for a split second and hustled to catch up.

Charlie walked to the middle of the sidewalk and stopped, a fair distance away but with a good view of the proceedings. He said something to the runner, who turned and jogged back to us. He said something to the linebacker, but I didn't wait for a translation. I pushed my way past the gauntlet that had been holding me at bay. I took three steps and stopped.

Charlie was looking hard at me. His squint compressed into suspicious crinkles, then eased some. The first signs of recognition must have been forming in his very suspicious mind, because the hard set of his mouth tweaked into the beginning of a smile.

I started toward him again. His lieutenants responded exactly the way I would have expected them to respond: they took two steps forward and positioned their feet the way men do when they're expecting a confrontation.

Charlie put his hands on their shoulders, whispered two words I didn't understand, and stepped between them. I pressed ahead, halting close enough to Charlie that I could smell his cologne.

I lowered my sunglasses.

He beamed a toothy grin, a crescent of bleached enamel and gold implants. "Jake fucking Conlan."

"Charlie."

He lunged forward with an embrace. "Damn, it's been years." He gave me a manly hug. "You look fit. Damn fit."

"And you look like you've been living the good life," I replied.

"There is no good life here in Tehran," he answered, without a hint of derogatory emotion in his voice. He studied me, nodding his head as if the curtain had just opened onto a scene that looked all too familiar. "My man Jake. Don't imagine you just dropped in for a quiet stroll through the park."

"Another time," I said.

"Okay. Okay." His smile evolved into a look of genuine curiosity. I saw a spark in his eye. "So, what gives?"

I motioned down the sidewalk. "Let's take a walk. Do you mind?"

"Do I mind taking a walk with a good friend I haven't seen in years? No, I don't mind." He smiled again. He gave an all-clear nod of his head to his guards, and we turned into the park. His lieutenants followed at a respectful distance.

I steered us to the fountain. The splashing water would mask our conversation from anyone hoping to eavesdrop, and Charlie seemed to understand.

When we were close enough to feel the mist, I glanced his way and said, "Charlie, you seem to have done well for yourself."

He shrugged, a tad embarrassed by the compliment. "*Inshallah.* I sell people what they want. Fortunately, there are plenty of Persians who want a taste of life before the mullahs."

"So you're selling the good life," I said.

"Well, that and a few of the essentials." I loved that. The essentials. Like guns and drugs and passports. Yeah, I got it. He said, "I can't tell you how much has changed over the years, Jake."

"You mean like the boy soldiers patrolling your streets?" I hoped I didn't sound too sarcastic.

"Tip of the iceberg, my friend." Charlie beat the air with his fist, a heavy gold bracelet sliding on his wrist. "The country is like a tinderbox waiting to explode. Ahmadinejad rants against the Israelis as if they were the source of our problems. He spends billions trying to develop weapons to wipe out our neighbors while our own country is in free fall."

"Which brings me to my mission."

"Mission? What are you talking about?" Charlie chuckled. Then he saw that I was dead serious, and he banished every ounce of humor from his voice. "Here? In Iran? That's why you're here? Hell, I heard you were retired."

"Was," I said.

"If you say so." He shrugged, but it wasn't very convincing. "And this mission of yours. What is it?"

I didn't say anything.

"And your team?" His eyes inched wider in surprise when he saw the tension etched across my face. "You're not acting alone?"

"No. There's a team here. Two teams, actually. I have MEK support and DDO backup."

"That's your team. Huh! You really know how to pick 'em, Jake," he said with the greatest of irony.

"Problem is, my op's been compromised."

Charlie shrugged. "Proceed without them."

"Easier said than done," I replied.

"Of course," he said, as if he'd just had a revelation. "They know too much, don't they?"

"I can't move forward without knowing who the traitor is, Charlie." He knew what I meant.

"Jake. My dear friend." He opened his arms toward the picnic area and the playground. Toward a family filled with kids and grandkids and a wife of thirty years. "Look, my friend. Look what you gave me. A man doesn't forget that. Not ever."

I heard the emotion in his voice. "You have a beautiful family, Charlie. You really do."

Now he looked at me, and his eyes were those of a man who knew the rules of engagement and had never been averse to breaking them.

"Anything I have is at your disposal." He opened his arms. "Men. Weapons. Money. You name it."

"Charlie, I've come to you because you have the one resource money can't buy."

"What is that, Jake?"

"Trust."

CHAPTER 15

Charlie Amadi and I were on the bottom floor of a dilapidated warehouse in Navvab, one of Tehran's southern districts. The warehouse was situated close to a cement factory and one of the city's wastewater-treatment plants. A train rumbled along on nearby tracks, rattling our windows and the overhead pipes.

The outside of the warehouse was blighted with stains and flaking plaster. Rusted appliances and stripped-down cars littered the weedy grounds, and dingy broken windows revealed a gloomy interior. The building didn't just look abandoned but forsaken. In other words, it fit our needs to a tee.

Inside, the warehouse didn't look quite so desolate, however. It was chock-full of cardboard boxes and sealed containers filled with things like fake Rolex watches and knock-off designer purses, sunglasses and leather jackets, Persian rugs and porcelain pottery, all part of Charlie's black-market inventory. The local street vendors must have loved the guy.

At the heart of the main floor, stacks of boxes had been pushed aside to accommodate a workstation hastily arranged atop four folding tables. Shop lamps had been clipped to the rafters, filling the space with harsh white light. A bank of five laptop computers rested on the tables, and their monitors flickered with the data steaming through my surveillance software. The laptops were connected to a router, which in turn was connected to my iPhone. A

139

handpicked team of Charlie's most-tech-savvy men sat at the laptops. Each wore a headset. I sat behind them, reading a text from Mr. Elliot: *Russian delivery in transit. Coordinates and specifics encrypted.*

I opened the encrypted e-mail, read the specifics, and transferred the co-ordinates into my map app. A pinpoint of red light settled over the border of Iran and Azerbaijan, on the shores of the Caspian Sea.

I left the screen illuminated, palmed the phone, and turned back to watch the op unfold.

If you looked up *counterintelligence* in the Agency's manual, the description was remarkably simple. Well, *concise* might be a better word. Counter-intelligence fell under the heading of actions taken by an intelligence apparatus intended to protect its own security while at the same time undermining any hostile intelligence operations. It wasn't just an agency or an arm of an agency that ran counterintel. I had become a master of it over my twenty-seven-year-career running outside paramilitary operations. So, while I was running intel ops targeting everything from narcotics trafficking and domestic terrorism to arms smuggling and cyber terrorism, I was also running counterintelligence on the DEA, the ATF, and Justice.

You have to remember, these guys had no idea who I was. In their eyes, I was one of the bad guys. I couldn't have them stumbling onto one of my ops and thinking they were in for a big-time score. The answer was to stay one step ahead of them, and the best way to do that was counterintelligence. Better safe than sorry. It didn't always work. Mr. Elliot had bailed me out of some very tight situations over the years, including several very nasty jail cells. One day I'd be behind bars, and the next day I'd be back on the street, doing my job. The boys from the DEA or ATF never knew what hit them.

So here I was again. Familiar territory. Protecting my mission with full-scale counterintelligence and the help of one of Tehran's most notorious crime bosses. I didn't care about Charlie's day job. I needed an ally. Somebody wanted me dead. If the rat was the DDO, then I was relying on Mr. Elliot's investigation back home to ferret the perp out. If the rat was inside the MEK, then Charlie and I needed to crack open their organization and find him fast. We started with Charlie's roster of known MEK operatives.

Charlie explained how he happened to possess such a list. "There's a lot of overlap between my import businesses and the interests of the MEK. Like most underground organizations, they finance themselves helping guys like me smuggle contraband." He winged a thumb toward the boxes. "The truth is, they need me a lot worse than I need them, so I take full advantage."

With as much sarcasm as I could muster and a crooked smile, I said, "You, Charlie? Damn, man, I would have never guessed." Then my expression changed. I held the iPhone up so that Charlie could read the coordinates from Mr. Elliot's text. "Know where this is?"

Charlie did little more than glance at the screen. "Anyone in my line of work knows where those coordinates are, my friend. Why?"

"Because I need you to make a pickup for me."

He stared. His eyes seemed to cloud over. "I have a feeling you're not smuggling Russian vodka into the country."

"It's a package from Saint Petersburg. A crate probably three feet square with the markings of an owl and a hawk. Nothing else."

"Arrives how and when?"

"By truck. Three hours from now." I gave him the rest of the specifics. Then I said, "I don't want to sugarcoat this, Charlie. This is serious business. All the marbles."

"That it's serious business is clear, my friend." Charlie lit a cigar. "I'll have someone there when the package arrives."

He blew smoke toward the ceiling and returned his attention to the work-station. Two dozen of his men had spent the last twelve hours planting GPS transmitters on MEK cars throughout Tehran. It was a start at least. Now, two of our computers were busy tracking the telltale blips crawling across the street maps of the city.

Next, we hacked in to Tehran's central phone exchange, using a contact Charlie had on the inside, and tapped in to as many MEK landlines and cell phones as we could locate. Snooping those phone numbers led to more phone numbers, and within twenty-four hours we had constructed a good schematic of the MEK organization.

I was pumped. On my own, this kind of op would have taken a month. Naturally, the song that came to mind as I was watching the monitors light up was the Talking Heads' "Life During Wartime." "Heard of a van that is loaded with weapons/Packed up and ready to go/Heard of some grave sites, out by the highway/A place where nobody knows." Very appropriate.

We had an avalanche of data pouring over the wires and from the cellular towers. Problem was, we couldn't listen to everything, even if we'd had twice the manpower. Never fear. My mission was top priority. Top priority meant that a thirty-second phone call to a certain three-star general in the Pentagon got us tapped in to the NSA's supercomputers. There were no machines on the planet better suited to listen to the cacophony of voices we had created and to sift through it all for telltale phrases, keywords, and names. When the NSA's computers shouted "bingo," metaphorically speaking of course, an alert would ping on Charlie's laptops and his men would put it on speaker.

Charlie looked over my shoulder. I had my iPhone in hand and was tweaking the connection between our laptops and the NSA. He appeared mesmerized by the capabilities of my iPhone. "Where can I get one of those?"

"When I get home, I'll FedEx you a spare."

"With all the bells and whistles, right?"

"Hell, I'll even hand deliver it, Charlie."

"Why do I detect a note of insincerity in your voice, my friend?"

Charlie had plenty of police on his payroll. But Charlie's connections were paid to turn a blind eye on smuggling things like booze and pot and caviar. They weren't paid to protect him from the kind of security breaches we were perpetrating at the moment. We figured to have another couple of hours before we attracted the wrong kind of attention, namely from the Vezarat-e Ettela'at Jomhuri-e Eslami, a mouthful of a name for the Iranian Ministry of Intelligence and National Security. Very nasty folks who had a license to drive people straight to Evin Prison, no passing Go, no get-out-of-jail-free card, no nothing.

As discreet as we tried to be, we were beaming gigabytes of data into space, an electromagnetic smoke signal begging for attention. Honestly, I was surprised that their security apparatus hadn't found us already.

Charlie had guards watching from windows in all directions. More stood vigil upstairs. He had men manning a perimeter several square blocks wide. He had a woman on his payroll called Janatta who worked in National Security's communications center and made more in a month just to keep Charlie informed than most Iranians made in a year.

I sipped absently at tea that had long ago gone cold. The remnants of a sack lunch lay crumpled on the floor next to my chair. It was one o'clock in the afternoon and we'd been hard at it since before daybreak. So far, we'd intercepted hundreds of calls and texts worthy of a second listen. We'd flagged three transmissions that were routed through Iranian government agencies, but in the end they hadn't amounted to much. We traced four calls between deep-cover MEK agents and police stations in and around the city, but these were clearly guys who were working the system and trying to build viable connections. There was an upside to these false alarms: we were identifying sources, and I would be tapping those sources in the coming days.

We were hunting a traitor. MEK, DDO, or otherwise. It was like searching for a needle in an electronic haystack, but all we needed was one good hit.

"Got something!" The young man sitting at the computer three seats down from me had scars running down the right side of his face, immensely dark eyes, and a black head scarf. He hadn't said a word all day. Now his hand shot into the air.

"What do we got?" The words had no sooner left my mouth than Charlie's private cell phone chirped. Everyone who was looking at the kid with the black head scarf and his hand in the air turned to watch Charlie.

"It's Janatta," Charlie snapped. As he listened, the corners of his eyes pinched, and his jaw tensed. He snapped the phone closed and jumped to his feet. His voice was calm, but filled with urgency. "Okay, people. We gotta move. There's a van headed our way, and it's not a tour bus filled with seniors."

Too bad. The clones from National Security were on their way, and whatever the kid in the head scarf had spotted was put on hold. The room became a beehive of activity of a completely different kind. I disconnected my iPhone. Men and women snatched headsets off their heads. They unplugged laptops and shoved them into briefcase carriers. Others collected the routers, cables, and shop lights. One jerked on the cable hooked to the satellite dish. The cable tore free and tumbled into the room. The man coiled it around his arm and stowed it in a canvas bag. Everyone folded tables and chairs and pushed them into one jumbled pile. The boxes and crates that had been pushed aside earlier were nudged back into place.

Less than a minute passed, and by the end of it Charlie's crew had calmly and efficiently erased all signs of anything resembling a counterintel op. Impressive.

"Get moving," Charlie said to me. "We're right behind you."

I went through the numbers: iPhone. Passports. Money. Backpack. Walther.

"See you at the next rendezvous," I said to him. We'd mapped out three contact points going forward, all buildings that Charlie owned, but none that could be traced to him directly. "Be careful."

"My middle name," Charlie said.

"Bad guys in two minutes," one of his guards called. He held a door at the rear of the building open for me. "All clear."

I halted in the shadow of the threshold and studied the alley. Nothing but trash and weeds. Trash and weeds I could deal with; going toe-to-toe with a van filled with National Security agents may have been tempting, but I figured I might as well save the bullets.

I ducked into the alley, went a block south at a run, then turned left for the rail yard. I spotted a freight train traveling north toward the city. *Perfect.*

I had to dash across an open lot and into the yard. I cut between an oil car and a flatbed, made a rather clumsy move in front of the slow-rolling engine, and caught up to the freighter. It was just beginning to pick up speed. I'd always had a fascination with trains, but I hadn't done the hobo thing since college, when Jimmy Benson and I spent a week riding the rails from New York to L.A.

We'd picked up an old Chevy his grandfather was giving him and took another week to drive back. Two of the best weeks of my life.

I imagined Jimmy would be proud to see me sprint alongside a line of boxcars, preparing my leap toward transportation nirvana. The air trembled and the ground shook from the violence of steel wheels grinding against steel rails, and I realized I was grinning. I matched my steps to the gnashing of the wheels, set my sites on a ladder fixed to the side of an empty boxcar, and jumped.

I swung onto the floor of the boxcar and congratulated myself on a nifty bit of improvisation.

One of the keys to success in any black op is flexibility. I was a manic planner, but a plan was merely a common point from which to deviate. Things can go wrong. You plan for that. Enough had already gone wrong over the last seven days, but the endgame of the plan remained the same. It was the details that had evolved.

That's why Charlie and I had identified rendezvous points throughout the city. The security apparatus in Iran was as thorough as it was brutal, but speed was not its forte. When the opposition has strength and size, stay nimble and fluid. No, that wasn't exactly the way Sun Tzu had drawn it up in *The Art of War,* but it was close enough.

I jumped off the train when it passed under the Azadegan Highway overpass and jogged three blocks to the east along Chitgar Avenue. I settled into a more casual walk when I turned onto Hesar Street. I paused out front of a ubiquitous downtown neighborhood market, smelled baking bread and roasted chicken on the air, and realized how long it had been since I'd eaten. I bought coffee from an open-air bakery and found a bench under a flowering ash tree.

I sent a text of my location to Charlie, thought about a quick update to General Rutledge, and decided against it. What was I going to say? *The dogs are on my trail*? Like that was some kind of news.

A half hour later, a bread truck pulled up to the curb directly in front of my bench, and one of Charlie's men glanced out the open door at me. He said something in Farsi, which I took to mean, *climb aboard,* and that's what I did. If the bread truck was meant as a diversion, it couldn't have been more realistic. The scent of freshly baked bread wafted through the cab and nearly made me delirious with hunger. I motioned toward the racks in back, and my driver shrugged as if to say, *Help yourself.*

I speared two dinner rolls from a plastic bag. They were soft and warm, and I wolfed them down like a man contemplating his last meal. I had two more. These I savored.

We drove deeper into the heart of the city. The streets churned with people. We arrived at the old Mansoor Hotel and parked down the street. The hotel, a broken-down three-story affair on the corner of Laheh and Shrine, was rendezvous number two and our base of operations for the next few hours anyway. I recognized a couple of Charlie's men loitering by the entrance; I wasn't keen on how obvious they looked.

Two black Mercedes sedans cruised by and parked in front of the bread truck. Charlie and his bodyguards. Again, way too obvious. I'd have to tell Charlie to dump the Mercedes and find a couple of beat-up Hondas. A moment later, a grizzly bear of a man emerged from the second Mercedes.

He walked up to the passenger side of the bread truck and gave me a tiny nod. I took the nod to mean, *Charlie wants to see you.* I climbed out of the bread truck and walked to the Mercedes. Charlie sat in the back, a laptop resting on his thighs. I slid in beside him.

"How did the raid go?" I asked.

Charlie tapped on the keyboard. He shrugged. "I was gone by the time they broke in. I'm sure they picked through the merchandise. They always do. Grab a couple of bottles of Canadian whiskey or bag some of the latest electronics. But if that's the extent of the damage, call us lucky."

"I wouldn't count too much on Lady Luck, my friend," I said. "She might take the day off."

Charlie turned the laptop in my direction. "Give this a look."

The screen displayed a fuzzy overhead shot of square buildings squashed together like tenements in Brooklyn. It was an infrared image that was mostly green and black with splotches of yellow, orange, and red that would have made a French Impressionist proud. At the heart of the photo, a yellow-and-orange blossom obscured the largest of the buildings. Charlie tapped the blossom with his index finger.

He explained, "It's the building you were talking about outside Qom. A school. One of my contacts in Iranian Air Force counterintelligence just provided it. He'll be hanging from a crane in Vali-e Asr Square if anyone gets wind of it. He didn't say what it was. Maybe he doesn't know. But he thought it was important enough to risk his life."

I studied the image and traced the outline of the bloom with a pen. "When was this taken?"

"Who knows? Not that long, I don't think. Two months max." Charlie shrugged. He pointed to the image. "What're you looking at, Jake? Any idea."

"This isn't the heat signature of any school." I hunted through my iPhone and sent an image via e-mail to Charlie's computer. When it arrived, he clicked it open and displayed a nearly identical image.

"Looks the same."

"There's a damn good reason it looks the same. What you're looking at there is a North Korean enriched-uranium-processing plant taken six months ago."

"Which means?"

"Which means there's more going on inside that school than a bunch of kids sharpening pencils." This was similar to the information that Chief of Staff Landon Fry had provided me four days back. Now I'd heard it from two different sources.

Charlie clicked back to the first picture. "Here's what my guy told me. He told me that Mahmoud Ahmadinejad knows there are American recon satellites photographing every square inch of our ill-fated country. No big secret there. And he's ordered the air force to take measures to camouflage the heat plume."

Problem was, this IR signature wasn't conclusive enough to order an attack. Not even close. You don't destroy a school filled with kids sharpening pencils based on something that could have been altered by a hacker with a couple of months' worth of Photoshop experience under his belt. I had to verify the source, up close and personal. To do that, I had to get to Qom and get inside the facility, assuming there was a facility.

Now things got tricky. Under ideal circumstances, I wouldn't even think about undertaking such a thing until I had the MEK traitor out of the way. Until that happened, he or she could very well checkmate every move I made. Under ideal circumstances, that meant working the counterintel until something popped. Too bad these weren't ideal circumstances.

"We're going to have to work this thing from two ends, you realize that, don't you, Charlie?" I said.

He shrugged. "We just hope the counterintel bears fruit before you get a bullet in the head."

I grasped the door handle. "Let's get to work."

Charlie palmed his cell phone and sent a text. Three of his men sprang out of the first Mercedes, laptop bags slung over their shoulders. I hustled out to join them. The raid earlier had cost us hours of precious surveillance time.

The men by the hotel entrance kept in the shadows. They both carried Scorpion submachine guns tucked against their sides. One of them shoulder checked the door and entered. His comrade followed. I was next in line.

I hadn't taken two steps when the world exploded in a ball of yellow light. A fiery blast knocked me backward six feet. Dust and debris pelted my body. I lay on the ground, stunned, choking, my ears ringing.

Someone grasped me under the arms and dragged me from the hotel. Smoke roiled from the shattered threshold in black waves. One of Charlie's men staggered out, blood streaming from his ears and gruesome wounds pocking his face, and collapsed. His partner didn't come out.

"Fucking booby trap," Charlie shouted.

Someone knew we were coming all right. And that someone had left his calling card.

CHAPTER 16

Three of Charlie's men carried me to one of his Mercedes. A searing pain stung the back of my eyes, like a flash of blue fire, but it was nothing compared to the throbbing in my ears. You don't realize how sensitive the auditory cells of the ears are until you walk into the shock waves of a bomb blast like the one that had just hit us. My world was more or less a blur, but my mind was already calculating. By the sound and the impact of the blast, I was figuring dynamite or plastique. Probably a half-pound satchel bag in any case. Anything more would have brought the roof down on top of us. I was thinking an M2A1 timer, but there were a dozen methods of igniting a satchel charge that were just as simple. Anyone with junior-grade demolitions skill or a copy of *The Anarchist Cookbook* could put together a satchel charge in about fifteen minutes flat if they had the right shit. No sweat.

The bitter taste in my mouth made me think of sodium nitrate, which made me think of dynamite. Throw in a little nitroglycerine and you're all set. Touchy stuff. Very touchy stuff. The problem with nitro was the very real possibility of blowing yourself up. I'd seen it before. Obviously, the bomber who'd lured us into his trap had some experience. I would still have put my money on plastique.

Charlie's guys laid me across the backseat. I rubbed my eyes and blinked

149

until my vision cleared. There wasn't anything I could do about the pain except put it out of my mind, so that's what I did.

Charlie leaned over me. I heard him say something so insanely out of place that I couldn't decide whether to cringe or shake his hand. "It just got personal."

His voice echoed with the kind of distance and composure that reminded me just how much violence had been a part of Charlie's life over the years.

I felt like I'd been pummeled from head to toe with a sledgehammer, but I managed to say, "What about your guys?"

"One down, and hurt bad. My nephew Azran," Charlie hissed. "One dead. Lukas. He's been with me forever."

Four of Charlie's bodyguards hustled toward us. They gripped the corners of a blanket with a badly wounded man stretched across the middle. This had to be Azran. He couldn't have been more than twenty-five and reminded me of Charlie in another lifetime.

They lowered him to the ground next to the car, and I heard a painful groan. It was the kind of groan you heard when the life was draining out of a man, and I knew he needed serious attention, and needed it right now.

Two more guards approached with a second blanket, this one dripping with blood. Had to be what was left of the guy who had entered the hotel on the point and taken the brunt of the blast. It was an ugly sight, and I felt a sour mixture of remorse and anger stirring inside me. The anger was winning out. The guy was dead because of me. He was dead because Charlie was repaying a debt, and his men were on the line for it. What did they know about the bond that Charlie and I had formed thirty years ago? What did they care? Nothing.

"Charlie, you have to get him to a hospital, and fast, brother," I said, nodding at the wounded man. He was clutching the blanket like a man dangling from a tightrope and blood foamed on his lips. I knew the signs, and it wasn't good. "The explosion tore up his lungs. I've seen it before."

I didn't really mean a hospital. I knew a hospital was out of the question. Even a hospital in the most democratic nation on earth would raise serious questions when they saw an injury like this. Here in Tehran, with national security a phobia infecting every fabric of society, the alarm would be deafening. But a man like Charlie had to have someone on the payroll, a doctor at a walk-in clinic or rehab center. Violence was an inherent factor in his business. You had to have contingencies.

Azran coughed. Blood flowed from his mouth and ran to his neck. His eyes clenched, and a painful wheeze replaced the coughing. Charlie braced himself against the Mercedes, like he had lost the strength to stand up on his own. Protecting these men was his responsibility. For a split second, he looked old and lost, but the moment passed. He gritted his teeth, and the color returned to his cheeks. His eyes burned like gimlets. He powered up his cell phone and began to dial frantically.

"I know a place," he snapped. He ordered Azran loaded into the backseat of one of the Mercedes. "You're going, too."

"No way," I said definitively. "We can't risk that. I'm fine."

I wasn't fine. I felt a wave of nausea rolling over me. A cold sweat had broken out on my forehead and was dripping into my eyes. Earlier, I had dismissed Lady Luck as a crutch for the lazy and the wicked, but the truth was that she had been faithful to me over the last week and never more than two minutes ago. A couple more steps, and it would have been me lying under a blanket next to Lukas, making a widow of my wife and leaving three kids fatherless. Or it could just as easily have been me squirming on the ground, throat scorched, lungs shredded like popped balloons.

"Have a couple of your boys take me to the safe house," I managed to say. "And make sure the safe house has a decent liquor cabinet and a hot shower."

"You look like shit, my friend." There wasn't an ounce of sympathy in his voice. The anguish and the anger had drained from his face. All that remained was a stoic mask. For a split second, our gazes met, but I didn't see even a hint of resentment in his eyes. I wouldn't have blamed him had there been.

Charlie shouted orders to three of his men as the wail of sirens harkened in the distance. Then he climbed into the Mercedes next to his nephew, and the car leaped away from the curb. We were only a matter of seconds behind him. But when Charlie's ride reached the intersection, they turned south. The

Mercedes carrying me went straight for two more blocks before swinging into a neighborhood filled with brick cottages. You couldn't call the pain in my head a headache; it was more like an internal train wreck. I didn't know whether to be sick or to put a bullet in my head. Instead, I curled up on the black leather of the backseat. I faded in and out as we rolled through the city.

I sensed the Mercedes slowing. I opened my eyes as it turned and plunged into a garage beneath a three-story building. Might have been an apartment house. Maybe a small hotel. The door scrolled closed, entombing us in darkness before a weak fluorescent light flickered from the ceiling. The guards hustled out. One opened my door and helped me up a short flight of stairs, across a carpeted foyer, and up a second flight of stairs, which seemed to go on forever. My knees felt weak. My eyes blurred.

I sensed a door being opened, but that was the last I remembered.

I came to on a surprisingly comfortable bed. I don't know what I'd been expecting; maybe a broken-down couch in a flophouse. I was light-headed, but I could feel the crisp white sheets and smell the fabric softener. Odd, what hits you first. What hit me second was that the nausea was gone. Okay, good start.

The room was dark, but the air, like the sheets, was remarkably clean. Something pressed across my face. I jerked my hand toward it. Then relaxed. There was a plastic tube lying across my upper lip. My fingers traced the shape of a cannula clipped under my nostrils. I followed the tubing to a green oxygen bottle on the nightstand. Night's purple glow outlined the dark curtains over the windows. And then the question: how long had I been here? I calculated. The bombing has occurred in midafternoon, around 1:30 P.M. I couldn't see a clock, but it had to be late evening, given the light.

In a span of two seconds, I self-diagnosed. Heart rate: fifty-eight. Decent. Lungs: not great; in fact, they hurt like hell. Obviously, the bomb blast had caused some damage. Flex index: 82 percent. Better than expected. Headache: throbbing, but better.

I groped the bedsheets and found my pistol tucked under the covers by my right side. I felt the pockets of my trousers. Thankfully, my iPhone was still there. Then a moment of panic: my coat, my passports, my money, and my back-pack. Where were they?

I tried to sit up. A nightlight along the baseboard silhouetted a man slouch-ing in a chair beside me. Charlie Amadi.

"It's all right here," Charlie said. He had read my reaction and hit it dead on. "The whole works. And I have to say, you've got a few toys in your pack that could make me a serious fortune."

"I thought you'd already made a serious fortune," I managed to say.

"Well, true. But a man can always find room for another serious fortune," he admitted. "How you doing?"

"Better. And yourself?"

Charlie kept quiet for a moment, as if an avalanche of emotion lay a little too close to the surface. Charlie was not the kind of man who benefited from a show of emotion. Or at least that was the prevailing thinking. Finally, he said, "Azran will make it. Just barely. Lukas had a wife and four kids. How fucked is that?"

"You'll take care of them." The words just came out, just one of those statements that really had no place in the room at that moment.

Charlie could have said, *How obvious is that, you stupid son of a bitch.* I would have understood. He didn't. Instead, he said, "I'll miss him," and bit down on the words.

"Yeah." Obviously my empathetic skills were not as highly tuned as they might have been. I changed the subject. "What time is it?"

Charlie raised his left arm. The gold band of his Rolex glittered on his wrist. "Eleven twenty-six." He lowered his arm. "I had a doctor check you out. You suffered a concussion. Maybe some lung damage."

"Tell the doc thanks." I took a long whiff of the oxygen. It was soothing and cool. I sat up, stripped off the oxygen tube, and detached the pulse monitor. I swung my legs off the bed. Back to business. "Listen, I know you lost a good man today. And I know you nearly lost your nephew. I feel responsible. Hell, I am responsible. But the only way we can make it even a little bit right is by finding out who planted that bomb, Charlie? Someone knew we were headed there. They had time to plan. Hate to even think it, my good friend, but it had to be an inside job."

"Thought of that already."

"Who picked the hotel?"

"I picked the hotel, Jake. Who the hell you think picked the hotel?" Charlie snapped. He squeezed off a quick breath, looking for a semblance of control. "I want the rat who planted the bomb as bad as you. Worse."

"Problem is," I replied, my voice measured and low, "we can't run out the clock playing cat and mouse with this guy. We don't have time."

"I'm not arguing," Charlie said. "What's the plan?"

"The plan is that I go forward with the mission. Get to Qom and uncover whatever the hell is going on there. Have your guys made the pickup at the border?"

"All secured. We choppered it back," Charlie said. "Now what?"

"We keep the counterop up and running while I'm making a target of myself. If our guy wants to stop me, the maggot will have to crawl out from under his rock. He does that, well . . ."

"You squash the shit out of him. Unless I get to him first."

"On the same page with that," I said.

"Good." Charlie's shoulders might have been sagging, and the weariness on his face was visible even in the dim gloom of the room, but he wasn't defeated. He might have taken a hit today, but someone was going to pay. If I didn't see to it, he would. Charlie stood up and made for the door. He paused, with his hand on the knob. "Put the oxygen back on, Jake. Get some rest. I got men all around this place. We start first light."

"First light," I said.

After he left, I shook out four Tylenol from a small jar on the nightstand and washed them down with water from a plastic pitcher. I replaced the cannula in my nose, laid my head back on the pillow, and savored the cool stream of pure oxygen. I still had a throbbing headache, but I was too exhausted to worry about it. I closed my eyes.

Two hours later, I woke up again when I felt my iPhone vibrating in my pocket. I dug it out and checked the time: 0218 local. There was a message alert from General Tom Rutledge: *Call ASAP.*

I sat up, removed the cannula, and shut off the oxygen. I poured myself a glass of ice water from a carafe on the nightstand. I took the glass, got out of bed, and padded across the darkened room to the window. I peeked through the curtain. My room was on the second floor. The building sat on a hill over-looking a sprawling carpet of city lights. I had no idea where I was, but I calculated a ten- or twelve-minute drive from the scene of the hotel explosion. Meaningless at the moment. I studied the street. Seven cars. No people.

I stood there for three minutes, sipping the water and trying to ease the tension in my shoulders and back.

My thoughts drifted. For ten seconds I was back home with Cathy. We were in the backyard. I could almost smell the barbecue. I blinked and saw Leila's face. Blinked again and steered my thoughts back to the most important thing in my world at the moment: the mission. *Stay focused on the mission or you'll never barbecue another steak as long as you live, Jake.*

I clicked on the iPhone to call Rutledge. The time in Washington, D.C. was 1724 hours. Knowing Rutledge, he was probably having the same fantasy as I was about a steak on the grill, while another fifteen-hour-day kept him locked away in a sterile office inside the Pentagon.

I speed dialed his number. He answered on the second ring.

"Damn, man," Tom said. "Your communication skills could give a man an ulcer if he gave it half a chance. I was getting worried."

"You had every right to be." I told him about the hotel bomb and kept it very short.

"Where are you now?" His voice had that even, almost indifferent tone that came with a full résumé in dealing with catastrophes.

I massaged an ache in my neck. I wasn't giving out that kind of information to anyone. Trace the call if you like, but don't expect any favors, even from a friend. "Out of harms' way."

"I need you at a hundred percent, and you don't sound like a hundred percent to me," he said in the same annoyingly unsympathetic voice.

Truthfully, I didn't care much for the comment, but I was also too numb to put up much of a fight. "Personally, I like being all beat to shit."

"Okay. Okay. I guess I deserve that." I could almost see Tom shaking his head. "You're the one dodging bullets, and I'm the one feeling the heat."

"Heat from where?"

"Our friend in Virginia thinks you're freezing him out," the general admitted.

"Hell yes I'm freezing him out," I said directly. "If you have a better handle on the trust level at this point, let me know."

"I don't imagine you're trusting anyone right about now."

I ignored this. "What do you have for me?"

General Rutledge grunted. Well, at least he didn't say, *Same old Jake.* I was getting pretty tired of that one. Instead, he said, "First of all, we've been tailing Sami Karimi, Kouros Moradi, and Ora Drago. That much you know. What you don't know is that all three of them disappeared twenty-four hours ago."

"Disappeared?" Karimi had been my MEK contact in Paris, Moradi and Drago in Amsterdam. "What the hell?"

"We found them again," Rutledge said, as if he hadn't even heard my comment. "Or the NSA did. They got a sniff from all the telephone traffic you've been forwarding. And guess what? All three are in Tehran."

"When did they get here?"

"Yesterday," Tom said. "So the question is, why now? And why all three of them? Me? I'm not big on the coincidence angle."

"It's no coincidence," I said. "They know why I'm here. They know that my op will do a helluva lot more than embarrass Mahmoud Ahmadinejad if it succeeds. Best case, I get enough intel to put the hooks into his government. That happens, and the MEK better be here to grab the reins."

"So they're consolidating resources," Tom said. "I'll bet they've got guys slipping back into the country from all over Europe."

"Count on it," I replied. "You can also count on the fact that there's not one in a hundred of them who isn't a cutthroat. Tried and true. And it would be a pretty safe bet that one of them is a traitor. That bomb was no coincidence."

156

"You're a master of the understatement," the general replied. Then he cleared his throat. "Listen, I know you've been running on all cylinders for the last week, but you should know, audio traffic between the Iranian High Command in Tehran and the Parchin military complex has slowed to a trickle."

Parchin. Iran's primary weapons-development facility. Damn. Not good news. "Means they're up to something."

"Means the clock's ticking." The general sounded like a man about to slug out the last laps of a marathon. "Give me an update tomorrow."

"Roger that."

The connection ended.

My communication with Mr. Elliot was less overt: *Headed for 1-bravo in short order. Package in hand.*

"One-bravo" referred to Qom. "Short order" meant within hours. "Package in hand" told him the Russian shipment had been received. I pressed the Send button. I took more Tylenol, drank another glass of water, and lay back on the bed again, waiting.

I made a bet with myself. Sixty seconds max before I received a reply. Let's see if the old man was on his game. I was ashamed of myself when my phone vibrated thirty-four seconds later. On his game? Yeah, I guess he is. The reply read: *Codes times three encrypted.*

I opened the encrypted e-mail. The first set of codes opened the packages. The second set of codes armed them. The third activated the self-destruct mechanism. Normally, I would have memorized the codes in a single reading and deleted the message. But a concussion can play tricks on the memory, so I saved the e-mail and put my head back against the pillow.

I didn't intend to sleep. My intent was to rest my eyes for a few minutes and then review all the documentation I had on the Iranian city of Qom. A few minutes turned into a few hours, because the next thing I knew it was 0440 and someone was knocking lightly on my door. I didn't panic. Didn't move a muscle. Well, except for my fingers wrapping around the Walther's pebbled grip.

A young Persian woman tiptoed into the room. She was carrying a tray. I

157

heard her whispering, "Sir. Sorry to wake you. Mr. Amadi's orders. I have breakfast."

I smelled coffee and scrambled eggs. Okay, maybe I could ease up on the Walther. Of course, I didn't. I looked at her through squinting eyes, actually nodded my head, and said, "You're an angel. Thanks."

Actually, she did look a bit like an angel, especially when she smiled, and I felt better, knowing my powers of fantasy were still intact. I watched her turn, her feet moving soundlessly across the floor, and was slightly disappointed when the door closed behind her.

Eat, Jake. Turn off the imagination and eat. That's what I did. I devoured everything on my plate and drank every drop of coffee. In fact, I was contemplating seconds when Charlie and two of his men entered the room.

He glanced at my empty plate, nodding. "You're better. Good. Let's get out of here. You've got ten minutes. Trim your beard, but not your mustache. It's just starting to come in. We brought you clothes. You need to start looking the part."

One of his men dropped a duffel bag on a chair, and Charlie pointed to the bathroom. "Ten minutes."

"Thanks for the grub," I said, swinging my legs off the bed and snaring the duffel bag. I stopped at the bathroom door. "I need more coffee, if you can manage it."

I found everything I needed in the duffel bag. I started with the shaving gear. My mustache and beard weren't particularly impressive after nine days, but they were enough to change my appearance slightly. I showered. Two minutes of scalding hot and a minute of icy cold. I felt almost human as I pulled on cotton drawstring pants and a loose-fitting pullover shirt.

I found my jacket hanging over the back of a chair out in the main room. I checked the pockets out of habit and hoped I wasn't insulting Charlie by doing so.

"Everything there?" he asked with a perfect dash of sarcasm.

Of course it was all there: money, passports, iPhone. I swung my backpack over my shoulder and said, "Road trip."

It was still dark when we went down the stairs—me on my own power this time—and out into the cool of the early morning. To the west, dawn's first light dashed the horizon with a tawny glimmer. I'd lost eight hours.

Charlie and I climbed into the back of a dust-covered Honda, and I was glad to see that Charlie had read my mind about the Mercedes. "Nice ride," I said with a crooked smile.

"Thought you'd approve," he replied, as his driver pulled away from the curb. "We have one stop to make."

"The MEK's on the move, Charlie," I said. I told him about my European contacts—Karimi, Moradi, and Drago—returning to Tehran over the last few days.

Charlie didn't look surprised. "Their boss knows you're up to something big, and he's lining up his chess pieces. Two to one you'll be hearing from him."

So, Yousef Bagheri, the head of the MEK, wanted a sit-down. This was actually good. I couldn't divorce myself completely from the MEK. At some point, I'd need Bagheri.

"He wants to talk, he does it on my terms."

"Couldn't agree more," Charlie said.

"Can you put the word out to him?"

Charlie nodded. "Done."

We drove toward the Amir Abad neighborhood, near the heart of Tehran, and parked at one end of a pedestrian mall in the business district. Charlie's guards were already in position. They loitered in a coffee shop, on a bench outside a clothing store, on the roofs. A dozen sets of eyes watching the area like crows around a cornfield.

Charlie led me to a shop that sold small electronics and appliances. A clerk ushered us behind a counter crowded with digital cameras and cell phones and into the stockroom.

Charlie's Internet team was there in full force. They had already set up their laptops and had hacked in to the telephone system. A satellite cable lay ready for my iPhone connection to NSA.

"How's it look, Amur?" Charlie asked a short, stubby man with round glasses, a rumpled gray suit, and a bow tie that would have made Charlie Chaplin proud.

"We've added some deflectors. It might give us an extra couple of hours before security gets wind of us again," he said. His English was educated and precise. "And we've got taps on the one hundred twenty or so MEK lines that caught our attention yesterday, some computers, some handheld devices. So we won't be blasting the airways like we were yesterday. That should make us a little less conspicuous."

"Good," I said. "We need to start separating friend from foe. Can you do that?"

"We already are," a voice at the far computer said. The voice belonged to the young man with the black head scarf. "I hit on an unfriendly yesterday just before security shut us down. I've been tracking him and his contacts ever since. The list of friendlies is longer."

"I guess we can take some solace in that," I said, without expecting anyone to appreciate my sarcasm.

"What do you think? Do we put the word out to the friendlies?" Charlie said to me.

"Damn right. We're looking for intel. Let's see what these guys know," I said. Then I looked at the men manning the computers. They were all watching me. "But it's got to be done quietly, gentlemen. Secure channels. Untraceable e-mails. The works."

I plugged the iPhone into the computer aligning the satellite cable and tapped in to my NSA source.

Once we had the connection, I downloaded the NSA's files that we already had in the pipeline, then uploaded what Charlie's men had gleaned overnight. My priority was getting counterintel on Karimi, Moradi, and Drago. One of them might be the traitor. I hated to think so, but you never knew. And if they weren't, fine. At least I could cross them off my shit list.

I went straight for the coffee. There was a huge pot sitting on a side table alongside a half-empty box of baklava and date-filled maamoul. I ate four more

Tylenol and washed it down with black coffee. My ears had finally stopped ringing. My headache had quieted to a near-tolerable throbbing.

I followed the proceedings, reading every piece of information and siphoning off what I deemed important. It was midmorning when Charlie pulled me aside. I followed him into the alley out back of the mall. He lit a black cigarette, offered me the pack, and wasn't offended when I refused.

I knew Charlie had news and said, "You talked with Bagheri, didn't you?"

"He wants you to meet someone," Charlie said without preamble. "You've heard of Professor James Fouraz."

My eyes nearly closed in concentration. I could feel my jaw jutting forward. "Fouraz? Guy died in prison, didn't he?"

James Fouraz was a nuclear physicist and former professor of quantum mechanics at Tehran University. Until a couple of years earlier, he had been one of the country's loudest critics of Ahmadinejad's nuclear program. Then he'd dropped out of sight. Dropping out of sight in Iran usually meant dead.

"Not quite," Charlie said. "They slapped him in jail for nearly a year."

"Evin?"

"Where else?" Evin Prison was the kind of place where women went for exposing their heads in public and men went for talking politics over coffee. It was world famous for torture at the highest level. "Apparently they released him after he signed some papers promising to behave himself, but he's been collecting information on their nuclear weapons program ever since."

My ears perked up like a dog's. "And Bagheri wants me to meet him. Huh!" Something this juicy drops in your lap, your first instinct is to give it the sniff test. I said, "Could be a setup," but I wasn't looking at Charlie when I said it.

He answered anyway. "You think?"

"How would you feel if you'd spent a year in Evin Prison with a broomstick up your ass? Would you come out of there swearing revenge, or would you come out of there praying for a way to get the government off your back? Make a trade? Me for him."

Charlie shrugged. "You know more about Fouraz than I do. What do you think?"

"I think the guy probably knows things about The Twelver's nuclear weapons program that even the mullahs don't know," I said without hesitation. "Set it up, Charlie. Just us and them."

Charlie nodded. He got out his cell phone and sent a text. I waited a few minutes, and when we didn't get a reply right away, I sent a coded message to Mr. Elliot. I asked him for a secure read on one Professor James Fouraz and tagged him with the code name The Wizard.

Mr. Elliot came back to me exactly seventeen minutes later and didn't mince words. His message read: *The Wizard checks out. Work him to the max.*

Oh, that's the plan, Mr. E. That's very definitely the plan.

I worked our surveillance until midafternoon. A little after two, Charlie tapped my arm. "Bagheri's in."

"When?"

"Forty-five minutes."

"Good. But we name the place, Charlie, not them."

"Already done." Charlie nodded. "Kheyrabad. It's a little village south of the city. My men are already on the way."

After I unplugged my iPhone from the satellite cable, I sent another message to Mr. Elliot: *Off to see The Wizard.*

The surveillance op at the back of the electronics store broke down in ten minutes flat. It was once again just an ordinary stockroom for a place selling digital cameras and dishwashers.

"The place is called Mad Khan's Coffee House. One of my less successful investments," Charlie said as we drove south on the Saidi Highway in a loose convoy of three vehicles, a mint-condition Chevy SUV leading, a less conspicuous Toyota hatchback in the rear, and our Honda keeping pace in the middle. Every vehicle carried at least two automatic weapons. Every man had a sidearm. Charlie didn't mess around.

As for me, my Walther remained tucked in my shoulder harness. Charlie carried a Beretta .380 holstered inside his jacket. The rolling armament might have saved us from an ambush like the one I'd survived in Amsterdam, but I knew damn well that we were dead meat if the ball breakers from Iran's Na-tional Security forces were waiting for us around the next corner. Worse yet if it was the black beards from the Revolutionary Guards.

The late-afternoon sun shrouded the hills of Tehran to our north. We entered a flat, desolate landscape that reminded me of the American South-west. We passed a wrecking yard filled with rusted cars and entered a forlorn neighborhood of squat, dust-colored buildings. I couldn't see Charlie's men any-where, and I was glad. No use making a show of things. And in all likelihood, Yousef Bagheri had his own eyes and ears in the neighborhood. He was, after all, the head of the MEK, and he had survived as an enemy of the state for nearly thirty years.

Our driver parked the Honda in a small lot next to the coffee shop, while the SUV and the Toyota went in opposite directions. Five other cars were parked in the lot, and I used three seconds to study them. Dim light spilled from the windows, and the marquee above the door read MAD KHAN'S COFFEE HOUSE.

Charlie's cell phone chimed, and he looked at the message appearing on the screen. "We're good," he said.

He and I went inside. The air was warm and smelled of strong coffee and scented tobacco.

To the right, five men sat around a hookah, sucking on the mouthpieces, blowing smoke, gossiping in low voices. Two were dressed in long robes. The other three wore Western clothes. When they weren't talking, they were tex-ting. What the hell had the world come to? Two couples, both middle-aged, and drinking from stubby, widemouthed coffee mugs, sat at tables near the window. On the left, a pair of men in dark sport coats sat opposite each other in a booth.

One faced the door. Round face. Dark complexion. Thick mustache. Heavy gold chain peeking from the open collar of a striped shirt. Eyes that took in everything. Fiftyish.

"Yousef Bagheri," Charlie whispered.

Bagheri saw us, gave a nod, and mumbled to his table companion. The other man turned toward us. He was older—in his earlier sixties if not more—grayer, and far more weather-beaten. Clean-shaven. Deep creases alongside his mouth and down the center of his brow. It wasn't hard to guess that this was Professor James Fouraz.

Charlie exchanged a brief nod with the MEK man as we approached. We stopped in front of the table, and introductions were made in low, cautious voices. Charlie used the name on my French passport, calling me Richard Moreau.

Persians are big on shaking hands, and I obliged both men. I kept it formal. "Professor Fouraz. Mr. Bagheri. Good to meet you both."

"Are you armed, Mr. Moreau?" Bagheri asked.

If a man asks, you tell him. "Walther." I gave him a peek under my jacket. I nodded to Charlie. "Beretta. We're not expecting to use them. Mind if we sit?"

"Of course," Bagheri said. I eased in next to him. I wanted a clear view of the door, just like he did. Bagheri was a hefty, muscular man and his power was as evident as his caution. I approved.

Charlie settled beside Fouraz, but the old man looked only at me, his eyes unblinking.

"You're American," Fouraz said in English.

"Does it matter who or what I am? I understand you have information that I need." I pulled an envelope from my pocket and laid it on the table. Ten grand in euros.

Fouraz pushed the envelope back with a trembling, clawlike hand. His fingers were gnarled, and his knuckles were misshapen. The fingernails were missing from his index and middle fingers.

"This is not about money." He lifted his hand and straightened his fingers as best he could. "I'm doing this to keep Mahmoud Ahmadinejad from doing to my country what he's done to me."

A convincing answer. I took the envelope and slid it back into my coat pocket. "No insult intended, Professor," I said to the man.

Fouraz dropped his hands to his lap. He lifted a square manila envelope that he struggled to open. He dumped a stack of photographs onto the table and pulled one free. It showed a convoy of cargo trucks. "That's a shipment of yellow cake uranium for the processing plant in Qom."

I said, "Looks like trucks to me."

Fouraz didn't bother to respond to that. He shared more photos. One was of a flatbed trailer with a cylindrical object as long as a telephone pole and as wide as a garbage can. "This is the upper stage of a Sejil-2 ballistic missile."

His comment plucked at my nerves. The Sejil-2 could reach Israel, all of the Middle East, and most of Europe. Fit it with a nuke and it's hello Armageddon.

"What's the yield of one of these Sejil-2 warheads?" I asked.

"Twenty kilotons. The Hiroshima bomb was sixteen kilotons," Fouraz answered somberly. "And sixty thousand people perished immediately. To comprehend the destruction, draw a circle with a radius of one and a half kilometers over any city and imagine that area flattened to ash and rubble."

I glanced across the table at Charlie; the color had been bleached from his face, and he was shaking his head like a dying man wishing he'd said *I love you* to his kids more often. "Where and when was this photo taken?" I asked the professor.

"On the highway to Natanz. Six days ago."

"Who took it?"

"Enemies of Mahmoud Ahmadinejad and his murderous plans," was how he answered.

Bagheri leaned toward me. "It's a race. You against Ahmadinejad. He wins, and the world loses."

CHAPTER 17

I used my iPhone to replicate the photos Professor James Fouraz had given me and stored them in a file marked "Recipes." I e-mailed the file in full to one of a half-dozen untraceable e-mail addresses that only Mr. Elliot had access to. The photos provided exactly the kind of pieces I needed to fill in the puzzle of Iran's secret nuclear weapons program: shipments of yellow cake uranium to Qom and the delivery of a long-range ballistic missile to Natanz. Huge. That's what intel was: first you unearth the puzzle pieces, then you put the pieces together so the naysayers don't have a leg to stand on when the bombs start to drop.

The clock ticking in my head just got a little faster. The photos were priceless, but they had to be substantiated. Time for boots on the ground in Qom and Natanz.

"Anything else?" I asked. Professor Fouraz had already written his death warrant. He wasn't going to hold anything back now. I could see it on his face.

"An audio link," he said. He held up a BlackBerry Curve, a generation old but still powerful. "Everything I know on one tape. If you could share an e-mail address, please."

Now it was time for a demonstration of good faith on my part. I gave him another of my untraceable e-mail addresses and then my assurance. "Only two people have access to it. Me and a man who'll know exactly what to do with it."

"It cannot be made public until the professor is safely out of the country," Yousef Bagheri said, pinning me with his dark eyes.

"You have my word."

"And mine," Charlie said. I was glad he chimed in. I could see that the MEK chief respected Charlie. They had probably done business a hundred times. When you're a renegade trying to fund an outlaw political organization, you naturally do business with a renegade who has the connections to do so.

Professor Fouraz collected his photos. "I should have more soon," he said. "People are coming out of the woodwork."

"Very good," I replied.

Yousef Bagheri placed his hands on the table. "If there is nothing else, then I'll ask you to keep me abreast of your plans, Mr. Moreau."

"I'd like nothing better. Only one small problem, Mr. Bagheri." Now it was my time to pin him with my eyes. He held them without blinking as I described the evidence suggesting a traitor in his operation. I gave him credit for that. I could also see his teeth grinding and the worry lines stretching out around his eyes.

"We're working it twenty-four/seven from our end." I tipped my head in Charlie's direction. "I want you working it twenty-four/seven on your end."

Bagheri grimaced. It was like someone had just sucker punched him. Eventually, he made a brisk gesture that might have been taken for a nod. "I won't sleep till he's found."

He reached out his hand to me. I shook it. Not that I was dying to shake the man's hand, but I had learned one thing in my years of running black ops: never alienate a potential ally, and never make an enemy unless it helps your cause.

I shook the professor's for the same reason. It wasn't about gratitude. I would use him until he had nothing left to give. And then I'd push to the edge and squeeze him one last time just to be sure he didn't have anything left to give.

I slid out of the booth, and Charlie followed. "Be in touch," he said to the MEK boss. He gave Fouraz a respectful nod. And then we were gone.

Charlie and I returned to Tehran and bunked in a new safe house in the Pamenar district, where the mix of old European architecture and corner markets gave you a feeling of prosperity that might or might not have been reality. Our rooms were on the second floor of an apartment house that looked like it had been transported from Paris. I half expected to see the Seine rolling slowly past when I pushed aside the curtain and glanced out. Instead, I saw an empty street that should have been alive with couples strolling hand-in-hand and street café's serving espressos and lattes.

One of Charlie's guys had left food and bottled water on the table. I cracked the water and drank half of it down. The food could wait.

I took out my iPhone. First, I sent Mr. Elliot a text: *Lazy day river, two-on-two*. "Lazy day river" was code for the Yahoo e-mail account that I'd shipped Professor Fouraz's pictures to. "Two-on-two" told him to look for a second e-mail with the audio link that Fouraz had forwarded. Then I sent the entire package on to General Tom Rutledge as well, with a note that read: *Visiting day tomorrow.*

The general would fast track the photos with the CIA's nuclear assessment team, and they would see exactly the same thing that I saw. Great stuff, but not enough to justify a military attack, no matter how smart the bombs or precise the strike. They would need two things: the exact status of the activities taking place in Qom and Natanz and specific attack coordinates that allowed for the most surgical strikes possible. Piece of cake.

I carried my food over to Charlie's room, and we ate in silence.

The one thing Charlie's guys had provided for him that they hadn't thought to give me was a bottle of brandy. He filled two glasses with two-finger measures, and we made a silent toast.

Charlie rolled the brandy around his glass and then held it under his nose. "Ah," he said, his first word in twenty minutes. Then he drank. I wasn't quite so sophisticated in my approach, but that did nothing to diminish my appreciation for the drink as the warmth of it spread in my stomach.

"So?" he said after another minute. "What's the plan?"

My first instinct was to keep everything close to my chest. The closer, the less messy, and things had gotten plenty messy over the last week or so. On the other hand, I still needed Charlie, and so far he'd been there at every turn. I'd asked him for his trust, and he'd delivered.

"Visiting day tomorrow." Same as my message to Rutledge.

"Qom," he said simply.

"No choice." I gave him a brief outline of my plans to infiltrate a facility that, by all evidence, was hidden beneath a high school housing a thousand students.

"A school. That's as fucked as it gets." He unwound from his chair and stood up. He padded across the room to a teapot resting on top of a hot plate. He poured two cups. He handed one to me and said, "Let's talk strategy."

"Qom is southwest some ninety miles. We set up shop outside the city."

"I've got a place," Charlie said.

"I go in a couple of hours after dark. Not so late as to pique anyone's interest, but not before things have settled down at the school." I glanced at Charlie. "You're my backup."

"Let's get a map in here." Charlie buzzed one of the guys in his crew and told him to bring in a computer. "With a plug-in," I heard him say.

In less than five minutes, we had a detailed map of Qom and the surrounding countryside up on the room's television screen. Charlie invited two of his team to join us. The first I had seen at the surveillance site this morning, the stubby guy with the bow tie. "You remember Amur." We nodded.

The other was a woman who couldn't have been more than twenty-five or twenty-six by my estimate. She was intense, sinewy, and tight-lipped. She wore canvas-colored cargo pants and an olive tank top. Captivating. She had *soldier* written all over her. "This is Jeri," was all Charlie said. "She's our eyes and ears from Qom. Runs my operation there."

We shook hands. Jeri settled in front of the map.

She pointed to a village on the outskirts of the city. "Seyfabad. We have a warehouse there with transportation and supplies. Your Russian delivery is already there."

"Excellent. Thanks."

"You have a French passport, yes?"

"I'm a tourist with a thirty-day visa." I opened my coat and extracted Richard Moreau's passport. I held it out.

She studied it like someone who had needed similar false credentials. "Good. Very good. There are a dozen French companies in Qom and who knows how many French scholars at the university. We also get a steady stream of French tourists."

"They're some of my best customers," Charlie said with a proud grin.

"Of course they are. Cheap bastards," I said, matching his grin.

Jeri handed back the passport. "ETD?"

I glanced back at the map illuminated on the television screen and said, "We'll leave in the morning, first light. I need some sleep. And we don't want to be on the road in the middle of the night. Too obvious."

"Agree," Charlie said.

We were on the road at 7:07 A.M. according to my watch. Jeri drove and seemed perturbed by our late departure. I took this as a good sign and apologized. She glanced at me in the rearview mirror and nodded.

She handed Charlie a manila envelope and said, "Photos of the school from twenty-two different angles. If there's a full-blown uranium enrichment facility somewhere in the area, they're doing a great job of concealing it."

Charlie sat in the front seat, smoking a black cigarette. Jeri kept the window cracked. We had traded the Honda for a Jeep Cherokee, and I was spread out in back with my backpack. Charlie's computer guy had forwarded a file containing the photos of the school, a blueprint of the interior, and a detailed street map of the area surrounding the school to my iPhone. I had added these to the aerial photos that the NSA had provided me.

"I thought you might want to see the originals," Jeri said of the photos.

Charlie broke open the envelope and handed me nearly fifty photos. Qom was ninety or so miles southwest of Tehran down Highway 7, a stretch of asphalt through flat and arid desert dotted with neat, two-story farmhouses amid groves of olives and pistachios. Seyfabad was eight miles closer.

"It's good you're going in as a researcher," Jeri said as I studied the photos. "Anyone with an interest in Shia studies is considered, well, I was going to say a friend, but that's a bit of an exaggeration."

"Less of an enemy?" I suggested.

Jeri shrugged. "Close enough."

We drove in silence after that. I placed the photos on the seat next to me and tried to match them up with the blueprint of the school's interior. We were halfway to Seyfabad when we spotted a convoy of panel trucks heading in the same direction. From a distance, the trucks looked damn similar to ones I had seen in Professor Fouraz's photos—trucks he suspected were carrying yellow cake uranium.

"Ease back," I said to Jeri. The trucks had an escort of unmarked Nissan SUVs, and it would not have surprised me at all if they were filled with men in National Security uniforms. "We know where they're going."

Jeri was not happy about slowing down, but she only had ten minutes to fume before reaching Seyfabad. It was a dumpy commercial hamlet that showed only mild signs of life at this time in the morning. Charlie's warehouse was one of ten or twelve served by a railroad. His stood out from the rest because there was a small helicopter moored on a concrete pad out back, a pen with guard dogs, and a man patrolling the roof.

Charlie Amadi ran a very tight criminal operation that moved everything from electronics to gourmet food, but he was also a serious businessman. One look at his warehouse and the store of legitimate and illegitimate wares inside—everything from athletic shoes to gas barbecues—told you that he could probably stay afloat for real even if the drugs, liquor, and arms went south. Which they never would, of course.

There were pallets stacked to the ceiling—I didn't ask what they contained—three forklifts, and a shipping office. That's where we huddled. That's where the crate from the Russian mafia had been stored. It looked pretty

171

innocuous from the outside. Jeri and I used crowbars to crack it open. Inside it were two very ordinary-looking metal suitcases banded with leather straps and brass buckles. The buckles may have looked ordinary, but without the appropriate codes, they couldn't be opened without rendering the device inside useless. Good thing Mr. Elliot had provided me with the codes.

"What do we got here, Jake?" Charlie's voice had a resigned and fatalistic edge to it. "You gonna tell us what we helped you smuggle into the country?"

"The Russians call them suitcase bombs. One-kiloton nukes, Charlie. Every intelligence agency's worst nightmare." Might as well spell it out.

"No way," Jeri said. She stepped up and ran a hand over the cases. "These things are just . . . just what? Propaganda, right? Legend?"

"Do these look like legends to you?" I said.

"And you're taking one of these inside Qom with you, aren't you?" Charlie said. Not even close to a question.

"It's just a backup, Charlie," I said. "Failure's not an option. If I don't get out, I take the place down with me."

"You're crazy," he whispered.

"No, not crazy. Brilliant," Jeri said. "I like it. Let's do this."

My kind of girl. I grabbed one of the suitcases by the handle. Hefted it. "Legend" had it that there were a hundred more of these in existence. Fifty-pound nightmares.

We spent the rest of the day finalizing my plan and talking about our communications pattern once I was on the move. Jeri equipped each of us with a prepaid phone straight from Charlie's inventory.

"Text messages only," I said. I thought about that for a moment and added, "Unless all hell breaks, of course."

At 7:00 P.M., Jeri and I packed the suitcase in the back of the Cherokee, and she drove me into town. She dropped me in the market district, which every tourist crazy enough to come to Qom was obliged to visit. Qom was the religious center of Shai Islam. The city was renowned for its architecture. The horizon in every direction was spiced with mosques and golden minarets, shrines and tombs, religious schools and government buildings. The city made little pretense of modernity the way Tehran did. It was the home of fifty thousand religious scholars from all over the world, including France. That was my cover: Richard Moreau, researcher extraordinaire, specializing in religious anthropology. I hoped I wouldn't have to lean on it too heavily.

I stopped in a market café to orient myself, set the suitcase on the floor next to me, and hooked my backpack over the back of my chair. I ordered a dish of rice with spiced chicken. I washed it down with a bottle of sparking water. Then I ordered coffee with cream, opened a day-old newspaper, and watched the sun begin to set.

Everyone knew there was a uranium enrichment facility in Qom. Three years earlier, French and English sources had picked up signs that someone was tunneling into the side of a mountain in the desert outside the holy city. And yes, there was a facility there. The debate was whether or not it was being used for peaceful purposes, as The Twelver wanted us to believe. But the size and configuration of this new find, disguised by the Vocational School of Engineering and Science, was completely inconsistent with a peaceful program. My job was to confirm the inconsistency.

I went into my iPhone and opened the photo files of the school and the processing facility, the one file from the NSA, and the one Jeri had provided me. I memorized the layout. The major heat plume recorded by satellite imagery pinpointed a source from inside—or under—the school's main building. A long, hot streak connected this building to an adjacent one, a student center according to the photos, and a very big student center at that. This was the building, according to Professor Fouraz, where the yellow cake uranium had been delivered. For all we really knew, the trucks were making a delivery of cheese pizzas to the school cafeteria. *Right, Jake.*

I was willing to bet my house that the long, hot streak revealed a tunnel connecting the two buildings.

The Agency forwarded what they had on the facility. The Iranian Ministry of Education promoted the place as a vocational school for young men and women. Though the school had been in operation for three years, there was no record of anyone who had yet graduated.

By this time, the market was attracting families out for the evening. Tots on bikes, men smoking, women in baggy abayas pushing strollers. It was a scene of urban tranquility, though I wondered about the scruples of a government that constructed a nuclear weapons plant practically under the feet of so many innocent people. Actually, there wasn't much to wonder about: evil was evil.

The crowd thinned out and night's darkness thickened.

At 9:15 P.M., I closed my paper, hailed a cab, and placed the suitcase on the backseat next to me. I gave the driver an address a quarter of a mile from the school, at the edge of a residential neighborhood. Simple logic: if you see a man carrying a suitcase, you assume he lives nearby and is on the way home from the bus stop. I hiked north in the direction of the school, my iPhone feeding me directions.

Considering the secrecy surrounding the uranium processing plant, the Iranians couldn't be obvious in providing security. If the place was meant to be a school, it had to look like a school. Couldn't be surrounded by a cordon of heavily armed guards. Security systems had to be discreet.

The school complex sat on the edge of the city, on the banks of the Qom River, the desert and low-lying hills forming a backdrop to the north. It was bordered on the south—my left—by a cramped neighborhood of typical lower-income homes. Flat roofs, tiny windows, and mud-stucco walls. A wide dirt road separated the neighborhood from a chain-link fence surrounding the school-yard, and I paused three hundred feet away. I set the suitcase down next to the trunk of an olive tree. I took my Zeiss digital telescope from my jacket pocket and connected it to my iPhone to survey the area.

The meager illumination came from light sneaking past the curtains of the houses and from the distant security lamps above a guardhouse along the front of the schoolyard.

On the other side of the fence stretched two soccer fields of scraggly grass. Two massive single-story buildings sat two hundred yards inside the fence. Both were constructed from cinder blocks and coated with reflective paint that gave them a reddish brown tint in the light of a new moon.

By my calculations, the school and all the acreage inside the fence—or what lay beneath it all—was probably large enough to conceal a facility whose sole intent was the enrichment of uranium, and not for the wholesome, peaceful purposes that Iran's government would have liked the world to believe.

I studied the fence. It was woven from top to bottom with innocuous-looking electrical wires that could only have one purpose: conduits for electric current. Probably not strong enough to harm either man or animal, but sensitive enough to set off alarms at police and security outposts both inside the facility and out.

From this vantage I could see an entrance adjacent to the nearest guardhouse. Parked just beyond the guardhouse and well inside the fence was a collection of excavators, trucks, and buses: not an assortment of vehicles you saw at every school in America, and probably not here in Iran, either. I spotted two other guardhouses, one on either side of the schoolyard.

The farthermost of these protected an entrance and road that curved away from the city in the direction of Highway 7. The road from this entrance seemed to fork at a point less than a quarter of a mile from the school. The left fork sloped into a tunnel, which disappeared under ground, away from the prying eyes of satellites hovering 150 miles out in space.

I was still staring at the images brought to life by my telescope when a low rumble shook the earth. I froze.

CHAPTER 18

QOM, IRAN—DAY 8

The rumble grew in volume and I felt the earth quiver under my shoes. From the east, a line of semi-tractors pulling flatbed trailers materialized along the dirt road separating me from the school grounds. Their huge tires tossed clouds of dust that shimmered in the darkness. Each trailer was laden with a massive amount of building supplies. I stepped deep into the shadows and counted pyramids of cement sacks, pallets of plywood, spools of cable, and stacks of concrete pipes. I counted seven trucks and trailers. Two hauled huge generators. One shouldered a mammoth earthmover.

The trucks rounded the corner and turned toward the first entrance. The lead truck stopped at the guardhouse.

A waiting guard checked the driver's paperwork. Another guard walked along the bed of the truck and waved it forward. The truck rolled toward the excavators. The parade of trucks moved up one truck, and the second truck stopped for inspection, this one heavy with plywood. This was obviously old hat for both the guards and the drivers. Their interplay had all the makings of a bunch of guys who saw one another on a regular basis and maybe even shared a beer after work. Hell, the beer probably came from Charlie's illegal stocks.

The guards weren't exactly cavalier about inspecting the wares, but they were certainly casual.

I stared at the last trailer in line. It was stacked high with concrete pipes twenty-five feet long and probably three feet in diameter. A long shadow fell across the back of the trailer as it inched forward and created a momentary blind spot between the driver and guards.

Sometimes an opportunity slaps you in the face, and either you recognize it for what it is or you pass it off as too good to be true. I opted for the former.

I shoved the digital telescope and iPhone into my jacket pocket, hoisted the suitcase, and started running. It wasn't the weight of the suitcase that hindered my progress as much as the awkward shape, but I still managed a decent pace and rambled up behind the trailer. I took the suitcase in both hands and hoisted it onto the bed. I grasped a handgrip protruding from the rear of the trailer and vaulted onboard. I grabbed the suitcase and ducked inside the center pipe in the middle stack. Eleven seconds. A lot of time. In the old days, it would have taken me nine.

I kicked the suitcase into a pocket of gloom halfway down the pipe and settled in beside it, as flat as a man could get in a concrete pipe. I readied my Walther, just in case. If a guard discovered me, the last thing he would see was the muzzle of my silencer. All well and good, except that the odds of surviving the ensuing gun battle would not be great.

The truck advanced. Jerked to a halt. Advanced and halted. Advanced and halted once again, this time directly alongside the guardhouse. Light from the overhead lamps fell in bright stripes between the pipes. I fingered the pistol's trigger and held my breath.

I heard the guards banter with the driver and suppressed the urge to shout, *Just keep talking, boys. Maybe we'll all live through the night*. A flashlight beam splashed along the pipes from the rear. I held my breath and prepared for a firefight, but then realized the guard would have to mount the trailer to see into my pipe. This guy didn't sound like the mountain-goat type.

Two very long seconds passed before he extinguished the beam and ordered the driver through. I let out a slow breath.

I heard the ugly sound of the driver grinding the gears and then the truck continued inside. I pictured the convoy of trucks crossing the open ground between the gate and the complex. Exactly fifteen seconds later, I heard the hiss of a hydraulic engine kicking in and the sound of a reinforced steel door rising. The truck inched forward. I could tell by the sudden hollowness of the sounds and a change in the light that we had passed through the door. We hit a downward incline and seemed to follow a tunnel a number of feet before we leveled off. The truck slowed, and I pictured the driver parking next to the other rigs. I expected him to shut down the truck's six-hundred-plus-horsepower engine, but he didn't. I heard his cab door open. Then I heard his feet hitting the ground as he jumped down. The next sound I heard was the grinding of metal and the *whoosh* of hydraulic release. And then it hit me: the drivers were helping one another unhitch their trailers. I couldn't understand a word they were saying, but I understood when they all climbed back into their cabs and drove off.

I was in. A silence followed the departure of the trucks that was slowly filled by the low hum of a generator. I listened for voices or footsteps, but heard neither. I traded my Walther for my iPhone, texted Charlie a brief *Inside,* and traded back. I crept on hands and knees to the end of the pipe and lay stomach-down again. Listen and learn, get the rhythm of the place.

The trucks had deposited their loads in a cavernous warehouselike facility that would probably be overrun by laborers come morning. I saw what looked like a boiler room off to one side of the warehouse, and it struck me as a good hiding place for the suitcase. My other option was to leave it right where it was. That's what I decided to do. If I was still inside the complex come morning, I was not leaving. And if I wasn't leaving, the plan was to take down the facility with me. A one-kiloton nuke would do that and a whole lot more. Talk about a worst-case scenario.

I used the code Mr. Elliot had sent me to access the suitcase: a series of six numbers that caused the buckles to pop open simultaneously. I was surprised at the size of the device. Nestled in the case was a cylinder that couldn't have measured much more than six inches by thirty inches. It lay diagonally inside the suitcase, surrounded by a circuit board and an arming switch. I ran a cable from my iPhone to the circuit board and used the keypad to enter the arming sequence, a twelve-character progression of letters, numbers, and symbols. The instant I punched in the twelfth character, a red light illuminated on the circuit board. The iPhone's screen simulated the red light alongside two triggers: Activate and Disarm. Activation took thirty seconds. Disarming was instantaneous.

I used the third code to ready the self-destruct mechanism.

I closed the lid of the suitcase, pocketed my iPhone, and crawled to the end of the concrete pipe. I studied the warehouse and spotted two swivel cameras positioned along the ceiling. Rudimentary. There was a stairwell against the near wall and no more than a thirty-yard sprint away. I timed my jump with the panning of the cameras and hit the floor running. I stopped inside the stairwell, threw myself against a wall made of damp concrete, and held my breath for five seconds, waiting for an alarm to sound. When nothing happened, I took the stairs two at a time to a pair of swinging doors.

I peeked through a head-high window into a hallway lined with lockers. School lockers. There was also a stream of people marching down the hall, but they weren't students. Some wore the casual clothes of office workers. Most were dressed like ordinary laborers. Clearly, the night shift.

When the procession ended, I ducked inside. It was a school all right. Classrooms, offices, labs, restrooms—and dosimeters hanging from the walls. What kind of school worried about radioactive contamination?

There was a bank of elevators farther down the hall, and that's where everyone was headed; the building was a single story high, so I didn't imagine the elevators went anywhere but down. There were two guards stationed at the elevators. They were checking ID badges.

I had to make a decision. There were doors on either side of the hall. The one to my right had a cutout of stairs on the front rising upward, which suggested a roof access. I made a quick turn through the door on my left, went down a wide hallway, and ran head-on into a man in a white lab coat coming out of a steel-framed door directly ahead. The door snapped closed behind him. I heard the magnetic lock engaging.

He stared at my face, and I stared at the ID card dangling from his neck lanyard. He did a double take and barked a question in Farsi. His gaze flickered across my chest in search of an ID badge.

Then his eyes went to the emergency alarm attached to the wall. He was reaching for it when I slashed an open hand across his throat. His cry ended in a gurgle. I punched him in the temple with a closed fist, and he crumpled to the floor.

I unclipped his ID badge and ran it through the magnetic card reader. The door clicked open. I dragged the unconscious man through the door with me. The door opened onto the landing of a staircase; I left the man there after deciding that another blow to the head wasn't necessary.

The staircase traveled down four flights to a second magnetically locked doorway and a sign that indicated an emergency exit. I used the ID badge a second time. The door accessed a narrow platform high above a cavernous room that was convex, like an airplane hangar only twice as large. My eyes widened in astonishment.

Pay dirt!

I was staring down at the Qom centrifuge plant.

A centrifuge machine looks like a tall silver cylinder the height of a tall man with silver coils spiraling toward the ceiling. I saw thousands standing like proud soldiers in perfectly straight rows that went on forever. I saw men in powder-blue smocks with handheld computers moving in and around the machines, but no soldiers.

I could climb down the ladders leading into the room, or I could use the digital scope. I figured that if I went down, I might never get out again, so I attached the Zeiss as quickly as I could to my iPhone.

I ran the iPhone camera for ten seconds on full zoom and then moved farther into the complex. I stopped when I saw a raised platform that housed what had to be the facility's control room. Beyond it, the room opened onto a cascade of smokestack-looking centrifuge machines that rose forty or fifty feet in the air; fewer in number, they looked many times more powerful.

I ran the camera again, thinking about what I was looking at. I got the process, more or less. Nuclear power began and ended with uranium. But the trick was separating the "useful" isotopes in the uranium from the "useless" ones. That took some serious machinery and engineering know-how. Nuclear reactors didn't need a ton of the good stuff, somewhere between 4 percent and 40 percent. A nuclear bomb, on the other hand, required 80 percent or more of the good stuff. Not easy. The first step was to turn the uranium into a gas. Then you spun the gas through the centrifuge tubes. The tubes siphoned off the "useful" uranium, tube after tube after tube.

I tried to do the math in my head, multiplying fifty rows deep of cylinders by at least four times that number long. Ten thousand centrifuges. Ten thousand!

No one on God's green earth needed ten thousand centrifuge machines for the kind of peaceful program that Mahmoud Ahmadinejad wanted the world to believe his country was engaged in.

I was looking through the iPhone's viewfinder when three men and two women walked into the picture. When one of the women looked up, the telescopic lens caught her scream even before the sound reached my ears. I was disengaging the Zeiss and jamming the phone into my pocket when the rest of them began shouting.

I didn't see which one of them pushed the alarm, but red lights along the ceiling began flashing even before I had my Walther out. Alarms wailed.

Get your ass moving, Jake!

I spun on my heels, used the ID badge to unlock the magnetic door, and dashed into the stairwell. I took the stairs two at a time to the first level. I didn't even look down at the unconscious body of the lab tech.

I crashed through the door. A guard with an AK-47 rounded the corner into the corridor. An AK-47 is an assault rifle. It's nearly three feet long and weighs more than ten pounds fully loaded. It's not meant for close-quarters combat. A Walther PPK/S is. He looked surprised at the encounter. I couldn't imagine why. He was trying to bring the rifle to bear when I leveled the silencer

181

at his chest and fired off two rounds. His surprise turned to astonishment and then he was face-first on the floor.

I grabbed his AK-47, cracked the door leading to the main hallway, and peeked around the corner. A trio of armed guards swarmed the entrance, and a metal gate slammed across the front doors.

I curled back inside the corridor, scooped the iPhone from my pocket, and hit the Send button on the emergency text Charlie and I had agreed upon earlier: *Shit hit the fan.* Pretty straightforward.

His came back to me five seconds later: *Roof.*

Rooftops are never a good idea. Rooftops are dead ends. I needed to get out, not up. I'd asked Charlie for one thing three days ago: trust. Now it was my turn. The stairs accessing the roof were across the hall. I could picture the stair motif printed on the door. The hall was four strides wide, by my estimate. The guards at the door also carried AK-47s, and a straight shot from a distance of, say, forty feet was exactly what they were designed for. Target practice.

I had to risk it. My heart rate had settled in at seventy-two beats per minute. Breathing steady and calm. I opened the door very carefully and used the body of the dead guard to prop it open. I took two steps back and set the butt of the AK-47 against my hip. Go!

I sprinted for the door. Between my first and second stride, I cut loose with two short bursts to keep the guards at the entrance at bay. Two more strides, and I had the door on the other side of the hall open. I lunged through and bounded up the stairs. The heavy metal hatch to the roof was secured with a padlock. One bullet from the AK-47 blew it apart, and I heaved the hatch open.

I climbed outside and into the light of the moon a day away from being full. I kicked the hatch closed and swung the handle to the locked position. I swept my gaze past the flat rooftop. Qom lay to the southeast. The spines of ragged hills to the west. Nothing but open ground to the north. Nowhere to run, nowhere to hide. No Charlie. I was toast.

The roof hummed with the echo of the alarms. Bullets thumped against the inside of the hatch. I had maybe fifteen rounds left in the AK-47 plus my Walther. The scene was about to degenerate into a very ugly shoot-out that I had absolutely no chance of winning, and me with a camera full of very damaging intel.

I scanned the landscape and the skies. I thought about the suitcase bomb two floors below. My heart jackhammered in desperation.

Charlie, where the hell are you? Don't make me activate that sucker.

CHAPTER 19

Alarms screamed around me in all directions and seemed to steal every ounce of energy from the air. I wanted to tell whoever happened to be in charge that everyone who needed to be alerted probably had been, so maybe he could hit the Off button.

Security guards rustled beneath the roof hatch. They were no doubt planning to rush me, but I also imagined that there was some debate about who was going to come through first.

There was a maintenance shed and three heating units near the center of the roof, and I ran in that direction. I pressed against the shed, circling it in a low crouch. More security guards scrambled onto the roof of an adjacent building to the south and started my way.

I flicked the safety from full auto to semiauto on the AK-47. No sense wasting bullets when I had to make every shot count. I brought the rifle to my shoulder, drew a bead on the leading guard—an easy hundred-yard shot—and squeezed off one round. He clutched his shoulder and crumbled onto the roof. It wasn't my best shot. The rifle obviously needed a site adjustment, but at least now I had it figured: four inches left, two down.

The guard's buddies saw him go down and sprayed the air with bullets that came nowhere close to hitting me. They grabbed their fallen comrade by the shirt collar and fell back. I had to give them credit. They might not have been very experienced, but they weren't stupid.

All well and good, but chasing them away was nothing to celebrate. Every minute I remained on the roof was another minute for the facility's security forces to gain strength and coordinate their attack. Soon, they'd have the numbers and the balls to come for me.

My pulse ticked upward. Eighty beats per minute. *Okay Charlie, where the hell are you?* I yanked the iPhone from my pocket. I stared at the triggering device: Activate or Disarm. Decision time.

The rotor blades of an approaching helicopter thrummed the air and drew my eyes away from the screen. Air cover. Now I was seriously screwed. A maintenance shed wasn't going to do me much good against a chopper with any sort of firepower.

Time to improvise.

The copter came straight at me. 500 meters and closing. A Bell Jet Ranger. I dropped to one knee. I hit the *Activate* button on my iPhone. I had 30 seconds. Might as well do some damage before the fat lady sang.

I sighted down the barrel of the AK-47. One shot each for the pilot and the co-pilot. I could picture the chopper crashing into the school and exploding in flames. One hell of a distraction. *But not from this range, Jake. Be patient.*

I counted off the seconds and calculated the distance: 400 yards. 350. The landing light under the chopper's nose began to flicker. *The hell?*

The Jet Ranger banked to the right, then orbited the building, the co-pilot in the left seat facing me. The cargo door was open. If the Ranger was armed— and every Ranger was—there would be a crewman hanging out the door with a machine gun. But the back seat was empty.

I glanced down at the iPhone's screen: 15, 14, 13 . . .

Decision time. 250 yards. *Wait!* I eased off the trigger. I'd seen the helicopter before, and now I knew where. On the landing pad outside Charlie's warehouse in Seyfabad. I lowered the rifle.

The co-pilot braced himself against the chopper's doorframe and leaned out. He raised his sunglasses and pushed a boom mike down from in front of his face. There was no mistaking the mustache and broad cheeks. Charlie Amadi. He signaled me to stay down and stay put. Yeah, as if I were going somewhere without him.

I dropped the rifle and reached for my phone.

Now it was down to 5, 4, 3 . . . I hit the Disarm trigger. The countdown froze.

The helicopter banked hard and swooped toward me. Now I recognized the pilot. It was Jeri. I was liking the girl better and better all the time. I pressed against the shed door and prayed that the guards in the stairway would hold off for three or four more seconds.

At the last second, the Jet Ranger flared upward to bleed off airspeed. A cloud of dust lifted from the roof. Jeri leveled the copter and raked her landing skids close to me, turbine engine screeching, rotor blades churning the air.

"What are you waiting for?" she shouted.

I dived onto the backseat. The helicopter accelerated upward. The roar was deafening. I rolled into a sitting position and snapped the seat harness over my shoulders and waist. I gripped my iPhone, stared down at the screen, and activated the self-destruct mechanism on the suitcase bomb. Thank God.

Wind whipped through the open cabin. I leaned to the left and glanced out the door. Security guards burst out of the hatchway on the school roof and began firing. Bullets sprayed us from the adjacent roof, wild shots that couldn't keep up with the forward motion of the Jet Ranger at full throttle.

I watched until we were well out of range. When I turned around, Charlie was holding out a headset for me. I slipped it over my ears.

"So?" I heard him say.

First, I held out the iPhone. He read the screen, and his eyes doubled in size. Then I pulled the phone away.

"Pay dirt," I answered, as we disappeared over the hills west of Qom and the first hint of dawn peeked above the horizon.

An hour later. Charlie handed me hot tea, Iranian style, in a short glass with one sugar cube. My hair was still wet from a hot shower and my face tingled from a welcome shave. He, Jeri, and I had just finished a late lunch of fried spinach and eggplant with yogurt, onions, and garlic. I was dying for a cheeseburger.

We hadn't gone back to Seyfabad, and we hadn't returned to Tehran. We'd gone south from Qom seventy or eighty miles to Kashan. Jeri had ditched the chopper at a private airport a mile from the city. The safe house was in an old neighborhood populated by painters and sculptors and papermakers, as Charlie described it.

He was expounding on Kashan's history. "Like everything in Iran, it's been overrun and pillaged by the best of them. Arabs, Mongols, Persians, and who knows all. That's what happens when you've been around for five thousand years."

Jeri wore the same tank top she'd been wearing during my rescue. It showed miles of skin the color of burnished walnut; I could have stared at her all day. She said, "If you had the time, you could walk into town and find a silk scarf for your wife unlike anything you could find anywhere else in the world. But you better get it quick before the mullahs make the arts a footnote in Iranian history."

"What's really special about Kashan is that Natanz is only forty miles away," Charlie said. He knew that was my next destination. "I assume that's the plan."

"Strike while the iron's hot, my friend. The Revolutionary Guards will know their security has been breached. I figure I have twenty-four hours max before everything within five hundred miles of Qom is battened down tighter than a drum," I said. I looked across at Charlie. He had chosen a hardback chair and a stiff posture. His cup and saucer were balanced in his hands like an artist with his brush and palette. "But you've done enough, Charlie. You and Jeri risked your necks for me back there. I won't forget. We're square."

Charlie looked over at Jeri. He was grinning. She looked like she was ready to take my head off. "He's no Persian, is he?" he said.

"No, but I like his style anyway," she said unexpectedly.

"In our country, as fucked up as it may be, it's the debtor who decides when a debt is paid. You've still got work to do, and we've still got a traitor to find," he said. "I'm in for the long haul."

"And I'm just beginning to enjoy myself," Jeri said. "But it's up to you, Abu."

Abu? What the hell? *Abu* meant "father" in Arabic. My eyes swept the room. Charlie must have seen it on my face. But he didn't say anything. Instead, he pulled a laptop from a case on the floor and set it up on the table.

While he was powering it up, he said, "I heard from Bagheri. You lit a fire under his ass. He's got people searching high and low for his mole."

I shook my head. "Bad move. All he's going to do is make it harder for us to find the bastard."

"Don't I know it. But there might be an upside. He raises enough hell, it might keep Security out of our hair for a while. My guys are narrowing things down. They're tracking twenty-six known MEK operatives who seem to have hidden agendas."

"Moradi?" For some reason, I didn't want it to be Moradi. He'd been chumming for the MEK in Amsterdam for thirty years. We'd partnered enough times to know we were on the same side. Or so I thought.

"Not Moradi. But Karimi and Drago keep coming to the surface," Charlie said.

"Okay. We have to flush our guy out," I said. "We have to set a lure for the twenty-six possibilities on our list. We have to use the communication links your guys have established to hint at various rendezvous sights around Tehran. See who bites."

"I'm on that," Jeri said, rising from her chair with the grace of gymnast on a balance beam. "I'll set up a video conference with Amur." She glanced at me. "Amur. The guy with the bow tie. We'll have something out on the wire in an hour."

"Keep it subtle, Jeri," I said. "This guy's smart. We don't want to spook him."

She nodded briskly—the soldier replacing the gymnast in the blink of an eye—and hustled out.

"Consider it done," Charlie said, as if I might have misgivings about a twenty-six-year-old screwing up our counterintelligence op. Nope, not this twenty-six-year-old. I'd share a foxhole with her any day of the week. Charlie turned the computer screen my way. "Professor Fouraz came through again. He sent another batch of photographs from Natanz and a couple of audio links."

Charlie put the photographs up on the screen. The first batch showed unmarked semi-trailers escorted by unmarked SUVs. All the men wore sunglasses and most weren't particularly discreet about hiding their weapons: MP5 submachine guns, Beretta auto-shotguns, and the ubiquitous AK-47s.

There had been times when I ran three or four ops at a time. I could have been circling the wagons on an arms-smuggling ring in Mexico and targeting a band of Chinese heroin dealers in Washington, D.C., while working the Iranian cartel in Florida and a trafficking operation out of Bangkok. The bottom line was always intel. Gather it, package it, send it off to Mr. Elliot to analyze and act upon. It wasn't my job to figure it all out, but figuring it all out more or less came with the territory. Figuring it out helped me plan my next move. Figuring it out kept me alive.

That's what I was doing now—staying alive, completing the mission.

"Knowing what we know now about Qom, it has to work this way," I said. I was really talking to myself, even though Charlie had settled in next to me on the couch. I jabbed a finger at the big rigs in the photos. "The trailers carry enriched-uranium ingots made in Qom. Once the ingots arrive in Natanz, they're fabricated into warheads."

I had transmitted the photos from the enrichment facility in Qom to General Rutledge and Mr. Elliot the moment we landed in Kashan, but I hadn't heard back from either of them yet. I knew it would take some time. I had handed them intel no one had ever seen before; they were probably creaming all over themselves trying to figure out what to do with it.

Charlie clicked to the next group of photos. This batch depicted a convoy of panel trucks, again escorted by unmarked SUVs. It came with an audio link. "Let's hear what the good professor has to say about these."

He clicked the link. I recognized Professor Fouraz's voice, and it didn't take a guy trained in voice recognition to hear the strain. He was saying, "These trucks are on their way to Natanz. That I know for sure."

"And the payload?" I asked, as if he were sitting across from us.

"From everything I have been able to find out, they're hauling special tanks containing deuterium. Collected in the heavy-water facility at Arak."

I waited for more, but the audio link had closed.

"That's deducing a lot from a couple of panel trucks," I said. Deuterium was a hydrogen isotope used to slow neutrons inside nuclear reactors: a good thing. More ominously, it was used to boost the yield of a nuclear bomb.

I clicked to a third series of pictures. These showed long cylindrical objects lashed to flatbed trailers and covered with acres of some reflective material. The shapes were identical to the one Fouraz had shown me yesterday. Sejil-2 ballistic missiles. Had to be.

But instead of speculating, I clicked a second audio link. In this one, the professor's voice was more clipped, more urgent. "These are casings for Sejil-2 ballistic missiles." Bingo. "Twenty-one such missiles were delivered this month to the underground facility in Natanz."

I shook my head, though it wasn't surprise I was feeling. "Ahmadinejad is fielding a strike force, Charlie."

"You need to get in there," he said. His cell phone rang. He came to his feet and put the phone to his ear. He spoke Farsi to whoever the caller was, and I sensed some annoyance in his voice. When he was done, he snapped the phone closed like a man who had spent too much time away from his business. He said, "I've got a problem with a shipment of Toyota car parts."

He turned on his heels and left me alone in the room. Good. I needed the privacy. I checked my iPhone. There was a call tag from General Rutledge marked "urgent alert." I guess pretty much everything was going to be urgent from here on out. I activated a secure video uplink. The general wore his gray camouflage uniform, and I could heard engines rumbling in the background.

He jumped right into the call. "Excellent intel. I won't ask how you got it."

"Your guys see it the way I did?"

"Roger that." In other words, proof positive that Ahmadinejad was manufacturing enriched uranium at a rate that far exceeded his domestic, commercial needs. "The son of a bitch finally did it. He's got nukes. We're going public with it."

He didn't mean "public" in the conventional sense. He meant that the information would be going to fellow intelligence groups in Israel, England, France, and probably a half-dozen other nations.

"There's more," I said. I told him about the deuterium, the enriched uranium, and a battery of twenty-one missiles that apparently had arrived in Natanz over the last month.

Rutledge squinted. I sensed his mind wrestling with the implications.

"Okay," he said. I heard the profundity in that one word and calculated the intensity in his gesture. Conclusion? He was about to hit me with another round of fun and games. Just what I needed. "The Iranians need more than enriched uranium to make viable weapons worth mounting on a Sejil-2 missile. You know that. They have yet to build a working bomb because they're not going to waste the time or money making a weapon they can't deploy."

This was all open-source information. You could hear it on FOX News. I waited for the twist. Tom said, "One bottleneck in fielding a credible strike force is collecting enough precision electronics needed to arm and fuse the ballistic nuclear warheads."

"I'm with you," I said, meaning, *Get to it, my friend. The clock's ticking*.

The general reached off the screen to touch an unseen button. "Which brings me to him. Take a look."

A jumble of colored pixels replaced Tom's image. The pixel resolution coalesced and sharpened into a photograph of a man standing next to an airline ticket counter. I recognized Atash Morshed, the online banker from Amsterdam responsible for laundering Iranian drug money and funneling it back into their weapons program.

"The photo you're looking at was taken at the Beijing airport six days ago. It took that long for the computers to put two and two together."

"That's why I'm *so* fond of computers," I said with razor-sharp sarcasm.

"Then you'll appreciate this," Tom said. "See his briefcase? Our agents in China have hard and fast evidence that our Amsterdam friend was in town, shopping product."

He didn't need to say that Morshed was shopping for special microelectronic circuit boards. The very type needed for finalizing the nukes. It was obvious.

"Our friend's face wasn't a priority fit until we finally got it on a fast track. Our guys in China made the connection the same day."

"Good work." I meant it.

"Our online banker has made a fortune laundering money and smuggling drugs using Iran as a conduit. At some point you have to pay the piper."

"So it doesn't take much to speculate that Ahmadinejad finally called in his marker and sent our friend on an errand to buy the components."

Tom nodded. "We need verification."

"You think he's in Iran," I said. I meant Morshed.

"The timing fits. And if he's in Iran with circuit boards meant for those Sejil-2s . . ."

"Then Natanz is probably on his itinerary," I said. "High stakes."

"The highest."

"It wouldn't hurt for me to have a picture of those circuit boards. Can you make that happen?"

"I'll send a close-up with the model number."

I stared at his face. "There's something else. What is it?"

"Our friend in Virginia isn't happy. You've cut him out."

"I'm not going there. He's compromised. Or someone on his team is." My voice could not have been calmer. "I'm more concerned about our friend on Pennsylvania Avenue." I was talking about Landon Fry, the president's chief of staff. "He jump ship yet?"

"He and I are having a face-to-face later today. A full update."

I shook my head. "That doesn't answer my question."

I hung up. "Politicians." The word came out more like a hiss. And why not. Snakes, every one of them.

I had no sooner disconnected the call with General Rutledge than my iPhone flashed two message prompts. The first was from Tom and contained a stock photo of the Chinese circuit board in question, listed as model number 378-98NB574. The Chinese didn't mess around. The 378 was a ten-layer board so thin and light that you would expect it to crumple in a stiff breeze. They were protected with some sort of laminate material that I didn't recognize and resistant to temperatures up to five hundred degrees Fahrenheit. The boards were ten-by-six, which meant Atash Morshed would need a small suitcase or a decent-size briefcase to transport them. This struck me as important. It meant that the product could travel from Beijing to Natanz and never leave his sight.

But maintaining anonymity in Natanz was not as easy as it might have been in a larger city. Natanz, for all its notoriety, wasn't much more than a collection of settlements a half hour southeast of Kashan, and an hour northwest of Esfahan. It lay at the junction off Highway 7, and no more than forty thousand people called the place home. The Karkas Mountains formed a rugged, ten-thousand-foot background to the town and its collection of shrines and ruins. Besides the nuclear facility tucked in the mountains south of town, the one thing the people of Natanz liked to brag about was the inauspicious fact that Darius III was murdered there. I couldn't find a historian who agreed with them, but why put a damper on their one claim to fame.

I heard a brief knock on the door, and Charlie peeked his head in. He had what looked like a diplomatic pouch in his hand.

"A courier from MEK chief Yousef Bagheri just dropped this off," he said, placing the unopened pouch in my hand. "It looks like Professor Fouraz came through for us."

I realized I was holding my breath as I broke the seal on the pouch, which suggested a reliance on an outside source that made me very uncomfortable. There were three pieces of documentation inside. The first was a single sheet of typing paper with six numbers laid out in a series of three written on it: *43-6-120*. A short note read: *Natanz entry code.*

The next thing the pouch revealed was an employee ID badge for the Natanz nuclear facility in the name of Avan Javaherian, complete with a magnetic strip and a photo: mine. Just as long as no one asked me to pronounce Avan Javaherian . . .

Charlie was right. The professor *had* come through. I let my breath out. At least this time I wouldn't be stowing away in the back of a semi loaded with concrete pipes and hoping the guards were too lazy to search them.

The last thing in the pouch was a delivery manifest for roofing tiles. I showed it to Charlie. "Leave it to me," he said, just as my phone rang. "I'll give you some privacy."

"Five minutes," I said. When the door closed, I picked up. It was Mr. Elliot.

"Your cover's all set," he said. His call was twelve minutes late, which was an eternity for my longtime case officer. I thought of chiding him, but detected a minor strain in his voice that convinced me otherwise. "I've arranged for you to join a group of Canadian archaeologists on their way to visit the Natanz ruins. But you've got to bus it. Their bus will be in Kashan in forty-five minutes. They've got a short stop at the Āghā Bozorg Mosque. That's where you get onboard."

"Nice," I said.

"What's not so nice is that, unlike Qom, security in Natanz is obvious and omnipresent, my friend. Cloak and dagger will only get you so far."

I told him about the security code and the employee ID, and a minute bit of tension drained from his voice. He said, "Okay. Good progress so far. Push, but don't press, right?"

I smiled. I hadn't heard that one in years. "Good advice," I told him.

By the time I signed off, both Charlie and Jeri were back in the room. Jeri updated me on the lures she and our counterintelligence team were laying for the twenty-six remaining candidates for traitor-of-the-year honors. "We're using physical rendezvous points tomorrow night that we'll be monitoring, all in central Tehran. I'm using every spare man we have."

"We'll have him within two days," I said confidently. Then I told them my plans for entering Natanz posing as a French archaeologist.

"I like it," Charlie said.

"But that doesn't account for my delivery into the Natanz facility, and it doesn't account for my other suitcase, Charlie."

"Jeri's taken care of that," he said, glancing her way.

Jeri used the computer to pull up a street map of Natanz and the access roads leading to the nuclear facility. She pointed to a warehouse district north of town and traced a route to a railroad siding. "Here. Look for a white pickup truck. A Daihatsu. Your luggage is already onboard."

She forwarded the map to my cell phone and said, "Now if you just looked a little more French and a little more like an archaeologist."

"And you're traveling too light. Looks suspicious," Charlie said. He went to the closet and came back with a rolling carry-on. He stood the carry-on in front of me. "It's got some extra clothes of mine and some toiletries. Nothing you can't pitch if necessary."

"And there's one thing missing," I said.

"Like what?"

"If I know my Canadian counterparts as well as I think I do, I imagine they might get thirsty on the long road to Natanz. Helping them out might be the neighborly thing to do, don't you think?"

Jeri grinned; she had an amazing smile. Charlie waltzed over to the room's liquor cabinet—an impressive collection of imported spirits that reminded me that Charlie had his hands in every possible form of contraband—and returned with a bottle of Knob Creek bourbon.

"Perfect." I packed the bottle in the carry-on and zipped it closed.

"One more thing," he said, nodding to Jeri. "Show him."

Jeri reached into her jacket pocket and withdrew a Fairbairn-Sykes fighting knife in a thin leather sheath. "A little added firepower," she said.

"Apparently," Charlie said, "an MI6 agent used this to settle a gambling debt. Said it once belonged to a British commando from World War Two. As the story goes, it drew plenty of Nazi blood over the course of the war. Sounds like a lot of value-added bullshit to me."

I inspected the blade. It was sturdy, razor sharp, and perfectly designed for close-quarters combat. I fastened the knife and sheath around the inside of my left ankle, tucked it inside my sock, and hid it beneath the pant cuff. "Let's hope I don't need it."

Charlie drove me to the Āghā Bozorg Mosque. I presented my Canadian passport to the archaeological group's minder, a woman from the Ministry of Tourism and certainly a part-timer with National Security. The head of the group was a balding, stooped man who introduced himself as Dr. Jeffrey Carlyle from the University of Manitoba. He was clearly suspicious of the latecomer to his entourage and asked too many questions too quickly.

"Thanks for having me onboard," was pretty much all I said as the minder herded all twenty-three of us—college professors, students, and a couple of amateurs—onto a very comfortable tourist bus.

I sat near the back. Dr. Carlyle took a seat across the aisle, where his game of stink eye continued. I didn't mind. I was more interested in the mounting evidence identifying the doctor as a day drinker: red nose, ravaged skin, spider-web eyes.

Halfway to Natanz, I retrieved my carry-on from the overhead rack and unzipped the bag; I made sure our minder wasn't looking. The bottle of Knob Creek bourbon lay swaddled in T-shirts, and I made sure Carlyle got a glimpse of it.

"If you should get a little thirsty." I gave him a nod. Not too subtle.

The doctor's gaze warmed. I guess he was easily impressed. He cleared his throat and whispered, "Splendid. Just the thing to cut the dust."

Suddenly I was Dr. Carlyle's best friend, and we chatted Iranian history until our bus pulled into a roundabout out front of a modest, three-story hotel situated near the edge of town and just off the main road.

We checked in and were issued old-fashioned brass keys to a string of rooms on the second floor. Just before dinner, there was a rough knock on my door. It was Dr. Carlyle, all decked out in a tweed suit that fit his ruddy complex to a tee. He had a glass bottle in his hand that had once contained pre-made green tea and the brilliant idea of using the bottle to transport Knob Creek whiskey to dinner. I acted like a man who would never have conceived such a clever idea, and together we congregated with the rest of our group in the hotel's cramped, but tasteful restaurant.

"The only decent place for dinner in all Natanz," our minder told us, as if the town was a disgrace to Iranian cuisine.

There were eight or ten other tables in the restaurant, all occupied, and all by foreigners from places far and wide: Russia, Germany, Japan, Sweden, France. As it turned out, Dr. Carlyle was not the only one who had arrived at dinner with a glass tea bottle in hand, and he was not the only one freshening drinks with the bottles' mysterious potions. After an hour, I understood why. The food was terrible. Some Knob Creek made it almost edible.

Dessert was being served when I saw him. He was passing through the lobby, a tall, rounded man with a trimmed beard and thick eyebrows. Atash Morshed, the online banker from Amsterdam. I nearly dropped my drink. Impossible. I took in details as fast as my mind would record them. Expensive suit and fancy shirt, but no tie, an omission that gave him an unkempt look. His eyes moved too quickly for a tourist. He looked too exhausted for a successful businessman.

He carried a large briefcase. The briefcase was identical to the one in the photo from the airport in Beijing. The briefcase was chained to his wrist. He stopped at the front desk and made a telephone call. His gaze skimmed the room and reached into the restaurant, hopscotching from person to person in suspicion. He exuded nervous tension like a rank smell, at least for someone with my experience. And my experience was giving very good odds that the Chinese circuit boards were in the briefcase.

Morshed said a few words into the phone, listened, and hung up. He checked his watch in a gesture that was equal parts impatience, discomfort, and distress.

I flexed my leg and felt the hilt of the F-S knife press against the inside of my calf.

The banker had two new items for his busy schedule.

One, he was going to lose that briefcase.

And two, he was going to die.

CHAPTER 20

NATANZ—DAY 8

The Iranian government had made Atash Morshed a wealthy man. They sold drugs in massive amounts, and he laundered their money using banking techniques that most bankers didn't know existed. He used the Internet. He covered his tracks by creating an online bank with thousands of legitimate customers. He funneled the money from Amsterdam back into Iran via the government's unmonitored Office of Business Development, and the OBD bankrolled nuclear energy development in places like Natanz and Qom.

It was hard to tell whether Morshed was on his way out of the hotel or waiting for someone's arrival. He wasn't very good at disguising his unease in any case, pacing the lobby floor with uneven strides and wandering eyes. I couldn't blame him: this was uncharted territory for a man more accustomed to penthouse suites in places like Geneva and Paris, a man more accustomed to gracing the business pages of the Amsterdam *Schuttevae* than to running errands for mullahs and demagogues.

When he turned suddenly toward the entrance, I rose from my chair. I was halfway up when Morshed pivoted at the door, did a complete about-face, and lurched down the hall to the elevators.

"Going someplace?" Dr. Carlyle asked me.

"I think I need some fresh air," I said. "If you'll excuse me."

Dr. Carlyle greeted this news with a hangdog expression that had far more to do with the bottle of bourbon up in my room than the sudden loss of a complete stranger's company. One part of me wanted to toss him my room key and say, *You need it a lot more than I do. Drink up.* A more prudent part of me wanted to keep the man at bay, so I said, "I won't be long. Maybe we can get a nightcap."

"Excellent," he said, as I lifted my hat from the back of the chair and moved away from the table, nodding with diminishing charm to the people at our table. I lengthened my stride when I reached the lobby, but by the time I got to the elevators, Morshed was already going up.

I hustled to a stairwell at the end of the hall. The black-glass ball of a security camera hung from the wall by the stairs, and I automatically pulled the brim of my cap down over my eyes. It didn't really matter. If someone wanted to know who the man bounding up the hotel stairs was in the middle of the dinner hour, there were twenty-three very high-strung Canadians who could probably have given them a fair description.

I took the steps two at a time to the second floor and peeked out the door in the direction of the elevators. No Morshed.

I lost a second huffing up to the third floor and a number on the door that looked like a hawk in flight. I put a crack in the door and scoped the hall. I heard a bell that signaled the arrival of the elevator. I heard the doors slide open. A man stepped into the hall. It was Atash Morshed. He turned to his left and walked away from the elevators with a quick, uncertain step. I watched his back for three seconds before stepping onto the floor.

Morshed veered to the left and down a second hallway. I knew the layout: it was identical to the second floor. I peeked around the corner and watched him. He was searching his pockets for a room key using his right hand while his left hand held firm to the briefcase. He stopped in front of a door halfway down the hall. Dropped his key. I heard an agitated growl as he bent down and retrieved it. It took him two tries to get the door unlocked, and he stormed inside.

I was moving down the hall when I heard the dead bolt click. A door chain rattled into place.

I yanked on a pair of thin leather gloves. I stopped at his door and listened. He must have gone straight for the telephone, because his muffled, agitated voice filtered through the door. Not a happy man, our Mr. Morshed. Well, what in the hell did he expect? Five seconds later, the telephone rattled in its cradle. Footsteps, like a man pacing. Water splashing in a basin. Silence.

I knocked softly. My Farsi sucked, but I managed, "Sir? Sir."

"What is it?" he replied, angry and nervous. His Farsi was worse than mine.

I thought about switching to English, but how obvious would that have been. English, in a town like Natanz, in a country that despised Americans? I wanted to say something enticing like, *Your car's downstairs,* but couldn't find the words. All I managed was, "Car. Outside."

Morshed cursed, no doubt concluding that the hotel had sent an illiterate bumpkin to deliver a message better suited to an eight-year-old. He stomped toward the door. I put a hand over the peephole and repeated, "Car. Outside."

He switched to Dutch and swore. I didn't bother trying to translate it, but suffice to say he sounded pissed. He snapped the dead bolt. Good. It was no fun dealing with a dead bolt.

I took a step back, palmed my Walther, and cocked my leg.

The door opened three inches. Morshed had stripped to a white undershirt and striped boxers. His bearded face appeared over the brass chain stretched between the door and the frame.

The instant his eyes met mine, I used the heel of my boot to kick the door inward. The brass chain snapped in two. The edge of the door caught him along the cheek and brow, driving him back into the room and drawing a painful groan from him. I stepped in, pushed the door closed, and secured the dead bolt.

Morshed lay on the floor, stunned. His stockinged feet quivered at the ends of spindly legs. Blood seeped from the vertical crease along the left side of his face. I had to search the room and couldn't bother tying him up, so I drove a foot into his crotch. His face withered in pain. He curled into a fetal position and whimpered. Okay, so maybe I overreacted, but I didn't have much respect for a man whose every move had dollar signs written all over it, even if it meant cashing in on weapons of mass destruction.

"Shut the hell up, Morshed," I growled, and it sounded so much better in English.

I followed the end of my gun into the bathroom, then did a quick search of the closet. Three seconds and I was back in the bedroom. The briefcase lay on the nightstand next to the bed. The open end of a pair of handcuffs dangled from the handle.

"Open it." I pointed to the briefcase.

He remained on the floor, twitching, breathing heavily, tears running into the wrinkles of his fat cheeks.

"Listen, Morshed. You wanted to play with the big boys and you got what you wished for," I said calmly. "Now I'm going to give you ten seconds to have this briefcase opened, or I'll put a bullet between your legs and you can see if that feels any better than my foot."

Morshed rolled onto his hands and knees. He brought his rheumy eyes up to me and asked in the most cultured English, "Who are you?"

"It doesn't matter who I am. What matters is what you've had chained to your wrist since leaving China six days ago."

He stared at me, and the skin around his eyes and lips quivered. He managed a tiny shake of the head. "I don't have the combination."

"Really?" I could have pried the briefcase open, but this was one of those instances when a lesson in high-stakes espionage was in order. "How about if I break your fingers one at a time until you remember?"

Morshed propped himself against the bed and struggled to his feet. Apparently he'd found his memory and the strength to stand upright. He staggered over to the table and gripped the briefcase by the handle. He stood it on edge. This was no ordinary briefcase. It was high-strength aluminum with two draw-bolt-style latches. The lock was a four-tumbler Vaultz. I watched his fingers work: 7-8-0-3. The lock popped. The latches sprang open. He glanced up at me. The Walther's silencer was an inch from his temple so fast that he didn't have time to blink.

"Maybe I should do the honors; what do you think, Mr. Morshed?" He took a step away without being told. I guess staring into the black hole of a 9 mm pistol was incentive enough.

I laid the briefcase on the bed. I lifted the lid. Packed inside were neat rows of Chinese circuit boards in clear plastic bags.

"Well, well, well. What do we have here?" I gestured to an armchair against the opposite wall. "Sit your ass down and put your hands on top of your head."

Morshed backpedaled three steps, sank into the chair, and interlaced his fingers over his bald head. The color had already drained from his face, and his expression went blank. He stared empty-eyed at the wall.

I looked back at the briefcase. I had to inspect the boards. Easy enough to believe these were the ones General Rutledge was hoping to find, but I had seen so much bogus merchandise in my day that it was second nature to assume the worst. But with Morshed sitting in that chair, wondering about his fate and scheming whatever schemes his mind could conjure up given the circumstances, I couldn't risk putting my gun down.

"Morshed," I said. "Look over here."

His eyes swiveled in my direction. I fixed my aim to the left edge of his sternum, directly over his heart. "You probably knew it was going to end this way, didn't you?"

He remained stone faced, hands on his head, the international criminal financier in his undershirt and boxers. Killing a man in cold blood was part of my job. I had no remorse. Sacrifice him and maybe I prevent a war that could kill millions, including his own countrymen. At least Morshed would die quickly and knowing why.

I fired once. The silencer coughed no louder than a baby. The bullet punched a neat hole in Morshed's chest. His jaw clenched, like something deep inside him had jerked tight. Whatever that something was crumpled an instant later and went slack. His mouth drooped. His fingers opened like a dying flower, his arms fell, and his hands slapped against the armrests. His head sagged forward until his chin rested on his chest. The crimson circle staining his undershirt stretched into an oval blossom crowning his belly. I didn't wait for it to stop.

I drew the F-S knife from the sheath around my ankle and sliced open one of the circuit boards. I withdrew a collection of wafer circuits and shiny metallic nodules glued and soldered to a green plastic card with gold connectors along the edges. The board had an aesthetic symmetry to it, a real object d'art. I flipped it over and read the model number on the product label: 378-98NB574. *Bingo.*

I counted twenty-four circuit boards, enough for Mahmoud Ahmadinejad's nuclear missile arsenal, plus three extra. I got out my iPhone and snapped photos of the open briefcase and circuit boards. I captioned the pictures: *Verified,* and texted them to General Rutledge and Mr. Elliot.

Neither had mentioned disposing of the circuit boards, but then we hadn't exactly anticipated events leading to a face-to-face meeting with the courier. I wasn't in a position to get them to Charlie, and I wasn't about to haul them around with me. Couldn't leave them for the Iranians. *Okay, Jake, so destroying the boards is on the house.*

First things first. Morshed's body. I had no way of knowing who he was supposed to be delivering the circuit boards to or when he was supposed to be meeting them, but at best it was a matter of hours, not days.

At the most, I'd have until tomorrow when housekeeping checked the room. The hotel would call the police, and the police would call Iranian security. Say fifteen hours max. Enough, unless someone stormed his room in the meantime.

I wrapped a bath towel around Morshed's torso to contain the blood and set him on the floor. I lifted the bed, dragged him under the mattress, and lowered the bed over him. I balled his shirt and jacket around his shoes and stuffed those under the bed as well. I studied my handiwork. Worthy of a casual inspection, but not much more. And if they didn't see him, they'd probably smell him.

I collected the personal items Morshed had dumped on the dresser: watch, cell phone, lighter, room key, bills, and coins. I dropped those into my jacket pocket.

I closed up the briefcase and tucked it under my arm. I spent three seconds with my ear against the door, listening. No footfalls, no voices.

I stepped into the hall, pulled the locked door closed behind me, and jogged to the staircase. I made a quick stop at my room to retrieve my backpack; I wasn't going anywhere without that. Then I took the stairs two at time to the ground floor. I turned away from the lobby, shortened my stride as I moved down the hall, and emerged out a side exit onto a small parking lot. Lampposts on either corner of the block spilled soft beams across the lot's broken asphalt. I counted six cars.

I crushed Morshed's cell phone under my heel and kicked it under a gray Toyota sedan. I tossed his watch, room key, and money into a Dumpster half filled with food wrappers, newspapers, cardboard boxes, and bundled trash from the hotel. I crumpled the better part of two newspapers into a small pyre. I opened the briefcase and laid it on the ground. I sliced open each plastic bag and tossed the circuit boards onto the crumpled newspaper. The briefcase wouldn't burn, but I threw it in anyway.

I took Morshed's lighter, reached into the bin, and set fire to the newspaper and several pieces of cardboard. Nothing fancy, but the orange flames skipped across the pyre and braided into a pillar of fire. I didn't expect much damage, but I did expect a nice mess that would go straight into the back of a trash truck and then into a compacter.

I hurried down the alley and found a secluded spot between a brick tenement house and what looked like the rear entrance to a bakery. There was a light burning inside the bakery, but I didn't see anyone inside. The air smelled of mildew and rain. It was chillier than I expected.

The iPhone's screen told me it was 9:23 P.M.

I opened the GPS app, tapped in to coordinates 33° 31' 47" North, 51° 54' 14" East, and mapped out my route. The nuclear facility lay just short of twenty miles north-by-northwest of town at the foot of the mountains. My first task was to locate the truck Jeri had left for me near the train depot.

I thought about jogging, but a Canadian archaeologist jogging through a Natanz residential area didn't sound like a wise idea. Especially one with a 9 mm pistol under his arm and a knife strapped to his leg.

So I started walking and thought about my target. This was what I knew about the Natanz plant: it was a hardened fuel enrichment facility. It covered one hundred thousand square yards. In other words, it was damn big. It was built twenty-five feet underground and protected by a concrete wall eight feet thick, which was protected by a second concrete wall. Serious business. The roof was built from reinforced concrete and covered with sixty feet of dirt. Overkill? Hell, they were building nuclear weapons. A little paranoia was in order.

The real work was done in two 75,000 square feet halls, and that's where I was headed.

The Natanz warehouse district was really nothing more than fifteen or twenty brick buildings huddled around a railroad depot, just as Jeri had said. I found the small Daihatsu pickup truck parked behind a stout two-story building with four very impressive chimneys. The bed of the truck was stacked with asphalt roofing tiles. I found the key inside the back wheel well, resting on top of the tire. I unlocked the door and peeked in. The suitcase, identical to the one I had transported into Qom, was tucked neatly behind the passenger-side seat. I hauled it out and spent just under two minutes entering the codes that opened the case and the sequencing that armed it. I tied the triggers into my phone and replaced it behind the seat.

I slid into the driver's seat. The truck started on the first try, and the engine sounded as if it had been tuned the day before. *Thank you, Jeri.*

Lights off, I eased down the street.

I decided not to risk the main highway. The back roads were dirt, but then desert sand was all you could see for miles. The road circled a hill and headed in the direction of mountains as black and ominous as a deep well. The sky was festooned with a million jeweled stars. The moon, shrouded in clouds, sprinkled tawny light over terrain that made Utah look like a tropical paradise, but it was just enough illumination to make navigating the dirt road manageable.

At the turnoff to the ruins, I continued north.

The truck crested one hill, then a tall ridge. On the other side, a smattering of lights sprinkled across a broad plateau. I eased the truck into a dry wash and kept the engine running. I climbed out. I found a vantage point that allowed me to peek over the bank of the wash. The facility was a half mile ahead and huge, but mostly what the eye saw was sand and dirt. I attached my Zeiss digital scope to the iPhone and did a preliminary scan. It was obvious the lights were coming from a cluster of administration buildings. Two ominous-looking concrete walls ran beyond my sight in two directions. A chain-link fence topped by razor wire surrounded the entire complex. Yellow lamps placed every one hundred fifty feet marked the perimeter.

More lights outlined a confusion of squat buildings that were part army barracks and part warehouses in appearance. Another building looked like a hospital or a prison, but maybe that was just the muddy, lackluster color. Another could have been a small factory by the look of the chimneys. Beads of reflected light followed shiny pipes clustered between a number of buildings, but I didn't get too excited by this. Machinery groaned in the darkness. Guard towers rose up against the horizon like floating apparitions. I couldn't see guards; that didn't mean they weren't there.

It was 11:17 P.M.

I turned the scope in the direction of the facility's main entrance. It dead-ended with the two-lane highway that ran north from the city of Natanz. I was hoping for evidence that deliveries were made at this late hour. If they weren't, all the paperwork in the world wouldn't help me.

I watched for nearly thirty minutes, and my patience was rewarded. Two vehicles used the main entrance during this time. Both were allowed in after what looked like a less-than-diligent inspection at the hands of the guards at the gate. Several other cars veered away from the main entrance, turning in my direction, and skirted the complex to the east. These didn't look like delivery vehicles. More likely they carried members of the night staff or workers returning from a night on the town in Natanz.

I'd seen enough. I got back behind the wheel again. I eased out of the wash and backtracked to the road that led to the ruins. I turned in the opposite direction. The road intersected the main highway not ten minutes later. I swung north on the highway, crested a low rise, and saw the entrance to the nuclear facility straight ahead.

I told myself not to hurry. I was 150 feet from the entrance when two guards materialized. They were armed, but their weapons were slung over their shoulders. I had my employee ID and delivery manifest in my hands as I eased to a stop. I held them out as the guard on my side stepped forward. He said something. I nodded and smiled and made eye contact. Always make eye contact. Never dip your head. Never turn away. Never let them see you sweat. Basic tradecraft. Don't drum the steering wheel. Don't lick your lips. Don't act impatient. Even more basic.

I expected him to carry my paperwork into the guardhouse, but he didn't. He positioned himself beneath the arc light at the entrance. He studied the ID first. Then he flipped through the three-page delivery order. He glanced into the bed of the truck, but that was the sum total of his inspection.

He returned to the ID again and was staring at my photo as he stepped up to the window again. Once again, he said something completely without meaning to a guy from New Jersey, and I responded by reaching out my hand. He looked bored, and I wanted to share his boredom, so I yawned. He laid the papers in my hands again. I nodded, turned in my seat, and put the truck in gear. I eased forward, an eye on the rearview mirror. *Stay cool, guys. We'll all live a little longer if you do.*

I eased the truck down a wide lane that fanned in three directions. Right seemed to track in the direction of the administration buildings I had seen. Left curled along the innermost concrete wall and along the perimeter. I decided to stay with the main road and eased through a concrete portal that led to a slab of concrete that fifty or so cars were using as a parking lot.

I debated stopping here until I saw a van rolling through a gated entrance at the base of what looked like an underground parking garage. It took sixty nerve-racking seconds to reach the entrance. I rolled up to the keypad. When I touched the pad, the numbers turned red. I entered the code: 43-2-156. The numbers turned green. The gate unlatched. An electric motor scrolled it open.

I eased the truck inside the garage and took a two-lane drive down one level, exactly as the guy in the van had done. I parked in an empty spot as far from the van as possible. I rolled up the windows, took a last glance back at the suitcase bomb, and made certain my iPhone was still registering the triggers: Activate and Disarm.

I went through the numbers before climbing out. Walther, iPhone, Zeiss, Fairbairn-Sykes fighting knife, French passport—as if that would do me any good. I left my backpack and the rest of my gear on the floor on the passenger side.

I climbed out like a man heading in for another long night shift, closed the door, and headed for the stairs. I exited through a door across from the building I had earlier pegged as a hospital or a prison. Nope. Offices. And most of the lights were out. I headed that way.

There was a chemical smell in the air that I couldn't identify. It seemed colder inside the complex, but that might have been the spike in my heart rate to an unsatisfactory seventy-six beats a minute. *Breathe, Jake. Turn on some tunes.* So I did. Golden Earring's "Twilight Zone." I heard the guitar, big chords. And the lyrics: "Soon you will come to know, when the bullet hits the bone."

I veered away from the front entrance and settled into a blind spot next to a window well. The harsh beam of a flashlight hit me straight in the face. I dropped down and pressed against the concrete wall. A guttural voice snarled a warning I understood only because of the universal tone every warning in the world carried.

Two soldiers approached, G-3 rifles at the ready, muzzles fixed on yours truly. *Way to go, Jake. Nicely done.*

CHAPTER 21

NATANZ—DAY 9

Two soldiers with G-3 rifles trained on me. A problem, for sure. But also an opportunity. The G-3 was a battle rifle developed a half century ago by a German outfit called Heckler & Koch. They made fine weapons. But a 7.62 mm battle rifle in close quarters—and a dark lane between two buildings definitely qualified as close quarters—was far from ideal.

I lowered my eyes and waved the flashlight aside, feigning annoyance and spouting a couple of harsh words in French just to confuse matters.

I got a good glimpse of the two. Both young, both bearded, and both rightfully amped up. Better yet. The one on my left was the shorter of the two and built like a wrestler who'd pumped a little too much iron. The taller one had three stripes sewn onto his upper sleeve. Unless my knowledge of the Revolutionary Guards fell short of what I thought it was, he carried the rank of *sarjukhe*—corporal. He held the flashlight in his left hand and cradled his rifle in an awkward right-handed carry.

He centered the light on my face again and barked something in Farsi. Probably something along the lines of, *Who are you? And what's that incomprehensible language you're spouting?*

I had several options. I could have hit them hard and fast and ended it there, but the odds of one of them discharging an errant shot and alerting the whole facility were too high. I needed a moment of confusion or minor distraction to level the playing field, so I acted like I didn't understand. Actually, it wasn't an act at all.

They separated, a step in either direction. This was a good move for them. Always create a wide V with your target in the center. But they didn't go far enough. I took a step to my left and narrowed the gap. Now they were too close together, more like one target than two. In the darkness, their ID badges seemed to shimmer against their dark uniforms. The corporal had a radio on his hip, but his hands were already full. I hadn't heard them sound an alarm or alert their superiors. *Big mistake.*

"Search him," the corporal ordered, bending his head in my direction. I understood the gesture, not the words.

The wrestler took a cautious step forward and carefully lowered his weapon. I chopped him across the throat, crushing his larynx. The rifle tumbled from his hands, and his hands automatically grasped his neck. His knees gave out. He stumbled, fell, and hit the near wall with an ugly thud.

I knew what was happening but really didn't see it, because I had already whipped to my right, seized the pistol grip of the corporal's rifle, and jabbed my index finger behind the trigger. He tried to fire but the trigger pressed against my knuckle, stopping the rifle from firing. I grabbed his other hand and drove my forehead into his nose: the hardest part of the head against the most vulnerable.

His nose exploded. The flashlight hit the pavement, and the sound echoed off the walls and died. I pivoted to the left, rolled him over my hip, and slammed him to the ground.

He lay still, his eyes wide circles of shock and pain. I braced my left forearm against his chest, slipped the F-S knife from my ankle sheath with the right, and drove the blade into his heart. No reason to sink the knife to the hilt. He stiffened for a moment and went slack.

The other soldier lay where he'd collapsed against the bottom of the wall. He cupped his throat and an ugly gurgle spilled from his lips. His feet churned spastically through the dirt. The flashlight illuminated his face, his features etched in agony. I sprang forward, put my hand over his mouth to shut him up, and shoved the F-S knife into his chest. His body jerked. I gave the blade a sharp twist and pulled it out, careful that blood didn't spurt over my hand. He settled against the dirt. I wiped the blade against his trouser leg and eased my knife back into its ankle sheath.

I turned the flashlight off and tucked it into the corporal's shirt pocket. I took his ID badge, struggled into his combat jacket, and traded my cap for his helmet. I clipped his radio to my belt. I thought about grabbing one of the G-3s, but I needed stealth, not a rifle capable of waking up every guard within a two-mile radius. Besides, I had my Walther, and a silenced Walther was as good a weapon as a man could have for this situation. I paused and reconsidered—a guard without a gun would raise a red flag in a hurry, so I slung a G-3 over my shoulder.

I dragged the dead soldiers deeper into the lane and down a narrow staircase to the landing. While I was there, I tried the door off the landing. It was locked.

I thought about the night's body count—three so far—but not from a morality standpoint. I had a mission to accomplish. The mission had direct consequences for my country. You start talking about dropping nukes on places like Tel Aviv or London or New York, you don't wait for it to happen. You get them before they get you. No, I was more worried about the attention I was potentially bringing to my mission.

I had destroyed the circuit boards Morshed was carrying, but that was a minor victory. It might have put a kink in the mullahs' immediate plans, but not in their long-term ones. Mahmoud Ahmadinejad's quest for nukes was not about to be stymied by the destruction of a briefcase full of electronics. My orders were to get inside the Natanz facility and see how far the rest of his program had progressed.

I stepped up to the mouth of the lane. I spent thirty seconds studying the aerial photo of the camp and used the GPS to target my position. Then I moved deeper into the complex. I needed to get underground. I could search every administration building and every warehouse from one end of the plant to the other, but I would need to get to the heart of the facility eventually.

I stayed in the shadows and followed an asphalt road deeper into the complex. A hundred or so meters farther on, the road forked. One side looped into a storage area with row after row of building materials. The other lane led to a vehicle entrance along the front of an immense concrete box a hundred meters wide and ten meters tall. There was a regular door on the right, a card reader beside the doorknob, and a security camera above. I decided to start there. Head down, I approached the door and swiped the corporal's ID badge. The door clicked open, and I walked in. So far, so good.

The door snuck into a narrow walkway. I dumped the corporal's rifle here, but not his jacket or cap.

The walkway merged almost at once with a concrete stairwell; I counted eighteen steps as I went down. The stairs accessed a tunnel a good thirty meters in length. Rows of dim yellow lamps on the ceiling illuminated the interior. The air had a diesel odor on top of the harsh chemical smell. A steel handrail separated a walkway from the vehicle concourse to my left. Rubber marks from extremely large tires marred the concrete. The whine of electric motors and the squeal of hydraulic machinery echoed from a cavernous room at the far end of the tunnel.

The walkway made a sharp right turn up ahead, and there was a door standing ajar at the far corner. I walked toward it at a brisk pace, my Walther palmed against my right side.

I was three strides away when the door popped open. A man in blue overalls with a device that looked a lot like an iPad in his hands emerged. His gaze flicked across me. My hope was that he would see a facility guard on the prowl, but it was not to be. Well, I wouldn't have believed, either. All he seemed to see was the muzzle of pistol and the silencer attached to the end. His eyes flared, and it wasn't anger; it was panic. I had to keep him quiet, but he didn't need to die. It was pure bad luck on his part that he'd stumbled onto me. Less an ill-advised act of heroism or stupidity, he might just live.

I pushed him back through the door. It turned out to be a generator room, and the noise was fierce. I closed the door and pantomimed the removal of his overalls. He got it. He stripped to his T-shirt and shorts. I used the tip of the Walther to suggest he get to his knees. He got that, too, though his hands were trembling, as if this might be his last moment. He shut his eyes tight and dipped his head.

I smacked him with the butt of the Walther, aiming for the hollow below his earlobe, the Kyusho Jitsu Dokko pressure point. Safe, but effective. He crumpled face-first to the floor. I touched his throat and felt a steady pulse. He'd wake up later with a gruesome headache, but at least he'd wake up.

I bound him with a section of generator wire and used a clean shop rag to gag him. I zipped on his overalls and made sure his ID badge dangled in front. I carried his electronic clipboard in my hand, walked out of the room, and locked the door behind me. So far, so good.

I rounded the corner, and things changed. The tunnel dropped even farther underground, and a room the size of two football fields gobbled it up. The walkway turned into a catwalk that traveled the circumference of the room and followed the tunnel. Placards warning of possible radioactivity decorated the walls. Cameras monitored the room from the ceilings, and I wondered briefly if any of these belonged to the UN inspection teams.

Pipes and ventilation ductwork crisscrossed the ceiling. The floor was crowded with some of the largest pieces of machinery I'd ever seen. Pallets were stacked high with metalworks, spools of cable, tubing, and steel drums as big as a man. The room stretched on and on for meters. It was hard to tell how far because of the dazzle of lights and a brown haze in the air. Men in blue overalls just like mine tended to the machinery. Others in exactly the kind of white smocks you'd expect to see in a lab moved like automatons. The activity was just as fierce as the noise. I was standing inside one of the most notorious nuclear facilities on the planet, but the intel wasn't right.

I needed to find the centrifuge plant, and this wasn't it. I needed to find the rocket assembly.

I followed the catwalk farther into the room, tracking the tunnel in the direction of a vehicle door large enough for a semi.

Twice, the vehicle door hummed and scrolled open. The first time, two forklifts loaded down with water-cooling equipment charged into the room. The second time, the bright headlights of a truck lit the tunnel and reflected off the catwalk. I faced an electrical junction box and feigned a workman's interest.

The truck rumbled through the tunnel and down the ramp into the room. It was a Russian military cargo carrier with drums lashed to the bed. A soldier sat in the back, a G-3 rifle slung across his chest. A worker in blue overalls guided the truck through a door to another room below.

I continued along the catwalk and found a niche between two vertical air ducts. I dug out my iPhone and surreptitiously engaged the recording app. I'd let the experts back home decipher the results.

I checked my watch. It had been nearly an hour since my arrival. I needed a way deeper into the complex. The catwalk farther on circled the room I was in, which made it a dead end. Trying to navigate the factory floor below would have been suicidal. There were maintenance ladders every hundred meters or so that traveled into the maze of ductwork along the ceiling, and I chanced a look through my digital telescope. I followed the nearest ladder up—the room's ceiling towered 150 feet into the air at least—and then traced the connecting skywalk to the far wall and a closed door.

Worth the risk.

It took thirty seconds to scale the ladder to the maintenance skywalk along the ceiling and another forty seconds to scurry along the skywalk to the door. I used the maintenance man's ID badge on the magnetic lock. It opened onto a second room, the convex shape of an airplane hangar only twice as large.

For the second time in two days, I'd struck gold.

Another centrifuge plant at least as large as the one in Qom. The tall, silver cylinders with their silver coils spiraling toward the ceiling looked like an army of clones awaiting their marching orders.

This was a place of serious business. The men and women monitoring the enrichment process looked like accountants and schoolteachers, not mad scientists with a mission of mass destruction. Everyone moved with purpose and calm, and, from what I could tell, I might have been the only one in this particular room with a weapon.

I ran my iPhone camera again on full zoom and stepped lightly along the skywalk. I knew I was already in way over my head, but intel was only as good as the pieces you put together into a cohesive whole. It might have been obvious to me what the hell was going on, but obvious wasn't what the politicians wanted. They wanted the entire picture. And since the guys I had to convince were politicians, that's what they were going to get. To hell with it.

I traveled through two more chambers before I found it. At first, I thought it was just another cavernous space laced with conveyor belts and roads and filled with cranes and trucks. But the security in this part of the plant was serious: guards in black uniforms with submachine guns stood at regular intervals.

I tracked the room grid by grid with the camera and froze when I saw the long, olive-green cylinders resting on the backs of seven flatbed trailers. Workers in blue overalls and technicians in white smocks climbed around the seven cylinders, busy as nursery ants tending their queen. In terms of size and shape, the cylinders mirrored those in the photos James Fouraz had shown me of Sejil-2 missiles, and I zoomed in to record as much detail as possible. The cap had been taken off the front end of each cylinder, exposing a concave circular plate with cable connectors and pipe fittings. I knew enough to understand that this was where the warhead and guidance system mated to the rocket.

All for nothing, right? After all, I had destroyed Morshed's circuit boards, and without them the Iranians were wasting their time. Well, I wasn't really convinced. That was far too easy and they could always buy more from the Chinese.

I crept farther along the catwalk. A twenty-foot-high white partition bisected the room, and the activity on the other side mirrored what I had just seen. There were workers and technicians fussing around seven more missiles.

One of the missiles seemed further along than the others: it had a conical device fitted to the front end. This had to be a nuclear reentry vehicle; I would have bet anything. Dozens of colored cables looped from the cone and the device inside to a battery of computers staffed by very serious technicians.

This had to be the nuke in the final phases of preparation. And there were six more cones waiting on trolleys next to their respective Sejil-2s.

I went into full evaluation mode, using rapid-identification techniques that had been ingrained in me over the last three decades and came to the conclusion that the men and women down there were acting as if these were live warheads. As badly as I wanted to believe that I had destroyed the critical electronic components that Morshed had been transporting into the country, the picture wasn't right.

All the intel I had collected indicated that the Iranians had twenty-one missiles. I had just accounted for fourteen of them. Okay, fine. Where the hell were the other seven?

I recorded as much as possible, then decided I should get the hell out while my luck was still holding. In case it didn't, I activated my iPhone to transmit the videos and photographs to General Rutledge. I don't know if I actually expected to get a satellite signal this far underground, but it didn't happen. Odd, but that made me more nervous than anything I had done in the last two hours. I took a deep breath and told myself to get a grip. Getting a grip really meant a steady, deep breath and driving my heart rate from seventy-six back to sixty-two. It took less than fifteen seconds but the pause still pissed me off.

The skywalk carried me back through four chambers and down to the catwalk in the first room. The catwalk and the tunnel merged again, and I jogged back to the rear entrance and outside. It was 3:36 A.M. The air bit into my skin, and I realized I was sweating.

If you expect the worst, there's probably a reason. The first thing I saw was a squad of soldiers hustling along the fence. It didn't look like your normal, everyday perimeter watch. Maybe because they were jogging, and maybe because I could heard their voices all the way across the compound. It was probably a safe bet they were looking for their two missing guards. Too bad they couldn't ask me, because I really could have saved them a lot of time.

I had a decision to make. Did I trust my disguise and my newly acquired

ID badge enough to use the old Daihatsu pickup truck I'd arrived in, or was that just asking for trouble? In either case, I needed my backpack, so I hurried across the compound to the door that led to the underground parking lot. I took the stairs two at a time and cut between three or four dozen cars to the parking space I had chosen more than two hours earlier. I was surprised how many cars had come and gone since I had ventured inside. For some reason, that didn't sit very well with me, and I decided against the truck.

I sidled up to the Daihatsu, keyed the lock, and reached casually inside. I hoisted my backpack. I went back up top.

I hadn't gone more than four or five strides when a man in overalls just like mine emerged from a side door of a detached, single-story office building on the far side of the lot. He had a courier bag slung over his back and was adjusting the neck strap of his helmet. He approached a Honda motorcycle and swung one leg over the seat.

There it was, my ticket out of Natanz.

The courier had the engine started and the headlight lit when he saw me coming. I raised my hand and called out to him like a long-lost friend, or at least a colleague in need of a helping hand or a cigarette. He eased back on the throttle and pointed to his helmet as if he hadn't heard me. He unsnapped the neck strap and lifted the helmet in two hands.

I smiled, said, "Good evening," in my best Farsi, and clotheslined him. He fell backward, and the motorcycle clattered to the ground.

He rolled to his side with surprising speed and drew a pistol from a belt holster. I had made a mistake: this was no ordinary courier, and I should have seen that even before I'd started his way.

Now I had to kill him. I kicked the gun from his hand and aimed mine at his head. One quick shot between his eyes.

I holstered the Walther, grabbed the collar of his jacket, and dragged him behind the building. I put on his helmet, goggles, and gloves, and slipped the courier bag over the shoulder opposite my backpack.

I walked calmly back to the Honda and jumped aboard. I turned the ignition. I'd grown up riding motorcycles. My biggest problem was always an

217

overwhelming urge to see whether a bike's speedometer was really accurate once you broke one hundred miles per hour. Of course, once you broke that mark, you didn't really care about the speedometer.

Not this time. I cruised along the asphalt lane toward the front gate of the complex at a crawl. I beeped the horn and flicked my high beams at the guards. I trusted my instinct that the guards were vigilant about keeping intruders out but not so vigilant keeping them in.

The security bar over the exit lane pivoted, and I scooted through. I goosed the throttle and headed back down the road toward Natanz. I reached the main highway and stopped long enough to access my iPhone, disarm the Russian suitcase bomb, and activate the device's self-destruct function. Then I turned north, toward Tehran. If I never saw Natanz again, it would be way too soon. Except maybe on the news, engulfed in the flames of a twenty-two-thousand-pound bunker buster.

I didn't stop until I got to Kashan. I parked the motorcycle a block from the safe house. It was still pitch dark outside and like a ghost town, so I used the alley. I jumped the fence into the backyard, followed a stone path through a rose garden waiting for spring to come, and stopped at the back door. I peered in. If Charlie and Jeri were still there, they were sitting in the dark.

I knocked softly. Knocked again. Jeri was all of a sudden standing behind me.

"Glad I'm one of the good guys," she whispered.

I turned my head. Smiled. "If you weren't, you'd be dead."

"Good to know." She brushed past me, all business. She turned the knob, and the door opened. "Charlie's inside. We didn't know when to expect you."

Charlie was in the kitchen. He was putting water on the burner of the stove. "Tea?" he said as if I lived next door.

"Hot. Very hot," I said.

They didn't say, *How'd it go?* or, *What the hell took you so long?*

We drank tea in silence for what seemed a long time. Finally, I said, "There's seven missiles missing."

"How inconsiderate," Charlie said. "Armed?"

"They were arming the other fourteen. I can only assume." I took out my iPhone. I gave Charlie and Jeri a blow-by-blow of the last twelve hours while I transmitted the videos from inside the plant to General Rutledge and Mr. Elliot. The files were huge. Even with compression technology, the iPhone's tiny antenna restricted bandwidth, and the process took agonizingly long minutes.

The transmission app finally beeped that the file transfer was completed.

Rutledge sent an alert. He needed to chat. No way he could have reviewed the videos already, so it had to be something else. I had a pretty good idea what it was.

"I saw the file," he said. "You got in." He didn't ask how.

"Academy Award–winning stuff," I said. "Party time."

"I'm on it as soon as we hang up." His face compressed into a ball of deep concentration. I'd seen the look before.

"Problem?"

"Yeah. Several."

"This have anything to do with Big Tuna?" I asked. We fell into basic tradecraft. Tag names only. Big Tuna: Atash Morshed. "I hope you don't want a word with him. He's under a bed in a hotel room. And the room probably doesn't smell particularly good right about now."

"It's about the aces," Tom said. He meant the circuits boards.

"Yeah, I know. The one's I took from him weren't the only ones, were they?" It may have sounded like a guess, but it wasn't. Not after what I'd seen in Natanz. "Spit it out. I'm a big boy."

"Big Tuna was a decoy. Six hours ago, we learned there were actually forty-eight aces. While we were busy tracking Big Tuna, another player hit the ground with twenty-four more."

"Makes sense. It was way too easy." I told him about the seven unaccounted-for Sejil-2 missiles.

"Okay, priority one is their TO," he said, meaning the missiles' targeting orders. Tom looked like he hadn't slept in a week, and his next statement sounded a bit like a man running on empty. "If there are any."

"I think it would be pretty dumb to assume otherwise, don't you think?"

219

"Roger that."

"I'm on it."

"I know you are," he said. "Keep the ball rolling, my friend."

"Fast and furious." We hung up.

I made a second call. Mr. Elliot must have had his finger on the Call button, because I heard his voice after a single ring. "You've been on with Orion," he said. Orion: General Rutledge.

"You've been eavesdropping."

"Which reminds me. Send a note to our friend in Virginia, will you? Catch him up before he has a heart attack," Mr. Elliot said. "And it'll give me a chance to see who he's talking to."

"Will do," I said. "Remember Panama City?"

I heard a short, discerning pause. Not a question, just a rapid shifting of gears that took him back nearly three decades. He said, "Oh, you mean when everyone and their brother showed up at our party uninvited." When he said *everyone,* he meant the ATF, the DEA, and a couple of guys from the FBI. "Jumped into our op with bullhorns blaring and bells clanging. What about it?"

"J.K." These were the initials of one of the Iranian drug cartel's bagmen at the aforementioned "party." His name was Jilil Kasra.

"Good-looking kid. Bright. Yeah, I remember."

"I need a photograph."

Mr. Elliot didn't ask why. If I made the request, it was important. He didn't ask by when. If I made the request, it meant as soon as possible. "Already done."

He hung up. I looked at Charlie and said to him, "Tell me about your eyes and ears in National Security." I was talking about the woman Charlie had recruited years ago to keep him informed about the comings and goings of Iran's infamous security service.

He nodded. "Jannata. What about her?"

"We need her to find an old friend of mine named Jilil Kasra."

CHAPTER 22

KASHAN—DAY 9

Mr. Elliot delivered Jilil Kasra's photograph in less than twenty minutes. It was a twenty-seven-year-old mug shot that the Panama City, Florida police had, by pure luck, transferred to microfiche twenty-some years back instead of destroying it.

That's where I'd met Jilil Kasra, in a Panama City jail cell after the boys from Alcohol, Tobacco, Firearms, and Explosives blew up an op I was running out of South Bimini.

The ATF didn't get the guys my op had been targeting; in fact, all they really managed to do was scare off the guys my op was targeting. Not their fault. Instead, they'd ended up with Jilil Kasra, two other twenty-something Iranian bagmen, and me.

They threw us into a holding cell. I had a couple of days to kill before Mr. Elliot did his thing and got me released, so I spent the time getting to know Jilil. No, I wasn't being nice. I was working. I saw a potential asset. In exchange for Jilil's cooperation, Mr. Elliot got two years trimmed off his four-year sentence.

I'd stayed in touch with Jilil even after he returned to Iran. I had kept track of him until the shah was deposed, and then he'd disappeared. Maybe he was dead. I didn't think so.

We transferred the photo onto Charlie's computer. He and Jeri stared at it. "We need to find this guy," I said. "He was government back in the shah's day. But he changed his name when the ayatollah took charge."

"Better than dangling from the end of a crane in the middle of Revolution Square," Jeri offered.

"I won't argue that."

"And you want me to show this guy's picture to Jannata hoping for what exactly? Like maybe she ran into him in some government cafeteria eating hummus and grape leaves?" Charlie said. The guy had a sense of humor, but I was too exhausted to laugh.

"I want her to run it through the government's labor-pool records. You and I both know that National Security watches their own people as close as they watch anyone else."

"Closer," Jeri said. "And a photo search wouldn't be that uncommon."

Charlie shook his head. "She'll need a reason. And a good one."

"Charlie. If you ask Jannata, she'll come up with a reason. That's why you pay her," I said. "And if you need to tell her how important it is, tell her." And then I thought to add, "Because it is."

We had to wait until morning before Charlie could make contact with Jannata, so we traveled back to Seyfabad via helicopter. The trip took an hour and thirty-five minutes, and Jeri kept the chopper so low to the ground that the barren hills off our port side looked like angry waves on a dirty brown sea. The girl knew how to fly.

Charlie made his call to Jannata as we drove from Seyfabad toward the city. They had a system. Jannata always carried a prepaid phone. Charlie's people smuggled thousands of them a year into the country, and the black market sold them like hotcakes.

"One of my really hot numbers," Charlie said about the phones. "I like my people to carry them, too. We change Jannata's out every ten days, just to be safe."

Charlie caught Jannata on her way into the office. It was a one-sided conversation, but I didn't get the impression that she was all that excited by his request. I heard him say, "I'm sending the photo over right now. Check your phone. Download it, and then toss it. Call me as soon as you get a hit. And, Jannata. Top priority."

Jannata called Charlie back from a bus stop across the street from the Ministry of Interior forty-three minutes later. By then, Charlie and I had twelve men in position just waiting for orders.

Jannata had chosen the location intentionally because that was exactly where Jilil Kasra acted as the department's deputy minister, a very powerful position. He was on the eighth floor, corner office, facing our way.

"His name is Pasha Fardin," Charlie said. "Any reference to your guy Jilil Kasra was lost during the revolution. Very convenient."

"He's done well for himself," I said.

"I wish he hadn't done quite so well," Jeri chimed in rather sarcastically. "A deputy minister? Sure be a lot easier to get to him if he was the janitor."

"But a janitor wouldn't have any information about an impending attack on Israel," I said without an ounce of emotion in my voice. "And that's exactly what he's going to tell me."

Charlie twisted his head around and stared at me from the front seat. I caught Jeri's reflection in the rearview mirror, and her eyes were cold and calculating. She said, "Your powers of persuasion must be off the charts, Jake. And I want to be there when you ask him."

Charlie was holding his cell phone against his chest. "So, what do I tell Jannata? I assume you have a plan."

"She needs to get Jilil a message without waking up the entire security apparatus. So it can't be sent electronically or over the phone."

Charlie shrugged. I loved it when he shrugged, because it meant the answer was as plain as the nose on my face. "She could hand deliver it. If someone's making inquiries about someone in the Ministry of Interior, she'd probably want to investigate it in person, wouldn't she?"

Jeri looked at me in the mirror. Her expression said, *And all this time I thought you were the expert.*

"Too easy," I said. But Mr. Elliot had a theory that he made sure I never forgot: the more complicated you make things, the more things can go wrong.

Charlie showed me his palms. "Jannata's waiting."

"Okay. This is how she does it. She walks in with her briefcase, laptop, files, whatever looks most official, most natural. She flips the light switch two times so we know she's in. Then she hands Jilil a business card and a disposable phone. On the back of the card, she writes, 'Remember Panama City? You still owe me a cup of coffee.' Then she hands him the phone, and I call it."

Charlie repeated the instructions into the phone. Before he hung up, I added, "Make sure she doesn't leave the card or the phone."

"She's on the way." Charlie hung up. He handed me a disposable phone with Jannata's number already on the screen.

Less than a minute later, the lights in Jilil's eighth-floor office flicked on and off twice. I counted thirty seconds in my head and dialed the number. Jilil Kasra answered. He said, "Yes?"

"Hello, my friend. It's been a long time. Time we caught up. Ten minutes from now at Café Rumi. You know where it is, I'm sure. Does that work for you?" Always polite, always mannerly. Basic tradecraft.

After a nearly interminable silence, Jilil Kasra answered, "Yes. That's fine."

"Good. Very good. And please talk to no one else in the meantime, my friend." I let the words sink in. "And now if you'll hand the phone back to my associate."

The phone went dead in my ear. "Okay. Good." I looked at Charlie. "Send a text to our surveillance guys. Game on. And Charlie, we don't let this guy out of our sight for even a second."

Café Rumi occupied a corner lot on Mir Avenue across from Laleh Park, and Jeri and I walked the last block while Charlie coordinated surveillance. You couldn't get away from people, which was exactly why I'd chosen it. The confluence of foot traffic from government buildings in either direction, shops and restaurants and apartment houses to the west, and the park to the east made it a free-for-all of tourists and town folk. Perfect. And no one would think a thing of a government employee like Jilil Kasra, aka Pasha Fardin, spending his break there.

My phone vibrated when we were three doors away from the café, signaling an incoming text message from Charlie: *All clear.*

The café was packed when Jeri and I walked in, but a table in the corner came open when a young couple—part of our team—pulled up stakes and walked out arm in arm. Jeri and I made our way to the table. I watched the door while she ordered coffee.

I was trying to imagine a fifty-year-old Jilil Kasra when a man in a very nicely tailored suit walked in with a newspaper tucked under his arm. He'd lost his hair and his mustache was gray, but there was still an air of aristocracy about him. Also an air of sadness. I tried to gauge the depth of his anxiety after reading Jannata's note and talking to me on the phone, but he seemed more raptorial than hunted. I took that as a good sign.

I didn't raise my hand. When his eyes moved across our table, I shared a nod so brief and nondescript that only a man in search of it would have noticed. He didn't come over immediately, which was smart. He went to the counter. When he looked over at me again, he had a cup of tea in his hand. I nodded again and pushed a chair out with my foot.

He was sitting across from us ten seconds later. The veneer of calm held up pretty well as we shook hands. "You've come a long way from Panama City," I said.

"You got my sentence reduced by two years," he replied. "I never had the chance to thank you. I suppose that's why you're here."

"I wish it were that simple." I nodded in Jeri's direction. "This is Rika."

Jeri reached out her hand. I had no idea where the name Rika had come from, but she played it well.

"It's a pleasure," Jilil said.

"Don't be so sure," Jeri answered, her smile beguiling.

"I only have ten minutes," he said to me.

I didn't mince words, but I did lower my voice. "I've been inside the underground facilities in Qom and Natanz, Jilil, and I know you're arming rockets with nuclear weapons."

His eyes nearly popped from their sockets. His surprise was completely genuine. "You're insane."

"The evidence has been transmitted to my government. They would agree that there is insanity at work here, but they don't seem to think it's me," I said calmly.

He saw the look in my eyes and knew I had used exactly two sentences to put a blanket over any argument he could possibly have made. He used two hands to lift his tea to his lips and still managed to spill it. He set the cup back down, leaned back in his chair, and crossed his arms over his chest.

The digital voice recorder that I took out of my pocket was hardly bigger than my index finger. It was podcast ready. It had a noise reducer and a bunch of recording modes I didn't care about. I set it on the table. Pressed the Record button.

I said, "You're planning an attack on Israel. When?"

He stared at me as if his world was about the come crashing down on him. He shook his head, three quick jerks, like a man warding off an attack. "I'm only the deputy minister of interior. I couldn't possibly know that."

I reached across and turned off the tape recorder. Kept my hand on it just to let him know that I would be asking the same question in a matter of seconds. "I could threaten you with the fact that National Security will put two and two together and conclude they have a traitor on their hands. I could also tell you that I can make sure they don't put two and two together."

I saw just a glimpse of hope, a blush touching high cheekbones and the minutest dilation of the eyes. *Take him, Jake.* "Instead, I'm going to ask you to save a few million lives, Jilil. Simple. No one will ever know except me, you, and Rika, but you'll be able to look yourself in the mirror every night and know you did the right thing. Oh, and maybe a few very important people in Washington. People positioned to make your life and your family's lives better than you could have ever imagined them."

I didn't wait for an answer. I turned on the voice recorder again. I said, "You're planning an attack on Israel. When?"

He stared at the voice recorder. He glanced at the watch on his left wrist. He said, "Three days and fifteen hours from today."

CHAPTER 23

TEHRAN—DAY 10

I slid a prepaid phone across the table to Jilil Kasra. He was, for all intents and purposes, a dead man. It was my fault. I had dragged a traitor into my op, something I would never have done had it been any other op. The reason was simple. Had it been any other op, I would have shut it down long ago.

"Don't go back to your office, Jilil. Under any circumstances," I said to him. "You have an emergency escape plan, right?"

"Yes." Of course he had an emergency escape plan. How silly. Every high-ranking official in every dictatorship in the world had one, because the moment a dictator fell, which they all did eventually, the witch hunt began. Get out or die.

I pointed to the phone. "Call me when you're out of the country."

He got up. I watched him until he was outside Café Rumi. I nodded to Jeri. "Make sure we're clean."

She jumped up and followed him out the door and down the street.

While she was gone, I downloaded the audio from the voice recorder to my iPhone, marked the file "Priority One," and transmitted it in separate e-mails to General Tom Rutledge and Mr. Elliot.

I didn't wait for a response. I took a last sip of my coffee, came to my feet, and sauntered out of the café as casually as possible. The kind of intel I had just extracted from the deputy minister of Iran's Ministry of Interior got the blood churning in a big-time way. It also made me realize there was still work to be done.

I was two steps from the door when Jeri reappeared. She caught me by the arm and steered me back inside.

"Problem?"

"Let's use the back door." We walked right past the counter and through the kitchen. Jeri smiled at a chef, two waiters, and a guy in a wrinkled suit. She said something in Farsi that I didn't understand, and the guy in the suit gestured toward the back door.

When we were outside in the alley, I said, "Jilil?"

"Not Jilil. He looked like a man headed back to work and hoping no one would know he was gone. But I saw a couple of cars that looked just a little out of place, and we've still got a traitor on the loose. Why risk it."

We hustled down the alley, and she placed a call to Charlie. "Abu. Head of the alley. A block east of the café. Just a precaution."

We were inside the car fifteen seconds later—Jeri in front and me in back—and Charlie, looking as fresh as a daisy.

"I saw them," he said as we worked our way through the neighborhoods west of the park. "Two cars that didn't belong. Our guys are on it. If they can pick up their trail, maybe we can pin them down."

I didn't say anything. Like Jeri had said, there was still a traitor out there, and if they tracked me to Café Rumi and a meeting with a government minister, then they were as good as in my back pocket. It took twenty minutes to work our way into the Ajoudaniyeh neighborhood. We dumped the car in a parking lot next to a busy market and walked three blocks to an abandoned warehouse. Charlie's IT team had already set up shop on the second story.

Six guys and two women were huddled over banks of laptops in the middle of the room. They had honed a routine of setting up and tearing down their equipment to a well-rehearsed drill. They could hardwire their laptops to a secure router and connect the router to a satellite dish in two minutes. And still have time left over to connect the entire setup to my iPhone when the need arose. They could dismantle the operation and be out the door in ninety seconds. What took the longest time was brewing tea and fixing kabobs for their breaks.

The guy in the bow tie, the one Jeri called Amur, gave me an update. "You know that we narrowed our search to eleven potential targets. All with MEK connections and four with substantial government interaction."

"We've got to get that number down fast," I said, looking from Jeri to Amur. "What's the plan?"

"Tell him," Jeri said.

"We sent out some electronic chatter that makes it sound like you're in for an important rendezvous later tonight. Places all over town. A coffee shop, an abandoned warehouse, a bazaar, a kabob stand, a late-night bookstore. Places like that. Eleven different places. One for each candidate. All at nine P.M."

"That's a lot of manpower. We got it covered?"

When I asked this, Amur deferred to Charlie. He said, "My guys will work in two-man teams, watching all eleven rendezvous locales. Should be enough. If someone shows, we'll pull in some other guys for surveillance. Sound good to you?"

"Your guys have been great so far, Charlie. I couldn't ask for a better team." I stole a deep breath and let my eyes travel around the warehouse. We had hacked in to Tehran's central phone exchange and Internet sites all over the country. We had tagged a half-dozen government databases. We had a direct line into the NSA and computers so strong that no one really knew their full capabilities; or at least I sure didn't.

We had gigabytes of data and some very sharp guys analyzing it. All this information at our fingertips provided the illusion of control. The operative word here was *illusion*. Because a whole lot of this mission remained outside my control. The MEK was a perfect example. They were birds of prey waiting patiently to strike. I was the guy providing the opportunity. They needed me, and I needed them, as much as I hated to admit it. They had contacts within the

Iranian military command and the upper echelons of the government. They had people in every university in the country. They had people in the media. They had eyes and ears on the street. But they also had someone in the high levels of their own organization playing a very dangerous game. And I was their target.

They had already missed me twice. A third attempt was inevitable.

"So?" I heard Charlie's voice and let out a slow, deep breath. Jeri, Amur, Charlie. They were all looking at me. Charlie put a hand on my shoulder. "You look a little frayed, my friend."

"Nothing a hot cup of tea won't mend," I said.

"I might join you," he said.

I turned and looked Charlie square in the eye. "How you feeling about Bagheri, Charlie? Gut feeling?"

Charlie raised his shoulders. "I wouldn't exactly call him a friend, Jake, but he's running too scared to be our traitor."

My eyes settled on Jeri. She gave me a curt nod, as if I were asking her opinion. I wasn't. I had already made up my mind. But it was good to know she was onboard. "Okay. Nine o'clock tonight. Let's see if we can sniff this guy out."

Amur, a guy who wore bow ties and pop-bottle glasses, didn't look like a man of action, but he snapped his fingers and started issuing orders to the rest of Charlie's team as if he'd been doing it his whole life.

I pulled Charlie aside. "Hey, I've been meaning ask. Your nephew . . ."

"Azran." The one who had caught the brunt of the explosion at the hotel three days earlier.

"Yeah. How's he doing?"

"Better. He'll even play soccer again if things keep going as well as they have been," Charlie said. "Thanks for asking."

One of his prepaid phones chimed. He dug it out of his pocket and stared at the incoming number. Looked at me and said, "Bagheri."

I nodded, and he answered it. They talked for sixty seconds, in typically rapid-fire Farsi. Then Charlie held the phone against his chest and said to me, "He wants to talk. Somebody high up the chain has information to share. Very big-time information."

"Who?" If there was suspicion in my voice, it was very intentional.

"Bagheri won't say over the phone. Too sensitive."

"How high up the chain?"

"Any higher and it would be Mahmoud Ahmadinejad himself, was how Bagheri put it," Charlie said. "How shall we play it?"

"Like we're in charge. And like we don't entirely trust anyone. Which we don't. Especially a guy with a mole running around in his organization," I replied. I turned to Amur and said, "Pull up a street map, can you?"

All Amur did was punch a single key on his computer, and a detailed map of Tehran was on the screen seconds later. "Okay," I said. "We move him around. Just like we used to do in the old days, Charlie. Tell him to bring Moradi. No one else. Not even his top lieutenant."

Charlie was shaking his head. "That's like asking your president and vice president to sneak out the back door of the White House without telling the Secret Service."

"Like we care." I didn't even bother to look Charlie's way. "And just for the record, I happen to know that the vice president is one badass driver."

We plotted three different points along Hemmat Highway, and Charlie relayed the first of these to Yousef Bagheri. He hung up and grinned. "He's not going to like the runaround."

"Listen. He's been compromised. So has Moradi. You think our traitor doesn't know that we're reaching out to these two? Of course he does. This counterop we're running is as much for Bagheri as it is for us. And if he expects anything less, then he doesn't know the rules of engagement."

Charlie held up his hands like a man surrendering. "You convinced me. Okay? I'm convinced." Then he gathered three of his bodyguards together and gave them their instructions. "When Bagheri shows up at our designated locations, make sure it's safe. If he has any baggage other than Moradi, the deal's off. If he's clean, we move him on to the next one. If the second one looks se-cured, we plan our meet for number three. *Tayeb*?"

"*Tayeb,*" one of them said.

"Good. Go."

I watched the three as they jogged toward the back stairs, then I discon-nected my iPhone and severed the uplink to the NSA. Charlie's IT team would remain in the warehouse for another hour before breaking camp. They'd set up again in another location just before sunset and monitor the movements of the eleven men still on our list of potential traitors. With any luck, we'd be one step closer to finding our guy. A very real alternative was that our guy would be one step closer to finding me.

Charlie, Jeri, and I returned to our car. Jeri drove, and I laid in back. We made a quick stop at a café that Charlie owned near the Goodarzi Market just off Daroos. I couldn't remember my last decent meal. We huddled in a private room off the kitchen. The chef brought rice, cheese, and apricots. Then he served a soup made with pomegranates, a stew he called *khoresht,* and a yogurt drink known as *doogh.*

Charlie didn't say a word. He wasn't particularly nervous or distracted, just quiet. Not Jeri. She went on and on about Iranian soccer and how the na-tional team had just pounded a team from Greece. I wanted to tell her that every-one pounds the team from Greece, but I was too busy keeping track of Bagheri and Moradi on my iPhone map.

We finished lunch just about the time the surveillance teams confirmed that the two MEK chiefs were alone and safe. *Safe* was the magic word. Time for a rendezvous.

We left the restaurant and drove to a parking lot next to a strip mall on east Damavand Street. Charlie was on his phone the entire time. His men had swept the area and given the all clear. No MEK. No National Security. They posted lookouts along a four-block radius.

Charlie hung up. He glanced over at Jeri. "Keep an eye out for a white Volvo."

"He probably took it through the car wash on the way here," she said with an abundance of sarcasm.

Charlie used a prepaid phone to dial Bagheri's number. "Park next to the curb. Grab a seat with us, and we'll get this done," I heard him say.

A moment later, a white Volvo sedan—spotless, as Jeri had predicted—cruised east on Damavand, slowed, and halted against the curb. Bagheri got out from behind the wheel, a big man in a maroon shirt with a big gold necklace, big sunglasses, and a big mustache. Moradi looked positively dowdy next to his boss.

We rolled out of the parking lot and glided up close to the pair. I unlatched the right rear door and threw it open. "Gentlemen. Climb aboard."

Moradi slipped in first and slid toward the middle. Bagheri threw his bulk in and slammed the door. Jeri had the car rolling even before the MEK chief removed his sunglasses, and we shot down Hemmat Highway.

Bagheri surprised me by saying, "Thanks for watching our backs. This situation is beginning to piss me off."

I wanted to say something terribly sarcastic, like, *That's what happens when you recruit second-rate talent,* but I didn't. Hell, for all I knew the office of the deputy director of operations of my own CIA was compromised. Who was I to talk? So instead, I said, "So? You mentioned someone way up the food chain. Who?"

Bagheri said simply, "Armeen Navid."

"Air force general Armeen Navid?" Charlie blurted. I was impressed that Charlie was so impressed.

Bagheri nodded. He said, *"Arteshbod."*

"Arteshbod?" I asked. My eyes flashed from Charlie to Bagheri and back again.

"The big cheese," Charlie said.

"The head of Iranian Air Defense Forces," Bagheri answered. "That enough cheese for you?"

"The head of the Iranian Air Defense. I see," I said. Yeah, I knew they could hear the skepticism in my voice. But intel coming from a source this highly placed was about as rare as finding a good bottle of single-malt scotch in a hamburger joint. "And this guy wants to stick his neck out why?"

"Navid is Persian first and Shia second," Bagheri replied. He must have see the skepticism flash across my face. "Yeah, I know. A rare bird. But General Navid is a pragmatist. He knows what a nuclear war will do to our country. And if stopping such a war means dealing with the Great Satan . . ."

"The Great Satan! You wouldn't be talking about my country, would you, Mr. Bagheri?" I interrupted.

Bagheri shrugged as if to say, *Who else?* Then he went right on, as if I hadn't said a word. ". . . And branding himself as a turncoat, then so be it. General Navid is ready."

"A man who takes the long view. I'm impressed," I deadpanned. Jeri had exited the highway. She was wending her way into a residential area, her eyes monitoring her rearview mirror as if the boogeyman himself might be lurking behind us. I asked, "How close are you to the general, Mr. Bagheri?"

Bagheri shrugged. "We're estranged acquaintances at best. He doesn't agree with my methods. I don't agree with his. But if your question is how much do I trust him? As much as you do your friend Charlie here."

"Okay." My voice might have been calm and collected, but that had nothing to do with the magnitude of the situation. A guy like General Armeen Navid was the mother lode. He was in a position to confirm everything I'd learned so far, and it sure as hell helped to have more than one source when the end game is a military strike. I said, "So what is it that brings you and Navid together?"

Bagheri didn't hesitate. "What brings the general and me together is an acute understanding that Mahmoud Ahmadinejad's proclivity toward the destruction of Israel and the unbelievers who support her will leave Iran in ruins."

There was a lot of danger here. A mild understatement if ever there was one. But there was also the greatest of opportunities, if the MEK chief was right. I looked over at Moradi. He hadn't said a word so far, and it was time to get a read on the man from Amsterdam.

"Kouros?" I used his first name. Very personal.

"We worked together how many times?" he said to me. "Five, six times?

Always with the same goals. We're not friends, but there is respect. And you're not leaving Iran without talking to this General Navid. I know you better than that."

I gave him credit for holding my eye. He wasn't lying. He was all in. Just like he'd always been for the last thirty years.

"Okay, but we use my rules," I said.

Bagheri shook his head. "No, I'm sorry. Navid's rules. He walks around with National Security draped around his shoulders. There are maybe three or four places where he can actually let his guard down, and one of those is his cousin's place in Mehran. And it's already arranged. The meet is scheduled for suppertime. Navid eats there a couple of times a week, so it won't raise an eyebrow."

"And what do you suggest I do? Walk up and knock on his cousin's door? That doesn't sound too suspicious." My cynicism was getting the best of me.

Bagheri handled it well. He gave me a cool smile. "You're a man of mystery. Be mysterious."

"A nice compliment, I suppose, but I'm actually very old-fashioned. I prefer a solid plan with a solid back-up plan,"

"So my friend Kouros tells me." He gave a twist of the head in Moradi's direction.

The man from Amsterdam reached into the inside pocket of his rumpled tweed jacket and extracted a single sheet of paper. It looked like a crudely drawn map. He said, "General Navid's cousin owns an herb-and-spice shop in the Grand Bazaar. Just off the main junction in Green Square."

Moradi didn't hand the map to me. He passed it to Charlie, and Charlie said, "We'll find it."

"Come at five o'clock this evening. Things will just be getting busy," Moradi said. He held my eye. "Come alone. Sorry, but that's the way it has to be."

"I think I can manage," I said.

Moradi had said, "Come alone," but he was smart enough to know I would have serious countersurveillance every step of the way. Were there risks? Sure. But at least I could feel pretty confident that I wasn't going to be driven out into the desert and shot in the head. "What's this cousin's name?" I asked.

"Sa'ra Milad. But she won't be there," Bagheri said. "Look for a man wearing a red-and-yellow soccer jersey."

"A man after my own heart," Jeri couldn't resist saying from the front seat.

"Ask him for blue ginger," Bagheri said. "He'll deliver you to the cousin's house in the back of a delivery van. It's a trip he makes three times a week, so there will be no suspicion. He'll also deliver you back to the bazaar after your meeting is concluded."

"I can live with that plan," I said. There was nothing in their voices that suggested a trap, and a man's voice was always the best barometer of deceit. A part of me wanted to issue some kind of subtle threat against any kind of treachery, just in case, but I was relying on my instincts. And my instincts told me the two MEK men were on the level. I caught Jeri's eye in the rearview mirror. "Let's get them back."

We had circled the neighborhood and returned to Bagheri's Volvo. The two MEK men wanted to shake hands and act as if we'd created some special bond. I just wanted them out of the car. I shook their hands anyway. I said, "General Navid's involvement doesn't go beyond this car, gentlemen. Maybe that goes without saying."

"Oh, it most certainly goes without saying," Bagheri said. The MEK boss looked as tired as he did determined.

Bagheri put on his sunglasses and got out. Moradi said, "Good luck tonight, Jake," and followed.

CHAPTER 24

We waited until they were in their car before driving away. Charlie's bodyguards appeared from both side streets, and we suddenly had an escort—an escort I could have done without. I didn't say anything.

"What do you think?" I asked Charlie instead.

"Bagheri's on our side. He's got as much to lose in this fight as anyone. Moradi doesn't impress me, but he didn't strike me as a threat."

"Moradi has been fighting the good fight since the ayatollah was in power. I don't think he'd know what to do if the tables turned."

"I think there's a lot of people in my country like that, Jake. Me included. You never get used to oppression, but it becomes easier to tolerate as time goes by," Charlie admitted. "Revolution is a game for the young. And I think the youth of Iran are ready."

"Damn right we are," Jeri said. She didn't bother looking at me in the mirror. I could hear the pride in her voice.

I wanted to say, *Let's hope to hell so,* but I didn't. Instead, I did a 180 and said, "I need to make a couple of calls, Charlie. Where can I get some privacy?"

"We need petrol," Jeri said. "Let's make a stop."

The gas station was nestled on one corner of an intersection in an old neighborhood not five minutes away. Both Jeri and Charlie got out, but not before his bodyguards were in place. She pumped the gas, while Charlie talked to the guy behind the counter. Charlie was smart. He did all his business with people he knew. Hard to get burned that way.

I opened a secure NSA uplink on my iPhone. I sent the information about General Armeen Navid to three-star general Tom Rutledge and Mr. Elliot. I tagged Navid "Bluebird." Then I called Tom directly.

"Bluebird's the real deal, my friend," Tom said, using Navid's tag. "If he's on the level, this will put us over the top."

"Get me everything you've got on the guy. He and I are going head-to-head in less than four hours."

"I'm going to need our friend in Virginia for this one," he said, referring to the CIA's deputy director of operations. "I know you think he's dirty."

"Our friend in Virginia isn't dirty," I replied, wasting time on a subject that needed no discussion. "But he's not running a clean ship. If he's not willing to do the legwork, they you're going to have to go over his head. You up to that?"

"I'll put in a call to our friend at Penn Central. He's got the pull," General Rutledge said. What Tom was saying was that it was not in his best interest to go over DDO Wiseman's head, and that made perfect sense to me. Chief of Staff Landon Fry, on the other hand, was in a position to do that.

"Roger that," I said and ended the call.

I called Mr. Elliot. I said, "Bluebird and I have a date this evening. Feedback?"

I could hear Mr. Elliot thinking; you didn't get a prize like General Navid very often. "Interesting. Trying to save his country's ass, is he? Good for Bluebird. He's just the man for the job."

"That's all I need to hear. I'll be in touch. And by the way, things are getting waist-deep in politics, if you wouldn't mind keeping an ear to the ground."

"Done."

I hung up and put the iPhone away. I knocked on the window to get Jeri's attention, and we were on the road again thirty seconds later. We dropped Jeri at an apartment building close to the airport, where our countersurveillance team had reassembled for the surveillance op on eleven MEK agents suspected of trying to sell out my mission.

"Bring home a traitor," I said to her. It was a long shot. Eleven was a big number. Maybe we'd get it down to three or four. Then we could do a clean sweep and apologize later for any collateral damage.

Charlie took me to the Grand Bazaar. I found the herb-and-spice shop near the main junction and the man with the yellow-and-red soccer jersey. The van out back had a cluster of spice bottles printed on the side below the word ADVIEH.

General Navid's cousin lived in a gated community twenty-five minutes north. The community had fortress written all over it, with the guards to prove it. They didn't even stop the van. The driver waved, just like he did every day, I imagined. I was in the back, gagging on the overwhelming scent of cumin. Sa'ra Milad's house was very modest. It was neatly tended with yellow walls and white trim. A small square of lawn was framed by neat gardens, with tall, leafy trees along the curb. Norman Rockwell would have been proud.

The van didn't stop until it was inside the third stall in a three-car garage.

Two armed guards were waiting for me at the entrance. They relieved me of my Walther but didn't bother about my digital recorder or my iPhone. Fine with me. I reached into my pocket and activated the recording app on the phone. A little backup never hurt.

Sa'ra turned out to be an older, slightly built woman, who seemed to appreciate the gravity of this meeting. She led me into the kitchen, where a man in his early fifties, athletically built, with closely cropped hair and a deeply tanned complexion, was brewing tea. He had a lean face and a hawk nose rounding the top of an impressive mustache. Despite his civilian clothes—a really uninspired ocher shirt tucked into blue trousers—he projected the confident bearing of a career soldier. No mistaking it.

He waited for me to speak first. I said the scripted words exactly as Bagheri had written them: "General Navid, a mutual friend sends his regards."

He reached out then and shook my hand. "Welcome. Sit." He pointed to the kitchen table. Very homey. I took my usual place with my back to the wall. I laid my digital voice recorder on the table. Navid served tea. He took the chair opposite me, his brown eyes troubled, but hardly conflicted. I would have given anything for a cup of really strong coffee, a dark roast with a good blast of cream. It was not to be.

I followed his lead, spicing the tea with honey and a cinnamon stick. Did I say very homey? It took a sip. Ghastly. Now it was my turn to wait, but I didn't have to wait long.

Without preamble, Navid reached into his shirt pocket and withdrew a gray memory stick. He placed the memory stick in my hand and wrapped his fingers around mine. The troubled look in his eyes vanished.

"Let me assure you of the moral dilemma this places me in." His English, though heavily accented, was precise. "I am no fan of the United States of America. I provide this information for one reason only: to save my homeland from disaster. Perhaps with luck, your country can use what I've given you to prevent a nuclear holocaust. To do that, you'll have to destroy the missiles on their launch platforms. Many of my fellow soldiers will perish." Navid squeezed my hand and let go. "Good men will die. By giving you this information, I'll be as culpable in their deaths as the pilots who drop bombs on them."

"We could talk about where the blame rests until the cows come home, General. And there's plenty of it to go around. But let's not. I might get pissed off." I held the memory stick between my thumb and index finger. "What's on this?"

"First, let me explain Ahmadinejad's strategy," Navid said. "He knows, should he launch an attack, to expect immediate retaliation."

"I think that comes under the heading of no-brainers, General."

"But he's hedging his bets by not expending his nuclear arsenal in one blow. He has twenty-one missiles in his strike force. These he has divided into three batteries of seven missiles each."

Navid pointed to the memory stick. "That lists the targets of the first two batteries. The first battery will launch missiles against Tel Aviv and Israeli military bases."

"Yes, I know. The attack takes place in two days." He didn't flinch when he heard this, nor did he ask where the information had come from. "I need confirmation. Two days from today. Yes or no?"

I waited. And waited some more. He looked at me, and all I saw was opportunity. I had no time for the anguish. Finally, he said, "Yes."

"And Ahmadinejad thinks he's going to get away with this." I didn't wait for an answer. "The second one of those nukes pokes its nose out of a silo, it's over. Israel will know within seconds, and they'll launch a counterattack seconds later."

"Of course they will. But our missiles will be airborne by then. That can't happen." Navid lowered his hand and his expression turned more morose. "The targets of the second battery of missiles include the U.S. Navy Sixth Fleet at Gaeta, Italy, and NATO bases around the Mediterranean and eastern Europe."

I tucked the memory stick into a pocket. "And the last seven missiles?"

"The third battery is Ahmadinejad's trump card. Those missiles are targeted at major cities within range." Navid's tone turned icy and foreboding. "Rome. Nuremberg. Munich. Istanbul. Vienna. Athens. And our president will settle scores against our Sunni brothers by wiping out Riyadh."

I wanted to say, *Never happen,* except that it was happening. One madman's definition of Armageddon and here it lay before us, as real as tomorrow. A nuclear inferno. Tens of millions dead. And for no other reason than to satisfy a murderous craving.

"Something else," Navid added. "When Ahmadinejad launches his attack, he, the top mullahs of the Revolutionary Council, and the senior officers of the Military High Command will be in a secret underground bunker. The coordinates of the bunker are on the memory stick as well."

The man had just signed their death warrants. *Nicely done, General.*

I said, "And you? You're in the high command."

"I'll be at my post in the Air Defense Headquarters at Mehrabad."

"That's got to be a priority target for a retaliatory strike if ever there was one."

"I won't abandon my men," he said.

Foolish, but honorable, I supposed. I tapped the memory stick. "None of this means a hill of beans without the launch-site locations, General. I assume they're on here."

He was already shaking his head. "The launch sites haven't yet been selected. When I get them, I'll relay them as fast as possible."

Unfortunately, what he was saying made sense. The launch sites would remain hidden until the very last. So be it. I was prepared to give him a secure e-mail address, when he shook his head and said, "Not electronically. National Security will be monitoring everything but my pacemaker. I have already chosen a courier. My most trusted envoy, rest assured."

A courier. His most trusted envoy. I didn't like it and said so. He didn't budge. "When I know, I'll have our mutual friend set it up." He meant Bagheri; and for me, just one more thing not to like.

He stood up and took my hand. "We'll see you back the same way you arrived. Please take care."

And just like that, the meeting with General Armeen Navid was over.

CHAPTER 25

When the job description says "collect intel," there is also an unwritten sidebar that says, "Don't think about it too much. Just deliver the goods and move on."

I wasn't all that good at the rules of the unwritten sidebar back when the bad guys were drug lords and cyber terrorists and arms dealers. Back then, Mr. Elliot and some other guys I never knew and never wanted to know were in charge of turning the intel into action; I rarely had the pleasure of taking down the criminals I'd set up. Now the bad guys were men with their fingers on the launch codes of Sejil-2 missiles with twenty-kiloton warheads in tow. Hard to be objective. Hard not to want to be the guy driving a stake into their hearts and stomping on their ashes.

The van delivered me back to the Grand Bazaar. I went to a cyber café on Green Square, prepaid for a connection, and downloaded the material from the memory stick directly onto my iPhone.

Then I opened a secure satellite link to the NSA. The files were text files and small. They transmitted in seconds.

No sooner had I unplugged the memory stick than my phone vibrated with an incoming call from Mr. Elliot.

I switched to the phone app, stood up, and walked toward the madness of the Grand Bazaar at seven thirty at night. Things were just getting started in

244

corridors lined with shops selling everything from children's toys and teak carvings to tripe and the spices to cook it in. I stopped to look at a copper urn and said into the phone, "Go."

"The files came through," Mr. Elliot said. The edge in his voice was as subtle as a blade of grass on a football field. I heard it. "I gotta say, the friggin' hair stood on the back of my neck when I read the hit list. Bad."

"Bad," I agreed. I tried looking like a tourist engrossed in the abundance of Persian artistry on display, moved two steps to my right, and settled in front of a glistening silver platter. "You get The Twelver's pond?" I meant Ahmadinejad's bunker.

"He and all his fat-cat buddies. Definitely. Bluebird came through on that one. That's a serious prize. Well done."

I wasn't all that taken by the compliment. I might feel better about it after a Tomahawk missile burned down the place, if and when that ever happened. I said, "How's our intel stacking up?" In other words, did we have enough to hit them before they hit us?

"We've got eagles and owls all over Europe and the UK locked and loaded," he said.

This was the real deal. General Rutledge called it "Big George." He'd been planning it for years. A single wave. A thousand targets. And Iran's nuclear capacity destroyed in one fell swoop by U.S. aircraft armed with the most powerful bunker busters ever created.

You make it massive, precise, and stealthy, and you light up the targets with boots on the ground. Can't have one without the other. That was my job.

Big George called for an initial wave of B-2 stealth bombers, F-117s, and F-22s, the "eagles" Mr. Elliot was referring to. Their job was to cripple Iran's long-range radar and strategic air defenses. The "owls" were carrier-based F-18s and F-15s, and F-16s launching from ground bases all over the Middle East with one goal in mind: to take out places like Qom and Natanz and to blow their missile sites to smithereens.

"But we need those addresses," I heard Mr. Elliot say. He was talking about the launch sites. "Hate to put such a fine point on it."

"Wish I had a back-up plan to Bluebird, but I'm playing all the cards I've got right at the moment. He promised me the addresses the minute they're finalized, and he's probably one of the guy's finalizing them," I said.

I saw their reflection in the flat surface of the silver platter. Two men. It was a flash that came and went in an instant, but I knew they were wrong for the bazaar. I yanked the silver platter from the rack and turned into the orange flash of an exploding gun barrel. I had enough time to decide that my attackers were less than fifteen feet behind me, and that they wouldn't waste a bullet on a head shot. Bad odds. No, a chest shot would give them three or four inches on either side of the sternum, and I'd still be dead.

I wrenched the platter around and took the bullet full force. It blew me backward into the shop display. Silverware and copperware flew in every direction. A second bullet missed by inches, but only because I was tumbling backward and hit the floor in a heap of platters and pitchers and teacups.

I was acutely aware of the noise—the roar of a third shot, a cacophony of screaming and shouting, the clatter of metal—but I turned all my attention to the one chance I had for escape. I rolled to my left, lifted a hammered copper plate in my right hand, and launched it like a Frisbee in the direction of the two men. Now I saw them. Dressed in black from head to foot, as if they'd just jumped off motorcycles. One wore a stocking hat. His gun was still smoking. The other was shouting and throwing a stunned woman with shopping bags in each hand out of the way.

The flying plate was enough to cause a hitch in their steps, enough for me to spring to my feet and dash to the back of the silver shop. I knew from my experience with the herb-and-spice shop not an hour earlier that there were loading platforms out back. I felt bad pushing aside the shop owner, but she was standing between me and the back door. Her scream told me she was more angry than hurt, which meant she might take it out on the two men pursuing me. Probably not.

I threw open the door. The platform was a narrow block of concrete. I took two long strides and jumped. I landed on an asphalt lane between a van and a pickup truck and three men with crates in their arms. I heard the door slam behind me and shouting. I glanced back as I raced along the lane, dodging delivery trucks. The man in the stocking cap was talking into a walkie-talkie. I didn't bother to reach for my Walther. A firefight was not something I would survive. I ran until the lane made a slight dogleg left, used a panel truck to shield me from my pursuers, and leaped onto the nearest loading platform. A door led back inside the bazaar and into an electronics store mobbed with customers. The store opened onto a corridor that was wall-to-wall people.

I eased into the crowd. I worked my way toward the middle of the aisle, where the traffic flow was a little steadier. If only I hadn't been taller than everyone else.

Fifty paces farther on, the corridor forked. I took the right fork into a long, narrow food court. I'd been in the Grand Bazaar only once before, and that had been two decades earlier. All I remembered for sure was that there were a dozen entrances and exits. Find one, and I'd be home free. Maybe.

I had the strangest thought as I carved my way through hordes of patient shoppers. Who knew I was going to be in the bazaar at exactly that moment? General Navid, General Navid's cousin, and the guy in the van. Charlie and Jeri. Bagheri and Moradi. No one else. It was an unlikely group. Allies, one and all, right? Apparently not.

I needed time to think, and Leila came to mind at that exact moment. She'd given me a key to her place. I hated using it. I wasn't sure I had a choice.

I saw the entrance up ahead. In the second-to-last booth before the entrance was a man roasting beef-and-vegetable kabobs over an open fire pit. I took the memory stick Navid had given me from my pocket. I slid up to the fire pit as the man was waiting on a group of three women and tossed the stick into the flames.

I hailed the first taxi that I saw. I handed him enough rials to get me halfway across town and gave him an address on Jalilabad Street, close but not too close to Leila Petrosian's market. I circled the block and entered the alley behind her place. Her car was not there, so I used the key she had given me to open the back door.

I eased the door closed. I called her name. "Leila. You here? Hey, it's Jake?"

247

I didn't need Rahim—clerk, protector, and jealous suitor—rushing in with a gun or a knife or the police in tow. "It's me, Jake," I said again, and moved from the entrance into the lounge that Leila used to introduce her customers to illegal contraband, which was her primary source of revenue. I could feel Leila in the room just by looking at the simple, classy way she'd arranged the velvet love seat and the leather chairs and the soft light spilling from perfectly placed wall sconces.

I went to the bar and poured single-malt scotch into a cocktail glass. The heat of the liquor exploding in my stomach wasn't quite enough to take the edge off the encounter in the bazaar, but it helped. I carried the glass to the love seat and settled in. I took a second sip and closed my eyes. I wrestled the temptation of a quick nap. Sleep and food had not been much of a priority over the last twelve days, and I felt the nerve endings in my arms and legs twitching.

Keep your mind on business, Jake. Figure it out. Who knew you were going to be at the bazaar at exactly that moment? I kept coming back to Bagheri and Moradi. They were MEK. Everyone they knew and trusted was MEK. Believing that there was a traitor among them stung. You naturally tried to talk yourself out of believing it could actually be true. You confided in people, never thinking the people in your confidence would betray you. Yeah, well, somebody did.

I didn't know Bagheri's hierarchy. I didn't know his top lieutenants, and that was a mistake. I did know Moradi's. Ora Drago was his second-in-command in Amsterdam and a rising star in the MEK upper echelon. Why would he kick away everything he'd worked for by pulling a Benedict Arnold? Didn't make much sense, but stranger things had happened.

I was about to call Jeri to find out how our surveillance op was shaping up—I wanted her to give special attention to Ora Drago—when my iPhone chimed. The number on the screen belonged to Professor James Fouraz.

I sat straight up and nearly spilled my drink. If it actually was Fouraz, he would never risk calling unless he'd come across information that couldn't wait. The other option was that he'd come across information he didn't care to share with anyone but me. Including Bagheri. An option I didn't want to consider was that the Revolutionary Guard or National Security had discovered the professor's duplicity, and now they were trying to get a fix on my location.

I activated the GPS-drone app on my phone and answered after the fifth ring. The voice-recognition app was already up and running, so I said, "ID?"

"It's Fouraz."

I didn't need the voice-recognition app. I knew his voice. Too bad he'd used his real name. Damn! "No more names. Do you hear?"

"Yes. Sorry."

"And your phone?"

"Prepaid. It goes in the trash after this call." he said. The stress level in his voice was like a 7.0 on the Richter scale. I heard a slow, deep breath and realized he was thinking about how to convey his message. "The dance has started. Three days ago. I just heard."

I got it. He was telling me that Ahmadinejad had started to deploy the Sejil-2 missiles from Natanz. That explained the seven missiles I couldn't account for during my unauthorized tour inside the facility. "How?"

"Wearing the most beautiful gowns you've ever seen." So they'd camouflaged the missile transporters and slipped them in with routine truck convoys; this was a guess, but an educated one. Did that also mean that the launch locations had been surveyed and prepped? I had to find out, so I said, "Does that mean the ballroom locations have been chosen."

"Not necessarily," Fouraz said. "They'll make that decision as late in the day as possible."

He was right about that. All we could do was to get a full satellite scan up and running, and I knew that had already been done. "Do what you can to get me that list, will you?"

"I'm using every resource I have," he said.

He severed the connection. I stared down at the phone for a good five seconds before putting in a videoconference call to General Rutledge. The local time was 8:42 P.M.; it was seven hours earlier in D.C.

From the shoulders up, it looked like the general had donned his dress uniform. I could see three silver stars glittering on each shoulder. He said, "Got your latest. Nasty. I'm on my way for a sit-down with Socrates." He meant White House Chief of Staff Fry.

"Good. Because I've got more. It's gotten worse." I told Rutledge in the most cryptic way about the deployment of the Sejil-2 missiles.

Rutledge's eyes shifted like the news had pushed him off-balance. "You sure? No one has seen a thing on our end. There's been no suspicious movement. *Nada.*"

"Then I suggest they go back and review the history books." I hoped that he understood that I meant every standard truck convoy that had gone out of Natanz in the last three days. I could hear the agitation in my voice and decided this was a pretty damn good time for it. "Not the best time in the world to start underestimating a bunch of lowlifes who have been pulling our chain for three decades."

"Agree," he said. "On it."

I guess that was Tom's way of saying, *I'll take boots-on-the-ground intel over eyes-in-the-sky any day, but I just need a reminder every once in a while.* Fine. I'm your guy, Tom.

I saved him the trouble of asking about the launch sites by saying, "No word from Bluebird yet, but I didn't expect it."

"No, it'll be a game-time decision." My old friend glanced off camera. I could see the set of his jaw and the tension stretching the worry lines around his eyes. He looked back at me. "Any news on your subterranean friend?" He was talking about our traitor.

"Yeah. He's close." I didn't tell him about the incident at the Grand Bazaar. The guy had enough on his mind. "But we've got a few tricks up our sleeve on this end, too."

"Stay frosty, my friend."

"Roger that."

He closed the connection. I stared at the iPhone screen. I had heard the frustration in Tom's voice. Nervous. That wasn't like him, but then he'd put all his eggs in one basket, and I just happened to be that basket. I knew one thing:

black ops was an inexact science. You could plan, but the only thing you could count on was the plan's changing. You could force intel only so far. If you pushed too hard, the whole operation could go south in the blink of an eye. The mission was 90 percent in the bag. But it was the last 10 percent that could spell the difference between life and death for some kid in Tel Aviv.

I heard footfalls on the other side of the door. In less than a second I judged their weight and consistency and decided they belonged to a woman. Leila. I put a hand on the grip of my Walther nonetheless.

The door opened. It was her. I tried to figure out a way not to scare her to death. "Leila. It's Jake," I said quickly.

Her breath caught deep in her throat, and she jumped. A hand covered her mouth. Okay, so I wasn't very successful. "Jake. My God. You're all right."

"I'm sorry. I didn't think it was wise to call. I needed a place, and . . ."

"It's all right." She managed a breathless laugh, and it may have been the most magical sound I'd ever heard.

I pushed the Walther back down in its holster and came to my feet. I pointed to my drink. "I sort of helped myself."

I came around the couch, and she fell into my arms. We stayed that way for five very satisfying seconds. Then she held me at arm's length and shook her head. "You look like hell."

I ran a hand over my three-day-old beard and realized she was probably right. "And here I am in the company of the one woman in Tehran whose opinion I actually give a damn about. Buy you a drink?"

"You found the scotch. Good," she said. "Make mine a rum and Coke, will you?"

Fixing a lady a drink. Now there was some normalcy that felt comforting, and I took my time doing it. We clicked our glasses.

"You're on the run," she said. "You wouldn't be here otherwise."

"I had a little encounter at the bazaar. You'll probably read about it in the paper tomorrow."

"No, we won't," she said, a harsh reminder of the censorship that ruled the media in Tehran. She set her glass on the bar.

She unzipped her abaya, shrugged it off her shoulders, and let it fall around her ankles. It was an innocent gesture so fleetingly erotic that a part of me wouldn't have minded a bit if she hadn't stopped with the abaya or the blue pantsuit she wore underneath.

Leila caught me looking and smiled. Then she picked up her glass again and shook her head. "You set the rules, Jake. Not me."

"That was dumb, wasn't it?" I was kidding. Well, maybe only half kidding.

We carried our drinks to the love seat. Leila had the kind of discerning gaze that suggested a woman with the ability to read minds; she had always been successful in reading mine. "So, should I be packing my bags and heading as far into the mountains as my broken-down Toyota will take me?" She was dead serious. "I don't fancy being turned into a pillar of radioactive salt."

I reached out and touched her face. Touched her hair. I said, "If Ahmadinejad pulls the trigger first, it won't matter how far up in the mountains you are, Leila. But if we shoot before he does, then Tehran will be the safest place you can be."

"A lot of 'ifs' and 'buts,' Jake," she said.

"Don't I know it. But listen, I'm . . ."

My iPhone chimed before I could tell her that I was doing everything in my power to make certain she was safe right where she was. It was a text-message alert from Charlie. It read: *If you're not dead, call. Priority one.*

"Charlie Amadi," I said to Leila and rang his number.

He answered after a single ring, saying, "I think we've got our addresses." The missile sites! Excellent. General Navid had come through. "But Bluebird refuses to send them electronically."

"Smart. If his people are monitoring him the way he thinks they are, they'd know before we did, and the addresses would be changed in a matter of minutes," I said. "How's Bluebird communicating?"

"Memory stick. It's been picked up now. We've got a rendezvous set. Honcho is sending a couple of his guys to pick you up. Where the hell are you?"

I wanted to protest using Yousef Bagheri's men for the pickup, but I didn't have a chance. Not a second after Charlie finished his question, a voice boomed from a loudspeaker hidden behind the bar. It was Rahim, Leila's eyes and ears at the front of the shop. He was shouting in Farsi. "Leila. Police. Revolutionary Guards. Front and back."

Leila was on her feet even before I was because I was still translating. My first reaction was to reach for my gun. "Your gun won't help. The Revolutionary Guards travel in packs. Very large packs." She grabbed me by the arm. "This way!"

"Trouble!" I shouted into the phone. "I'll get back to you."

I hung up, and Leila grasped my hand. She pulled me to the door at the front of the lounge. The door led to the same hall I had come down the first day I'd been here. This time, we scurried in the opposite direction. A door halfway along the hall opened onto a large storage closet. Leila flung it open, crouched down, and started pushing aside crates filled with canned fruit. I knelt down next to her and helped. When the crates were out of the way, Leila peeled a square section of linoleum off the floor. Below was a square section of hinged wood with a handle embedded in the surface. A trapdoor.

Leila grabbed the handle and raised the door, her face glistening with perspiration. There was a meter-wide hole in the concrete beneath the door. The hole dropped to a tunnel three meters below. Handholds had been molded into the concrete.

We heard banging at the other end of the hall and shouting.

"Quickly, Jake," Leila said. She pointed to the tunnel. "It leads to a storage room at the end of the alley."

I lowered myself into the hole. I reached up and kissed her lips. "I won't forget this."

I dropped into the tunnel and heard the trapdoor close above me.

CHAPTER 26

Darkness swallowed me.

I reached into my pocket for my iPhone. In the pitch black, the screen's light had the power of a single candle. The tunnel ran straight out in front of me, rough concrete that looked as if it had been poured in haste many years ago. Condensation dripped from the ceiling. A dank, musty smell weighted the air.

I didn't wait for my eyes to adjust. I fell into a low crouch and followed the light. My feet scraped along the floor, and my lower back took the brunt of the punishment. I tried to envision the distance from the market to the alley.

Lengths of rebar curled along the walls and ceiling, like the exhumed bones of corpses buried long ago. A fine glaze of dust ran out ahead of me. I saw no sign of footprints or any other evidence that the tunnel had been used recently.

I counted my steps, as abbreviated as my stride might have been. My vision improved.

At thirty paces, the passage made a right turn. I stopped and listened for five seconds, but the only sound was the drumming of my heart. Seventy-two beats per minute. A little high, but not bad.

I peeked around the corner and gazed into total darkness; a buried coffin didn't have a thing on this tunnel. I switched on my iPhone and pressed ahead. Another thirty-five paces, and I felt a slight incline beneath my feet.

I switched off the iPhone and listened. This time I heard the murmur of conversation wafting from somewhere above. I felt my way to the top of the incline. The murmur grew in volume. I could just make out the distant chatter of men and women speaking Farsi. It sounded like the casual talk you'd hear in a shop or a café.

I felt along the wall and crept forward. I took my Walther in hand and clicked off the safety. The incline emptied into a crawl space six feet long, twenty feet wide and not quite three feet high by my estimation. Light trickled in from a small ventilation grate on the right and two thumb-size holes at the far left of the crawl space. I smelled coffee and sweet spices. Shadows flickered across the grate and I heard the rattle of plates, the splashing of liquid, rapid conversation, and laughter. Definitely an outside café.

I holstered the pistol, crawled in complete silence toward the grate, and peered out. Strange, seeing the bottoms of shoes, the occasional bare ankle, and trouser cuffs. I heard the scraping of a chair as someone sat down, the click of a glass, laughter. All routine activities for a café doing a fair run of business for a Thursday night. Or was it Wednesday? It didn't matter. What mattered was the normalcy. You wouldn't hear laughter if the Revolutionary Guards were parading about.

I moved away from the grate and crawled toward the holes on the left. I put my eye up to one of them and saw cardboard cartons. More cartons sat on shelves along the wall at the opposite side of a narrow floor. There was a door to the right, which was closed. This had to be the storage room Leila had mentioned.

I used the light of my iPhone to get a better view. The holes ran along the top of a shoulder-wide board. I stuck my fingers into the holes, gave a gentle tug, and realized the board was loose by design.

I gave it another tug. If there was anyone in the stockroom, I thought, it would make for an interesting encounter, but I didn't have the luxury of waiting. Dust sifted from the edges. This time I put a little more weight behind it. The board pulled free, but not without a painfully loud squeak.

I froze. I counted to five. Nothing.

I gave a last tug and the board gave way. I pushed aside the cartons concealing the entrance and snaked out of the crawl space. I replaced the board and yanked it firmly into place. I returned the cartons and felt the strain in my knees as I struggled to my feet.

I was brushing dust from my clothes when the door opened. A man wearing a white apron stepped in. He did a double take. There were about two seconds during which his brain tried to decide whether this guy in the rumpled coat, cross-trainers, and baseball cap really belonged in his storeroom. I used the first of the two seconds to grab a large burlap bag filled with coffee beans. I used the next second to thrust the bag into the man's hand. This created an extra moment of confusion, enough time to put my hand on his neck and pinch the pressure point at the side of his throat. He gasped; this was normal. His eyes bugged out, which was also normal. He crumpled to the floor, the bag split apart, and beans spilled out all around him. He wouldn't be out long.

I walked out the door, closed it behind me as if I'd done so a thousand times, and entered the open-air café. No one noticed. I wove in and among a dozen tables until I was outside on the walk.

I put my sunglasses on and spent five seconds studying the street. I glanced in the direction of Leila's market. Two white Toyota HiLux vans marked with the words SPECIAL POLISE on the side were driving away. I saw Leila standing on the curb with her arms crossed. They must've searched her place from top to bottom and come up empty. Otherwise they sure as hell would've taken her away, and who knows what would have become of her.

How do you say thank you from a hundred yards away, knowing someone just put her life on the line for you? How do you say thank you to someone you'll probably never see again, never hear her voice again, never know her fate? I guess you don't. Which made that last kiss that much more special. I kind of hoped she felt the same.

I hoisted my backpack and headed in the opposite direction. I walked two blocks east and then a block north, just to get off the beaten track. I ducked into a crowded bistro. I took a corner table with a view of the street and quick access to the kitchen, worst-case scenario.

I sent a text to Charlie with my location at the corner of Jomhouri Eslami and Felestin.

He replied, *Honcho's men are on the way. White Nissan van. Two of them. One dressed in black. Will ask if you want a ride to the airport. Say that you can only pay in rials.*

I should have ordered something to eat, but I didn't. I drank coffee with cream and sipped a bottle of mineral water. *Real healthy, Jake. Real healthy.* Not to worry; I'd put a steak on the grill the day I got home, and Cathy could whip up one of her world-class tomato salads.

I paid my bill and crossed the street to a newsstand. I stood off to the side, pretended to browse, and texted General Rutledge a short update. It didn't say much, only that things were "progressing."

I knew that wouldn't satisfy Tom, but I had learned something about intel over the years. Don't anticipate. Don't hope for the best. When you have the intel in hand, say you have it in hand. Otherwise, just keep digging.

I knew Mr. Elliot would understand this, so I sent him the same message. Maybe he'd give the general a call and tell him to sit tight.

With any luck, I'd have the launch sites in hand by nightfall, and then the air force could do their thing. I didn't often feel nervous about an op. Anxiety was a red flag when you were dealing with the scumbags of the world. But so many things hung in the balance on this mission. I'd been dodging bullets—literally, in some cases—since the beginning. I didn't believe much in luck, but I had a bad feeling that what luck I had I'd used up. And now I was waiting on two guys I'd never met before, two guys who worked for an organization with a traitor in their midst.

Tehran was lousy with white vans—at least that's the way it seemed as I thumbed through a magazine dedicated to Iranian soccer—and they paraded north and south on Felestin Street along with a scattering of taxis and buses and cars manufactured in places as far away as Korea and Sweden. After a good forty minutes, one rusted junker with TAXI printed on the sides slowed in front of the bistro and halted. A man wearing a black coat over blue jeans dismounted from the front passenger's side. Thick mustache. Twentysomething. He had a definite edge to him. He waited as the van sputtered away, then glanced into the bistro.

This had to be the one Charlie had referred to as the man in black. I went to the next corner and crossed with a half-dozen other people when the light changed.

I watched as he drew out his cell phone and made a call. Ten seconds later, the van returned from an apparent trip around the block. The man in black had his hand on the passenger-side door when he saw me coming. He didn't wave, and he didn't stare. Good. What he did was smile at several other people coming his way, gestured toward the van as if it were the best taxi in Tehran, and apparently offered them transportation, which none of them seemed inclined to accept.

I was liking how this guy handled himself. When I approached, he went through the same routine. A smile, a nominal gesture in the direction of the van, a polite invitation in surprisingly polished English: "You would like a ride to the airport, sir?"

We made eye contact. I studied his face for less than a second and drew on thirty years of stress-recognition training. Tension, but not anxiety. Focus, but not trepidation. Good. "That would be nice. But I can only pay in rials."

"Rials are fine." He opened the passenger-side door. "Please. Get in."

I climbed aboard. Duct tape crisscrossed the cracked and tattered vinyl seats. Ragged holes dotted the rusted floor panels. A slab of plywood had replaced the window behind my left shoulder. The rearview mirror was a small bathroom vanity mirror wired to the ceiling post. I settled onto the seat, and a spring dug into my ass. Apparently nothing was too good for an American with rials to spend.

"Nice ride," I said. "What took you so long?"

"Our guy's on the run," the man in black said from the backseat. "We finally got a fix. He's headed for a warehouse in the Old City."

I nodded. He wasn't lying. I said, "You guys got names?"

"I'm Giv. Your driver's Zand."

Zand was probably about thirty, but the graying temples added ten years.

And the exaggerated worry lines that creased his forehead and branched out around his eyes added another ten. He held out his hand. It was the hand of a laborer. His grip was aggressive and sure.

He shifted the van into gear, and we rumbled from the curb.

Giv pointed to a bundle wrapped in canvas by my feet. I bent down and flipped a corner of the canvas aside. A pair of Russian AK-47s with the tubular stocks folded against the receivers stared back me. The MEK didn't care where their armament came from. Carrying a Russian rifle had no bearing on their loyalty, any more than carrying a German handgun or a Swiss blade. The MEK was loyal to only one cause, and that was their own.

"Insurance once we get to our destination," Giv said.

I wanted to say that if AK-47s were necessary in the next hour, odds were very high that we were all dead and that the mission had fallen short.

Giv fell silent. He watched the traffic behind us like a man expecting the worst. He watched the people on the walks as if everyone of them had it in for us. Zand concentrated on the road, a hand on the wheel, a hand on the gear-shift. I powered up my phone and texted an update to Rutledge, this one more detailed than the last. I used the most basic tradecraft lingo to tell him where I was going and why and what I would do the minute I had the launch sites for twenty-one Sejil-2 missiles, each capable of delivering a nuclear weapon twelve hundred miles with accuracy.

I pressed the Send button. I looked up from the phone and glanced across the seat at Zand. "How'd you two rate this assignment?" I asked.

Zand gave me the benefit of a mild shrug. "Mr. Bagheri has seven daughters and six sons-in-law. We're two of the six. We'd die for him. Which means we'll die getting you where you're going if we have to."

He cast a glance my way. I answered with a short nod and bit of sarcasm. "Seven daughters. That must have made life interesting."

Giv didn't get my humor. He said, "He wants them to know what a free Iran feels like."

"I don't blame him."

We drove north three more blocks. Then we turned west onto Enghelab

Street. A small white Mercedes coupe came south on Felestin Street and accelerated around the corner. The car lunged after us like a dog chasing a rabbit.

"Zand." Giv nodded toward the rearview.

Zand glanced into the mirror and shook his head, pissed, but not panicked.

Red lights flashed inside the grille of the coupe.

Giv cursed, *"Polise."*

The Walther was in my hand even before the word left his mouth. My heart rate jumped three beats a minute. Music filled my head. George Thorogood. "Bad to the Bone." Fighting music.

CHAPTER 27

Giv reached out and gripped my shoulder. "City police. Not black beards," he said.

That was the Revolutionary Guards' trademark: their black beards. Well, their black beards, their patented scowls, their battle gear—anything that heightened the fear. I saw the white Mercedes closing in on our rear bumper, lights flashing. The Revolutionary Guards I had seen outside Leila's place drove the bulkier, more ominous-looking Toyota HiLux.

"Let's see what they want. We run or put up a fight, we got no chance of making our rendezvous."

"Yeah, and if they haul us in, we have even less chance of making our rendezvous," I said. I glanced at the AK-47s wrapped in the canvas by my feet. Okay, so if it did come down to a fight, at least we had the firepower to make it interesting.

"Please put your gun away, Mr. Moreau," the man at the wheel said. He was already rolling down his window. "They may have recognized our van."

"What's that mean?"

He glanced at me. His expression only reinforced that I clearly had not had time to grasp the unwritten rules that governed the underground in a city run by fanatics. He said, "The Guards we cannot buy off. We don't even try.

It's the next best thing to signing your own death warrant. The police, they are a different story. Most loathe the current regime. Most have families."

Zand eased the van up to the curb and rolled to a stop.

Have at least two contingencies, Mr. Elliot used to say. Contingency number one: a viable escape route. I spent three seconds building a visual map of the neighborhood. There were small shops and apartments jammed together on either side of the street. But there was a florist on the immediate right, with the front door propped open with a plastic bucket that held fresh bouquets. Assuming the florist had an exit onto the alley—nobody likes assumptions, but this seemed like a pretty safe one—I could be out in the alley in ten seconds and improvising my next step. Contingency number two: incapacitate the police, relieve them of their weapons, and trade the van for their police car. I liked this one better, though I didn't know if Giv and Zand were up to it.

The Mercedes halted behind us. The frantic rhythm of its red emergency lights screamed danger. I watched in the van's side mirror.

The driver got out. He adjusted his uniform and hitched up his pistol belt; in other words, he could have been any out-of-shape cop in any city in the world. He walked toward the left side of the van while his partner stayed behind in the sedan. Zand waited, his gaze shifting from the rearview to the outside mirror. He prepared himself with a deep breath.

By this time, I'd decided on contingency number one if things went bad. If push came to shove, the cop approaching Zand's window would get the first bullet. I'd roll out the passenger-side door, drill the other one with a couple of shots through the windshield, and sprint into the florist. It wasn't a great plan.

I scoped the area, looking for unmarked cars or suspicious figures among the pedestrians. I saw none. So, if it was a trap, it was a well-disguised one. If the Revolutionary Guards were onto me, they would never send just one squad car. They'd send two dozen commandos. That was how they operated.

The cop sauntered up to the window. He peeked in, his dark, pointed face charged by an elongated nose and a poorly trimmed mustache. Sunglasses covered his eyes, even though the sun had long since hidden itself along the western horizon. He eased an elbow onto the doorframe and smiled the kind of smile that a banker shares with a customer seeking an embarrassingly high-interest loan.

He and Zand exchanged greetings in relaxed Farsi, and I had to wonder what the hell was going on. He glanced into the back at Giv. He said, "Pleasant day, no, Giv?"

"Not a bad day, Farid," Giv replied.

Very chummy. If this cop was after me, he did a great job of hiding his jitters.

Farid looked at me now. He lifted his sunglasses. His brow cinched and the edges of his mouth quirked. His gaze traveled to the canvas bundle on the floor and returned to me with an amused grin.

I smiled. It wasn't a particularly friendly smile because I was also calculating the geometry necessary to plant a 9 mm slug in his forehead.

Giv coughed, loudly and deliberately. I saw him turn a palm up at the cop. He said, "What do you want, Farid?"

The cop turned from me and replaced his sunglasses. "I was getting worried you had forgotten me."

"We've been busy. What do you need?"

"What I always need." The cop rubbed his fingertips together. This wasn't about me after all. It was about his regular shakedown. Yeah, I was relieved, but a guy on the take was no better than a cockroach on the sidewalk. Both deserved to be squashed. Maybe I'd shoot him just on principle alone. His grin widened. "Could be your boss' warehouse is overdue for an inspection. What do you think?"

It was no secret that the MEK smuggled contraband in from Europe and the Far East. They were one of Charlie's biggest competitors.

"Can't have that, can we?" Giv said. He reached into his coat and retrieved his wallet. He counted out all the bills that he had, euros, not rials. He held it out. "I'm short. You're not gonna make an issue out of it, I hope."

Farid gestured for the money. Giv reached across Zand's chest and gave it to him. Counted it. Then grinned. "Nah, this'll hold you till next week." He slapped the money against the doorframe and turned back to his car.

"Baksheesh," Giv said to me. "Protection money."

"Yeah, I got it," I said. The question was, did I believe it? This op was so full of smoke and misdirection that an elaborate double cross would not have surprised me.

The three of us were watching as Farid got back inside the Mercedes. The windshield threw shadows across his face, but there was no mistaking the smirk as he showed off the payout to his partner. The emergency lights stopped flashing.

Zand put the van in gear. We lurched away from the curb and back into traffic. If I hadn't been so exhausted, I probably would have burst out laughing at the ridiculousness of what had just happened. On balance, we'd just lost ten minutes, and I wasn't sure we had ten minutes to lose.

I felt my iPhone vibrate. An incoming message from General Tom Rutledge read: *Need to talk.*

"Problem?" Zand misread the expression on my face.

"I need two minutes," I said to him. "Find a place to stop."

Zand swung onto a side street and pulled up next to small, neighborhood park. Before I climbed out, I looked back at Giv. "Check with your boss. Make sure we're on schedule."

Then I glanced at our driver. "Keep the engine running."

I connected an earpiece to the phone and put some space between myself and the van. I stopped under a shaggy plain tree, engaged the secure-call app, and called General Rutledge's number.

On the second ring, he answered, his voice brusque and strained. "I know you're on the move, but I wanted you to know what we know."

"Go."

"You were right," he said, and then confirmed that everything I'd sent him since day one had been verified, including the fact that satellite recon and sources on the ground had established that all twenty-one Sejil-2 missiles were on the move.

So, Professor Fouraz's information had been spot on. "Okay. What else?"

"Listeners picked up chatter bouncing between major players"—meaning all branches of the Iranian military—"which means the clock is seriously ticking."

I wanted to say, *It's been seriously ticking for the last eleven days, General,* but I didn't. Instead, I said, "It's showtime. What else?"

"Ever since we got your note about The Twelver's pond, we've been keeping tabs on the area," Tom said. "And there's been an increase in traffic there, just like Bluebird said there would be."

The Toad's pond: Tare Ankaboot. The secret facility where Ahmadinejad and the mullahs were set to ride out a nuclear exchange. "The Toad and his friends are on the move. Chickenshit bastards," I said. "How much time do we have?"

"Safe to say that the margin of error between success and catastrophe is thinner than thin," he said. "Yoda has ordered Big George."

So the president had set the wheels in motion on Tom's attack plan. And it went without saying that if we missed the window to hit the launch sites, any number of the Sejil-2 nukes would get away. I ran their target cities through my head: Tel Aviv. Rome. Vienna. Istanbul. Athens. Nuremberg.

"ETA on the party?" In other words, when would our bombers be in the air?

"Six hours."

"What's my data exchange?"

"We've got a link that will route you through the listeners and right to the eagles and owls," he said. "Hey, do me favor, will you? Try not to cut it too close." He hung up.

Six hours. So I had provided enough intel to set a preemptive operation in motion, but not the most important piece of the puzzle, the one that could save how many millions of lives? *Well done, Jake.* I shook my head in disgust. *Get your ass moving.*

I jogged back to the van, threw open the door, and jumped in. "How we doing?" I said to Giv.

"We've got our coordinates. A warehouse on the edge of the Pameran district. We're fifteen minutes away." He showed me a map as Zand urged the van forward. "We have to come at it from the south. Across the railroad tracks from the public market and over this bridge."

He jabbed a finger at the map. A two-lane bridge ran parallel to a foot-bridge spanning a river that apparently wasn't large enough to warrant a name, at least not on Giv's map. I didn't like the bottleneck created by the bridges, but the next crossing was a half mile east.

"How well do you know this guy we're meeting?" I asked.

"His name is Aiden. His driver is Sui. We've known them both forever. I trust them with my life," Giv said.

I hated when people said that. *I trust them with my life*. Trust was one of the greatest gifts on the planet, but it was also one of the most abused. Trust gave you a license to be careless and sloppy, and careless and sloppy got you dead.

"I don't care how much you trust them," I said. I pointed to the AK-47s. "We go in armed. And we go in expecting the worst."

"Got it," Giv said.

I vouchsafed Zand with the coldest eyes I could muster. "Got it, Zand?"

He shrugged. "I don't go anywhere unarmed, monsieur," he replied.

We rumbled toward the Old City. The nervous tension in the van wasn't a bad thing. The hard part was finding a balance between raw nerves and height-ened senses. I had made an art form of it for nearly three decades, which was damn near longer than the two guys in the van with me had been alive. The diamond-hard resolve I was feeling grew even harder with every passing block, and the resolve also fueled a growing sense of calm.

The problem with the MEK was that they were used to creating conflict, not confronting it. They were two entirely different ball games. I saw Zand's viselike grip on the steering wheel: he could have been riding a bucking bronco. I watched Giv's head swivel, taking in every building and every window as if they bristled with binoculars and video cameras and rooftop snipers.

"Relax, boys," I said calmly. "The fun's just about to begin."

Tehran for the most part was a juxtaposition of the modern against the ramshackle. Brand-new high-rises and four-star restaurants stood cheek-tojowl with shabby apartment buildings and decrepit shops. But the Old City was a grand pile of neglect with no pretense of gentrification; that's what happens when you have mosques from the Qajar era, tombs from the thirteenth century, and churches from the 1700s. Were there Islamic fundamentalists obsessed with the fall of mankind back then? I didn't think so.

A wide boulevard fronted the area like a moat. Dilapidated buildings sagged against one another like weathered cardboard boxes. Zand guided the van onto a street with mixed commerce and apartment living that seemed more like a funnel with crooked walls that might teeter over on us, like the last stand of a house of cards.

Tangles of electrical wires crisscrossed the street. Rusted marquees and hand-drawn signs dangled from storefronts. Knots of pedestrians strolled along uneven sidewalks. Bearded old men sat inside open windows, nursing cigarettes and watching the world like grizzled house cats. The air was saturated with the funk of musty blankets, stale tobacco, dust, diesel, and rot. Which fit perfectly with the infestation of pollution that hung like a pall over Tehran day and night.

Our van joined a procession of carts piled high with produce and a flock of sheep on the way to slaughter. The mist hung over the open market directly ahead, and Giv made a quick gesture to his map.

"The warehouse is just beyond the market," he said. "Three, maybe four minutes."

"Let Mr. Bagheri know where we are," I said. "And make sure he keeps Charlie Amadi in the loop, hear?"

Three, maybe four minutes. I was thinking about the bottleneck at the river. I should have been thinking even further ahead than that, because in the next ten minutes Giv and Zand would both be dead and everything I had worked for over the last eleven days would be on the verge of falling apart.

CHAPTER 28

Dusk.

The worst possible time to be moving through the streets of Tehran's Old City.

A half mile stood between me, a warehouse, and a memory stick containing the launch sites. The trouble was, dusk made that half mile seem like a marathon. Too many shadows. Too much broken light. Not enough people in the streets. Or too many if I decided to use the street bazaar for cover, which was exactly my plan.

An hour later and night would have been my ally. Too bad I didn't have an hour to burn. The mission would be over in a matter of hours, or I'd be dead. I didn't plan on being dead. General Patton had it right when he told his troops, "No dumb son-of-a-bitch ever won a war by dying for his country. You win a war by making the other dumb son-of-a-bitch die for his country." Yeah, I'll try to remember that, George. Great advice.

Until then, I would follow my three golden rules: take nothing for granted, expect the worst, and trust no one. That included the two MEK agents riding with me in the broken-down piece-of-shit van that was supposed to deliver us to our warehouse.

"Park here!" I shouted to my driver suddenly. I used Farsi even though

Zand understood English a whole lot better than I spoke his native tongue. When I saw the confused look on his face, I pointed to a gravel lot wedged between a machine shop and a plumbing-supply house a half block from the local bazaar. "There! Right there."

"Why here?" Zand didn't wait for an answer. He jammed on the brakes, cranked the van's wheel, and found a spot between a flatbed truck loaded with plumbing supplies and a pickup truck that had more rust around its wheel wells than our van did.

Zand looked into the backseat at me. He opened his palms. "We're four blocks from the bridge."

"We walk from here," I said calmly. I rested a dirty white headdress on my head and wrapped a scarf loosely around my neck. I had already mapped out our approach to the warehouse using the bazaar as cover, but I hadn't told Zand or Giv. "Bring your weapons. Put them under your coats. We're going shopping."

I didn't wait for a reply. Zand apparently liked to argue; I didn't, especially when there wasn't anything to argue about. I threw open the door and jumped out. Zand shrugged his shoulders in the direction of his younger companion. They both jumped out behind me and quietly closed their doors. Giv's dark face gave nothing away, even as he slung the AK-47 over his shoulder and threw on his jacket. By all rights, Giv should have been chasing girls instead of fighting in the underground, but this was his life. He'd probably been carrying a gun since he was twelve.

"Ah!" Giv said, as the smells of the bazaar filled his nose: curry, boiled lamb, damp textiles, sheep dung, exhaust fumes. He nodded his approval. "The market. Good cover."

"Not so good if someone starts shooting," Zand replied glumly. Unlike Giv, he looked like a traditional academic, with a Sarbards wrapped around his head and a wrinkled black sports coat over a denim shirt. His coat wasn't bulky enough to completely conceal his automatic rifle, but it would have to do.

I slid past a flatbed truck and peeked down the street. The bazaar filled the entire square and spilled out along the narrow side streets to the east and the west. Throw up a table, put up a tent, and lay out your wares: everything from beaded jewelry and woven blankets to handmade musical instruments and cane baskets, tripe and canned olives to freshly baked bread and wind chimes. I estimated two hundred merchants and five times as many people. Perfect. Or at least as perfect as a bad situation could be.

The upside was that markets like this one were only moderately policed. The security *polise* and the Revolutionary Guards relied on informants instead. The locals had learned: don't talk politics in the square. They'd seen too many of their compatriots hung up by their necks in the streets. Save the rhetoric for discreet coffee shops and underground meetings.

I glanced back at my companions. "Take your time, but hurry. We rendezvous at the fish market."

The MEK agents understood what I meant when I said, "Take your time, but hurry." I didn't need to explain.

I entered the flow of people pressing toward the bazaar. I knew Giv and Zand would follow suit, a dozen or so paces between them and headed for different sides of the square. I hated the feel of the headdress and scarf, but the last thing I wanted to look like was a tourist. My mustache had grown in nicely and a three-day-old beard sprinkled my sunburned face with traces of black and gray, and this helped.

I needed to add to my disguise, so I stopped at a fruit cart. I threw down ten thousand rials in exchange for a net sack filled with undersize apples. I plucked one from the sack, took a bite, and kept walking. All for show.

Halfway across the square, I paused at a stall selling hand-stitched leather satchels. Beautiful; my wife would have loved them. Funny how a guy just hoping to escape with his life can have such random thoughts; but then, maybe it was the random thoughts that kept you sane.

I glanced back and saw that Zand had purchased a woven poncho and thrown it over his shoulders. *Good,* I thought. *Smart.* Now the AK-47 was completely hidden. Giv was sidling along the other side of the square and seemed far too tense for my liking. I shook my head and looked away; nothing I could do about it.

I squeezed through the crowd, saw a pair of riot policemen coming my way, and ducked into a tent selling chelo and kebabs and doing a landslide business. I put my hand inside my coat pocket and curled my fingers around the Walther's handle. I watched the entrance out of the corner of my eye, expecting the worst, but it didn't happen. The *polise* passed with little more than a glance. I loosened my grip and followed two women back into the square.

I didn't stop again. *Take your time, but hurry.*

When I reached the fish market on the north side of the square, Giv and Zand were already there, lingering at stalls thirty feet apart. We made eye contact for an instant. Then the three of us joined the stream of people following the lights toward the river and the railroad tracks. The sun dropped below the horizon. A blustery wind kicked a dust devil into the air. Night descended.

The men guarding the bridge were Revolutionary Guards, the worst of the worst and the bane of every man, woman, and child in the country. I followed the crowd onto the footbridge, munching another apple. A stream of cars and trucks exiting the market was consuming most of the Guards' attention, and abandoning the van looked more and more like the right decision.

My feet hit the pavement on the far side of the bridge. Like everyone else who wanted the Guards as far behind them as possible, I picked up my pace. I crossed the railroad tracks before looking back over my shoulder for Giv and Zand. In evening's last light, they were just part of the crowd, two Iranian men heading home after a long day. So far, so good. I kept moving.

A quarter of a mile from the river, a cluster of warehouses played host to panel trucks and flatbeds, cranes and forklifts, and freight cars as massive as small houses. I heard the voices of the dockworkers before I saw them.

Giv moved up next to me. He pointed to a squat brick building made red by the setting sun and crouching like a little brother between two larger buildings with busy docks. "That's the place," he whispered. A sign that read CRIMSON FREIGHT COMPANY in three languages—Farsi, French, and English— hung across the gate, but the warehouse looked like it had been abandoned for at least a year.

Giv disappeared into the shadows next to the building on the right. Zand took up a position alongside one of the freight cars. I stopped next to the docks fronting the warehouse on the left. Yousef Bagheri had placed two men inside the warehouse. They were waiting for my call. I opened my cell phone. I texted a one-word message: *Clear*. There were security lights burning from a half-dozen fixtures surrounding the building. Two blinked suddenly. The blinking lights were the first of our all-clear signals. The secondary signal was a half-drawn shade in an office on the first floor that rose and fell a moment later.

When Giv saw this, he jogged to the front gate. He keyed the lock, opened the gate a foot, and gave Zand and me a quick wave.

"Let's move!" His voice was a low hiss, filled with energy. Too much energy.

"Take it easy," I said to him as I squeezed through the gate.

We jogged to a concrete dock with three huge, sliding doors that were heavily padlocked. A set of stairs rose to the dock and a narrow door led to a small office. Giv was first in and clearly relieved. "We made it. God damn!"

Zand followed, his AK-47 cradled in two hands just in case. "Aiden? Sui?" he called.

"Where are you guys?" Giv said, pushing through the office and into a compact two-story warehouse littered with empty boxes and stacks of wooden pallets.

"Wait!" I shouted, but it was too late.

Zand had already followed Giv in, and the roar of gunfire filled the air. I heard Giv groan and Zand crumple to the floor. I barrel rolled into the room with my Walther in my right hand, saw a puff of smoke up in the rafters, and ripped off six shots in three seconds. A man tumbled from the rafters, screaming, and hit the floor with a ghoulish thud. I rolled again, came up on my knees next to a concrete support pillar, and caught a rifle butt straight in the face.

It was a staggering blow, but not enough to put me down. A second blow, from behind, caught me right above the ear, and I collapsed in a heap. A foot in the chest drove me onto my back. Four bearded men with rifles surrounded me, all wearing the gray-and-blue uniform of the Revolutionary Guards.

A fifth man walked casually into my line of sight. He looked down at me.

He opened his hand and showed me the memory stick cradled in his palm. "Is this what you were hoping to find?"

I lunged for him and was driven back by the hard steel of four gun barrels. "Traitor!" I shouted, my eyes burning holes into him. "You better kill me now, because there's no place on this earth that you can hide."

"It will be a pleasure killing you. *Mr. Moreau.* Or whatever your name is," he said.

He took a quick step and kicked. I saw the blur of his black boot coming toward my head. I turned away, felt a sharp pain, and the world went black.

CHAPTER 29

Here's the problem with torture. If you want information from a guy who'd gone through the kind of training that I'd gone through since the ripe old age of nineteen, you should probably plan on a very long wait. Give up my mission? Do you really think a little shock therapy or some unimaginative waterboarding is going to make me give up my mission? You have to do better than that.

That was the thing about the Revolutionary Guards. They were used to dealing with ordinary citizens and common criminals. Put a gun barrel up to their heads and they'll tell you anything you want to hear. Fear had always been their greatest ally.

I wasn't afraid. I was prepared to die. That was a fairly insurmountable position when you're up against the clock like the Guards were. They had resorted to pain. I'd been trained to compartmentalize pain, and it worked pretty well. But the wire cutting into my neck was on the verge of crushing my esophagus, and I had passed out three or four times by now. They'd broken three of my fingers, and they'd broken my nose, which really pissed me off.

Ice-cold water splashed against my face. I woke with an angry, confused start. I jerked against restraints holding my arms against my sides. A headache sagged in my skull like a heated iron weight. My insides lurched like those of a man coming off a really bad drunk. They'd shot me up with something, but all it had done was make me sick.

I heard my name. Actually three names. The three names on my passports. Green, Swan, Moreau. "Well, which is it?" The man's voice sounded dirty and smug. Did he really have time to be smug?

I turned my head, saw shadows, and tried to blink my eyes into focus. There was something filmy and wet pooling in my eyes. I didn't know it was blood until it ran down my cheek and over my lips. I'd tasted blood more times than I cared to admit, and this was it. Coppery, salty, sickly sweet.

I got my bearings. I was propped up in a chair. The chair was wired to a concrete pillar. My torso, legs, and arms were wired to the chair. A garrote wired my neck to the pillar. My arms were locked behind the chair. My hands were wired together. The memorial bracelets on each wrist cut into my skin. My elbows and shoulders had gone completely numb. How much time had passed?

"Mr. Moreau," the voice repeated.

He loomed before me, one light-colored shape in the middle of four similar silhouettes in the deep gloom.

I backtracked. My MEK compatriots and I had been lured into an ambush at the warehouse across the river from the street market. Giv and Zand had been shot dead. I'd taken a boot in the head, care of . . .

Ora Drago. The MEK's second-in-command in Amsterdam. And the traitor Charlie and I had been tracking since I'd arrived in Tehran. We'd been so close. But close doesn't count for much in a counterintelligence op. Close got you dead or captured. Dead may have been the better alternative in this case.

But it occurred to me that the situation wasn't hopeless. They'd kept me alive. And they wouldn't have done that without a very good reason. Obviously they needed to know how much I knew. And just as obviously, I hadn't given them anything yet. Okay, so the odds weren't exactly even, but long odds were better than none.

I'd trained with some of the toughest sons of bitches who'd ever served Uncle Sam—U.S. Navy SEALS, Army Rangers, Green Berets, Marine Force Recon, Air Force Pararescue, Delta Force—and I wasn't about to stain their reputations by giving in to a bunch of lowlife thugs. Oh, yeah, and then there was Mr. Elliot. I couldn't imagine what he would think if I knuckled under, and I

275

didn't want to find out. He'd know by now that something was wrong. He'd have pulled out all the stops, trying to find me. That was our deal. I go in; he makes sure I get out. A good guy to have on your side.

I willed myself past the headache and the nausea, tried to lift my head, and nearly choked myself to death on the neck wire.

"I bet you'd like us to loosen that, wouldn't you, Mr. Moreau?" The accent was Persian, but there was the hint of a European influence. I clenched my eyes and filled my lungs with a slow breath. It felt like my insides were on fire, but when I opened my eyes again, my vision had cleared enough for me to make a split-second assessment of the situation. I was in a warehouse, but not the one where the ambush had occurred. The room was large and dank and made for this kind of thing. I saw a water tank. I saw an electrical generator. I saw a table lined with surgical equipment like scalpels and clamps and hypodermic needles.

A viciously bright light poured down on me from the exposed beams in the ceiling, and Drago and four black beards hovered just outside the light.

Drago glowered, the set of his narrow face as menacing as a truncheon. His eyes were hooded by wiry and expressive eyebrows that cinched together like the ends of a frazzled cable.

"Turncoat!" I was proud of myself for getting out at least one word before a fist shot out from the shadows and exploded against my cheek.

"How imaginative. You've gone from traitor and rat to turncoat."

I didn't remember calling him a rat, but that sounded like me. "How does snake in the grass sound?" I hissed.

"Show him," one of the Guards said. He stepped forward, shading the light, as if he wanted me to see him. I blinked away the blood and squinted. He was the slightest of the four Guards, with an equine face, bulbous nose, and uncomfortably black eyes. "Show him."

Drago held a bundle of documents in his right hand. He held my iPhone in his left. I was more interested in the memory stick I'd been after when all hell broke loose. The locations of the Sejil-2 missiles and their warheads were all that mattered. Every other piece of intel I'd provided had been confirmed and verified. Why was it that the most important piece of the puzzle was always the last piece? Without that, all the bunker busters in the world wouldn't be enough to stop Mahmoud Ahmadinejad's nuclear offensive. Armageddon. Our worst nightmare.

Two of the Guards closed in on me. I could smell their sweat, and that was probably the idea. Intimidating the prisoner as the interrogation intensified—or so they thought.

"Let us start with the phone," the skinny man with black eyes said. Drago aimed the screen of the iPhone at me. At least now I had the chain of command: Drago was someone the Revolutionary Guards would use, and when he had nothing left to give them, he would end up hanging from his neck in a place where every member of the MEK could see him. "What is the access code?"

I didn't answer. I ground my teeth and stared. Finally, I said, "I can't think with this wire around my neck."

"Maybe it's not tight enough." The man with the black eyes snapped his fingers. The soldier on his left moved up so fast that he was grabbing the garrote and ratcheting the tension on the wire before I had time to fill my lungs. The wire cut into my neck. I gagged and coughed and felt the pressure building in my head. I was on the verge of passing out when the echo of the man snapping his fingers hung in the air. The man behind me gave the wire a centimeter or two of slack. I coughed so violently that my insides turned to knots.

They waited until the coughing stopped. "The code or the wire. It makes no difference to me," I heard the man with black eyes say eventually. "What will it be, Mr. Moreau? Choose."

"Okay," I croaked through the spittle bubbling on my lips. Giving them the code would probably seal my fate, but at least I could see the look on their faces.

"I didn't expect you to break so easily," Ora Drago said with a sneer. "How disappointing!"

"Shut up," the man with the black eyes said. He put a fist under my chin and lifted my head. "The code."

"One. Nine. Backslash. Two. Eight. Backslash. One. Eight."

"You Americans," Drago said. He entered the number, his fingers jabbing the screen, a man eager to prove to his superiors that he had thwarted the Great Satan and captured one of its demons.

The phone emitted a low beep followed by the wail of a high-pitched alarm, and I knew the self-destruct app had been activated. Drago's eyebrows settled low over his eyes as the phone's screen began to erode. "What's happening?"

"What do you think's happening, Mr. Phelps?" I couldn't help the *Mission Impossible* reference even though my throat burned with every word.

The man with the black eyes snatched the iPhone from Drago's hand. He stared at the corrosion eating the screen. His fingers opened. The phone clattered to the floor. The screen cracked. Smoke curled from the broken glass.

He kicked the phone and sent it spinning across the floor. He glared, his eyes sharp with malice. "Don't be so proud of yourself, Mr. Moreau."

He turned and whispered a command to his fellow Guards. They moved with the precision and speed of a well-oiled machine. One released the wire pinning me to the pole. The other two yanked me to my feet, hoisted me onto the table, and pulled me across the rough surface until my head dangled over one edge, my legs over the other. They tightened the wires around my chest, wrist, and neck and held me down. I knew what was coming.

The man with black eyes walked around the table, a bucket in hand, water sloshing over its rim. He set the bucket on the floor between us. "Waterboarding. Such a twisted creation. And I applaud the twisted minds inside your CIA for its invention. Almost the perfect torture. Leaves no marks and breaks all resistance."

He had it pretty much right. I guessed I could start talking and save myself the trouble, but I was probably dead in any case.

He barked another order. The Guard who responded had a blank face and a surprisingly pale complexion. He fished a towel from the bucket. He wrung the towel and water rained back down. I heard Drago laugh.

Time slowed. I reached deep inside myself and called on whatever reserve of determination and grit I had left. Every detail came into sharp focus. The drip, drip, drip of water splattering on the floor. The dank odor of decay. The pockmarks on Drago's bladelike nose. The dull luster of his crooked teeth. Dust motes circling the bare light bulb like crows above a carcass.

"You can beg for mercy," the man with black eyes said. "Or you can endure the terror. In any case, you will answer my questions."

The man with the towel draped it over my face. It smelled of mildew. I filled my lungs with air an instant before water drenched the towel and forced it heavy and flat against my features.

Someone came down hard on my midsection with his fist. My stomach seized. I gasped, sucking in air . . . and water.

The water gushed up my nose, down my throat, and into my lungs. A lever tripped in a distant part of my brain that went straight to survival mode.

More water drenched the towel, and I convulsed.

Pain control has very little to do with this. With some pain, you can retreat deep into your soul and fend off the most brutal blow. But there is no such pain in drowning. It's a gigantic monster of terror that rampages through your consciousness. Your mind flails. Panic seizes your soul.

I thrashed against the table. My lungs screamed for air. A veil of darkness descended inside my head an instant before the towel was pulled away. The pain of coughing was almost unbearable. I tasted something salty in my mouth. I turned my head and spit water and blood.

"We're going to do this all night," a voice whispered. It was Drago. "First we'll break you. And then we'll break you into a million pieces."

He was a complete blur, but I couldn't let that go unanswered. "Rat." It came out a raspy croak, but at least it came out.

The man with the towel yanked my head straight. He draped the towel over my face again. The material was as cold as a drowned corpse.

I readied myself for the onslaught. And then I heard the Voice. It was hardly more than a whisper. It was telling me to save myself. It was saying, *Tell them what they want. You've done enough. You've given enough.*

We're told about this—that if things got bad enough, the Voice was inevitable. I had never believed it. The Voice was for others, not me. Not bad-to-the-bone Jake Conlan. But they also said that the Voice wasn't necessarily a bad thing. It was a defense mechanism. You could suppress it, but it would return, louder and more insistent. It was how you dealt with it that counted.

I gulped air, buying a few precious seconds.

Water sloshed from the bucket and soaked through the towel like a flood. It pressed against my eyes like thumbs of steel and clasped my face like dead fingers. I puffed hard to keep my airways clear.

I knew the bastards would hit me again, and I readied my stomach for the blow. It came hard and metallic: the butt of a rifle. I fought, but it wasn't enough. My lungs exploded. A howl traveling through my throat and mouth was swallowed by the onslaught of water. Water flooded my nose and burned my sinuses. I bucked against the table, my body screaming for air and release, panic driving me toward the edge.

The Voice returned, louder and more insistent. *Save yourself. Tell them. About the attack. About Fouraz. About Charlie and Leila. Denounce the lot of them: Rutledge, Elliot, the Great Satan. All of them.*

The water stopped. The towel fell away. I gagged and coughed and felt pain in places I hadn't even known existed. Complete and utter exhaustion. Not defeat. But close.

I needed something to hang onto, something to focus on, something to fight back with. Anything. So I crashed through a door in my memory and came away with a picture of home, of Cathy and the kids. But the picture hurt too much, so I pushed it aside and crashed through another door. I found myself standing in Arlington Cemetery. The gravestone staring back at me belonged to my dad. This picture didn't work any better than the one before it, but it served a purpose. I was suddenly back where I had begun and every ounce of my focus was centered on the memorial bracelets cutting into my wrists. My hands were soaked with sweat and water, but I knew the Semtex coating the bracelets was insoluble. So was the primer. The problem wasn't the weapon; the weapon was a thing of beauty. No, the problem was gaining enough leverage to ignite it. Then again, even if I did succeed in igniting it, the explosive would probably blow my hands off, and then where would I be.

What the hell! Go for it, Jake. If nothing else, die trying. Hard to argue with that, so I tugged furiously at the wire binding my wrists and felt the brush of metal on metal.

"I know why you're here," the man with the black eyes was saying. He set a fresh bucket of water by my head on the table. "We know you entered the facilities at Qom and Natanz without invitation or authorization. We know that you left a trail of dead bodies in your wake. We know that you have been colluding with traitorous elements throughout our country. What I want are names."

A sound like the whoosh of a hydraulic motor echoed throughout the warehouse. The man with the black eyes looked in the direction of the sound and smiled. "For you, things are about to get much worse."

CHAPTER 30

I put a name to the sound: hydraulic doors opening. Then a second sound filled the air: distant footsteps echoing down a long hallway.

"My comrades have arrived," the man with black eyes said.

"Now you'll talk," Ora Drago said, his voice painted with intense satisfaction.

I twisted my wrists and snapped one bracelet against the other. Come on, goddamn it! It did it again, heard a pop and a hiss, like a match bursting into flames. The primer ignited, the Semtex detonated, and my skin began to melt. That was the bad news. The good news was that the explosion had also turned the wire binding my wrists into molten metal. My hands were suddenly free.

I did three things so fast that the blackbeards hardly knew what hit them. I grabbed the garrote controlling the wire around my neck, spun it clockwise, and pulled my head free. I drove my knee into the stomach of the man with the black eyes and sent him sprawling backwards. I rolled off the table, grabbed the AK-47 that one of the Guards had stupidly left leaning against the pillar, and barrel-rolled across the concrete floor. I came up firing. Three shots in less than a second erased three of my captors and made me feel ever so much better.

Behind me, Drago started to run, confused and panicked.

I spun around and saw the man with the black eyes tracking me with a

282

9 mm pistol. A burst of orange fire erupted from the barrel, but I was already moving. I dove behind the pillar and rolled to my right, using the waterboarding table as a shield. I came up in a low crouch, put a shoulder against the edge of the table, and sent it flying in the direction of the man with the black eyes. He backpedaled and stumbled. The table caught him in the mid-section and drove him to the ground.

I stepped toward him. More than anything I wanted to savor the kill, but I didn't have time. The footsteps pounding along the corridor were seconds away. I heard shouting. I raised the AK-47 and fired once at the man with the black eyes. He slumped forward.

I took up a position behind the pillar. I put the butt of the rifle against my shoulder and sighted the barrel in the direction of the approaching footsteps. I didn't mind dying like this. Me against them. A fair fight, more or less.

I saw a shadow materialize at the entrance, then a person. I was a blink of an eye away from pulling the trigger when I realized it was Jeri. She was jogging deeper into the room, two hands gripping a machine pistol and a look so intense that it made me glad she was on my side.

"Jake!?" Her voice echoed throughout the warehouse and I thought to myself that never in my life had I heard a more welcome sound. I saw Bagheri and six of his men a step behind Jeri, Uzis raised and ready.

"Here," I called. "I'm here."

I waited until the barrels of their guns were at a less-threatening angle before tossing aside the AK-47 and stepping out from behind the pillar.

Jeri raced up to me. "Oh, my God. You poor man. Look at you."

"I feel better than I look," I said, a lie of the highest order. The words felt like glass raking across 50-grit sandpaper, and I knew they'd done serious damage to my throat and lungs.

"Don't talk," she said and instinctively laid fingers gently across my lips. She put her arms around me, and I let her. My gaze settled on a man walking into the room, a pistol at his side, as calm as if he were being escorted to a table in his favorite restaurant. It was Charlie. A sight for sore eyes, if ever there was one.

"Jake! My good friend," he called out. "You're alive. Thank God! Where's Drago!"

I motioned toward the far end of the warehouse. Bagheri and his men had Drago cornered. The MEK traitor had made it as far as a locked door, and now he was shrinking like a shriveling fig in the face of his own capture.

Bagheri's men dragged him back. "You want him?" Bagheri asked me.

I wanted him, all right. Mostly I wanted him for the men who had died keeping my mission on track: Akbari in Amsterdam and Charlie's man Lukas. And when Drago's lips curled with contempt, his last attempt at justifying his miserable existence, I wanted him even more. But I didn't have the strength.

"He's your traitor," I said to Bagheri.

"I was hoping you'd say that." Bagheri marched forward, raised his pistol, and aimed it at Drago's forehead. He fired once. A red dot appeared in Drago's forehead. He rocked on his feet and toppled backward, dead before he hit the floor.

Bagheri shook his head in disgust and turned away. "Way too good for him."

Charlie shared a crooked smile with me. "You look like shit."

He wrapped an arm around my shoulder, and he and Jeri helped me into my shoes and jacket. He added, "I'd shower you with endless amounts of sympathy and pity if we had the time, but we don't."

"I screwed it up, Charlie. They got the memory stick," I said. My voice wasn't much more than a whispered croak.

He shook his head. "Actually, they didn't." We started down the hall toward the door, with Bagheri supporting my other shoulder.

"What do you mean?" I felt a ray of hope.

"I mean Bagheri's man was smarter than you. She managed to avoid the ambush that you walked right into," Charlie said.

"She?"

Jeri held the door open for us. She said, "Actually, Bagheri's man isn't a man at all. That's how we found you. She followed Drago and his Revolutionary Guard friends here. And thank God she did."

"They had two truckloads full of men headed your way, and we had to intercept them before we made our move," Bagheri interjected. "A serious body count."

We stepped out into the night. A panel truck and a black Mercedes sedan idled in the darkness. Leila Petrosian stood in front of the truck. She held up a memory stick.

I limped toward her "Leila?"

"Jake. I'm sorry I lied to you," she said. "Or at least that I wasn't completely honest with you."

"You? You're . . . ?" My eyes shifted from her to Bagheri and back again. "You're MEK?"

"For the last ten years. I knew you wouldn't want me involved in your mission here, so I pretended that I wasn't." She laid the memory stick in my hand, wrapped my fingers around it, and touched my face. "So many have died to bring you this. I hope it's worth the cost."

"Let's make sure it is." I looked at Charlie. "They took my phone. I need a computer."

"I figured you would. In the back of the truck." With Charlie's help, I hobbled to the back of the truck. Jeri threw open the door and climbed in first. By the time Charlie and I were inside, she had a briefcase open on the side seat that ran the length of the bed. She pulled a laptop from the briefcase and powered it up.

"Internet ready," she said and turned the screen my way. Despite my broken fingers, I managed to insert the memory stick into a port. The screen flickered to life. By all rights, I should have felt a wave of emotion; I'd come a long way in the last eleven days, and here was the payoff at my fingertips. But mostly what I felt was a meld of irritation and urgency while the computer identified the single file with an unknown name attached to it. I hit the keypad, and the file opened. There they were. The locations for the Sejil-2 missile launch sites. Twenty-one coordinates. All within latitude coordinates 32 and 38 and longitude coordinates 50 and 57.

In a perfect world, I would have sent the information directly to the NSA, but I had to settle for one of my secure e-mail accounts. I knew Mr. Elliot and General Rutledge would be monitoring every one of them. I attached the file and clicked the Send button. The computer confirmed that the message had been successfully sent. The question was, had it been successfully received?

That wasn't my only concern. If the Revolutionary Guards were onto me, then maybe they knew that I'd made contact with General Navid about the launch sites. Maybe the launch sites had been changed at the last minute and without Navid's knowledge. And maybe the coordinates in the memory stick were pure fantasy. A man could worry himself sick about such things, but it was out of my hands now. I'd played my last card.

So I waited. I looked from Charlie to Jeri and then to the rear of the truck, where Leila was standing. The computer pinged. The messages came one right after the other. General Rutledge's read: *Roger receipt. Well done.* Mr. Elliot's was not quite so complimentary: *About time.*

They all saw my smile. "You gonna share the joke?" Charlie said.

I turned the screen so he and Jeri could see it. " 'About time.' " Jeri read it out loud and shook her head. She said, "My thought exactly."

Charlie said, "Time to get you out of the country. I've got a plane waiting. Sorry it's not a bit fancier. But I think you'll approve of the pilot I chose."

I looked at Jeri. Her grin had turned into a smirk. "Guess who?"

"He's right. I approve."

Charlie threw the computer back into the briefcase, and we exited the truck from the rear. I could almost walk on my own. Bagheri shook my hand, and he and his men took our place in the truck. I put my arm around Leila, and she walked me to the Mercedes. The world that she lived in would never be the same from this night on. But I guess that's what she'd committed herself to over that last decade.

I didn't kiss her on the lips this time. I kissed her forehead. She said, "Thank you," and I wished she hadn't. I didn't feel like a man worthy of gratitude.

I hunched into the backseat of the Mercedes, and one of Charlie's men joined me. He had a first-aid kit in his hands. He did what he could to pack me up and gave me something for the pain. Jeri drove. Charlie rode in the front and made three calls on his cell phone. I didn't ask where we were going. Ten minutes later, we were on the open highway going toward Shahr-e Qods, a suburb west of Tehran.

Another ten minutes passed before the Mercedes slowed and angled across the highway for a southbound dirt road that eventually veered west. Once it did, Jeri doused the headlights. The road ran straight and level for a kilometer. Charlie made another call. He spoke in crisp Farsi. A pair of parking lights flashed farther up the road. Jeri pointed the Mercedes in that direction, slowed to a crawl, and came to a halt next to a black SUV.

A single-wing Cessna 172 was parked in the middle of the road. The propeller was already turning. "That my ride?" I asked.

"We'll need a couple of stops," Jeri said.

We bailed out. Five of Charlie's men were waiting for us. I walked on my own toward the plane, but it wasn't easy. Prop wash kicked up dirt that beat against our faces and clothes. Jeri climbed into the pilot's seat. Charlie and I paused under the wing beside the co-pilot's door. Charlie brought his face close to mine and shouted over the roar from the engine.

"Until next time, Jake." He offered his hand. We shook, then embraced. I looked into his eyes. Who knows how my mission would have fared without Charlie. He seemed to read my mind. "I know," he shouted. "Now get out of here."

I let go and climbed onboard. Jeri was all business. I put on a headset and fastened my safety belts. She revved the engine, then advanced the throttle. The airplane trundled forward. She accelerated, and the plane bounced along the road. If Jeri was concerned about taking off in the dark, she didn't show it. Me? I was just glad when the Cessna lifted off.

She pulled on the controls and kept the nose at a low angle until we gained airspeed and altitude for a turn to the northwest.

We were over the Alborz Mountains when I saw the bomber. It was a Northrup Grumman B-2 Spirit, aka the Stealth Bomber, like something out of a science fiction novel, breaking through the clouds. I saw two others in close formation and knew there were twelve others headed for targets all over Iran. Sixty seconds later, six F-117s filled our window to the west, high above us and moving incredibly fast. The bombers thundered overhead, and our little 172 rocked in their wake like a cork in a stormy sea.

Big George had been unleashed.

I looked at Jeri. She bit down on her lip and pushed the throttle as far forward as it would go.

People were about to die. I knew that. I was more concerned about the people who were going to live. Millions of them.

CHAPTER 31

General Tom Rutledge wanted to take me to lunch at the Capital Grille, a Pennsylvania Avenue mainstay a stone's throw from the U.S. Capitol. Fitting.

The weather outside was gorgeous; for some miraculous reason, the humidity had lifted and the air had a balmy, tropical clarity. A shame to spend the time inside, but then, lunch at the grille never disappointed.

I'd spent six days debriefing. It should have taken six hours. But everyone wanted a piece of the action. They always did when things went well. And things had gone very well.

Big George had been a success. The bombers had knocked out all but one of the Sejil-2 missiles. That one had been attacked and destroyed on the orders of three rogue generals who wanted no part of watching their country get blasted into a radioactive parking lot. Smart thinking.

Mahmoud Ahmadinejad, an undetermined number of mullahs, and half of his high command were in their bunker hideout when a twenty-thousand-pound bunker buster drilled a hundred feet into the ground and incinerated the place. Well, at least that was the hope. The Twelver's death could not be confirmed. Nor could the mullahs or the members of the high command. A 20,000-pound bunker buster didn't allow for confirmation; it didn't allow for

289

much of anything except rubble and complete annihilation, and that bit of uncertainty left me with a queasy feeling in my stomach.

Of course, the Muslim world condemned the American attack, though behind the scenes every government from Istanbul to Rabat scrambled to prop up the alliance formed by the renegade generals and the MEK. Would they be an improvement over the insanity of their predecessors? Well, it would take some real doing to be any worse. And now Iran's young people were swarming the streets and stepping into the void, and that might just be enough to bring back the engineers and the doctors and all the other professionals who had abandoned the country over the decades.

Truthfully, my concerns were all selfish. I wanted Charlie and Jeri and Leila to have what they'd been striving for going on thirty years: a place they were proud to call home. I wanted to know there wasn't some self-inflated fanatic holding a gun to my country's head.

"You feeling any better?" Tom said. Neither of us had bothered to open our menus.

"I'm fine." I really wasn't fine. The waterboarding had left some serious scars on my lungs; no telling if they would ever completely heal, one doctor had informed me. In other words, don't plan on running any marathons in the near future. The three fingers broken on my left hand during interrogation had been rebroken and set with tiny screws that would come out in another four weeks; same prognosis. The good news was that I played tennis with my right hand. The wire they had used on my neck had apparently been rusted, because I'd been given tetanus shots on three occasions; so far, no lockjaw.

"What are you eating?" Tom said. I hadn't seen the waiter coming.

I had to smile at that. We had been ordering the same damn thing since the day we'd started going to the grille. "How does sliced filet mignon with cippolini onions and wild mushrooms sound, Tom? Something new and different."

He looked up at the waiter. Held up two fingers. "And two coffees. Black for me. Cream for the wimp."

"Yes, sir," the waiter said.

"How's Richard?" Tom asked. He meant Mr. Elliot. He'd gone into the hospital three days after I returned home. Cancer.

"Not good. Damn cigarettes," I said. I'd been to visit him every day since my debriefing ended. Funny, he was really the only one I really wanted to brief. He was the only one I'd ever briefed. "Amazed he lived this long."

"He cleared the DDO's name. You know that, right?" the three-star general sitting across from me said. "The investigation punked two guys from his staff. Charges pending."

"Yeah, well, they were still on his staff," I said. Actually, I was glad Wiseman hadn't been implicated. That would have been a disaster. A couple of guys going down from his staff was only half a disaster. "What about Landon Fry?"

"He put in his resignation as White House chief of staff," Tom said as our coffee was served. "He's running for the U.S. Senate in Ohio. And after all the praise the press has been heaping on him, he's a shoo-in."

"Terrific."

"He stayed true to his word, though. He got your intel on the president's desk."

I smiled out of the side of my mouth. "He got the intel on the president's desk, Tom, because only a fool would have ignored it. It was politics from the get-go, and you and I both know it. We sat in that meeting with him at the Old Ebbitt, and he tried to make us believe that he was all in. Behind us all the way. Hell, he might as well have said, *Hey, listen, Jake, you bring me back evidence even my mother couldn't ignore, and I'll get it in the hands of the president. And then, if the bombers are already in the air, I'll make sure the president takes your intel seriously.*"

"Hope you're not expecting me to give you an argument." Tom looked over the rim of his cup at me.

I caught the look in his eyes. "So the bombers were already in the air, weren't they?" I said.

"Well, more or less." He held his cup out to me, and I clicked it with mine. He said, "We made heroes of them all, Jake. We made heroes of them all."